A SONG

.

A SONG

A life story is like a long poem;
with a voice it becomes a song.

DAVID TURNER

Matador
9 Priory Business Park,
Wistow Road, Kibworth Beauchamp,
Leicestershire. LE8 0RX
Tel: 0116 279 2299
Email: books@troubador.co.uk
Web: www.troubador.co.uk/matador
Twitter: @matadorbooks

ISBN 978 1789016 031

British Library Cataloguing in Publication Data.
A catalogue record for this book is available from the British Library.

Printed and bound in Great Britain by 4edge Limited
Typeset in 11pt Minion Pro by Troubador Publishing Ltd, Leicester, UK

Matador is an imprint of Troubador Publishing Ltd

For Emily, my daughter, with love

When we are young the words are scattered all around us. As they are assembled by experience, so also are we, sentence by sentence, until the story takes shape.

The Plague of Doves
Louise Erdrich

Why would things happen as they do and history read as it does if inherent to existence was something called normalcy?

The Human Stain
Philip Roth

There are places I remember
All my life though some have changed
Some forever not for better
Some have gone and some remain
All these places have their moments
With lovers and friends I still can recall
Some are dead and some are living
In my life I've loved them all.

In My Life
The Beatles

Contents

1

Providence Road

Jim is comfortably ensconced in his favourite café. It is a summer's day and with the lunch-hour crowd departed there are now only few. Light tinkling sounds of a piano are playing, and the large windows slid open allow a pleasant breeze – an atmosphere conducive for reading and writing, some quiet conversation.

Pascal arrives with his smiling, gentle-mannered expression and places Jim's usual *café noisette* and croissant and a glass of water.

"*Bonjour, monsieur, ça va?*"

"*Bonjour, Pascal, oui, ça va, merci.*"

He is the eldest waiter, and his formal countenance and politeness are those of an English butler of the old school, or a chauffeur, foppish perhaps outside his black-tie uniform. Despite his middle-aged stoutness he is light and agile on his feet. Jim told him once that when he is rich, he would like him to be his chauffeur. Sundays he would be free to drive the Rolls up and down the Champs-Élysées. Pascal was not sure.

On the table, too, are the pages of a letter from Ingrid, Jim's daughter, with the photos she enclosed of her son Peter on his fifth birthday, a joyful occasion by the look of it. In her letter she reminds Jim of her own fifth birthday party when he jumped up onto the table and danced to Elvis Presley, upsetting a bottle of lemonade that disgorged with funny glottal gulps into the bowl of jelly beans. Some of the kids squealed with laughter, others were dumb with wide-eyed disbelief. "You're crazy, Dad," Ingrid cried with embarrassment. "Get down!" Then the first of a dozen or so grown-ups arrived, those invited to see the performance of *The Magic of Spring*, a birthday treat choreographed by Ingrid and her best playmate, Cindy, music by Vivaldi. They gave out tickets for admission and served drinks and cakes and cups of tea. Some surreptitiously smoked pot. The children sat around on rugs. The production included a skip-on part for Dad in green tights and a crown of leaves – as a good father he had to do it. During the performance there were good-natured chortles and playful sniggers, and with the final bow, cheers all round. In the bathroom afterwards, even though their steps didn't go exactly as rehearsed, they were delighted. It was Cindy who went on to make acting her career.

She remembers also their breakfasts on the front veranda from where they fed the carp, the trickling sounds of water, and from within the jubilant sounds of Vivaldi. At some later time, another memory, the thrill she felt when they climbed together to the topmost branches of the plane tree in the back yard. Those were the innocent days of 1979, when excitement of happiness was everywhere.

Then the not-so-happy times: about a year later, when Ingrid was six, and when her mother fell in love with another, an Englishman. They went to live far away in northern Queensland. The separation broke his heart, but we won't go into that now. During her early school years Jim managed to see Ingrid only half a dozen times. In later years his letters were longer and more thoughtful, ranging freely about his travel experiences – things he'd seen and people he'd met. He hoped that one day she would be inspired and want to reach out and see for herself. She was, of course, still only young, and so reciprocity on her end had been sporadic. Their birthdays are two days apart, so there was that at least. But he remained dedicated because he loved her and feared being forgotten. As a little girl she was joyful and lively, the sun shone out of her; in adolescence there was some deep soul-searching; in adulthood, talk of adult responsibilities; and then parenthood – well, that has been an on-going dialogue. It is because she herself is a parent now, I think, that their bond seems stronger than ever, and she is ever more persistent with her inquisitiveness about his past. She is eager for him to go over it all again, to tell the whole story this time. He is to include all the juicy bits, she says, and not spill a single drop.

And so it was, that with the letter put to one side next to his notebooks and pencils, he leaned back and closed his eyes. He felt a kind of swoon tumbling back into the obscurities of the past, probing the far reaches of his mind.

One by one revenants came to light, some of whom were living still and others who had gone – a resurrection of a sort. In brilliant summer sunshine Jim's mother appeared. She was in her floral dress – roses? I seem to see roses – with one hand shading her eyes and in the other the hand of a child. She was smiling, she looked bemused; there was some background traffic noise, and the tambourine rattle and trombones of the Salvation Army. It must be him – it was the same navy-and-white sailor's suit. Oh, he will never forget his dearly beloved mother.

Like most women of her time, Jim's mother had her favourite film star. He had the air of a suave, aristocratic gentleman. Debonair is the word. His name was Clark Gable. What she would have done for Clark Gable was in her wildest dreams. She saw *Gone with the Wind* two times. Lots of kids were named after Hollywood stars in those days, so Jim might just as easily have been called Clark. Robert, her uncle, lost on the 'field of honour' was also on the cards. It was James Stewart, however, another heartthrob, who won the Academy Award for his role in *The Philadelphia Story* in 1940, the year Jim was born. When *Casablanca* won three Academy Awards two years later, he might have been called Humphrey – lucky, that. His sister got Lauren Bacall. His full name is James Turner, though to most he was just plain, ordinary Jim, and Turner because he comes from a long line of English wood-turners.

Journeys rarely begin where we think they do. Jim's began that day in the backyard, in his eleventh month, with a blunder and a stumble. He picked himself up, took a deep breath then staggered on. When he reached the back gate he squeezed himself through and then out into the world.

There is in every child this essentially human urge to explore, to go where no child has ever ventured, where angels fear to tread, or, in his case, crawl. On the linoleum dining-room floor he could feel the vibration of footsteps and hear from behind the glass-fronted dresser the rattle and tinkle tattle of crockery and glass. He entered the cave under the table and skulked his way through the labyrinth of chairs. He stopped to take stock and discovered he was in a burial ground of dust, flies scattered here and there like dead soldiers. He inspected one between his fingers, muttered to it, tasted it, and spat it out with revulsion.

"James, where are you darling? What are you doing under there, who are you talking to?" his mother always keeping an eye on him.

He crawled out, feeling disgusted, aware that his hands and knees were unusually black. He knew to keep well away from the cupboard under the stairs where the dreaded vacuum cleaner lived. He was headed for the back gate again.

One warm night about a year later, we find him in his crib on the second floor of their dark-brick tenement in Rozelle, in Sydney. The room is dark and full of silence, only the robotic tick … tick … tick of a clock, sometimes a rustle – an insect perhaps, or a small rodent – the sporadic swish of cars and flashes of light across the ceiling; a repetition of some sibilant preternatural sound; again the darkness; a bumping sound, whispers; the landing door opens and gently closes; footfalls on the stairs; time suspended; with a light breeze the curtains swell and ebb and his sudden fright when something with wings and claws flaps at the edge of his sleep. His sheets are wet. He longs for his mother's warm embrace; he yearns for the morning light.

His fears and uncertainties were probably not much different to those of others of such an early age. By trial and error and guidance we make the adjustments necessary to conform and fit in.

His mother wanted to move him up in the world.

"One, two, buckle my shoe,
Three, four, knock on the door,
Five, six, pick up sticks..."

Ten, wonderfully, was a big fat hen!

She liked having him in the kitchen; and each time she made a cake she lifted him up onto the bench so he could watch her break eggs into a bowl then beat them.

He liked to lick the wooden spoon.

Picture now the road outside busy with trams and buses, and below them in the gloom of dim white bulbs the clanking and hammering of machines all day long, welders in grease-stained overalls and hoods that look like the helmets of Crusader knights fizzing and showering sparks, and listen – a radio is on at full blast. Jim can actually taste the smell of oil and metal. Beside them, too, on one side, is the old stone church, Baptist, I think, that gives weekly services, and on the other, set back from an asphalt parking lot, an austere black-glass-fronted parlour with gold Gothic print –

KINSELLA FUNERAL DIRECTORS

(which also gives weekly services, in one door and out the other). Across the road is a Resch's pub. A sign on a window above says *BILLIARDS*.

The trams were nightmarish. They came round a bend then bore down on him like great limbless monsters, heaving from side to side, clanging their bells and clashing their antennae with wires that sparked and sizzled; their step up and handrails were too high off the road, and their wheels just inches away from his toes. His mother had to lift him, urgently, before they pulled away – clang! Clang! And it was fascinating living next to a funeral parlour, peering through the paling fence at a real person being carried, dead in a box, then slid into the back of a hearse, the mourners outside bowed in black and whimpering, overwhelmed by grief.

Rozelle was a gritty inner-city suburb, and it was where, on the main Darling Street, Jim's father ran his butcher shop. He worked long hours and employed a staff of three. Everybody ate meat in those days so the shop made enough to get by on; fish on Fridays. Laurence Turner was popular in Rozelle. He was roguish with rugged good looks, and strong – he could easily heft a hindquarter of beef up to the rail. His uniform was a shirt and tie, a white coat and a blue-and-white striped apron. What gave him a jaunty swashbuckling look was his wide, thick belt and sheath of knives, and on his left side, like a sword, his sharpening steel; no gold earring but perched there was his short red pencil for adding up. He was normally easy-going, and had a way with his customers; he could be playful and make them laugh.

"Tender, lady?" proffering a cut of prime sirloin, frowning, his dignity offended. "Tender? It's as tender as a lady's heart," he would say. Sometimes he would throw in a bit of mince for the dog, and with the children he teased them with a pig's head.

Punctually at 10.30, most mornings Matilda would dutifully

deliver to her hard-working husband his thermos of tea, his slice of fruitcake and his impressionable young master Jim. She loved dressing him up to show him off. On this day, in his stroller, he is dressed in his navy-and-white sailor's suit. He has his whistle. He is excited to be on the voyage again that will take him to the outer limits of his world.

It is a day of brilliant sunshine.

To enter the lane he is pulled backwards up the three steps, the sagging gate then scraped closed behind them. The lane is quiet, narrow, and clean-swept with tall paling fences along each side: on the right are small backyards, some pegged with washing, shirts inhaling the breeze waving their arms, legs doing a funny little dance. One gate, displaying a thick, hand-painted number 6, is oddly coupled and evenly matched with its hand-painted number 6 garbage bin, and sprawled on its lid, hairless and naked and with a look of fixed abandonment, is a tiny plastic doll; a baleful, sick-eyed alley cat is foraging for scraps. On the other side of the lane are the grounds of the church and above them a huge canopy of rustling fig leaves. The lane then turns to the left, still the high palings as far as the main Darling Street.

"Good morning Mrs Turner," red-haired Mrs Fairweather says from her gateway, holding a cigarette and shading her eyes. You can see greyhounds in wire cages in their backyard.

"And how's the little man today?"

Her husband is away for a while and the whole neighbourhood knows why.

Jim loves being steered on his morning outings like this, blowing his whistle.

The same two fat men are seated on the same public bench. They are veterans of the First World War, holding forth and puffing pipes, each wearing grey sweat-stained hats and grey waistcoats, one with a silver watch chain, the other with a crutch and only one leg; with identical freckled hands they might have been brothers. It was the war that was raging across the front pages of all the newspapers then that they mostly talked about – the Luftwaffe had bombed London and the Americans Dresden, the German Army was in retreat, the Japanese were in on the act, Mussolini's bombing of Ethiopia and eventually dragooned and hung upside down in the main square of Milan. It might all come to an end soon, they reckoned.

To Jim's mother they nod a polite hello.

'Whippersnapper' is what the jovial one calls him. "Well now and look who we've got here today. How are you young whippersnapper?" he says, poking his pipe at him. Jim recoils in shyness. "Are ya gonna give us a tune then, are ya?" An Irish accent I now recognise. Whilst his mother exchanges pleasantries with one, Jim watches the other inspect the bowl of his pipe for ash, scrape and tap it clean, check it with an experimental puff, then with a pinch from his pouch stuff it with his blunt stump finger. A match is struck, the tobacco catches and glows red, and when he exhales smoke and extinguishes his match he is ready then to continue his conversation. Fascinating. He produces a penny from behind his ear and blows on it to make it disappear. With a click of his fingers he deftly brings it back. He offers it to Jim as a gift. Jim looks at his mother and she smiles a nod of approval.

And just there at the kerb are a horse trough and two magnificent chestnut Clydesdales. They have just made their deliveries from the railway goods yard to the grain and produce store and so are damp with salty sweat and smell of wet leather. To this day Jim can evoke both of those smells at will. Slurping gallons of water through their thick rubbery lips their bridles jingle and their tails swish away the flies. Matilda lifts him and, curiously, while stroking the bony box of one's forehead it plops a mound of yellow vegetal-smelling stench on the road – *non sequitur.*

Under the horse trough is a dogs' trough. Led by dry noses investigating pockets of air for smells, their tongues hanging out like red rag, thirsty, packs of warring feral dogs prowled the scorching asphalt streets in those days. Their fighting – snarling, biting, ripping one another apart like that – was a terrible, frightening experience for a young child. The winner would then go to claim the nearest telegraph pole, and to prove it was his, raise a back leg and scribble his signature all over it. Fascinating. And it is near here at this time each day that a fat old woman in an oversized woolen blue cardigan feeds crumbs to the pigeons.

The sun bears down, the road already quivers; it will be another very hot day.

The main road now is busy with activity.

Ha, Tony, the barrowman who sells fruit on the Woolworths corner comes into view. He is an excitedly happy handsome young man who speaks a funny accented English. Above his mosaic of fruits dangle bunches of bananas. He likes Jim's mother and makes sure she gets the best.

"*Buongiorno*, Tony," she says. "*Va bene?*"

"Ha, Mrs. Turner, I keepa these tomatoes specially for you."

He puts them in a paper bag.

"*Pomodoro*," he says, responding to her enquiry, which is her way of being friendly and welcoming.

"*Ciao, bambino*," smiling down on Jim, "*sei bellissimo*", and then offers him something rich red and apparently meant for eating. Its juicy softness leaves his mouth flooded with its succulent sweetness; a trickle runs down his chin and spills onto his front.

"*Fragola*," Tony says.

Jim smiles at his first word in Italian and the taste of his first delicious strawberry, the Proustian madeleine he will never forget.

"*Arrivederci, grazie, à la prossima.*"

They enter Woolworths to buy some skeins of wool and come out with colouring books and pencils and a bottle of glue.

Sounds of a mouth organ rise above the street noise. A whiskered old man, lean as a prairie dog with a green, pink-faced parrot on one shoulder, is scampering a merry tune. When Jim drops his penny into his tin he raises his eyebrows and gives a friendly nod; there is a sparkle in his eyes, he must be kind. And when he stops playing one hears the squeals of children in the school opposite, which, in years to come, Jim will also attend.

The footpath now is mercifully shaded with awnings. The hardware store displays shiny pots and shovels and balls of string; set back for the steps that lead up to them and closed are the doors to the bank; the barber shop with big chairs. Smells of mouth-watering deep-sea frying come from the Greek's fish-and-chip shop, and Mr Douglas' cake shop smells of hot buns and sugar-sprinkled sponges. They go in and buy a vanilla slice.

On another corner, Harris' Grain and Produce Store, where a short, stout, elderly man is sweeping the floor – Mr Harris, I presume – smells dry and musty of buckwheat and bran. Chalked on his stonewall outside, at child's height, is a white tree with white fruit, and on the footpath below, chalked in elegant cursive, is the word *ETERNITY*.

Others doing their shopping smile at Mrs Turner and wish her a good morning. Those also wheeling strollers stop, look down and then gush. They share what all women know about raising children. Jim, meanwhile, at the same eye level as his peer, making his inspection up and down with silent curiosity, wonders what all the fuss is about. He feels as if his ship has run aground, marooned. His father's tea is getting cold. But he is an angel cherub, his pretty face white with rosy cheeks, blue eyes and long golden ringlets, on loan from the Sistine Chapel, the daughter his mother still hadn't had.

Hand-cranked cars rattle by, trams clang their bells, horses clip-clop and jingle and cyclists tingle. Once there was the blaring siren of a speeding fire engine, and once, even, marching in their uniforms, the rattle of tambourines and blowing of trombones of the Salvation Army. A chugging steamroller, like a monstrous rolling pin, rolls smooth, thick black pastry; the fishmonger throws a bucket of ice in the gutter; two men push a car that has no one in it.

From the distant goods yard come the shrill whistle of locomotives and the shunting sounds of freight cars. The acid air pollution stings his eyes and the swamp of radiating heat reddens his face. You can see it in the sky, the yellow smudge of sulphurous smoke from the tall brick chimneys of the Colgate soap factory and the black coal smoke from the goods yards. Everybody suffered, but his mother, with bronchial asthma, was an extreme case.

Finally and wonderfully it is his father's butcher shop that marks the journey's end. Laurence is always delighted to see Jim. He lifts him and gives an abrasive kiss, then gleefully throws him high into the air, his face stricken with fear. Then, more gleefully, he throws him a second time even higher, his face stricken with even greater fear. He carries Jim to show him off, one by one, to each of his customers. "This one's cut out for Prime Minister," he boasts. They adore him. Matilda stands back to let him have his day. Jim is then let down to crawl on the floor. It is a soft, thick, yielding carpet of pine-fresh sawdust, and for sensitive young hands the texture is exquisite. He crawls to the refrigerated display cabinet to cool his face on the glass and is confronted with folds of white tripe and rows of plump pink sausages. In her dress of many lovely colours Matilda is laughing as she stoops and picks him up and dusts him off. And it is there that the memory of being wheeled to his father's shop fades. But wait, a little bit more: there was the bicycle ring of the cash register too, and the keening sound of his father's knife on his steel, and the wooden chopping sounds of the wooden chopping block.

Now, why that day in particular, I wonder? It was as any other, nothing untoward: floral-print dresses were what Matilda loved to wear, her laughter as she lifted and enfolded him, the sweet smell of her scent ... Ah, yes, now I know – the memory suddenly reveals itself. It was not the smell of his mother's scent but the smell now from this box of Faber pinewood pencils, the same unforgettable pinewood smell of sawdust on his father's butcher shop floor.

"Pascal, *un verre d'eau, s'il vous plaît.*"

I see him now one Sunday morning a few years later, sitting on the steps of the church. Baggy shorts, a button wrongly button-holed, no shoes, sticking plaster on his big toe, and a nuisance fly buzzing at the scab on his right knee. I see he is missing a tooth. He has his bag of marbles. Nobody else has noticed him. He is casually observing them, the small congregation of worshippers (simple pious folk), and the Reverend Donnelly (a kind face), all feeling relief from the sun's golden warmth, smiling and nodding to one another, dark patches of sweat forming beneath their armpits. There is Mr Grimshaw, the undertaker from Kinsellas, and Mrs Kilborne, a customer who once complained about his father's sausages. He perceives a mysterious blend of smells – the boxy odour of old-age decay, stale flower water, thumb-smudged prayer books, and the deodorant sweetness of frankincense. Inside, in the cobwebbed gloom relieved by bright colours of tinted glass, he can't believe it: down past the rows of pews, near the altar, he can make out a man almost naked, thin and deathly white, nailed to a cross.

He liked Sunday school in the church's annexe, playing games with others, games with building blocks and bottle-tops, colouring in with crayons depictions of parables from the Bible, cutting out pictures to paste in his book, or, on the wall next to other drawings, pin the tail on the donkey. And singing songs – *Yes, Jesus loves me* ... With the doors wide open the floor was awash with lovely warm sunshine, and on the end table was a large vase of yellow flowers and plates of cupcakes and bowls of jelly beans; looked down upon from above was the kind-face of Jesus surrounded by his flock of benign white sheep. He felt here that life was good. It was where he first met Eunice. She was wearing a flared bright red dress matched by her shoes and ribbons and her peachy red cheeks. She was the minister's daughter. She attended ballet classes and was learning the piano. She was gorgeously pretty. Jim adored her.

At the risk of getting caught, he sometimes squeezed through a hole in the fence into the grounds of the rectory where the Reverend Donnelly lived with his wife and Eunice. The rectory itself was a solid mansion with a gabled rear porch with filigreed columns, and sometimes from within the tinkling sounds of a piano could be heard. The grounds were a wonderful unkempt forest of magnificent Moreton Bay figs, massive, swaying, a rustling, gesticulating canopy pierced by flashes of blinding sunlight. The ground cover was of twigs and dead leaves in wild grasses. The only human incursions were a few tilting moss-blackened gravestones, or sometimes the vicar himself, who advanced on Jim in his clerical collar, growling and brandishing a leather strap: "You're not supposed to be in here, get out!" One day he found a pigeon lying in the grass. It was stiff and pallid, its eyes like shiny black beads, its wing he spread like a fan; how beautiful and fine its feathers, its throat colours of blue and crimson and purple sheen like the brilliant tints of acetylene flame. From the beak of its averted face emerged a tiny, frenzied black ant. Eunice, hanging upside down from a branch with her arms splayed, was laughing.

Not yet seven, another place to satisfy his prying nature was the pub opposite. Sometimes in his pyjamas and dressing gown he sneaked downstairs and crossed the tramlines to catch ten o'clock closing. It was like a lunatic asylum in there with all those bellowing scorch-faced bullies, supposed to be home with their wives, falling about drunk, laughing their heads off and singing songs:

"Show me the way to go home,
I'm tired and I wanna go to bed.
Had a little drink about an hour ago
And it's gone right to my head.
Show me the way to go home..."

Mr Tyndal, a gunner in the First World War, was never seen without a glass in his hand.

"Hey, Jimmy," he said, "Have a glass of beer. "

"I am too young to drink beer, Mr Tyndal."

"Well, I'll be buggered. Take a look at this then," he said.

He flexed his muscle to show Jim how a scantily clad lady tattooed on his arm could wiggle her hips. Jim laughed.

"You like her then, do you?" Mr Tyndal said.

A fat one, laughing his head off fell against a wall and slid down onto the floor. Two other fat ones tried to lift him but then they too fell, and so now there were three of them bellowing with laughter, sprawled on the beer-spilled floor. What a sight, like three beached dugongs. The barman was shouting loudly that it was time please for everyone to go home.

They were always decent and friendly to Jim. He went around the bar with a cupped hand and begged them, "Please mister, Can I have a penny?"

Some took the tips from the bar.

Mr Cooper took a penny from behind his ear.

"I know that trick," Jim said, and thanked him.

He'd done pretty well. He sneaked his way back up the stairs and into his bed.

He cashed in empty drink bottles to buy vanilla slices; the tooth fairy left him pennies for vanilla slices.

"What'd you buy?"

"Not for you."

"Show me."

"Not for you. Get away."

It was a Saturday afternoon and Jim had his pennies jingling in his pocket. The pictures at the Kings cinema were what he lived for. All the burgeoning stars of Hollywood were there then. He joined the queue on the hot footpath, and one by one they stepped up into the foyer where they bought tickets and liquorice straps or Jaffas (red-coated chocolate balls). From the foyer, then, through a heavy-curtained doorway, he entered the coolness of the magnificent picture palace. Its interior was fabulous – glittering chandeliers; the ceiling frescoed with heavenly angels and cherubs; naked ladies in protective veils stood in niches holding urns, and high up, crouched on ledges, folded like bats, demonic ghouls glowered down on him. All the kids were as excited and restless as ants. You found a seat, the house lights dimmed, the curtains drew slowly, teasingly slowly, apart, and then, ta-da, the show began – how incredibly exciting.

Firstly, everyone had to stand for *God Save the King*. Once a boy behind Jim pulled him and punched his back. "Stand up!" he growled. Next Movietone reported the news: there was a dogfight with a Spitfire that sent a Luftwaffe plane trailing black smoke plummeting into the sea, and bombs seen from above, drifting in quiet unison, exploded like sparks on cities below. Pretty ladies paraded in swimsuits for a beauty pageant, and Donald Bradman, with his famous cover drive, scored another

Test century against England. The cartoons, which came next – Mickey, Donald, Pluto, Goofy or Porky Pig (none of them except Goofy wore pants) had the whole house in stitches; some wet themselves. The feature film could be the slapstick antics of Charlie Chaplin, his funny long shoes and cane and twitching moustache, his comical wound-up way of walking, or the maniacal Marx Brothers in *Duck Soup*, or the hilarious fatty-and-skinny duo of Stan Laurel and Oliver Hardy, or *Batman and Robin*, or *Tarzan and the Apes* – incredible. It seemed anything could happen in those days because everything was possible. They were days of miracles and wonder. Hordes of mad screaming Indians could come galloping across the screen. They did. And for Superman, who could *fly faster than a speeding bullet*, the excitement pitch would rise and kids jumped up and down and their Jaffas tumbled and rolled all the way down to the front. Jim often dreamed he could fly, high above some metropolis, arms outstretched, looking down on all those upturned faces, their mouths agape, pointing. Nobody could hear what was being said on the screen but it didn't seem to matter very much – it was the occasion that made it so exciting, being able to laugh and scream in the dark.

Lines marked in pencil on the kitchen wall showed how tall he was growing. He was nearly seven now and had just begun his attendance at primary school. His mother covered all his new exercise books with different coloured paper, and printed on each with care his name in blue ink – name, grade and subject. Timid and uncertain at first, he managed to overcome his shyness and joined in. He discovered a new world of play-acting. In 'Pandora's Box' was a wonderful array of fancy dress costumes. Rummaging through he found he could be a pirate, a prince, a cowboy, a jester or an old man with a stick. The plays they rehearsed were to be performed at the end of the year, when all their families would be invited to come along. It was on a Saturday afternoon his mother took him to see the new French film called *Les Enfants du Paradis*, starring Jean-Louis Barrault. When Jim saw how wonderfully he mimed Pierrot, the beguiling, sensitive white clown, he knew that was the role he wanted to play. His adventurous young art teacher encouraged and directed him, while his mother made his costume.

I see now the first big night is a full house, the families all gathered, the air charged with happy anticipation. Jim's performance will be the last one of the evening. It is called *A Street in Paris*. His rehearsals had gone well; he was calm and confident.

The others' performances before his brought much jollity and appreciation.

And now, finally, it is his turn.

With the curtain raised we see him standing at the front of the bare spot lit stage. He looks quite wonderful in his white satin costume and matching cap, his face white-painted, his eyes darkened and his lips shaped with red. All is perfectly quiet. Then he turns and is caught by surprise at his audience. He touches his mouth roundly open like a fish's. Who are you? Why are you here, his expression seems to say? He looks at one, then another, then another. He points to one further back. Why are you here? Nobody answers. Someone giggles. Oh well, he shrugs, then slowly makes his way to centre stage.

He is clever at conjuring mystery and making the invisible visible. After all, isn't magic the work of the charmer?

We are to imagine a crowded, narrow street scene filled with the merriment of revellers. It is a celebratory occasion of some sort. For the pleasure of our amusement a rounded trombonist comes rolling by, and a playful jester tweaks someone's nose; a lady tap dancer and a clever juggler, and a bent old man with a stick begging for money are performed, and others, too, just being who they are. He delicately removes the old man's glasses, gives them a rub, puts them back then gives him a coin. *Be careful*, he warns him, *pickpockets*. A bosomy lady calls to him from a window above and he waves back. With a grandiose bow to a pretty mademoiselle he graciously presents a nosegay, and for a boy's civility a big red balloon. Sniff, sniff – ah, there is the smell of fresh-baked bread. He enters a tavern, sits and takes a glass of ale. He gives the barman a tip. He takes a sip and turns. Oops – he presses four fingers over his open mouth again – his audience is still there. His expression softens. With his arm on the bar he rests his chin on his hand, bats his eyes and gives them all a beguiling, self-satisfied smile. They are captivated; they gasp and giggle. The curtain falls and there is loud, rapturous applause.

"Oh yes," his mother whispers, "and how deserving."

Afterwards she took him in her arms and held him close. She adored him. His teacher told him his performance was faultless. He was conscious of all the smiles and stares and you could see he was proud. Eunice was there. Someone took his photo.

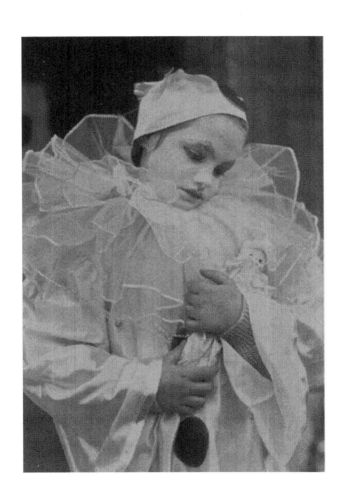

Not long after the war, Jim fell in with some pretty bad company. Diminutive, pugnacious, white-skinned redhead, good with his fists, always looking for a fight and something to steal – you wouldn't have wanted to cross Keith Fairweather, not back in those days. He took after his father. His father was in for stealing, and his uncle, a shifty greyhound punter, was tarred with the same brush.

Keith was a barefooted runner for a greyhound bookie – he collected from the losers and made pay-offs to the winners and the cops. Short for his age, his pants had to be rolled and tucked under his belt. And he was a shrewd kid with initiative. Each Saturday morning he set himself up near the horse trough with a bicycle-tube repair business, puffing cigarettes, loutish. You left your bike, and with his tools he would have it all done in a matter of minutes. He charged two-pence. Once, a big guy with rolled-up sleeves came up to Keith and called him a smart-arse. Keith quickly got his measure. He lunged at him, gave him a swift smack in the mouth and assumed the crouch of a boxer. The bully glared at him, thought better of taking him on, then turned and lurched away. Keith let out a resounding fart. He was always able to take care of himself.

Another brainwave was his seesaw. All he needed was a large steel drum and a long plank. This monkey business caused more trouble. Jim was too young, and being flung so high scared the wits out of him. When he slid off the low end, it rose and struck a severe blow beneath his chin, causing him to bite his tongue. "You bloody idiot," Keith shouted. Jim was rushed to hospital and had it stitched. The scar is still plain to see.

Anyway, Jim and Keith were both larrikins and they fought in the same street gang together. They threw stones and bottles and insults, wielded sticks and kicked over garbage bins. Keith was impudent to the mothers and got reprimanded by the police. They let down car tyres and threw stones onto the tram tracks to watch them derail; they removed covers from manholes and peed in them; they unlatched the pigeon house; they burned German effigies and even skewered dead rats. They got their share of cuts and bruises. The money cadged in pubs went mostly on cigarettes; they pilfered chewing gum and comics. Eating liquorice straps, smoking and reading comics on Keith's floor stifled the tedium of having nothing to do.

The community, though, were mostly decent, good-hearted folk, the men mostly living the quotidian routine of unskilled manual labour in factories or on the wharves or in the coal-yards, some of them as foremen; the women: shopping, washing, ironing, cleaning and cooking. They occupied identical semi-detached brown-brick homes behind brown-painted picket fences and small flower plots. On their sills and doorsteps lay the grimy windblown dust. But they didn't complain and they stayed together. Tabloid newspapers provided them with the enormous scope and range of human folly – the war, hideous murders, titillating sex, rumours of scandal in high places, horse racing and rugby, births and deaths and funeral notices, etc. It was legendary still, after all the years, the Barrets on Beattie Street winning third prize in the lottery. She died just after and he drank the money away and died of a liver condition. Billy Reynolds on the same street won enough to set himself up with an ice-cream shop on Bondi Beach.

Jim's dear mother, frail and gentle, was one of the domesticated. She'd had her five boys in six years (the twins died at birth and Jim's two brothers, John and Edward, were the eldest), which even for a strong, healthy woman would have been quite an ordeal. It was not that she really wanted such a large family but that she longed for a daughter, the daughter that by then she had gotten to know by heart. Certainly her husband wouldn't have wanted a large family, struggling as he was. None of the relatives on both sides were well-to-do, nor were they religious, and I don't think any of them lived to be a ripe old age, but then, during those years not many did.

It was the multifarious activities like these that made Jim's childhood so unforgettable. Sure, he got roused on a lot and often walked around with skinned knees and once with his arm in a sling, but that was all part of it. He performed daredevil feats that sometimes brought him to within an inch of his life; he met with drunks and lunatics and also the friendly and good-hearted. Every day was a new adventure. He was never lonely or bored, and he will never forget the day his father took him to see Jimmy Caruthers become the new bantamweight champion of the world.

After the arrival of the fifth child there wasn't the space any more. With the war over things were slowly getting back to normal. There was time to think again; there was the air of a new beginning. With the young men returned there was new employment; the tram conductors were more chirpy with the ladies; the ladies dressed more stylishly and showed a bit more leg; shop-fronts were painted in new colours; butter was no longer rationed; chromium plating, extruded plastic and asbestos sheeting were the new materials; more and more new-model cars came on the roads; memorials to those who had fallen were erected in public places, Lest We Forget. Housing sites on new subdivisions of peripheral bush land came up for sale. It was much fresher and cleaner out there. The site they chose was marked out with white stakes at the end of an un-named dirt clearing that one day would come to be known as Providence Road. Who their neighbours next door would be was as unpredictable as the ones who would lie beside their graves in another future.

They were the pioneers in that part of the world. The axe striking the trees alerted birds that had never heard that sound before: rozellas, rainbow lorikeets, mountain parakeets, sulphur crested cockatoos, galahs, wrens, and finches, all of such resplendent colours. The kookaburras were hilarious, a real treat for a city boy. It was evening dusk, everything peaceful, when they came home to roost. Perched on branches, they would suddenly go berserk and the trees shook with loud, contagious laughter. They cackled like maniacs, all getting the same silly joke in some loony bin it seemed, and on and on it went until eventually they settled down, ruffled and shuffled their feathers, a bit of a wheeze, then finally they nodded off to sleep. Down at the creek dragonflies with iridescent limpid wings, quivering with lambent beauty, hovered above shallow rock pools, over which small black beetles darted back and forth, making small ripples of the sun's bright reflection; frogs and crayfish thrived; spiders' webs suspended from ferns, fine as gossamer silk, motioned to each passing breeze.

In their imagination they had ideas of what their new home would be like: a straightforward plan of simple rectangularity, not too modern, timber-framed, asbestos-sheet cladding painted a pale yellow, and the roof of the local Marseilles tiles, reddish-brown; in the lounge room would be a coke fireplace with a mantel, a spare nursery room just in case, in the entry floral carpet and a fan-shaped mirror – in other words, suburban vernacular. A builder, a friend of a friend, studied the plans and saw no problems. Afterwards there would be room for a front lawn with a round fishpond with a sprinkling fountain and four cement frogs, the backyard would be rows of vegetables and fruit trees, and a penned-off run for laying-hens and ducks.

They drove to their site on weekends. Taking in the new fresh air and carrying rocks and wheel barrowing the land improved Matilda's strength, and the sun ripened her complexion; blackberry thorns clutched at her garments and scratched her skin, dry earth-dust clung to her and got caught in her hair, as if the wilderness was trying to claim her as well, as if this was where she was meant to be, what she should really look like. Snakes and lizards slithered. Laurence was used to hard labour but never before as hard as this with his sleeves rolled up perspiring in the sun, hammering and sawing studs and rafters, as the first Colonial settlers had done. It was Jim's job to punch the nails in the tongue and grooved pine flooring, and to keep the fire burning with the logs of felled trees. At the end of each day's hard labour Matilda filled the billy for tea. Laurence sat like a swagman and rolled a cigarette while he waited till it boiled. He looked with pride at his new construction. He felt good. With the sun bedded down and the air cooler the crickets started up again. It hadn't rained for six months.

The first thing all young wives love to do in their new home is to make the curtains. Jim has a particularly happy memory of when the house was finally finished, that first night, the meal of expertly carved roast lamb with sauce made from the mint he'd picked that afternoon, potatoes roasted with pumpkin, parsnips and onions, and the rejoicing when his father took his bride once again, and when he slept and dreamed between crisp new sheets. And there was big celebration not long afterwards when Matilda finally had her longed-for daughter. They called her Lauren, after Lauren Bacall.

It was a long walk to the nearest shop, school, cinema and bus stop. The summer heat was oppressive and unrelenting, the drone of cicadas monotonous and constant, and the isolation and boredom unbearable. Through the long still nights two faraway heart-wounded dogs howled to one another, at dawn the jagged retching sounds of faraway roosters; then the quiet-rain sound of his father taking his shower. Jim got up and put on his dressing gown to go and make the porridge. He watched his father in his singlet making funny faces in the mirror while he scraped away his lather.

After school he played marbles or climbed trees to catch cicadas. As a cowboy he galloped madly around the bush on his broomstick horse and single-handedly picked off Red Indians; as a soldier with a wooden rifle over one shoulder he marched straight-backed in a straight line – left, left, left, right left. He catapulted rows of bottles, picked blackberries for jam, and loved fresh-bread peanut butter sandwiches. His hobby was collecting stamps.

The only other settlers then were the Thomases next door. They had lived there reclusively for years, miles out of town. Another mile away was the Italian flower orchard and the Chinese rhubarb garden. The Thomases' home was a faded-grey weatherboard shack with a red-painted corrugated iron roof; the roof drained into a large rainwater tank. The old house was well grounded with a rubble-stone fireplace and chimney. Muscatel grapes shaded their rear terrace and throughout the day there was the creak and slap of a fly-screen door; flypaper coils hung from their ceilings; there was a smell of wood smoke. Leonard, the father, was stoical by nature, didn't talk much but he could recite by heart the ballads of Banjo Patterson and Henry Lawson. He had a set of encyclopaedias he studied each night. By day he drove a delivery truck for Tullochs – shovels and forks and other heavier hardware. They sowed tomatoes and lettuces, peas, beans and strawberries; had a run of laying-hens, a milking cow they called Daisy, and a playful red setter they called Ted. Sometimes in their backyard at dusk the idyllic scene was redolent of a Tom Roberts painting: Leonard in his braces and collarless shirt chopping wood or turning the soil with a long-handled shovel; Bella, his young wife, reclined on a grassy mound holding their baby, or shelling peas; and, weightless in the cool blue evening air, rising from the chimney like a fine brush stroke, a ribbon of milk-blue smoke. The Protestant shibboleth that the sweat of the brow from an honest day's toil, daily prayers, total abstinence and chastity guaranteed a virtuous life was the upbringing Leonard would inculcate into his children. Discipline, too, to keep them in line. A tyrant with a leather strap, he made them dig for potatoes and pull weeds till dark, always snivelling and miserable, always smelling of soap.

On Sunday mornings Leonard and Bella and their three children – William, like a little naval officer in his black suit and glaring white shirt, black spit-polished shoes, hair wet and waved and meticulously parted, a smaller version of his father; and Judith and Beatrice like cute little dolls in bonnets bowed with pink ribbons, smaller versions of their mother – went chugging off to church, upright in their T-model Ford, usually with the canvas hood folded back, not for worship so much as for moral rectitude.

The two women yearned for friendship. What separated them was the rusted barbed wire boundary fence that over the years had grown a hedge of tiny pink roses. One day, hanging out the washing Mrs Turner said hello and commented on how nice the day was. Mrs Thomas agreed and advanced slowly to elaborate, treading her way carefully around the rhubarb patch, like a timid animal being coaxed with a biscuit, to the rose-covered fence. Their words met and mingled among the flies; they helped one another in forming a friendship, mostly by being agreeable. Mrs Thomas cut a slightly queer figure – bovine, with thick waist and ample breasts, her arms warding off the flies, her hair escaping in grey wisps from her frayed straw hat, a gaping hole in one elbow of her husband's grey woollen cardigan, her muddied Wellingtons, and pink rubber gloves holding a knife and stalks of red-blushed rhubarb. She was good-natured though, a heart of gold, and together, whilst batting away the flies, they found they had a whole world of things to yarn about, be serious about, and even laugh about. They knew all the things women know yet seldom talk about: warm eucalyptus oil as an analgesic for earaches was a new one for Mrs Thomas, as was a frozen hot water bottle when the nights got up over a hundred degrees Fahrenheit for Mrs Turner; elixirs for mumps and measles and chicken pox, lotions for insect bites and scratches; recipes for blackberry jam, scones, bread pudding and fruit preserves in jars, how cloves gave pears a certain flavour. Ted, sitting still and regal as the Sphinx with his paws stretched out on the cool grass, he just listened. Sometimes they slipped into the undercurrents of their pasts, touched on the maiden sides of their family histories. Mrs Thomas recalled how when she was in school a farm boy once put her up against a wall and told her he wanted to marry her, and she confessed how once she got a bit tipsy on a taste of beer.

"In old England the family name was often taken after the family trade," Mrs Turner explained. "Smith is common because forging horseshoes and farm implements was one of the most common trades, and there were the Farmers and Taylors, the Carpenters and Cooks. The Hargreaves were the hedge-growers; we Turners turned the legs of tables and chairs. I don't know about the Thomases."

"Well I never – you live and learn, don'cha, eh?" Mrs Thomas remarked about such things.

"To tell you the honest truth, I'm not really one for books," she said when Matilda offered her the one on poetry she had on loan from the council library.

When their friendship grew from one of acquaintance to something more intimate, when their inner natures had been revealed, they leaned to one another to talk about the men, their husbands, in complicity. Some things, of course, could never be talked about. Hearing the kids' cries home from school and the squawking galahs coming in to roost, they said their farewells till another day. In season Mrs Thomas gave some of their leftover strawberries and muscatels. Laurence, in turn, gave the extra sack of chicken feed he picked up from Harris' Grain and Produce Store. To be invited in for a cup of tea, well, that would have been stretching things a bit too far.

They mourned the King's passing and were enchanted by the Coronation and the Royal Wedding.

One winter's evening in the lounge room, Matilda was at the fireplace darning the heels of woollen socks. Feeling fresh after a nice hot bath, Jim was in his dressing gown and slippers, sitting on the floor, content with his head cushioned on her lap, his arm around her waist. It was such a comfort to have the warmth of the coke fire, to be able to see the glowing embers shuffle and subside into different forms. There is nothing like a home fire. On the mantelpiece Christmas cards were still arrayed, and above the mantel hung the framed still-life print of a vase of magnolias in bloom, beside which three fallen petals lay. Only for the hiss and shuffle of the coke everything was quiet. He gazed at her. There was grace and mystery in her nature, and he could see on her face her expression was thoughtful, she looked beautiful – another treasured memory.

She put down her needle and thimble and took out a book and candle. She lit the candle to read by. She began to recite with feeling poems by Shelley, then The Ballad of the Inchcape Rock:

"'Come back! Come back!' he cried in grief
'Across this stormy water;
And I'll forgive your Highland chief,
My daughter! O my daughter!'"

He loved the longing in her voice and the skipping, rhyming sounds of the words. She loved poetry not just for its imagery and musicality, but also because it brought with it the kind of gentility belonging to the more privileged class.

She closed her book and smiled down on him.

"Your hair looks nice like that," she said.

The dramatis personae in Jim's memory are a disparate and sometimes bewildering lot. Some come to him in dreams, others when he cannot sleep. In one dream he remembers, he was sharing a box carriage of a clackety train with a blind old man he had never met before, hands of a farmer. They were both travelling to Paris. He said he was going to visit his brother in hospital.

Lying awake, in his mind's eye they come wearing the same costumes they once did, each removed from the details of before and since, none of them aged. Some smiling reach for his embrace; Mr Dudgeon, his choirmaster – he is sure it is him – reaches out and tells him to sing C, then, sotto voce, he melts away; the Reverend Donnelly and others like him come on and scowl with pursed lips; some in formal costumes deferentially bow, and, oh no, not Keith again: bare-footed, a fag in his mouth, fists clenched, posed as a boxer. Memory prefers to hold things still. And now there is Aunt Bess, poor Aunt Bess, sitting on the loo with the door open, a newspaper spread on her lap, shelling prawns, a plop sound.

With nobody else willing to take her in she one day landed on their doorstep wearing a blue dress and muddy shoes, having walked a mile from where a tow truck had dropped her. She was drenched to the bone. It was six in the morning. Holding only a half-filled suitcase and something edible in a brown paper bag she tapped on the door.

Matilda saw her sister through the window.

"Oh, no," she said.

Jim was twelve years old at the time and had never heard of her.

In her mid thirties, immaculately done up, Aunt Bess had made a lot of money gambling on horses and men, most of which she squandered on opiates and Barossa Pearl (a bubbly pink wine). Destitute and lonely now, she drank only cold black tea. You could tell by her features that she must once have been quite good-looking, and it was said she had once been an impressive ballroom dancer. But now she was just skin and bones. She sat as still and pale as a marble statue, blank-faced as a cloth doll, hardly ever saying a word. She never wore her slippers, nor, apparently, any underwear, only her pink satin dressing gown – a vestige of her boudoir – and a pair of thick grey woollen socks.

With her legs crossed her eyes sometimes darted about or stared back in on herself as if listening to something that was or wasn't there, or, without blinking, at the veins that stood out like leeches on the backs of her hands. She shunned the company of others and insisted on having the radio off. Her gold ring reminded her of Bill, whom she once loved and did still, but all she could remember was his name and something about a car crash. Sometimes she would wake up in the night and leap out of bed calling out his name, convinced he was still alive. Matilda guided her back to bed with a sleeping pill.

Jim was oddly touched and at the same time bemused by her moods. He never saw her laugh or cry, except once. She was staring ahead, chuckling to herself and nodding with approval – dry sarcasm, it seemed; or spite; possibly something mischievous, or malevolent even, who knows, as if it was *she* who was humouring *him*. And then suddenly she threw her head back and gave this loud, shrill whinny, like something out of a mad scene in an opera, which nearly scared the wits out of Jim. She had never done that before.

And she was skittish: the face in the mirror intimidated her, its putty-coloured skin; the wild, sad look in its eyes; the mouth sometimes smeared with lipstick trying to smile; the hair unruly – someone she barely recognised. She reached out and touched its cheek and saw it do the same, its fingers stained with nicotine. She whimpered and released herself and scuffled away.

At the table Jim stared with fixed fascination at the way she squashed and screwed each cigarette, her thumbs and fingers then wrestling to roll another; then the disarray of broken matches, the first deep inhalation, one eye shut against the smoke, then the flicking of ash in the direction of the ashtray, and threads of tobacco clinging to her lips. Would she like him to read to her, he asked, a cup of tea, perhaps? She seemed not to recognise him. Or was it the idea of a cup of tea that confused her? What might one have found seething there in that dark well of her mind?

He made sure that she took her pills with each meal. The only foods she seemed to enjoy were prawns and chocolate bars and the sweet biscuits she liked to dunk in her cold black tea. Feeding the hens and collecting eggs would have given her something to do, but she didn't understand.

"We can't keep her!" Laurence declared.

One morning soon afterwards, after a fit of despair in the bathroom mirror, pills scattered everywhere, she was escorted off in an ambulance.

Aunt Bess was never talked about after that.

I wonder whatever became of her?

Her slippers were later discovered hidden in the biscuit tin.

Ah, those days – the ones you think about when you can't go to sleep, usually in the wee small hours, around three or four when all others' lights are out, in the day's silence before the first bird sounds, only the fridge mumbling nonsensically to itself over there in the corner. But he was reluctant to go to sleep anyway, to close the door on another light-filled day and enter the dark world of slithering, weird and wonderful dreams. Hours would be stolen from him and never given back.

Now, Aunt Bess, poor Aunt Bess, she was one thing. Memories of her come with sadness and some amusement. Hers and so many others should all, like pressed flowers and postcards, be tucked away and protected; some are as vague as the vestigial chalk markings of some carelessly erased clause; too many, alas, have been erased altogether. There are others, too, best forgotten, that will never go away. Jim's classmate Phillip Whalen, for instance, when they were both running for a bus that day and Phillip slipped on the loose gravel and fell, the wheel running over his hand, the imprint of the tread and the gravel embedded in his hand, his face turning white as a plate … *Too awful, go away* – and Jim holding the hens getting their heads chopped off. They possess. They cling like scar tissue, those horrible ones. Do we belong to them or do they belong to us?

Another incident was with his father, a few days after his sixteenth birthday – the deep shame mostly. Who was to blame? Who was responsible? We are talking now about a miserably unhappy time for Jim. The new school wasn't going well, his mother's health was getting worse, the boredom of living in the bush, another black eye after sticking up for himself in the paddock after school, no girls. Well, there was Deirdre Jackson, the bus driver's daughter, older by two years and considerably larger. She wasn't bad looking but boy, was she difficult. As a child she'd been given to tantrums and flashes of bad temper and she could still punch her way out of any argument. There was a small, permanent scar above one eyebrow, and sometimes, unexplained bruises. She cut her hair short as a boy's and painted her fingernails purple. He could tell by the way she teased him that she seemed to have taken a bit of a shine to him. 'Lover Boy', she called him. He was lean and slow, had stubbornly unkempt, longish, rope-coloured hair and eyes of blue, a few pubescent pimples. In the bush there weren't many other males around. Given half a chance she would wrestle him to the ground, pin him down, and with her tongue poking out on one side and laughter in her eyes, sit on him. "I surrender, I give up, I give up," he cried in pain, her chewing-gum breath in his face and the smell of crushed weeds. Then she lifted him and gave him a big bear hug. He liked the smoothness of her skin and her soft breasts. Late one night he heard the rattle of a handful of gravel on his window and knew it was she. He imagined in bed she would have the strength of an octopus. But her heart was kind. She rescued a sick, abandoned terrier once and cared for it till it died in old age. Jim caught her stepping out from behind a bush one day, hitching up her knickers.

But I digress. That incident with his father, senseless and wilful, and never talked about:

"I feel rotten," Jim said, moping around the house feeling constipated, he couldn't help it. His father in a pair of shorts and a singlet, a hammer in his hand, was sitting on the back step cobbling the boys' shoes. He was in his early forties by then and developing a paunch. He had only one face around the house, which was sullen. He looked tired and needed a shave.

"Buckle up son, get over it," came the stern rebuke. "Now go and do the dishes."

Standing at the sink, looking at the backyard, he thought, *what a mess*. It had gone to weeds, rusted sheets of iron and leftover timber stacked against the garage (its floor stained black with sump oil), the moulting white cockatoo trapped in its cage squawking its head off (one wing clipped in case it ever managed to escape), the door of the dunny hanging askew on one hinge, and piled against the fence the tangled wire of the demolished fowl pen. Several flies lay comatose on the window sash (their repeated head-butts against the pane), the carapace of a glassy green beetle, and to add to that small menagerie, the ruin of a daddy-long-legs spider. The gravy-coloured washing-up water was warm and greasy. It was another day of a heat wave. He was sweating like a pig.

At that time doing some interstate trucking, his father thought a few days break from school might give Jim some respite and help to improve his morale. They would drive up to Moree in the far northwest of New South Wales, a small grazing town, and to make Jim feel more the man his father wanted him to be he had him sit with a .22 rifle on his lap. "In case we see rabbits," he said.

Well, a definitely unforgettable experience it was: Jim marvelled at the vastness and flatness and emptiness of the parched red desert floor; the huge void of silence; suspended primordial time; and the night sky an extravagance of scintillating diamonds that seemed like pinpricks into the light of the universe. The east-west highway ran straight for hundreds of miles with only a single diner and petrol station; road signs showed names of towns hundreds of miles away. They took the dirt road north, past tall grain silos, abandoned mills and sheep and cattle stations, and left clouds of red dust billowing in their wake. There were kangaroos by the thousands, and huge flocks of emus that scattered with fright. But most memorable was that day when squatting at the roadside ahead was one kangaroo, a joey, and how when they slowed down and stopped beside it his father said to shoot it.

"Shoot it? Jim said. "Why?"

He commanded him, "Go on, shoot it! Shoot it!" trying to teach him something, I guess: How to be a man.

This is the worst part – he shot it.

They drove away.

When he looked back, the poor creature, still standing and swaying from side to side, seemed confused. Jim felt a tightness in his chest and his eyes begin to sting. He hated his father for this. He thought of his mother. His father leaned to the radio and snapped off the idiotic chatter of a disc jockey. Then there was the silence again, and the desert, and a terrible feeling of shame. For five days they had breakfasts together and slept in the truck but they didn't talk about it. His father's big hands heavy on the steering wheel, his mind numb with tedium and fatigue, unshaven, for hundreds of miles they didn't talk about anything, they couldn't – a time long ago that he is still living through, another scar on his memory.

There were days, of course, when things weren't so bleak. Take the year before, when he was fifteen, when he was doing well in his class. The maths teacher from 4B in the adjacent room came to see if anyone in Jim's class could solve a quadratic equation that none of his boys could. Apparently there was some friendly kind of rivalry between the two teachers. The equation was chalked on the blackboard, the class was given five minutes, then pens down. You could hear them mucking up next door. With clear logic, Jim's method proceeded step by step until finally he arrived at the solution. He was the only one. He was then asked to go to the blackboard to write it out. Mr Ferguson, whom he liked, touched his shoulder and smiled down on him.

"Well done, James," he said, "you can feel proud."

The saddest news he ever got was that of one of his best classmates, Harold Plummer, asthmatic and painfully shy, hardly spoke a word because of his awful stammer. His mother and father were always fighting until one day his father packed up and left. Harold was too poor even to wear shoes and barely had enough to buy chips for his lunch each day. He was always there, close to Jim, like a sad little puppy needing to be stroked. At his home in the bush he had a phobia of spiders, in the classroom he found numbers impossible – dyslexia, I guess. Seated next to him, Jim could sometimes feel Harold's gaze on the page he laid open for him. He regrets terribly that he didn't help him more. But then, how was he to know that one day Harold would get up from his desk, walk home and hang himself in his toilet? Poor Harold. His eyes were always so sad and watery.

Laurence arrived home from his shop punctually at 6.30. When she heard her father's car, his new daughter shrieked "Daddy! Daddy!" and ran for his embrace. He put a parcel of meat in the fridge, kicked off his boots and then took his place at the head of the table. He was dog-tired. The home became quieter with him there. His dinner was always hot and waiting for him: fried steak or sausages, sometimes mutton chops, rabbit or tripe, calf's liver or lambs' brains, served with mashed potato and steam-bleached cabbage or spinach, or stringed beans with carrots. Sliced bread lay stacked on the breadboard, beside it some butter, a bowl of sugar and blackberry jam. The pepper and salt were placed within his reach. He was a great one for pepper and salt.

They ate in silence except for the scraping of knives on plates or somebody asking to pass the tomato sauce. On the dresser sat a brown Bakelite radio emitting a barely audible crackle of talk or faint music. Jim began to talk about the flooding down at the creek, higher than it had ever been before, the waterfall crashing in full flow.

"Jim, take your elbows off the table, and don't talk while you're eating," his father said.

"Eat your carrots."

It was considered bad manners to talk at the table, especially with your mouth full, and when you were finished you placed your knife and fork together on the plate.

"You'll have to get some more sauce, Dad," Jim said, shaking the last of the bottle.

"I won't *have* to get anything," he rebuked him, glaring at him.

Jim felt guilty and sat red-faced, awaiting any further punishment, but none came. Tapioca or sago, or canned peaches with custard, or pear preserves from the pantry were served for dessert. Then Laurence took his cup of tea. Matilda told him quietly, that the hens have got lice. "Another three died," she said. His jaw set, his eyes closed, he nodded slowly, breathed deeply, then sighed. They were his Christmas orders. It was Jim's chore to feed them each day and collect the eggs. He had names for some of them. At Christmastime he had to hold their heads on the chopping block.

Usually, for anybody who wanted more there was leftover mashed potato. Laurence poured himself another cup of tea. He liked it dark brown and steaming hot. After dinner he belched quietly, pushed out his chair and shuffled off to bed. He never said goodnight. He would be up at five to face another twelve-hour working day. One evening Jim saw tears on his mother's cheeks. He wanted to put his arms around her – their lives weren't meant to be like this.

With the washing and drying of the dishes done, Jim sat at the table to do his homework. He could hear his mother treadling her sewing machine. Or he climbed up on a chair and pressed his ear to the radio, holding the thin aerial wire to make the sound more properly audible. Gliding the dial across stations 2UE, 2GB or 2UW gave quiz shows and half-hour episodes of *The Lone Ranger* or *Charlie Chan*, and later on plays, which he enjoyed most of all: dramas with creepy gangsters and clever detectives, the sound effects of doors creaking open or slamming shut, running footsteps and speeding cars, sometimes gunshots. He was there alone in the dark. Everyone else had gone to bed, but he kept mostly to himself anyway.

The playground was a maelstrom of frenzied, overactive boys, shoving and shouting their heads off to let off steam. When the time approached for assembly Jim stood anxiously beside the school bell, waiting for the teacher's nod. Then with wild excitement he rang down and up, down and up as loud as he could, down and up, riding the rope like on a runaway horse, he rang and rang, and seeing all the boys suddenly desist, coming round and falling into regiments according to their classes, made him feel imperious. It was like a call to arms.

"That's enough!" the teacher cried out loud, "That's enough! Enough!"

In assembly the summer heat was hard to bear. Boys without shoes gathered fig leaves to protect their feet on the stove heat of asphalt; some had glued cardboard soles. The air smelt of melted asphalt and the pungent, sulphurous gas spewing from the chimneys of the soap factory nearby. It stung your eyes. While the boys sweltered, their headmaster out front, like a buttoned-up parade-ground sergeant major, droned on and on about Memorial Day celebrations, or sporting fixtures, or new rules that applied, or complaints of student behaviour that had come to his attention. Peter McGregor fainted and collapsed into a heap. Then, at last and finally, they filed into their classrooms, where it was cool and smelled of chalk.

There were thrills to be had in the bush. From a certain large boulder on one side of the creek Jim could swing on a long rope, like Tarzan, to a landing station on the other side. And he loved climbing trees, the tallest ones – angophoras with smooth pink bark, ideal for carving hearts and initials. Like climbing mountains they were an enormous challenge. To reach the first branch, or base camp, it was necessary to throw and climb a rope, then, with the branches alternating each side of the trunk, it was possible to go all the way up. As naturally as a mother teaching her child his first steps, his tree seemed to want to teach him to climb, coaxing him on, giving him the courage and confidence to go higher and higher, which he did, and finally, one day he sat cradled in the topmost branches, listening to the leaves' rustle of applause and the beautiful sounds of birdsong. Sometimes he was high in the rigging of a tall-mast galleon with wind-mastered sails, swaying with the ocean swell. And being able to see so far gave him such a feeling of triumph and exhilaration. You could talk to God up there. Gazing heavenward, Jim said, "Bruce Nelson said there is no such thing as God, but what would he know? I believe in you. Someone must have made the world and the stars. I saw some shooting stars. I think they could be angels throwing stones to frighten demons trying to listen to secrets being told in Heaven. Is it true there are mountains under the sea?" he asked. Jim told Him his best subject at school was drawing and that, one day, he would like to be an architect.

As months and then years rolled by, the Department of Main Roads poured concrete gutters and tarred roads; the Electricity Commission planted hardwood poles and strung overhead wires; the Metropolitan Water, Sewerage, and Drainage Board came and laid pipes; and planted at a street junction was a splotched red-and-black-painted telephone box that took pennies. Delivery trucks loaded with furniture, washing machines, Venetian blinds and new kitchen appliances backed into driveways of brand-new homes; milk and cream were delivered in canisters from Mr Budd's horse and cart; warm bread from a closed-in van; letters by a cycling postman; and melons, skinned rabbits and clothes props by blokes with baritone cries from the backs of trucks. The rolled-up weekend newspapers landed with uncanny accuracy on front porches. The new sound that filled the streets was the weekend lawnmowers.

For some pocket money Jim got a job delivering local newspapers, and each weekend got up at four o'clock to help Mr Budd with his milk run. On Guy Fawkes Nights, in Deirdre Jackson's backyard, a bonfire of car tyres and a forest of sapling gums went up in smoke.

At fifteen, on Sundays, Jim relished lying in bed reading the weekend comics. In the age of chivalry there was Prince Valiant, Knight of the Round Table, lover of Queen Aleta, and wielder of the Singing Sword, clashes that rose audibly off the pages of two-handed broadswords on armour and shields, the screams of falling horses, all fabulously illustrated by Hal Foster; and Ginger Meggs, the street kid who reminded him of Keith; and Superman, the hero who could scoop up good-looking ladies falling in mid-air. Or his books: *The Canterbury Tales, Moby-Dick, The Adventures of Huckleberry Finn*, or the air adventures of Captain Biggles.

One particularly luxurious morning, resting on his elbow, basking in an unusual euphoria of lightness, he felt an intoxicating sense of well being, the forces around him all seeming to be playing for his attention. A grasshopper, like a curious little friend, sat crouched on the windowsill beside his bed, inspecting him.

"Hello, Jiminy," Jim said with a smile, "Paying a visit are we?"

The leaves just outside were rustling for his attention, waving to him it seemed, or were they beckoning, saying, *Come away, pack your things and come away*? The thin curtain inhaled a northern breeze and it rose and billowed above his pillow, remained suspended for a moment, then floated down and ebbed away, as if luring him on as well – such a beautiful gesture, so light and gentle. He lay back with his eyes closed and tried to imagine what it would be like to venture out as an errant vagabond to faraway places, exotic places, like India, to follow in the steps of the savant Krishnamurti, or to Morocco in the steps of Rimbaud and Delacroix, or to walk the streets of famous cities like London on the Thames, or Paris in the spring. *Bonjour, mademoiselle,* he said in his thoughts, and, with a smile, *Comment allez-vous?* He tried to imagine how beautiful the streets must be with Belle Époque and Art Nouveau architecture, and the Moulin Rouge and Folies-Bergère. He sighed. It was the sounds of Greensleeves and the jingling bell of the ice-cream van that brought him back to his pillow; his thoughts floated away like bubbles. It was time to get up and feed the fowls. He kept his pajamas neatly folded under his pillow.

Maria Stefos was a kind, serious-natured girl, and as Jim could see, she was also very beautiful. She was his half-Greek cousin, sixteen years old, slim with milk-pale skin, straight black hair with a raven's-wing lustre, dark brown eyes, downy forearms and a seductive, faintly shadowed upper lip. The dark colours she wore suited this particular physiognomy. Her beauty was all the more enticing for her seeming unawareness of it. She was spontaneous and natural, not at all shy. Her most remarkable feature, perhaps, was how she reached out for and embraced life. Jim thought, felt, for the first time he was in love. Certainly he was infatuated.

She played piano, the only member of her family that did so. The *Moonlight Sonata* and some of Chopin's nocturnes held him enthralled. The songs she sang, her show of excitement and joyful laughter were captivating. She also had a novice's interest in astrology – she could name all the signs of the zodiac in order – kept silkworms and studied nutrition. She loved Shakespeare's sonnets and Elvis Presley. Her ambition was to become a doctor. Hoping he would make a good impression, Jim showed off his meagre drawings and some photos he had taken, including the one of Merv with the dead snake round his neck, which made her laugh out loud. They talked for hours; they complemented one another. He could not, of course, profess his love for her. It was a passion in his mind of which she was completely unaware.

Her mother, his Aunt Rose, was strict when it came to boys. Even with her vivaciousness and sweet nature, Maria, it seemed, was less loved than most. Her father, his Uncle Angelo, a kind man, ran a Greek restaurant in the city, and during a Christmas rush, for a bit of pocket money gave Jim the job of washing dishes. He remembers he tried his first ever oyster there, in the kitchen, and spat it out.

At about this time Maria was sent to Athens for a few months to stay with her father's family – aunts and cousins she knew only from photographs. Practising the little Greek she knew, treated with typical Greek hospitality, and profoundly affected by the discoveries she made among the ruins of her classical culture, she loved it. On her return to Sydney she began her medical studies and rose to become a senior nurse in a repatriation hospital. Seeing her as a bridesmaid at her older sister's wedding, and then as a bride herself two years later in her long white wedding gown, Jim fell in love all over again. The lucky man, a tall, very handsome Greek, was a doctor. A nicely descriptive postcard from Poros, written beneath a tree beside the sea, told of how they were now settled in Athens. Sadly, Jim never heard from her again.

On rare occasions adult friends, two or four at most, were invited into the home for dinner. Roses or mimosa were suitably arranged in the vase at the entry, white table-linen serviettes that Matilda herself had needle-worked were laid out, cutlery from their wedding box was selected, the cruet stand assembled, and wine glasses never normally used were arranged. Roasted leg of lamb was usually the choice.

One evening the guests were Mr Wolfram, the German joiner who had built in the new wardrobes, his wife and their four-year-old spastic son, who for the whole evening never spoke a word. They had driven a long way and arrived punctually at the appointed hour. He was typically German, serious, blond, blue-eyed and handsome, a trim body with an immaculate wheat-ripened complexion. At the table Jim observed that his neat blue shirt accentuated the blueness of his eyes, his hair so fine and soft he wanted to touch it, and around him was a fragrance of sweet cologne. It was his European-ness that made him unusual, Jim thought – different, in a way superior. Mrs Wolfram, a nurse, cared for returned soldiers in the Moorebank Repatriation Hospital. She was gentle and quiet and you could tell by her face that she was kind. Mr Wolfram brought a bottle of wine. Laurence never touched the stuff.

Plates were served, and as talk got started Laurence edged away to the record player and put on some mood music, Paul Robeson singing *Old Man River*.

Matilda asked why they had chosen to live in Australia. Mr Wolfram ate slowly and chose his words carefully. In good German-accented English he spoke of how in Dresden he had been a bookseller and now here he could turn his hand to whatever odd jobs came his way. They left Germany, he explained, because their city was bombed, and because they felt ashamed. His brother and his brother's family were all killed. Matilda felt sorry for them, and their poor young son. Laurence asked if they liked living in Australia.

When they arrived they were camped in a migrant shelter in Villawood, some miles out of Sydney. Not long afterwards they drove along the northeast coast and into the rain forests, and then ventured inland to the central desert. Mr Wolfram described with enthusiasm what they saw in the rainforests of northern Queensland – birds and butterflies of extraordinary colours, orchids of such rarity, and how they had sampled the various smells of crushed leaves. They met welcoming ranchers in outback cattle stations, saw kangaroos and camels in the wild, and the incredible vastness of the desert and its subtle changes of colours and range of small delicate flowers; the profusion of starlit skies he never imagined possible, their constellations nothing at all like the northern sky. The foreigner's voice with its accent was enthralling; his eyes bluer than anybody's Jim had ever seen. Laurence's face tried to show interest, but actually he was never inclined to drive all that way into the bush and the outback. During dessert Laurence got up and put on Richard Tauber singing *Girls Were Made to Love and Kiss* and Mr Wolfram immediately recognised the wonderful tenor voice. Tauber was born in Austria, and with the outbreak of the Second World War he fled to Britain, where he made his living making recordings and conducting orchestras. He loved his voice. He himself had once sung in a choir, he said. He thanked Laurence.

On leaving, Mr and Mrs Wolfram agreed the lamb was the most delicious they had ever tasted.

On another occasion, one of Laurence's shop customers, Mrs Young was also invited and came with a man he had never met before. She was widowed, and he was a try-on. His name was Roy. He liked beer. Jim thought they didn't really suit one another. Matilda chose her floral dress each time. This lively choice helped to fill the gaps Laurence's personality sometimes had difficulty filling, and it was she mainly who carried the evenings. Talk around the table seldom came to much but Jim sat back and listened to every word. He liked adult conversation. After the roast, peaches and cream were served. Then, when he was allowed to stay up late, they all gathered around the pianola with Laurence pedalling, close to one another so they could all read the words, singing golden oldies like *Roll Out the Barrel* and *Happy Days Are Here Again*.

Matilda played the piano well enough to teach Jim scales and some simple exercises, which each day he was encouraged to practise. The home, sometimes, was able to give more than it was.

During the difficulties of those years, there were certain intermittences Jim remembers with some fondness.

When his father rolled up his sleeves and brought out his brushes, coloured powders and saucers, he knew it was to write up his tickets. Jim sat by his side to watch. He worked with water-soluble powders – red, yellow and blue; when yellow and blue were blended together they magically made green.

With his italic brush and a ticket-writer's hand Laurence skilfully printed the name and price of each cut of meat. Jim was very attentive to the precision and gracefulness of his thick and thin brushstrokes and saw that there was an art to it, and also that it expressed a side of his father he admired. He definitely had an artistic flair. Laurence was pleased to have his son's interest and admiration. He reminisced about his early vocational years. He had tried his hand in a few directions: car mechanic, pastry cook, signwriting, and then finally, butchering. It was the signwriting he was naturally good at. That was in the early '30s, a period of austerity, the height of the Depression, people still rebuilding their lives after the First World War, a second one brewing on a distant horizon. He was married by then and had his first child, so to serve his apprenticeship as a butcher was a practical thing to do, rather than attending college studying manual arts, even if that was what he really wanted to do. Jim secretly experimented with his own signature – one that he thought expressed his individuality in an artistic way. He also had his own sketchbook, in which, with a pencil and ruler, he copied photos of houses, one designed by an American architect named Richard Neutra, a very modern one with a flat roof and glass walls that slid open onto a wide terrace with a blue swimming pool. His drawings weren't quite right but that was to be expected, he had not yet learned the rules of perspective. He also sketched animals and sports cars, and copied the drawings by Hal Foster of castles and horses and men in armour in Prince Valiant comics.

The tickets were laid out on the table to dry.

Laurence rinsed his brushes and, in packing them away, he said,

"You're fifteen now, Jim; you need to think about what you're going to do. I wouldn't advise you to go into butchering, it's bloody hard work and long hours. See if you can get a certificate of some kind, wear a suit and work in an office."

He sat down, took out his tobacco pouch and rolled a cigarette.

Jim said he loved the idea of designing houses and that, one day, he would like to be an architect.

"Hmm, well, the trouble with that," Laurence said, "you'd have to go to university."

Jim said that didn't matter.

"And who do you think is going to pay for that?"

"I can work," Jim said.

Laurence struck a match and lit his cigarette. He had his doubts.

Each Friday night after Laurence closed the shop he would take his staff to the nearby pub for a couple of beers and smoke cigarettes. One of them, Mr McKendrie, ginger-haired, florid-faced with a funny strong accent, arranged once to take Jim to the Sydney soccer ground to see Scotland play Australia. It was one of the most raucous, exciting days of his life. It was rumoured that Mr McKendrie once fell over in a public place while under the influence of strong drink.

Oh, and that Sunday afternoon when Elvis Presley was singing *Blue Hawaii* on the record player and Laurence appeared from the bathroom in just a towel wrapped like a sarong. Like a ringmaster introducing a circus act, he announced, "Ladeeez and jelly beans, presenting to you, direct from America, for the first time ever, the never-to-be-repeated performance of … Carmen Miranda!" then did his version of what was supposed to be a sexy hula dance, swaying his arms and waving his hands like water waves to the voice of Elvis Presley, and everyone laughed.

"Disgraceful," Matilda had to say, holding back a giggle when Jim pulled away the towel and he dashed back to the bathroom with his hands over his privates. But it was his hairy paunch mainly, and his beard of shaving lather that made it so hilarious. And there were his silly jokes: "A lunatic looking over the fence of the asylum asked a man who was shovelling horse manure off the road why he was doing it. The man said it was to put on his strawberries. The cross-eyed lunatic with the drooping lip said, 'Oh, you should come in 'ere, we have cream on ours.'" And with his nose up, the way he could put on the airs of an upper-class English snob: "Oh, I say old chap, how awfully, frightfully, bloody decent of you."

Laurence cut Jim's hair with old scissors and blunt hand clippers cruel army style – short all round with a bit on top. He cobbled his shoes. Jim remembers, when he was little, about six, his father let him light his cigarettes for him. He put fairy lights on a small Christmas tree, mowed the front lawn every second Sunday, and played cricket with them. For his tenth birthday Jim got a cheap watch which soon stopped, on his eleventh a fold-up penknife, and for his twelfth a fountain pen. The greatest gift of all, when he was fourteen, was his green, size twenty-four, Malvern Star bicycle. Where his mother's soft voice chided and forgave them for their silly mistakes, Laurence roused on them, as often they deserved, but he was never violent, and he was a faithful husband, though was never seen to give his wife a kiss or put his arms around her. Poor Matilda, she was so affectionate, she needed affection.

Laurence had worked hard all his life. Had he reached old age Jim would have forgiven him for his small indiscretions, shown his gratitude for the sacrifices he had made, and shown his appreciation for how he had provided for them. He would have cared for him, cooked and shopped for him, wheeled him around parks and gardens and along the harbour shore.

Family crowds and girlfriends came to see their boys play soccer each Saturday afternoon. From the side lines fathers shouted abusive language at blameless referees who were volunteers and doing their best. Despite playing in a goal-scoring position, as far as I can remember, I don't think Jim ever scored a winning goal.

A condition of playing with the Methodist Soccer Club was regular church attendance. Jim had never been a churchgoer; nor had the others. On Sunday nights they and the righteous, pinched-looking congregation had to sit through interminable, sententious sermons. You wouldn't have thought that Reverend Jenkins, of such meagre stature with a small button nose and little round spectacles, could raise Hell, but he could. He could snap them out of their daydreaming. He was a Methodist with method. From his pulpit, in his dog collar and his satin vest smooth and black as a raven, with open-palmed gestures and almost a whisper, he could entice you to near his bosom. There was promise of a glorious afterlife, he assured them, if you were good and obeyed the words of the Almighty. He leaned closer in complicity to give fair warning that God was ever present and was watching your every move, knew your every thought. Thinking lustful thoughts, he warned, was sinful. One who looked with adulterous heart upon another had as good as committed the act. Then suddenly, he would rise up and bellow and spit like a mad zealot, wave his arms like an impassioned dictator, and then bash his bruised fist down on his splintered pulpit because for those who transgressed there would be damnation in Hell! His voice sometimes broke under the strain. He could be frightening if you sat too close. He looked mad – it was part of his fascination. The impression he gave of Hell was the gruesome deformed world of Hieronymus Bosch: seething groaning bodies; the scaled and fish-faced; the armless and web-footed, gawky, beak-faced monsters flapping about. How could anybody be so deluded and so mean-spirited, Jim wondered? He usually found a place with his mates at the back of the congregation. The jokes they made about the reverend made them giggle. Looking over his spectacles, picking Jim out as the mischief-maker, he glowered.

"Daniel was cast into a lions' den for breaking the decree forbidding prayers to God. Dare to be a Daniel!" he adjured with raised eyebrows and pointed finger, "Dare to stand alone! Let us pray: *May Thy holy angels dwell herein to preserve us in peace, and may Thy blessings be always upon us through Christ our Lord. Amen.*"

Before the last hymn, and having fulfilled his obligation, Jim slipped out without attracting attention. Funny, after the service, at the doorway with each of his congregation, Reverend Jenkins was avuncular and sweet as pie. It was noticed he had great bunches of hair sprouting from his ears.

The milk bar afterwards, that was the main attraction – the girls in pink, dolled up with lacquered perms and bright lipstick; the boys quaffed and in shoulder-padded sports coats, smelling of Brilliantine hair oil; all of them awkward and segregated. Jim had a soft spot for Robin, and she seemed to feel the same for him. He was young and fit and tolerably attractive, but when it came to girls he was just as insecure and self-doubting as the rest of them. Robin was pretty and also shy; she worked as a checkout girl and stuck on prices in the local supermarket. The jukebox played syrupy love songs where 'moon' rhymed with 'June', about summertime blues, broken hearts, unrequited love and love that will never die.

Saturday-night parties were sometimes held in private homes, when parents went out to let the youngsters be themselves. A favourite game was Spin the Bottle, a kissing game of chance where you could get lucky. In the next-door room with the lights off Robin gave Jim the best time of his life.

For Saturday-night barn dances the Scouts Hall was made to look like a barn: wagon wheels and streamers and pennants hung diagonally above a hay-strewn floor, a soft-drinks stand set up near the door. On the stage a trio of old-fashioned men in boaters and braces beat out old-fashioned tunes. Everyone was meant to dress the part. Usually about sixty turned up. Jim knew all the dance steps – the barn dance, square dance, gypsy tap, pride of Erin and the Canadian three-step. Cheryl, the prettiest cowgirl, got rushed for dances. Boys raced to her like a dog on a bone, sliding on the hay-covered floor then grabbing her. Jim managed one waltz with her and with his arm around her he could feel her bra strap and smell her mix of scent and shampoo. Kate, a wilting wallflower, tiny and meek as a mouse, in a flared, frilled, pink skirt and white cotton blouse, twisting her handkerchief around her finger as she was wont to do when she felt left out, had a complex about her looks, which, I have to say, were not her strong point. Whey-faced and with a red nose she was snuffling with a cold. She looked pathetic. Seeing that nobody else had asked her up, Jim felt it was the right thing to do. As the band struck up for a square dance he took her hand and swung her onto the floor – *Allemande left, do-si-do, promenade down and off we go*. He escorted her back to her seat. There was perspiration on her upper lip and her palms were clammy. He bought two Cokes and sat with her while she fanned herself. The band was now playing *How Much Is That Doggie In The Window?* As she talked she picked at a loose thread in the hem of her dress. She said she was down in the dumps because she was in love with Mr O'Gorman, her biology teacher, a married man. She asked Jim to promise he wouldn't tell anybody.

Dutiful fathers came to pick up their daughters at midnight.

In one of those wonderful mysteries of nature, Kate, over time, was transformed into a shapely, gorgeous beauty, which occasioned surprise and comment by all. She preferred to remain unmarried. She became the target of some cruel gossip about her affairs with married men.

A few months before their first was born, Deirdre moved in with a draftsman, a nice, decent sort of fellow. He quietened her down. Poor Deirdre. It was not long afterwards she came to a sad demise: one day seen pushing a pram, the next killed in a car accident.

It was about this time Matilda presented Jim with a second-hand Box Brownie camera. Taking photos became his hobby. Composing photos, he realised, was like writing a good sentence: you put in only what is essential and keep out what is not. He experimented with light and shade: shots of his father cobbling shoes on the back step, the half-lit portrait of decrepit, old Mrs Keegan – blind, alcoholic and a chain smoker – and Merv with his unusual looks. He got Merv one day at the shed where he kept his reptile collection, looking heroic with a dead snake round his neck, holding his rugby ball.

I have to tell you about Merv. I have a fascination for human curiosities with marked idiosyncrasies.

He was living nearby, he and his mother, and had been for some years. Jim sought him as a new friend. It was a strange friendship because Merv himself was strange, as we all are in our own ways. Everyone round about thought he was touched in the head. 'Mad Merv' they called him; 'a dill'. Deirdre reprimanded them, said they wouldn't like it. He was unusual, that was all. He was a man-child in his mid thirties, younger than his age, and, with a thick equine neck and the shoulders of a rugby forward, he was strong, big jawed, his head was like an anvil. His physical disadvantages were his spastic leg and a similarly afflicted left hand that was clutched like a hen's claw. His baggy trousers, hitched by red braces, reached up to near his armpits and covered his chest; his flannel shirt smelled of body salt and soap, his skin like sour milk; his breath like the taste of a penny; and his clumpy black leather boots with thick soles were specially made for him. Shy by nature, he always seemed to be shying away, as if the sun was in his eyes, or someone taking aim at him with a camera, his taut, thin-lipped mouth slanted down to a little bit of spittle. I know I shouldn't say it, but when he had a fit of sneezing it was just the funniest thing, his convulsions, his arms flailing and moths of spit flying everywhere. He limped pigeon-toed, clutched a pet rugby ball close to his chest, and grabbed at flies. Each Saturday afternoon watching the Balmain Tigers he went crazy. It was how he knew what day it was. It was what he lived for.

Merv felt at ease with Jim. He called Jim 'Boy'. He dropped in sometimes to be neighbourly, sometimes to practise passing his ball around, sometimes to charge like a wounded bear on the front lawn wanting to get tackled. Sometimes they would parody a boxing bout, feinting and jabbing, him laughing maniacally, then Jim would have him on the lawn and they wrestled like two puppies. Sometimes on the hottest days he came for just a cold drink. Jim tested him on the rules of the game, and how

good he was with numbers. He asked what Merv knew about his
father, and about his interest in girls. Such was Merv's difficulty
in forming his words he was difficult to understand – his voice
had the gruffness of a sick old dog, way out of tune. With his
mother's help he could modulate it a bit, but it didn't make much
difference. It turned out he did know the rules and had a head
for numbers – could remember the scores. Who his father was
he had no idea – he may even have come from the soil, and
regarding girls he just looked both ways and chuckled.

He and his mother lived on Providence Road on land that
had been cleared of all its trees. A wire and privet hedge served
as their front fence, their gate was braced and ledged hardwood
palings hinged on a jarrah hardwood post. Their home, at the
end of a long, meandering dirt pathway, was a shack of old grey
weatherboarding, the iron roof stained in parts with red ochre
rust, its front veranda stacked with logs of firewood, and its front
door peeling with what looked like scabs of blue paint.

Inside, the day room was wallpapered and lit by a small
window where, on its sill, green peaches lay to ripen. It was
furnished with a table and two chairs, a pinewood dresser, an ice
chest, a sink in one corner, and a big wood-fired cast iron stove.
On the table sat a vase with flower cuttings, usually of golden
wattle. The room smelt of years of wood smoke, cooking steam,
stale vase water and, on this day, fried eggs and toast, none of
which deterred the small black ants that trailed throughout the
cupboards, nor the termites that burrowed in the woodwork,
nor the few small lizards and mice that darted back and forth.
The rustling noise in the roof was the possum. The summer heat
and the wood stove made the inside like an oven; it made the
iron creak.

Merv's mother – I never got to know their family name –
was the opposite: thin, neat, straight-backed, self-possessed
with a pinched unsmiling mouth; a disciplinarian. In most other

ways, however, she seemed quite normal. She was clear in mind and had good elocution, an inherited voice. She could once have been a schoolmistress or a matron. Her skin had turned olive. She never took much interest in Jim.

She was a dutiful, caring mother, if not a loving one. Her affection for her son, though never physical, was a kind of watered-down love. Once a week she gave him a shave and each few weeks cropped his head close to his scalp; she sewed his buttons and tied his bootlaces, and each Christmas he received a small treat of one kind or another – one year a penknife, another his football.

Merv is sitting now at the table for breakfast.

She brings him his eggs and toast.

"Mervyn, I have to have a talk with you," she says, scowling with pursed lips.

He dreads these confrontations. She has discovered something. She will admonish him for it. He cowers.

"I have found money to be missing from my purse," she said.

"It could only have been you. Now if there is one thing I must insist on, Mervyn, it is honesty. If you are in need of some spending money you must come and ask for it. I won't have you going through my purse. Is that understood?"

Shamefaced, tight-lipped, he nods slowly.

"It won't do you any good because you will get found out."

The two fried eggs look accusingly at him.

In a milder tone, she says, "The other thing; you must remember to wipe your boots before you come in. And close the gate."

She turns to make his tea.

On a hot Sunday afternoon, in men's grey trousers, garden gloves, frayed straw hat, and about her face, wispy grey hair, she looked and sounded rather like a creature of the bush as she wheeled a squeaky wicker pram piled high with the blackberry bush to be burned in the backyard. Magpies squawked at this strange sight. There she had a tethered goat, a worm-riddled peach tree, a wattle tree, staked tomatoes, lettuces and a strawberry patch, but mostly it was weeds and thistles and dry, unkempt grass. What was once a corrugated-iron tool shed Merv now used for his found objects and reptile collection. Once he brought back a particular handheld stone and fragments of flower-decorated crockery; another time a broken piece of dark blue bottle-glass with air trapped inside bubbles, and a fledgling that had died freeing itself from its shell. In jars he had lizards and snakes and centipedes. One day in the rubbish dump he found an old, visually impaired mongrel dog. They spoke the same language. He coaxed him home to show to his mother. With consideration to both their pleading eyes, she yielded.

"Very well, Mervyn," she said sternly, "you may keep him, but his welfare shall remain solely your responsibility. First thing he needs is to be fed, then a good wash. And teach him where to do his business. Now," pointing to the door, "outside." The dog's rheumy eyes looked up at Merv's and gave him a matey, conspiratorial wink. Merv called him Dog and they became the best of friends, loved as only mongrels can be.

Merv felt at home in the bush. Even with his infirmity, every so often he and his sidekick went on walks further than anyone else had gone. There were no tracks to follow, only signs. He limped, drag-footed, through undergrowth, over rocks and along the creek, stopping when he felt like it to pick a few blackberries or lap at the waterfall or to urinate. Rabbits scurried away. Way beyond the creek was a huge rock, in form not unlike a broken molar, and in its cavity a once-inhabited cave. There were the remains of bones and fire ash and childlike wall paintings. It was cool. He could feel the sweat running down his neck. He lay down to rest; closed his eyes. A black man in a scarecrow suit came into his dream.

He continued his exploration of the damp, dark netherworld under rocks: he rolled them over and found startled cavorting worms, thick white grubs, and dark poisonous-green centipedes – the biggest ones he sometimes coaxed into a jar. His best find was a three-foot-long non-venomous pink snake. Out of respect, he always rolled the stones back. And he paid due deference to the spiders he encountered, and to the big blue-tongued lizards that hissed and lashed their tongues at him. He wasn't afraid of things people were afraid of. It amused him to whip up ants' nests into a mad frenzy. Under a tree he discovered, half consumed by the earth, the repetitive pattern of bleached rib-bones and a grey skull with a rictus of white teeth – a wild dog or dingo, probably; the pelt now like a long-discarded doormat. He eased a tooth out with his penknife and put it in his pocket.

When he returned to his mother in the late afternoon, salty with the sweat that stung the scratches on the back of his neck, they didn't say much. He showed her his new tooth and a brown-speckled magpie's egg; he gave Dog a bowl of water, and from the ice chest took out a bottle of milk. In the laundry he hosed himself down while she scrubbed his back. She stoked the fire for a cup of tea and brought out some rock cakes. He liked the sweetness and texture of warmed rock cakes. They sometimes gave him the hiccups. She wiped his face of crumbs and kept the rest for the birds. He went to his room to lie down. The possum was playing up again. The wattle on the table, she noticed, needed replacing. She opened a tin of sardines.

On some days he might be sent out with a shovel and a hessian bag to collect horse manure for the tomatoes and strawberries. Or, like on this day, she would give him a shopping list and money to go on the long walk to buy some tea or sugar, or potatoes or matches, scraps for the dog, or tins of sardines. She tied his laces.

As Merv dragged the gate closed behind them, Dog lifted his leg on the gatepost and nearly fell over. They set out along Providence Road, Merv limping, clutching his football, Dog with his hangdog look, doggedly following, his nose like a soiled truffle close to the ground. The din of cicadas amplified the summer heat and crows watched with suspicion. Merv happily jingled the pennies his mother had given him to buy picture cards of football heroes. He chewed the succulent end of a stalk of grass and every now and then gave a spit.

There was nothing Merv could do about their immersion in the cloud of dust kicked up by the rattling old dust-coloured bus heading to Parramatta. And then a truckload of cauliflowers kicked up more. He narrowed his eyes, wiped away the sweat and plodded on.

The right turn at Quarry Road brought them to the new brick-and-tile neighbourhood. As illustrated in the brochures, concrete driveways lined with roses swept up to double-shuttered garages, sometimes with an outboard motor boat parked inside. Toy-coloured gnomes welcomed visitors, and each letterbox gave each house its number. Water sprinklers, twirling and flinging with delirious delight, painted lawns a grass-green gloss and air the colours of a rainbow; there was the smell of fresh-mown grass; chimneys sprouted spindly, insect-looking antennae; windows flickered with TV. One woman doing her ironing flung open her window and hurled abuse at Merv for kicking a tin can along the road. Dog didn't have the fortitude to bark back. The window closed, then everything was back to normal.

They arrived where there was a kernel of a few shops: a general store with a farmers' co-op, a butcher and a postal service. Among the other shoppers Merv felt called upon to perform social customs he had learned but not fully understood, such as offering his hand for someone to shake. Old Mrs Brown, the postmistress, scratched her head trying to understand him being sociable about his dead snake. They found him strange. Some lowered their eyes in passing, then looked back; some deliberately turned away. It was they, he thought, who were the strange ones; it was difficult to know what attitude to adopt next. Dog had given up on people a long time ago. It didn't matter. Merv packed his shopping bag and they hobbled away.

The boys in the auto repair shop were friendly enough.

"Hi, Merv!" they cried, "'Ow ya goin' mate, orright?"

They made fun of him and chuckled, but he didn't mind. Bill was his best mate. He was fullback for a local club, and once rode Merv round the block on the back of his motorbike. Once, even, he rode him to see the Balmain Tigers play the Parramatta Giants. Merv proudly showed them his new picture cards. Bill tied his laces for him and gave Dog a bowl of water. Merv felt at odds with most but with his football mates he felt a sense of camaraderie.

There was that curious incident later, in November 1954, when Merv, who never gave any trouble, started putting it around that down near the creek, wedged high up in the fork of a tree, was the decomposing body of a middle-aged woman. Nobody believed him; they told him to grow up. It didn't matter. Her dress was torn, one leg was broken, and she was wearing a plain gold ring.

"Well, I never," Mrs Thomas said. "You wonder what goes on in some people's 'eads. It gives you the creeps, but what can you do?"

The evidence showed the woman had run away from a brother, a banana grower recently buried in a cemetery up near Townsville. The post-mortem concluded that she had died of a heart attack; the police sergeant said there was nothing suspicious. With consideration to the contents of her basket and the nest in the tree it was thought she might have been after eggs. "Death by Misadventure" the newspapers called it. That was the same year Jim's best classmate, Harold Plummer, was found hanged in his toilet.

Laurence found a new and important social life playing golf. Jim learned what it was to be a caddie and to fish in ponds for lost balls. After a day's round his father allowed Jim to use his clubs to play a few holes. He was not aware that other club members had gathered behind the clubhouse window to watch him hit off on the first tee. With a cane-shaft number-four wood driver, the ball left the face with a sweet click, rose, hung suspended, became microscopically smaller, alighted, then bounced and rolled to where any of those watching, including his father, would have been satisfied. Matilda, too, eventually became a member and she loved it. She was given her own little Austin motorcar to get around in. And Jim loved being her caddie. Her game improved and she got her handicap down to twenty-two, which was very good. They stopped one day at the ninth hole to take a cold drink and a sandwich. Jim tasted his first glass of nice cold beer; the beef sandwich had an awful, tainted taste he was told was mustard.

On the club's social evenings Jim sat and gazed at his mother's reflection in her dressing-table mirror. She was at her best in her white satin petticoat getting dolled up. She was meticulous with her hair, her face powder, rouge, brown eyeliner and brushed eyelashes, and the cerise lipstick that matched her fingernails. Jim wondered which feature it was that in particular made her beauty so remarkable. He watched her paint a perfect pair of lips then take from her small jewellery box, her pearl earrings, and thread them in her ears. She turned to him. Posing alluringly one side then the other, enticing him by batting her eyelids and giving a sexy wink and a come-on smile, she said, in not her usual voice, "Hey, mister, you wanna come and have some fun?

The drinks are on me. No hanky-panky." Marlene Dietrich, I think. She took his breath and made his heart fly.

It was her smile, he realised. Her face was everything he couldn't put into words. He loved her so much. *La Donna*, his mother.

Laurence, who never liked to wear a suit, uncomfortable in buttoned-up collars, awkward in his black bow tie and matching cufflinks, paced impatiently, complaining that they were going to be late. But she wouldn't be hurried. When finally she stepped out in her gorgeous gown and fox stole, her matching pearl necklace and, on these occasions, her small gold watch, Jim told her she looked absolutely gorgeous, like Ingrid Bergman. And she really did, smelling of perfume, that beautiful smile. She loved dancing, her favourite the waltz. She knew the quickstep, the foxtrot and the pride of Erin from the early days when she and his father used to dance at the Trocadero. Jim kissed her lips tenderly, wished her a wonderful evening, and reminded her of the fate of Cinderella coming home late after midnight. She smiled once more her loving smile, her perfect white teeth.

Then began a period of decline. There were days, now of increasing frequency, when Jim would have to stay home from school to minister to her. Her asthma attacks became more severe. He took to her bedside her breakfast tray, made sure she took her medication, measured the drops, attended to her chamber pot, and kept her out of draughts.

The Rialto cinema was designed in the Art Deco style, and sometimes it was where Matilda wanted Jim's company to see love stories. She had already seen *Gone With the Wind* twice, but she wanted to see it one more time. When the lights went down she put his hand in hers, and he could feel her pressure in the poignant moments; she was living the story again, and near the end, yes, she had tears on both cheeks. She was such a hopeless romantic.

They strolled home arm in arm through the empty moonlit streets, only their shadows and the chirping sounds of crickets for company. Her mood was quiet at first, and then she began talking about romance, of Rhett Butler and Scarlett O'Hara and their sad, ill-fated love affair. She reminisced about how she and his father had first met, on that day of the Cross-Country Cyclists' Club picnic, when he looked so sportive and dashing, straight and tall, his hair wavy and combed back. She remembered with a smile their wedding day in the stone church in their small hometown of Bundanoon – a beautiful spring day it was, the daffodils out in profusion – and how the whole town, it seemed, had come to cheer and clap and throw confetti. It was her best friend who caught her bouquet, and for those who cared to make the walk to the house, sandwiches and cakes and cups and saucers were laid out, beer for the men. They drove away trailing streamers, him tooting the horn, she in her virginal innocence, to the Jeanne d'Arc suite in the Hotel Majestique up in the Blue Mountains. Eventually, after a year or so, Laurence bought a butcher shop in the city and they began a family.

"If you are sincere, and you must always be," Jim's darling mother said, "love will always win in the end." She confided how she had once loved a boy named Ben, the same age as Jim was then. Ben knew how much she loved poetry and for her sixteenth birthday he gave her a leather-bound collection of Shelley. He wrote in it that Shelley expressed better the words he wanted to say. In it, too, were faded pressed violets. She dreamed of marrying him one day, but when the time came he chose another instead. She remembered how he could make her laugh, and wondered whatever became of him. Someone said she heard he got killed in the War. It was when Laurence was doing his apprenticeship that he had teased her into marrying him, when she was twenty-one. She was working in a haberdashery at the time. She was the first of her sisters to go. She told him her maiden family name then was Williams. As they turned into Providence Road, Jim said he thought he would never want to marry because he would never want to leave her.

"Oh, one day someone will come along, you'll see," she said with a smile, holding him with tighter affection.

But it was she who would leave him, when one of God's satanic angels would sweep down and in a moment of weakness seduce her with his violet-flavoured kiss and steal her away and she would never be seen again.

At fifteen Jim received a letter from the Education Department saying he was selected to go to Drummoyne Boys High School, a school with established traditions and a reputation for being able to elevate reckless boys of a certain class into responsible young men. Jim was an obedient type, considerate and reliable. The school uniform was a college-grey suit (including, for the first time, long trousers), the lapel badge a shield – *Vincit qui se Vincit* – and the tie red-and-blue striped. The architecture was cheerless and perfunctory, like the brick blocks and cloisters of Victorian England, except that having been built recently, there was no hint of embellishment or religion. Gilded on the roll of honour in the main entry, were the names of all the past headmasters, and next to it, sitting on her throne in all her regalia, a photo portrait of the Queen. From there he could see a long, prison-lit corridor which smelled of linoleum polish, along each side numbered doors, and behind each door a room of regimented seating. Outside, in the recreation ground there was not a single tree, not a single blade of grass, just the severely brick-enclosed quadrangle with bench seating. Beyond was the lavatory block – the only place where there were taps for drinking water; where boys, in flagrant contravention of the house rules, sometimes smoked; and where there was a revolting pungent smell of urine.

In attendance at his first lesson the teaching was strict and his classmates snobbish and unfriendly, though it was surely more to do with him, his feeling of inferiority and thus timidity, and the sadness of his home that he carried around inside him like a sickness.

It was expected that he would excel in French and Latin, as well as physics and chemistry and advanced mathematics, the disciplines of which all those who aspired to become lawyers or doctors or engineers would need to know. French and Latin were difficult – the accumulation of conjugations, which didn't make sense, overwhelmed him. In the front row of each classroom, Jim concentrated on every word. The chemistry teacher – 'Dr Jekyll' they called him, a mad professor with wild electrified hair – chalked madly on the board chemical formulas everybody else madly wrote down. For Jim they were like meaningless hieroglyphics: *$CaCo_3$ reacts with H_2SO_4 and froths and fumes and forms $CaSO_4 + CO_2 + H_2O$*, or something like that. It seemed to Jim that private tuition was what he needed. Sometimes he raised his hand to ask a question that caused some to groan, others to laugh – mirthless, malicious laughter – so he stopped doing it. For the first time in his young school life he began to sense failure. Was it because the headmaster had had a word with Graham Frazer, the head prefect, Jim wondered, that Graham showed kindness and took him under his wing? *'Tries hard'* were the words written on his school report.

It is the role of every good teacher to get his pupils fascinated with the subject. Imagine Jim's surprise when his physics teacher turned out to be the one who had captained the Australian rugby team, the Wallabies, champions of the world. Mr Davidson demonstrated that physics is a fascinating subject that could be easily understood. He was personable and spoke with clear articulation. He sat with his feet up and talked about the nature of things, what they are made of and the laws that separate and bind them. It was to Jim he seemed to be talking. The world is made up of the tiniest particles, he said, smaller than microscopic, known as atoms. Each atom is a tiny spot nucleus with electrons spinning around it. Each atom is defined according to the number of electrons orbiting its nucleus. He got up and sketched a diagram to illustrate.

"Hydrogen, you see, is the simplest. It is called hydrogen because it is an atom with only one electron. Helium, he said, making another sketch, is a similar atom that has two electrons, lithium 3, beryllium 4, right up to uranium, which has ninety-two. Atoms lock into one another to form molecules, and molecules combine to form different substances. These substances are all around us – this wooden desk, for example, is made up mostly of carbon atoms, each with five electrons, glass is mostly silica, water is hydrogen and oxygen combined, and so on. When seen from this perspective it explains the physical nature of the universe. Simple." He had everyone's attention.

"Anybody not understand?" he asked.

He went on to explain the not so easy subject of friction.

To study for exams Jim visited the huge, cool atmosphere of the Mitchell Library, a favourite place for university students. He was drawn to the philosophy section again to re-read pages of a book he one day discovered whilst browsing there – Will Durant's *The Age of Reason*. Philosophical reasoning was new to him and it awakened a new inquisitiveness.

"What is it, Jim?" his mother asked. "What's the matter, darling? You've been so sad lately."

She gently stroked his hair. His dejection then had to do with his latest chemistry exam results.

Bless her she came to his pillow late at night to give encouragement. She told him she would discuss with the headmaster a transfer to another school. He lay awake thinking of those who lived on streets in dirty clothes, those who had lost their ways and fallen. He remembered the old music man with his parrot, playing for pennies, and one day he saw him picking up cigarette butts. He wondered if that poor old man might even have died homeless on a street somewhere, found lying in the rain. Jim could feel the seconds of his lifetime passing with each pulse of his heart.

It was during this transition period, when Jim was taken away with his father for five days, that the transfer was arranged without complication.

For his new school in Rozelle Matilda had his new uniform laid out for him – his shirt nicely ironed and his yellow-and-black striped tie, his shoes polished. He shaved for the first time.

Rozelle was another non-religious, boys-only school, more technical and of a lower standard. Remember, he had previously attended the infants' section of this school. The caustic air of his early childhood was still in evidence. The buildings were of the same institutional, liver-coloured brick, and the playground blistering-hot asphalt. There was one large fig tree that provided shade for him to sit with thick white-bread sandwiches he himself had made, of Marmite or peanut butter or baked beans, or, if he was lucky, newspaper-wrapped fish and chips. Those around him actively played but he seldom joined in. The curriculum was less demanding and the teaching less disciplined, less concentrated on scholarship and more on manual arts, less learning by rote and more manual training. The physical education classes he enjoyed. I can see him now, straddling the vaulting horse from a springboard, landing squarely on the mat with perfect equilibrium, then diving cleanly into a forward roll and up to attention, shoulders back, head held high. And he felt easy with the friendships of his new muck-about classmates.

In elementary maths and trigonometry he excelled, and in all subjects he was soon topping his class. He was selected head prefect and wore his badge with pride. He talked with some he knew were struggling, like Graham Frazer had done for him when he was struggling. In woodwork he constructed a cupboard with dovetail drawers, and in technical drawing – his favourite subject – he learned the principles of perspective and isometric projection, how to plot and draw ellipses with a pair of compasses, and parabolas and hyperbolas using French curves. These skills would serve him well when eventually he entered university to study architecture, the mother of the arts.

And, improbably, there were music appreciation classes. Mr Maldoni, serious, very neat, a young man of considerable passion, the greater part of which lay in his love for opera, Verdi and Puccini in particular, was fresh out of teaching college. He so much wanted beautiful music to be a good influence on his boys. He used to bring his own recordings in his polished black leather attaché case. With very black Italian hair oiled, combed and neatly parted, he wore shiny black elevated shoes because he was short and meticulous, and in his buttoned-up double-breasted suit, with a flower-coloured bow tie and pocket handkerchief, and smelling of eau de cologne, the class never really took him very seriously. 'Mr Macaroni', they called him, and other names far less charitable. Even in the staffroom he was fair game.

Every Thursday after lunch, when the boys were still hot from handball and war games, it was hoped they would relax and enjoy the lyricism of stringed concerti and the glory of symphonic compositions. Mr Maldoni's voice was light and vibrant as a 'cello, a singer's voice. "Let your spirits be free," he intoned with a gesture of imploring outstretched hands, "let your hearts be gay, let the music carry you away." During Vivaldi's spring season they might imagine themselves skipping through the Elysian Fields, enjoying the trilling sounds of birdsong and murmuring brooks; then the following week he would compare it to Beethoven's *Sixth,* the *Pastoral,* and then his coup de grâce, the Ninth, when the class would, he hoped, be ultimately raised to Heaven. A new composer each lesson had been his way. He liked Borodin and Prokofiev as well. For Jim it was the first time he had heard the romance of strings and the trill of a silver flute and he found it truly delightful.

There was a spoiler in the classroom. There always has to be a spoiler, it seems. Ronnie Wiseman refused the school uniform and dressed instead in a black leather coat and a smelly unwashed T-shirt. He was tall for his age and gangly like a comic Giacometti, his face badly blemished beneath pubescent hair, his goatish buckteeth always chewing gum, and he stammered and had bad breath. He was from a troubled home in the rough part of Rozelle, He got the nickname 'Gawky' and it was generally known that he had once been found out for shoplifting cigarettes. With Jim he was OK, but with others he was a bully. At lunchtimes he coerced kids into giving him chips; in class he was disruptive, always wanting attention. The boys giggled at his loud, derisory clowning, and the quacking sounds he made with his armpits during the quiet moments of Beethoven. Mr Maldoni pleaded with him then tried to ignore him. One day, however, when he realised it was hopeless, instead of raising his voice above the general disturbance, Mr Maldoni broke down and wept, packed up and walked out, which only made things worse. Jim felt sorry for him. As head prefect he felt it his duty to have words with Ronnie. But it didn't make any difference – Ronnie was expelled from music classes. The following term Mr Maldoni was no longer in attendance. His preferred milieu was the Conservatorium of Music where he taught voice and regained his confidence and dignity. Ronnie's initials must still be carved somewhere on one of those desks.

The day of her death was like any other school day, except for an unaccountable disturbance in Jim's mind. He sensed something was wrong. He was doing a sum at the time and found it difficult to concentrate. A boy came from the headmaster's office and gave Jim's teacher a message. The teacher called Jim to him. He said quietly he had just received word that Jim should go home. That was all he said. During the bus ride and then the long walk, he was filled with dread and fear. It was an oppressively hot November afternoon. His relatives were there. His father's car was parked in the driveway and others' on the street.

It was at the front gate that his Aunt Rose gently touched him and told him his mother had died. A spear pierced his heart. His voice was choked. No, she couldn't have, he reasoned – he was with her the night before and she was well.

"She died this morning," he heard his Aunt Rose speak again. Rose was the eldest sister, always close, now trying to be strong, doing her best, repressing her tears. "We all have to die sometime, James." She was saying something more, words that might console him – lame and useless words, something about God, poor woman – but he didn't want to listen; he turned away. He knew that the dreadful words she had uttered could never be undone. He could see the bedroom curtains were drawn. If only they'd had a telephone. The rest of time would begin on this day.

But even if life for him had been irrevocably changed, life elsewhere would surely be the same, normal, as if nothing had happened. Rinny, his dog, came by his side and followed him down to the creek. He seemed to understand. The creek was in full flow, blackberry bushes beaded with dark berries abounded in barbed hoops along its fertile banks, climbing vines forced their way through the mass of trees along trunks and beneath lifeless bark; flowering, thick grasses provided a place for myriads of crawling insects. Dragonflies hovered, and in the warm golden haze above rock pools motes of sand flies had gathered, weaving their mysterious patterns. And yet everything *was* different.

He sat exposed on a bare rock. A pure white cloud moved to one side to allow the sun its warm condolence; the pool sparkled with white light, and the shadows in the underbrush kept their dark secrets to themselves. That warmth, he felt, was her warmth, the spirit in the living things her spirit, the scent in the sweet flowers her love. A host of dragonflies shimmered around him in ritualistic formation and the sand flies presented their wreath embroidered in invisible threads of gold and purple; there were the faint sounds of the creek and of small living things, on a breeze the faint, imagined sounds of a stringed adagio. There would be no birdsong on this day. His poor darling mother: when the mind deserts the body there is no Heaven to reach for, there is no God, he thought bitterly, only nature, deep, unfathomable, remorseless nature.

With eyes tightly closed he saw her again from just the night before, when he lay by her side, her sheet turned and folded neatly across her chest, his arm around her waist, the scent of her hair on the pillow. His father was in the lounge room watching TV. She had on her reading glasses and was reading a book. Jim asked her to tell him what the story was about.

"A dark love story which begins in 1802," she said. "A handsome, villainous ruffian with a dark complicated nature named Heathcliff, grown out of the harsh craggy landscape of the Yorkshire moors, and Catherine, a genteel city girl, who finds his wild ways irresistible and falls madly in love. It is beautifully written." She turned to a page near the beginning. "Here, let me read about the setting: *Wuthering Heights is the name of Mr Heathcliff's dwelling, 'Wuthering' being a significant provincial adjective, descriptive of the atmospheric tumult to which that part of England is exposed in stormy weather."* The author's name, she said, was Emily Bronte. Jim laid his cheek against hers and kissed her goodnight. He told her, in the words of the song, it was *a kiss to build a dream on,* and then, when she smiled, he left her.

"She died this morning," he heard his Aunt Rose repeat in his mind.

Oh, why did he leave her?

Why did she leave him?

He wept.

The coroner's report showed she had been suffering from pleurisy, scarlet fever and pneumonia as well as bronchial asthma, but it was her heart that finally gave out.

There was a soft nasal droning sound of the organ. Standing by her casket, Jim was stunned by her changed appearance. She looked beautiful and noble, a martyred saint carved in marble, her face white and cold, beautifully at peace. Small white blossoms had been placed along her hairline. He kissed her cheek, told her once again that he loved her, and with aching heart bade her a last farewell.

Whom now would he love, and who would love him?

The hearse and its cortège were noticed as they proceeded slowly along the main road and through the streets. It was sprinkling rain. An old man stopped and removed his hat and placed it over his heart. He bowed his head. Jim wanted to thank him for his mark of true respect.

In the twilight chamber
She lay white and serene,
As on stone-carved sepulchres
The stone-carved queens.
Her eyelids closed
In this final hour,
Her cheeks like dew
Upon a sleeping flower.
On her bosom, her palms laid bare,
White blossoms braided in her hair.

In the entry of the home, where it was intended that guests would be ushered in, the carpet design was of red roses. On the wall to the left was the fan-shaped mirror. Below the mirror was a mahogany-veneered writing bureau, and on the bureau, on a doily, was a cut-glass vase, beside it a stained wooden elephant. The door of the bureau hinged down and formed a felt covered shelf on which she wrote her Christmas cards. She had lovely prim handwriting. Inside were pigeonholes for writing paper and envelopes. There was a bottle of blue ink, an inkwell too, and a glass tray for dip pens and nibs. You could actually smell the ink. At one end of the bureau, on shelves, was the twenty-volume *Encyclopaedia Britannica*; at the other, the *Webster's Illustrated Dictionary*; next to it a slim copy of *The Facts of Life*; and next to that another volume: with faded pressed violets a leather-bound collection of Shelley's poems. Inside the cupboard below, behind a pair of doors with a key, were bundles of official documents, receipts, school reports, postcards – one of the Hotel Majestique in the Blue Mountains – and, to Jim's surprise, some of his drawings of animals and the pencil-ruled house with the swimming pool. A shoebox contained Box Brownie snapshots and sepia photos – family and friends mostly, some faded like the memories, others he had never met. As he sorted through them he saw his father as he had never seen him before: young, straight and dashing with wavy hair at a rally for cross-country cyclists; in another, rather heroically striding in his butcher's coat and apron, his swashbuckling belt that held his sheath of knives, rolling a cigarette; a less flattering one of him when he was older, in his shorts and singlet, holding a big fish he'd caught on a holiday up at Forster. Aunt Jessie was there too, in her white lace bridal gown and a veil, Uncle Jack by her side. Also, in her high-school uniform of a black tunic, white blouse and striped tie, brimmed white felt hat, and with her lovely, ineffable smile, forever young, was a studio portrait of his mother. How little he knew of her. She is over there now, on his wall.

The following year, the day before Jim's eighteenth birthday, his father died of a broken heart.

2

The Halcyon Years

He felt totally bereft. The passing of both parents in such short succession and then the sale of the family home seemed to be losses too hard to bear. His consolation was his cherished and much-coveted university scholarship.

He wanted to live it up in the bright lights of Kings Cross, reputed to be Sydney's night-time den of iniquity – the cinema, strip shows and fancy boutiques, bookshops, honking taxis and crowded footpaths, Hungarian brasseries and Russian bistros, the kosher delicatessen, hamburger joints, and the dimly lit underground caves where long-haired men in black leather jackets stayed up all night listening to black jazz, drinking black coffee and smoking rolled cigarettes. In that realm of flashing neon there was room for all kinds. He was inexperienced and naïve and couldn't with any certainty recognise a prostitute in the streets and didn't even know the meaning of the word 'transvestite'. Most importantly, he wanted a place of his own, where he could discover and develop his own individuality, where he could begin to grow. He would make something of his life. He was, after all, eighteen now, ready to reach out, as well as knuckling down to some serious study.

Behind the busy main streets of 'the Cross' were also the quiet, tree-lined streets of gracious, elegant Victorian terraced houses. In former times these would have been occupied by wealthy merchants and landowners, now they were single-room lets. Jim favoured Victoria Street, its plane trees down each side so large that each summer their reach formed a shaded tunnel from one end to the other, in autumn leaves piled ankle-deep and covered almost completely all the parked cars. Marvelling at their voluminous atrium interiors and their oceanic swaying brought back memories of the ones he used to climb, high in the rigging of tall-mast ships. He had the notion now of wanting to live high up in a garret somewhere because that was where impecunious young artists famously lived, on stale bread and wine, closer to God.

In the small front garden of Number 67, behind a steel picket fence, two colourful bearded gnomes were tending a dainty arrangement of violets and pansies. Strands of maidenhair ferns hung from baskets above, a jasmine vine had made its way up to the balcony, and hanging on the doorknocker a *Room To Let* sign. He rapped a couple of times and waited. He was about to leave when the door opened slightly and out peered a face, a wrinkled old face, her hair like a mass of dashed spider web, so old and worn she might even have been dying. Wearing a blue chenille dressing gown and holding a cigarette, she winced at the extent of the day. Ah yes, the room. It was small, she said; she could let him have it cheap. She invited him in.

A hallstand served as a poste restante as well as a place for a vase of pallid plastic flowers. At the stairs she paused for a moment to grip the handrail. Then she began her slow ascent. The staircase was carpeted, each landing a mismatch of dark floral reds, balding in parts, and it creaked all the way up. Past the mid-level bathroom with a coin-operated shower, they finally reached the room at the top, the attic. She opened the door onto what he knew straight away was his: whitewashed walls, a plain-covered bed tucked under the low side of the roof, a wooden two-door wardrobe, a small table and chair, bare floorboards – it gave a monastic simplicity. A small dormer window was beckoning him to come and take a look. The view it gave through the topmost branches to the other side of the street, with its brown-and-yellow dappled brickwork, its dark slate roof and stained-glass windows, was St. Vincent's Convent.

On the stair landing outside was a coin-operated gas ring with a kettle and beside it a sink. On a shelf were two battered saucepans and the blue-painted wall showed traces of previous tenants. Yes, he thought, looking around him, this was all he ever wished for. The rent was cheap, the location perfect, and a motherly old landlady. "If you want to entertain girls," she said, "well, that's your business." Her only stipulation was that rent would have to be paid on time each Saturday morning. He told her he loved the room and wanted it. He said his name was Jim.

"You will be very welcome, darlin', everyone calls me Bubba."

He moved in the following weekend.

Jim felt he had never before lived so close to heaven. He laid the floor with sea grass matting and next to his drawing board he fitted shelves for books and a cassette radio, two coffee mugs and dishes; outside he fed pennies into the gas meter to toast crumpets on the gas ring, boiled tea, and filled the stairwell with the smell of scrambled eggs and fried onions. This was where he would stay during his next five years of university.

Naturally he wondered about who occupied the other eight rooms. It is always other people that interest us most.

Bubba occupied the two-room apartment off the hallway from the front entrance door, made more spacious with her two internal doors folded back. He knocked to pay his rent each week. Always a delayed silence, then there she was again in her blue dressing gown and fluffy pink slippers.

"Come in, darlin'," she would say, then step aside, seat him on the sofa by a low gas fire and put on a cup of tea. She remembered how he took it. With heavy double curtains of faded velvet and half-drawn lace in the front room, the light was dim and the atmosphere warm and stuffy with a strong smell of cigarettes.

On the wall above her mantelpiece was a large framed mirror that saw all the comings and goings, on the mantel a frilly lamp with a dim bulb, a plaster figure of the Virgin, and a goldfish bowl with two small guppies – Bernard and Lilly. With its tail in the air conducting a slow-time waltz, her black cat waltzed over and smeared its fur on Jim's trouser leg. He was never really one for cats. He thought them too haughty, selfish, cunning and manipulative. He was a dog man.

She always wanted to talk about the ever-present past, people mostly: the Queen, how lovely she looked in pink that day in the motorcade; the thrill she got when she saw Frank Sinatra leaving the Chevron Hilton in Kings Cross, next to where the Beatles stayed; and Rudolf Nureyev window-shopping in Macleay Street – so gorgeous, every step a dance. She smiled at the memories of the Americans – she loved them, she said, the boys when their ships came in for rest and recreation from Vietnam, their accents, the fun she and her sister and two girlfriends had with them, how they threw their money around, the nylon stockings and chocolates, the jokes that made them laugh their heads off, the songs they sang, and card games that went on all through the nights. "None of them said they were married but we reckoned they were," she said with a smile, nodding. And there were street gangs, too, and the Mafia – Juanita Neilson, just a few doors away, leader of the protest movement against high-rise development, murdered; Saturday-night dancing in the glitzy ballroom of the Trocadero; and the famous boxer, Jimmy Caruthers, her brother's best friend who, after his fight in the Sydney Stadium in 1952, became the bantamweight champion of the world.

"I know," Jim said, "I was there. My father took me. I was only twelve. He was incredible. It was one hell of a fight."

She stirred the tea in the pot, shuffled to the low table and placed the tray next to the vase of dried flowers and her ashtray. She was tired. She put two spoonfuls in her tea and a dash of milk. The biscuits were for him. To let her cup cool, she lit another cigarette. Her match was trembling. She inhaled deeply and then blew the smoke away from her face.

"Oh, and the girls' nights out," she recalled, more spirited now, her eyes brighter. "The night before Maggy's wedding at the ice-skating rink, all of us tiddly on champagne, slipping over, laughing our heads off. We were totally bonkers, we should have been locked up in a loony bin."

Then she paused and sighed. There had always been the girls, their good times together, before they got married. There was a time when she thought she might have married, she said, but she let it go.

Her hair, her face, her eyes the colour of pale blue milk were all drained, and her fingers arthritic – ugly, she thought. She had stopped her medication; there didn't seem to be any point.

"Can't do it any more, darlin'."

She looked away. Another wistful memory saw her as she was, as they were.

"He used to insist that I was fairer than all the buds in May," she said, a blank gaze, "and that I was the pick of the bunch." She leaned forward and crushed her cigarette. What brought that on, she wondered? Was it something Jim asked? She couldn't remember. Her mind was beginning to play tricks now.

She said she wanted only young people in her house.

The air was getting hard to breathe.

Standing, he asked if she needed anything from the shop, and would she like him to let in a bit more light, lift the window a little?

"No, don't worry, leave them darlin'."

Then, just as he was leaving, John knocked and was invited in. He hadn't met John before.

"Come in darlin'," she said in her usual tone of voice.

It never seemed necessary to ask for a receipt.

There were evenings when, from St. Vincent's Convent, strains of angelic choral voices drifted through the trees and into his window. The autumnal leaves one by one had let go and fallen. He converted his dormer window into a pair of French doors and constructed a small wooden deck with a bench seat. He was able then to sit on the parapet sipping tea, skimming opening lines of obscure poets, or strumming his guitar while looking down on the street below. After a lapse of some weeks and a short period of rain there appeared green buds on twigs that the day before were bare. Their swelling was his swelling.

Sometimes, passing the door off the next landing, he heard the muted sounds of a cello, someone practising. One morning she was rushing out and they met briefly on the stairs. She was friendly and said he should drop in sometime for a coffee. She said her name was Karin.

In the early evening a few days later, he knocked and with a pleasant smile she welcomed him in. Her room was warm, a smell of patchouli incense, on her radio something Baroque; drawings were spread out on her desk. She was tall, pale, dark-eyed, heavy spectacles, and with long black hair. She put on a kettle, brought out some cake, asked where he was from, how long had he been living here and what did he do. Her accent was German. She had perfect European taste for dark chocolate cake, strong coffee and Renaissance art; her collection of classical music was prodigious.

She took out her long thin pipe. In guttural syllables, Karin talked about her own history, about when they'd arrived two years ago, she and her family, and where they had lodged, in an inhospitable migrants' camp in an awful outer suburb called Villawood. She managed to escape and found this room.

The escarpment on which their row of terraces stood provided for her a view to the rear, of Woolloomooloo bay, and beyond the bay the city skyline and setting sun. She was happy, she said, to be in a country that seemed so easy-going and the weather perfect. Would he like some Mozart, she asked. She put on the Clarinet Concerto. She and a partner had recently created a design space, and the modular furniture they manufactured was displayed in a city showroom. Her catalogue showed sophisticated, minimalist designs: tubular chrome and polished black leather chairs, and matching tables with plate glass tops. Her record collection, arranged by composers, was Bach, Beethoven, Handel, Haydn, Mozart, Vivaldi, and many others too who, for Jim, were names he didn't know. After the *Clarinet Concerto* she played Beethoven's *Fifth Piano Concerto* – the adagio movement sublime – and then Vivaldi's Four Seasons. Mr Maldoni played this in school, he remembered. *Let your spirits be free, let your hearts be gay, let the music carry you away.* He let the music carry him away. It was wonderful.

It was Karin's suggestion that they go to Rhapsody, the Hungarian restaurant up on the main road. This would be his first ever dinner in a restaurant. Red-carpeted and tastefully furnished, the lighting was subdued and pleasant, as were the background violins. They were seated far enough away from the sounds of traffic. A candle shone softly upon white napery and silverware, winking in the slender stems of their glasses, and single red roses in slender vases were placed on each table. Other diners – Hungarians, he guessed, men in smartly tailored suits, some in evening dress, and the ladies elegant in fine dresses and modest jewellery – spoke quietly and courteously with continental charm. Karin was comfortably at home in such surroundings, and Jim felt at ease. A German waiter, Karl, known to Karin, handsome in black vest and bow tie, ran his finger down the menu to make suggestions. They each chose the goulash and Karin asked for a white wine so that on this occasion Jim would have his first taste. When they touched glasses it made him feel regal. The taste, though not unpleasant, was one he thought he might need to acquire. After a while he felt different, which made him think, delightfully, that he must be a bit tipsy. It was funny that she pronounced 'finger' as in 'singer'.

"The plate is hot, sir," Karl advised him.

Jim waited to see which piece of cutlery Karin picked up before risking his own. Mmm, the goulash was delicious, the mushroom ingredient another first. He chose the subject for conversation, her life in Germany. She described the different conditions under which East and West Berliners lived, and the insidious wall that kept them apart – she was from the Western side – while across the road the flashing flesh-pink neon sign over the hamburger joint was teasing him shamelessly with GIRLS … GIRLS … GIRLS. Apple strudel with cream was ordered, and then *café crème*.

On some evenings, when sketching furniture designs, Karin was not bothered with Jim's company in the corner, listening again to Vivaldi, or Bach or Mozart. She wanted to expand his listening repertoire with some of the lesser known, such as harpsichordist Wanda Landowska playing Scarlatti, or flautist James Galway playing Quantz. He was moved almost to tears when he heard the beautiful, haunting Albinoni adagio, remembering the one he imagined at the creek the day his mother died. Karin once took out her cello and played some Bach suites for him, pausing at certain moments, articulating each theme variation for his better understanding of structure and composition, and to explain hidden subtleties. He felt inspired and could sense similarities with the compositions and proportions of classical Palladian architecture, which was also concerned with the golden mean and natural order, as perhaps every great work of art is. He liked the idea that architecture could seem to be frozen music – ice crystals geometrically locked together, or solid forms as variable as instrumental sounds, spaced like notes, each composition a coherent, balanced whole that had a quality of inevitability. Schopenhauer, wasn't it, who said that all arts aspire to the condition of music?

Jim's appreciation for music began in this small chamber, and during these sessions there was nowhere else in the world he preferred to be. Under von Karajan's baton, Beethoven's *Ninth Symphony* was at times slow and calm, then it gathered momentum, louder and larger, bearing down on him like a great locomotive, reached its crescendo and held it there aloft in triumph. And then, like a leaf floating down from side to side, it settled gently and quietly again, back into serenity. With the finale, the choir of a thousand voices singing the *Ode to Joy*, he looked up and gazed into the white infinity of the ceiling and it opened like clouds drifting apart – there was the blazing light of glory, hallelujah! He breathed out and slumped. He said he thought he'd had enough for one evening. "Let's go for a walk," he suggested.

One day Jim and Karin took the slow train ride to the Blue Mountains. In the rainforest coolness of moss and fern, seated beside a babbling stream and reading Goethe's poems descriptive of a similar earthly paradise, he felt euphoric. On one sunny Sunday afternoon later, resting on his pillow reading *Portrait of the Artist as a Young Man*, when he came to the seaside where Stephen was *alone and happy, near to the wild heart of life, and young and wilful and wild-hearted, alone amid a waste of wild air and brackish waters and a sea-harvest of shells and tangle and veiled grey sunlight,* where *a girl stood before him in midstream, alone and still, gazing out to sea,* changed, it seemed, *into the likeness of a strange and beautiful seabird* he felt light-headed, as if bewitched by the inspiring power of the Muse.

He discovered Dylan Thomas under milkwood, Garcia Lorca in the bullring, and Kafka's fantastic idea that Gregor could wake up one morning unable to get out of bed because he had metamorphosed into a monstrous, gangling cockroach; Alice's fanciful wonderland inhabited by white rabbits and a caterpillar flopped on a mushroom smoking hashish from an oriental water pipe. Everybody was free to invent any kind of fantasy they liked and share it with the world.

Other friendships had ripened by now. One by one he discovered that nearly all the others in his terrace were involved, one way or another, in the arts. Lucy, in the next door attic, a violinist and close friend (lover, it was thought) of a well-known Sydney composer, was the youngest member of the Sydney Symphony Orchestra; Nico and another Lucy were pursuing arts degrees at Sydney University; David, Kahil and Stasia, all budding actors were attending the National Institute of Dramatic Art. In rehearsing their parts they asked Jim to sit as their audience, not for comments so much as just a presence:

> *"What a piece of work is man, how noble in reason, how infinite in faculty, in form and moving how express and admirable. In action how like an angel, in apprehension how like a god! the beauty of the world, the paragon of animals."*

They were learning that the art of acting is to pretend not to be yourself but to impersonate others, to be as believable as the couples you see conversing in coffee shops – their body language, their natural gestures, no script, improvising, just being themselves, their own personas. So, being a voyeur was part of it as well. A shameless duplicity, acting, but really just a harmless game of make-believe. All the world's a stage: streets full of strolling players dressed in costumes of … business executives in smart suits, children in school uniforms, tourists in a palm beach shirts, policemen, or, if you like, actors on a stage, whomever, whatever.

In rehearsals he commented that they seemed unconvincing, they sounded theatrical and moved like actors on a stage, and of course having to throw one's voice only added to the difficulty. After rehearsals, in conversation over coffee, they came back again to being convincingly who they really were, their own personas. One could tell Kahil might not make it, though he was not bad with Pavarotti in the bathroom. His penchant (and maybe his nemesis) was for Lebanese hashish.

The big end-of-year performance was a packed house. They were all brilliant. David as Hamlet and Kahil as Rosencrantz were absolutely brilliant; the audience was clamorous. In the crowded foyer afterwards, and then in their company at the celebratory dinner, Jim felt proud as Punch.

John in the room below, spectacled young office clerk in the Department of Works, became Jim's closest friend. His biggest night came when he smoked grass for the first time. He stared at Jim with puzzled amazement and then laughed uncontrollably. They hopped into a cab to a city cinema, bought double ice creams and sat in the front row before a panorama screen just in time to see the opening scene of *2001: A Space Odyssey*.

All were fledgling paragons then, callow and ambitious, and it was wonderful how friendly everyone seemed to be, slipping in and out of one another's rooms like young novices do, the magical, mutual bliss of the first passionate embrace.

Now, Basil, in Number 65 next door, he was an actor with experience – passionate, capricious, impetuous, even villainous at times. He was well known in the theatre world, tall, good-looking – a poor man's Laurence Olivier, some said. He had won acclaim in Shakespearian roles and had just finished a season to good reviews and packed houses at the Theatre Royal in the role of Algernon Moncrieff in *The Importance of Being Earnest*. He loved early Hollywood films and adored the famous drama queens, Harlow and Garbo, and the sultry femme fatale, Marlene Dietrich.

He possessed a sixteen millimetre movie projector and each Thursday evening his ground-floor apartment, with its doors folded back revealing two marble fireplaces, walled mirrors, some Aubrey Beardsley prints and apocalyptic scenes of Piranesi's Rome, was transformed into a private-house cinema, or sometimes a music salon, where on his baby grand, with the charm of Liberace, he played Debussy and Ravel, or Chopin or Satie. The musical evenings usually led to late-hour drinks and badinage. In a gay mood, making flamboyant gestures in his dandyish smoking jacket, he regaled them with stories and ribald anecdotes, garnished the gossip and scandal that surrounded the rich and famous – Lord So-and-So and the pretty boys. Sometimes, pale and Satanic, with a glass and tapping his black cigarette holder, impersonating himself, he could also be cruel, brutal even, a crown of thorns to some who had been his intimate acquaintances.

"There should be an Inquisition," he said with the narrowed eyes of a villain, "and some of them burned at the stake. I don't know about God, but by Christ, I believe in the Devil."

His first stage appearance, he recalled, was at the age of eight – pantomime, when he was made up as a fairy and played Tinkerbell in *Peter Pan*.

"Darling, you look absolutely scrumptiously bumptious," was what he said.

Jim arrived in a masquerade of a colourful buffoon. Basil himself was a bare footed Vatican padre in a cassock, a white skullcap and a black eye-patch, a long peacock's feather in one hand to bestow absolution, and vodka in the other to get drunk. It was the evening of his *La Dolce Vita* party, a warm summer's evening with all the windows and doors open to catch some harbour breeze. The season of summer parties had begun.

His eyes slid past Jim through the doorway.

"Good man, bring it in here."

"'Scuse me, mate."

It was a delivery of a dozen crates of alcohol, then after him, the pizza boy.

There were many guests – the cultured, the successful-looking, the arty-farty glitterati, femme fatales and anointed virgins, alcoholic poets, ego-driven theatricals, a nun in a wimple smoking marijuana, a bosomy wench a fishmonger's wife, and a gaggle of shy, inarticulate hangers-on. One was wearing an executioner's hood, another the striped shirt and boater of a Venetian gondolier. Barry Humphries, in his top hat and black tailcoat, wearing a monocle, looked like Mandrake the Magician. Some had chosen bizarre Fellini-esque costumes with masks and wigs and tinsel, tooting whistles, snapping paper streamers and throwing confetti. Nino Rota's music from 81/2 was playing at loud volume – Carnivalesque you could say. At around midnight, quite suddenly like the pop and froth of corked champagne, the foyer filled with cloying after-theatre guests and rowdy gatecrashers. In the study, in the hallway, all the way up the stairs and crowding the bar there was much banter and loud, squealing laughter, some confusion, one or two bitchy snarls, and some, but not much, spillage. A girl in heavy make-up, a blonde wig and crimson corset, her head in her hands at the bathroom doorway, was quietly weeping. It was becoming noticeable that Basil was drinking too much again, but he wouldn't listen. His eye-patch was swivelled over one ear and he was perspiring.

"Don't be diriculous old girl," he said contemptuously to Mademoiselle Fanny, who said she thought he'd had enough.

"Not even close, not by a long chalk."

He played indignant, and perhaps he was. He could be anything at any moment and often several things at once, yet deep down, at the core of his being, one could detect the vulnerable little boy.

"*Cherie* I beseech thee, *laissez moi tranquille, s'il vous plait,* much rather a bottle in front of me than a frontal lobotomy."

Mademoiselle Fanny rolled her eyes and turned to Jim. She was a black witch with a pointed hat, black eyes, black lips and black fingernails. Exhaling smoke, she said in her French accent, "And what is it zat you do, monsieur?"

"Well, if you really are French you will understand, though not believe, *Je suis funambule.*"

"A tightrope walker! I don't believe you."

"I said you wouldn't. Actually, I do whatever I like. *Je suis libre comme le vent.*"

She said she did acting.

Basil turned around. "Jimbo," he said, "be a good sport and replenish this like a good man will you? Not that vile red stuff."

And with that, he plopped on the piano stool and began to sing out loud:

> "*Roll out the barrel,*
> *We'll have a barrel of fun,*
> *Roll out the barrel,*
> *We've got the blues on the run,*
> *Zing boom tararrel,*
> *Ring out a song of good cheer,*
> *Now's the time to roll the barrel,*
> *For the gang's all here.*"

And one by one, everybody joined in.

At this hour, about four o'clock with only a few left, the plain and peevish old dowager above hammered on her floor.

Basil, hopelessly drunk and maudlin, actually crying, was helped up the stairs and put to bed in the arms of his little Italian catamite.

"Ah, come and give poor Granny a kiss, dolce, dolce ..," Then with a purr and a sigh, he deflated into deep sleep.

Jim, the last to leave, locked the door behind him.

The next morning, maybe it really *was* an accident that a flowerpot fell and grazed Basil's shoulder. There was nobody there when he looked up.

Jim sailed through his first year's full-time attendance at university and passed all his exams. For others it proved to be more challenging. After the first few months the student dropout rate was increasing; by the end of the year the class number had fallen from 160 to about one hundred. Those who found they were not gifted with artistic talent mostly re-enrolled in engineering, or law or medicine. Jim's optimism remained undiminished, confident still that he had made the right decision. He loved it. He could feel the change, it seemed he had grown an inch taller; he grew a stubble beard for a while and wore the red woollen university scarf with pride. He was on his way. The curriculum included the arts, design, engineering, mathematics, and building science, all well within his grasp. The history of architecture itself was a monumental subject. With freehand drawing of solid forms in light and shade he was a natural, and for pen-and-wash renderings of the streetscapes around Moore Park he scored top marks. At home, sketching plans and sipping coffee through the late nights, in the silence and silver brightness of the moon and the tinkling sounds of Chopin's nocturnes, there were moments of inspiration when he could feel a stirring in his heart, a seed beginning to swell.

He was introduced to many great architects: the Neoclassicist Palladio, of course, Le Corbusier and Walter Gropius of the Bauhaus school; and the great Modernists: Frank Lloyd Wright, Mies van de Rohe, Alvar Aalto, Eero Saarinen, Louis Kahn,

Richard Meier, et al, and the first of the Postmodernists, Robert Graves, for example, who didn't accept the Bauhaus rules against ornament or historical pastiche. The most avant-garde was the genius Danish architect, Jørn Utzon, whose 'frozen music' sculpture for the Sydney Opera House had now taken form. It was rhapsodic. The concept was a variation on a theme of the billowing white sails Utzon had first observed on the harbour, and poised on the harbour peninsula it gave the impression of the fullness of a magnificent three-mast galleon on a high sea, its composition as unified and irrevocable as a Beethoven symphony.

The second and subsequent years involved part-time attendance at university, which allowed time for office experience and night work that would earn him some pocket money.

Peter, a colleague in his final year – intelligent, good-looking, son of an eminent architect – received the hand in marriage of the daughter of the Spanish Consul, the ring selected from a tray at Cartier, the marriage in St. Mark's Church at Darling Point, and the reception in the lush banquet hall of the Wentworth Hotel, three hundred guests, at least. It was a great celebration – the cacophony of cutlery and clashing plates and feasting; loud, joyful sounds of talk and laughter; aproned waitresses swishing around servicing the tables. Floating above it all like a mist were faint sounds, beautiful sounds, of a stringed instrument. Jim thought he recognised Bach. His eyes found a classical guitarist seated out front. Without excusing himself, he was lifted and lightly transported to sit by his side. His appearance was that of a Catalan prince; darkly handsome; cascading oily black curly hair; his shirt blousy black silk and his instrument a priceless handcrafted Ramirez. But it was the fingering on the neck of the guitar that held Jim's gaze, each resonant note and arpeggio pure and sublime. The maestro was too imperious and dignified to show any awareness of his young admirer's presence or infatuation.

At the end of the evening the prince and the pauper found themselves standing apart at the same taxi rank. In deference to him, Jim didn't say a word. When a taxi finally came along, however, they each insisted that the other should take it. When they found they were actually heading in the same direction, to Kings Cross, they agreed to share it. Jim told him how much he loved his playing. He said his name was Antonio. When it transpired that he was living just around the corner from Jim, they got out together. Jim pointed to up there behind the parapet, past the second chimney, and asked Antonio if he would like to join him in a coffee.

On the roof the night air was still and pleasant, the lighting a couple of candles and street lamps that filtered through the trees below. The setting seemed to please Antonio and a warm, friendly manner began to emerge through his princely haughtiness. Sitting on the parapet, they sipped coffee and shared some weed.

Jim recalled for him that day recently when, travelling by train somewhere in Andalusia, on the top of a distant hill there appeared what looked like an ancient relic – the ruins of a castle, and down its hillside the spilled remnants of a medieval town. His adventurous spirit rose to an impulse so that when the train slowed enough he jumped off and headed in that direction. He crossed a field of tall grasses and a bleating herd of goats. A young boy brandishing a stick barked a command to one who strayed, setting off a tremolo of bells. He stopped at a watercourse to drink. He hopped across the stones. He then began his ascent along a stone path that stepped and curved upwards. Some walls were continuous with the bare, vertical rock face. He could see evidence now that these stone-age dwellings were actually inhabited.

On entering the town it seemed deserted; all its window blinds were drawn. A faint, eerie wailing sound of a voice seeped through the alleys and rose above the rooftops. He followed the sound to where all the townspeople had gathered, under a large oak in the main square. There, in a coffin, was the laid-out body of a young boy. His father was crying a lament.

"*Si,* flamenco is the cry of death and unrequited love," Antonio said. "*Digo mis penas cantando porque cantar es llorar.*" (I tell my sorrow singing because to sing is to cry.)

Antonio touched on Lorca's theory and function of the duende – the spirit of evocation, the emotional response to art, especially in poetry and music, especially flamenco.

After coffee Jim appealed to him to play again some Fernando Sor studies, and the Bach *Preludes*, and *Recuerdos de la Allhambra*, and *Asturias,* and, and … Antonio smiled and said he would be happy to do so. And so he played, more and more of his repertoire, one rapturous piece after another, with duende. He played until across the street above the convent rooftop was the beginning glow of a golden new dawn, then the tolling of the first Sunday bells.

Walking with him to his home, Jim noticed Antonio had a limp. More humble now, able to smile, he said, as he always did, it was retribution he deserved for his momentary lapse of concentration one day in the bullring. Poetic justice, he called it.

"*A las cinco de la tarde?*" Jim asked.

"*Si, eran en punto las cinco de la tarde.*"

And it transpired that Antonio was not a Catalan prince after all; he was actually a music teacher from Madrid. Jim became his pupil for the next two years.

Being one of the only two females enrolled in the course, Heléne Dubois, a pretty bluestocking of some petit bourgeois French provenance, held her self rather precariously aloof. Surrounded by so many males her inhibitions were understandable, and the visible fact that for the first few months she wore a silvery wire clamped to her teeth didn't help matters. But what distinguished her most were her excellent exam results. Her father, Monsieur Dubois, champagne merchant, dead now, had been the wealthy one but it was her mother who had the brains and the good looks. Her mother still looked good – youngish, dressed extravagantly and made up her face with precision. Heléne's academic success earned her good employment with a respected firm of city architects. 'Mummy' she said, was having an affair with the senior partner, who drove her around in his Porsche. Prospects for advancement for both of them were good.

For her Jim was special. She chose him as her friend and confidant, the one with whom she could speak most easily, and one she admired for what she thought were his dashing good looks. I am reminded of long summer afternoons they spent in the Botanical Gardens, where they picnicked together on the grass beneath the Moreton Bay figs near the harbour's edge; small boats with their spinnakers straining to full tilt sailed by, their soft slow dip and splash; the cries of gulls. While Heléne read the diaries of Virginia Woolf Jim sketched some botanical specimens. There was once the majestic arrival of a big P & O liner from London, splendid in its whiteness, her deck crowded with all the excited incoming passengers, marvelling at Sydney's magnificent new Opera House. The sun set slowly over the western suburbs and then in its wake the long sultry hours of twilight. There was a sort of luminous enduring calm that seemed to extend to endless tranquillity. The slow walk home would include their favourite coffee shop, where there were always friends to greet them.

On some Saturday evenings they went to restaurants and theatre together. The all black American Modern Dance Company, whose principal dancer and choreographer was Alvin Ailey, happened to be performing in their Sydney season at the grand, old Tivoli Theatre. Jim made the reservations. It was a full house. The choreography to native drumbeat music was incredibly, wildly, exciting and the audience applause was rapturous. So moved was he that the next day Jim enrolled in the Martha Graham School of Modern Dance. After many months of strenuous effort and perseverance, pleasure and pain, he found his centre by finding perfect balance. And his gracefulness of movement he could feel in his walk.

He performed in a number of very amateur stage productions to music by Bartok, Stravinsky, Dohnanyi, Carl Orf and others. He was in his prime.

At about this time Jim met by chance a Londoner called Martin. It was in Vadim's, a sophisticated, softly lit, lace-curtained side-street café in Kings Cross, which attracted mostly after-theatre couples. He went there sometimes after midnight when he needed a coffee break from his drawing board, and in the hope of making new friends. Vadim, himself a white Russian blue blood with aristocratic good looks, snobbish and humourless, had a scholarly interest in Chekhov and Shostakovich. He wore prim bow ties.

Martin was reading a book when Jim walked in. He looked up and indicated to Jim that since all the other tables were occupied, he was welcome to sit with him. He was wearing a tweed coat with patched elbows and bulgy pockets, pale corduroys baggy at the knees, and a daring, red, John Wayne neckerchief, that gave him a touch of derring-do. Lard-faced and roundly overweight, short curly dark hair and moustache, he slightly resembled Dylan Thomas with a moustache; behind the moustache his smile revealed he had a chipped front tooth; he was snuffling with a cold. They ordered coffee and apple strudel; Rachmaninoff was playing.

Martin's voice was roundly English. He revealed he had an almost childlike interest in, of all things, fire engines. He spoke firstly of how he had been raised in a London orphanage, had become an intelligence officer for the Royal Air Force, couldn't stand the weather, and then about the new-model fire engines he'd seen that afternoon at the central fire station on Castlereagh Street – with the new ersatz skyline of higher office buildings, ladders with extended reach and sturdier stabilisers, apparently, were their main features. He claimed to know the workings of the London underground sewerage and drainage system. He fancied himself as a good cook, liked English pub fare and had an interest in Test cricket. Maybe he had been at some time, Jim thought, a riverboat gambler as well. Some cream of strudel like toothpaste was caught in his toothbrush moustache.

He came for the sunshine (snuffle) and to make money, though not sure how; possibly to open a restaurant or a bar. So far he had gotten only a cold. He was surprised, he said, that unlike in London, there were no wine bars in Sydney, nowhere to go with a lady between finishing work and attending a show. With a growing white-collar middle class, a wine bar, he thought, could be a good business. The book he was reading was *Quite Early One Morning* – the BBC's breakfast broadcasts of Dylan Thomas. He asked Jim what line of business he was in.

"Architecture, eh? I need an architect. Do you know Hudson's furniture store that closed down in Oxford Street? I think that could be a perfect location for a wine bar, it's on the way to Paddington. It's big enough." In drying his nose with his handkerchief, it was a relief that he wiped away the cream. When asked if he would like to have a look at it and give him some ideas, Jim said he was sure he could – his first professional assignment. Jim gave him his number then left to go back to his drawing board. Martin stayed with Dylan Thomas.

He liked Jim's ideas, went ahead with the proposal and called it Martin's Bar.

Membership was exclusive, the music kept discreetly background and the lighting discreetly low. Good Australian wines were provided and, new to Sydney, alcoholic apple cider, and generous servings of English Cheddar with baguette and Branston pickle.

As Jim was looking for night work at the time, Martin offered him the job of barman. Georgia and Julie, the two delightful bar girls who worked by his side were topless. He took to it straight away. He soon got to know the members by name and they got to know him by name. He made friendships easier by introducing them to one another. The less socially adept officiously curried favour with him, single young women flirted with him. He had the feeling that his standing in the world had gone up a notch or two. He was actually being sought after. Martin's Bar became well known as a place to be and, therefore, was often crowded. Jim became as well known outside the bar as inside.

Gabriella, a demure classic Quattrocento Florentine beauty, one of Botticelli's maidens with blonde ringlets, and also an Alitalia airline stewardess, sat only at Jim's end of the bar. She didn't want to be talked to or served by anyone else but Jim. Leibfraumilch was her choice, a sweet white wine. She always dressed very smartly. One evening she was dressed in a navy blue linen skirt that fitted tightly to just above her knees, and a matching jacket, and a white silk low cut blouse; her lips were always drawn perfectly with strawberry red lipstick. Even without any jewellery she looked immaculate. She looked like a model for Alitalia Airways.

One of Jim's duties at ten minutes before closing each evening was to ring loudly the brass bell. It was his idea to then put on the dramatic first movement of Beethoven's Seventh Symphony at full volume, whose duration, conveniently, was about ten minutes. The crowd anticipated it. They took up their instruments of choice and played with enthusiasm, many conductors conducted, and so on it went, until the evening was brought to a resoundingly joyful ending, when everyone had to leave.

One evening, with his takings counted, the empty bottles taken out and the floor swept, he had some last words with Martin then left to go home. He found Gabriella outside huddled in the cold waiting for him. She told him she was in love with him, which was very flattering. She knew nothing about him, other than that he was the luminary on stage at Martin's Bar. She put her arms around him and kissed affectionately, which put him in a spin. She wanted a commitment he didn't want to give to anyone. He did, however, he couldn't help it, take her to his chateau and she was very lovely indeed, another notch on his bedpost, so to speak. Some time afterwards, when Jim finally resigned from the bar and became just another one of the customers, Gabriella continued to sit in her usual place, not wanting anyone's company but the new barman's.

The weekends were to do what Jim liked most of all – to walk with his camera between small brick-row cottages in the narrow streets of Woolloomooloo. They were occupied mostly by Italian migrants and painted in remembered colours of emerald seas and Prussian skies, the doors and window frames tomato red or chrome yellow, on windowsills bright splashes of potted geraniums and sometimes the yellows of caged canaries; the air was the salt-sea smell of the harbour flavoured with rich, herbal smells of Mediterranean cooking. Derelict winos sat quietly around campfires in the backyards of some of the boarded-up houses.

But it was a fishing community mostly, their boats moored at the wharves, and in the early evenings their nets spread out on footpaths for repairs. Loud voices of family and television gushed through open doorways. Behind the high wire fence of the basketball court boys kicked a ball around, and girls, squealing like mice, hopscotched and skipped. Some of the very young crawled around like spiders, trailing lines with coloured chalks, and with each new shape and change of colour they told fantastic stories. Kites were picked up by the harbour wind. The photographs he took would serve as illustrations in his final-year thesis on architecture for children. Mothers cherished the photos and sometimes, for gratitude, invited him into their homes as a special guest, on two occasions to celebrate Christmas, a festivity that brought all the families together. The women loved to cook their traditional dishes. Such were the privations of their different languages that conversation never really came to much. Getting slowly and happily drunk on red vino, hearing their loud conversation and not understanding their laughter put him at odds, but he managed to find his place. He felt privileged as the only non-Italian guest, and they, in their own humble way, showed they felt the same.

Giovanni, solid as a trunk and short as a stump, was a fisherman with six kids, all girls, aged from three to fourteen. He was the life of the party. He captained his own boat. His English wasn't bad. Jim sat next to him and asked him to describe a day's catch. It was white bream, whiting and schnapper mostly, sometimes baby shark, some blubber, and many undersized that had to be thrown back. And what happens when the sea gets rough? "That is the fun of the game," Giovanni said with a laugh. Each morning at around 4am, they would take their nets and lanterns, kick over the motor, weigh anchor, cast off, then head for the open sea. They spent up to five hours out there trawling. Jim expressed his desire to go with them. If he could be at the wharf by 4 o'clock on any morning then, yes, the fisherman said, they would be happy to take him on board. Look for Esmeralda. He would be given a job to do.

There was something wonderfully refreshing about bobbing out there on the ocean swell in the first light of dawn, the salt-sea smell, the steady pulse of the engine's heartbeat and the hull's shudder; long deep breaths of fresh air. The sea was calm this time and the boat fed out its long net for an hour or so. Then, making a big sweeping arc, the boat began its long trawl back. The net was gathering and slowly decreasing and tightening into a noose. The hauling in was most exciting, the sea convulsed with frenzied netted fish. The net was raised and momentarily hung as a bulging writhing mass above the deck. Then it was released. It splashed and flooded to the gunwales. It was a treasure trove it seemed, of precious silverware and a thousand glinting coins. Each enraged fish fought in its last desperate bid for the sea. Jim, with the others, waded among them to sort out the ones too small and to throw them back. The frenzied gulls swooped and shrieked like mad.

Then they headed home. From the boat's cabin, on a light facing breeze, there came the spaghetti smell of breakfast and the doleful strains of Mick Jagger singing, *I am the little red rooster, too lazy to crow for day.*

On one of his street walks he sometimes stopped to admire a very old house. It was situated on the corner of dead-end lane and all that could be seen behind its tall privet hedge was its steep-sloping, rusted, corrugated iron roof. It was a simple brick colonial cottage of only two rooms, 150 years he reckoned, very old indeed for Sydney, one of the first. It was known as the Gatekeeper's Cottage because once upon a time it was the gatekeeper who granted access to Crown land as a more direct route for wagons hauling goods from the docks at Rushcutters Bay to the goods trains at Central Railway Station. Now an old lady was living there.

On a spring Saturday afternoon in 1967, he saw the *For Sale* sign displayed. The old lady must have died. He immediately rang the agent to tell him he wanted to buy it, without first of all enquiring as to the price. He had the terrible fear it might already have been sold. It was only $9,800. The reason it had not sold was its state of dereliction: the timber floors were rotten, as was the roof structure; the window panes were smashed, the walls water stained, and there was no kitchen or bathroom to speak of. Since Jim wanted to do a completely new renovation anyway this was not important, except that it made the price more affordable. The site was a triangle and the particular placement of the house gave a small triangular front yard, a larger one to one side and another at the rear – three potential courtyard gardens. A tall deciduous tree growing over the house, *Ailanthus altissima*, (common name, Tree of Heaven), whose male flowers have potentially allergenic pollen (it was a male), seemed to him to augur both portentousness and propitiousness.

Some weeks later, two days after his graduation, he moved in and began his life as a hermit. This would be the test of his learning. Little did he know that his labour of love would last for the next five years.

The architect he was most influenced by was Frank Lloyd Wright, an American pioneer whose homes hugged the earth with a strong horizontality, seeming almost to have grown from roots in the soil. Open-planned, they allowed internal spaces to flow or step up or down from one level to another, and then open out to a sunny courtyard garden. Wright was influenced by principles of the traditional Japanese home: its sense of scale and proportion, simplicity of planning, the relationship of unity between house and garden and garden and house, and the use of natural materials such as wood, plants and water, as well as the inclusion of winter sun. These principles Jim would apply to his new home, and as much as possible to each new commission.

Jim employed Glen Bacon, a young blonde carpenter, for whom building a new home was his biggest and most exciting challenge. Each morning they discussed the details Jim had drawn the night before. Jim gave him all the assistance he could with labour. He engaged bricklayers and plumbers and electricians when he needed them. His savings from his bar work and his inheritance were sufficient to pay the costs.

During those early days of renovation he cooked his meals under the stars, on earth floor over an open fire.

The old home began to reveal some of its hidden secrets: underneath the corrugated-iron were the original cedar shingles, broken and in splinters; in the accumulation of dust in the roof was a hand-forged slater's hammer, and up there in the dust also, wrapped in 1939 newspaper and tied with string, was a thin oak-framed sampler, the words cross-stitched on hessian, their colours faded now by time and light:

Jesus, permit thy gracious name to stand
As the first effort of an infant's hand
And as her fingers o'er the sampler move
Engage her tender heart to seek thy love.
Abigail Stone
Age 10
1849

The two interior brick walls that formed the hallway and front room he demolished and reused for the kitchen extension. This left just one big room contained by the four external walls and the exposed roof, a cathedral space in which music could be played at volume. Good use was made of the roof space with a new mezzanine bedroom with a small shower room en-suite. Desirable sunlight was gained by incorporating a large fixed window glass into the rear roof plane with rolling shutters. The Tree of Heaven could be seen. The two integral fireplaces gathered into a single chimney. Between the two fireplaces he built in his discotheque of LP recordings. His centrepiece was the heavy, thick wooden bench table similar to that of a priory refectory, with six high-backed armchairs. A small but adequate extension to the side boundary became his studio. In his kitchen, above the sink, a niche with a stained-glass window contained a precious traditional Japanese salt-glazed teapot, a gift from an eminent Sydney potter. The windows generally were of stained glass, the ones he had salvaged from various demolition sites around Paddington. In accordance with an overriding design philosophy and themes of simplicity and unity, all new interior elements built of substantial timber and rooted firmly in place gave a sense of permanence – an exercise in perfection. His collection of Persian and Baluchi rugs were spread about. He hung the sampler above a fireplace mantel. The three external spaces contained by high brick walls became garden sanctuaries.

Finally, on completion, to arrive at the stone veranda from the front gate one crossed a simple wooden bridge over a deep, carp-filled pond shrouded in bamboo, a stone-carved Balinese Buddha secreted within and a real sleeping tortoise by its side; a faint trickling sound of water. There were days – beautiful days, magical days in the fresh morning coolness of that space, sitting in the shade at the pond's edge, leaning against a veranda post sipping tea, the carp gathering for titbits, a dragonfly shimmering in golden sunlight and Monteverdi's *Vespers* or Gregorian chant or Handel's *Largo* rising from within – when Jim felt that same mysterious, light-headed feeling again of wellbeing, beholden with the precious gift of life.

> *"There sometimes arise moments in the lives of men when there is no human power or human art or human skill, whether of painter or sculptor or musician or poet or teller of tales, that could possibly do what Aristotle called "imitate nature", or what Goethe called "realise the intention of nature", or what Shakespeare and Rubens did without thinking of what they were doing. There is for them, when they appear, a total absence of every*

conceivable recording and of every possible reflection or memorial. (John Cowper Powys)

It didn't occur to Jim then but soon he would realise that in building his home he was also feathering a nest for a family to come. The seeds of future events are carried inside us and they unfold according to the laws of their own nature.

In the mid to late nineteenth century there was a large British migration to this southern arcadia. Jim's grandparents had arrived in 1902 via Suez on a three-mast, two-funnelled steamship. Australia was a lucky country endowed with vast mineral resources, and fertile land that was good for every kind of farming; the air was pure, the skies blue and starry, and the sun shone all the year round. There were good employment opportunities and the promise of a fresh beginning. It was a courageous thing to do, to pack up your belongings and make the voyage half way across the world by steam or sail.

Between about 1860 and 1900 mostly, a few miles inland from the harbour shore, two- or three-storey brick terraced homes designed in the Victorian style formed the new inner-city suburbs. The streetscapes were like in London. Over the following hundred years, however, those suburbs, due to lack of proper maintenance, fell into dilapidation. They became slums occupied by a new population of immigrants and refugees, poor pensioners, and rats that crept up from old railway tunnels.

This was the state of affairs when Jim began his home practice in the late 1960s – the beginning of a period of renewal and restoration. Many worthy heritage homes were being demolished and the apartment blocks that replaced them were typically artless and perfunctory (the 1960s was a low point in the history of architecture). The new city skyline was of boxy, high-rise office blocks, banks, offices for government departments and insurance companies, a new stock exchange, and many long-armed cranes. This new breed of white-collar office workers found that terraced houses in the city, in their run-down condition, could be bought very cheaply, and moreover, restored to their former glory with a new bedroom or two, plus bathrooms and kitchens, they were very profitable investments. And of course you could get tax credits. Prices rose slowly at first and then skyrocketed. Thus it was that suddenly there was much work for bricklayers and carpenters, plumbers and electricians, Italian marble workers and plasterers, as well as solicitors … and architects. Restoration became Jim's speciality, not through choice so much as by circumstance.

In 1973, the year of the inauguration of the Sydney Opera House, Jim's house was awarded the "House of the Year" prize by the Royal Australian Institute of Architects. It was this success that confirmed in him what became his career, and the publicity brought more work than he could handle. How much he would have loved for his mother and father to be guests for Sunday lunches; how proud they would have been.

Toffee, Jim's new adopted friend, yelped with delight chasing after a ball he threw down the lane. Halfway down one couldn't help but notice Number 21, a stately Victorian mansion, set back, uninhabitable, much in need of restoration. In its backyard, where the laurel's leaves lay scattered among flowering weeds, was a small white-painted outhouse. There, alone, sometimes on her windowsill her stockings laid out to dry, lived Leticia. Jim knew her by sight long before they first met. She was one of the made-up meretricious theatricals he saw on the crowded streets after midnight, a dancer, one of the strippers at Les Girls. Sometimes late at night he heard the clicking clacking of her high-heeled shoes outside his window.

She was delicately made, a transvestite, tall and slender as a lily, pale as a nun, her Virginal face soft and kind as a saint's, her eyes dark, deep ponds of sadness. At home she wore no make-up except a touch of mascara, which emphasised the darkness of her eyes and, by contrast, the whiteness of her skin. Her hair, naturally long, was that gorgeous Pre-Raphaelite colour of crushed cherries, her dresses – dark blue or burgundy – were simple and flimsy, and round her neck she wore strands of small black rosary beads, or more frequently a simple gold cross. At times she really did have the look of a saint. For a while she had thought of becoming a nurse but decided against the idea. Religiously, Leticia attended St. John's church service every Sunday morning.

For her performances she dressed and made up with care, almost as a ritual. They first met by chance in a small late-night coffee shop when between acts she with two other performers burst into the Picolo coffee shop. In their flamboyant costumes they seemed to fill the place. Vittorio loved them all but it was Fi Fi Lamour (Laeticia's *nom de théâtre),* to whom he paid a fawning deference. On his wall, with other stage personalities, was a signed photograph, "To Vito, Love Fi Fi".

Jim at first had been wary of her, thinking her too much. For one thing, in high heels she was taller than most, but it was her crazed histrionics, her shrieks and raucous laughter, her crushing put downs of loutish insults and her wild drug-induced eyes that made her seem so formidable. She fidgeted, flicked her cigarette, and one could see behind the façade of *maquillage* the hidden identity of the frightened little girl.

Jim happened to be seated next to her when a joint was being passed around. She offered it to him with a smile. They found that they had grown up in the same outer suburb, and now they were a pair of émigrés living in this same den of iniquity, in the same dead-end lane a few doors away from one another. She knew his house and asked if she could drop by sometime to see his building work and the plans. She was attentive when they talked about a design philosophy that included the aesthetics of Zen simplicity. Her musical taste was Monteverdi's *Vespers*, Indian ragas and cool modern jazz.

For her stage work she embellished her costumes with feathers and sequins, and for the weekend street market she crafted pots and made jewellery of jade and turquoise and sometimes opal; on her pots she applied single calligraphic brushstrokes. Her love poems carefully hand-printed on pages of coloured silk were dedicated mostly to her mother, who was still living a lonely existence somewhere in outer suburbia. There had always been affection, and pity, she felt for her mother (a lock of her hair was enshrined in an onyx locket). They spoke on the telephone for hours.

One day Leticia came bursting through Jim's doorway – she was in a hurry – apologised for her intrusion, borrowed a teaspoon, melted some heroin then injected her self. She rinsed the spoon, put it back, and then, in a flurry of departure, she was gone. That was her way – she was in the early stage of her addiction.

Sometimes for a dinner invitation she would spend nearly a whole afternoon meticulously preparing a meal, and her presentation was always as special as she could make it: candlestick lighting and red chiffon draped over lamps, light stringed music, a trace of sandalwood incense, a glowing wood fire on the hearth. On her walls were a Turner sky and van Gogh's *Starry Night*, bookshelves – feminists and heroines mostly: Virginia Woolf, Camille Paglia, Sylvia Plath, etc. – and, spread out as wall hangings, a Spanish mantilla and the white lace shawl she'd picked up on a recent trip to Athens. Curiously, in obscurity beyond the lamp lighting was a beautifully crafted wooden rocking horse, and sometimes, curled up on the red velvet chaise longue near the fireplace, were Pyramus and Thisbe, her proud and devoted Siamese cats. Everything was neat.

On this particular evening she was white-robed with a wide scarlet sash around her waist, her only jewellery her gold cross necklace and a turquoise ring; her perfume just a touch of jasmine. Centre table was a vase of orchids, each one at the climax of its beauty, and on each side a candle. Cold cress soup was served in bowls she herself had crafted, followed by sole cooked simply in a wine sauce, then lemon soufflé, and to drink, a nice chilled Chablis.

Across the table talk was mostly about the goings-on in the neighbourhood: demolition and rebuilding that was changing its scale and character; rents being raised to unaffordable heights – some of the poor and elderly, including friends, being forcibly evicted; more drugs and more frequent burglaries; the new city rail link about to open, and how work was progressing on Jim's house. She raised a glass to her courageous friend Juanita Neilson, whose murder, after ten years, was still unsolved; "a cover-up," she said. She divulged, surprisingly, that she with Juanita formed the protest movement that blocked the demolition of homes for the redevelopment of Woolloomooloo.

Coffee was served.

She put on some Miles Davis.

They repaired to the fireplace.

Reclined on the chaise longue she proceeded to prepare some hashish. More of the latest events in her life unfolded – films she'd seen at the Valhalla, events in *Rolling Stone* magazine that had not yet found their way into history, and some lines of just-written poems she recited. "And these," she sat up and reached for them, "from Hydra" – a pack of mostly overexposed snapshots: sitting straddled on a mule, shielding her eyes, looking genuinely happy (she laughed remembering the old muleteer pleading her to stay and be his wife); the fishing boats moored at the quay, the wives bickering with the fishermen; the dozen or so cats there hungry for the viscera; Patrick, an English novelist she befriended; the house where Leonard Cohen once lived; the

Armenian cook. She saw there was an art to trussing the mules that hauled everything up the narrow lanes, from milk churns and pots and pans to bags of sand and long lengths of timber. In the tableau Jim saw there was background obscurity. Beside the draped embroidered mantilla, she was lit between firelight and diffused lamps, her scarlet sash set against the bright red velvet, her cherry coloured hair, her blushed cheeks and white skin, the points of reflection dabbed on her eyes, the violet-blue of her ring and the gold cross, on the mosaic table-top the bowl of oranges and grapes and the silver ashtray, the smoke, her gesture – in just a few moments of stillness she was a Caravaggio.

The fire hissed and crackled with satisfaction. The final delicacy was the pistachio halva. She inhaled some more smoke.

The two weeks away in Greece had done her some good, but now she was pale again and thinner. In removing the plates, she knocked over a glass.

As Jim rose to leave she insisted that he come to Les Girls the following Saturday to see her new stage folly. She gave him back one of the orchids and, on the porch, a short farewell embrace. "You must come," she said, "it's a real hoot."

He did go that evening and sat secluded at the back. He waited till the last act but she didn't appear. She had phoned, apparently, to say she wasn't well. Her lights were off when he passed by.

Then there was that unforgettable evening in the Don Quixote, the new Spanish restaurant, his thirtieth birthday party, and the woman he met.

Not two hundred yards away from the City Hall, it was off a dark, cobbled alleyway down some stone steps into a spacious stone-vaulted cellar. Large wooden barrels were stacked against one wall, the usual dramatic bullfighting posters, rows of bench seating at long candlelit tables, bare floorboards, and it was crowded, full of wild, loud merriment – shouting and laughter above the frantic singing and strumming of the Gypsy Kings, plates clashing, the *vino rosso* cheap and plentiful. His friends were all expecting him. He took their cries of "Happy birthday", and made his round of embracing them all. Bill, an old codger and bearded friend, called out and beckoned him to come and join his rowdy bunch. A place was made for him next to a woman he had never met before. She smiled and said her name was Grace. She was dark with facial features that looked American Indian, wearing jeans and a simple white cotton blouse.

"We've been waiting for you, Jim, where have you been?" Bill said. "You have some catching up to do." He then commanded a bottle and asked the guests for quiet. He handed Jim a full glass, which he drank slowly, all in one long draught, feeling the champagne bubbles bursting in his nostrils, and then he held the glass high in triumph. Everyone clapped and cheered.

The speciality was roasted suckling pig. The clashing of plates continued, the talk got louder, and Bill cried out for more wine and more music. He called for Flamenco. *"Bueno! Bueno!"* He was on his way to becoming very drunk, as everybody seemed to be. Even the candle flames seemed to be jumping out of the wax-dribbled Vat 69 bottles. It was difficult to make oneself heard. The waiter came and Jim and Grace both ordered grilled fish and wine. They leaned to one another to talk, and soon Jim became aware that they were no longer part of the crowd. Her eyes were amazingly dark. She was attending the art college, she said, and Bill was her teacher; she loved the course. She used to paint when she was younger, and then left off when she married and had to make a living. In Canada she had worked in a photo studio, enhancing old black-and-white family portraits with hand-applied colours. Friendship came easily and Jim found he could make her laugh. For dessert the waiter placed two plates of strawberries.

After dinner they slipped away and walked through the busy streets to Vadim's in Kings Cross where he knew it would be quiet and candlelit. Vadim ushered them to one of his tables on a raised level from where they could see and be seen. Jim wanted to be seen. Albinoni's *Adagio* was playing.

They were both the same age. There was much to talk about: the wilds of Thunder Bay in Ontario where she was raised; her father, a native Cree, a tough lumberjack and heavy drinker; hardships in the logging camp; her mother long gone, her two sisters married, and she herself once married to a Canadian photographer, now free to do what she liked. Australia seemed to be a good place to make a fresh start, she said. She was rekindling her passion for art, her fascination for landscapes and love of nature. The painter she admired most, she said, was J. M. W. Turner – a temptation for Jim, wanting to make a good impression, to tell the same fib that, by the way, Turner, born in 1775, happened to be his great-great-grandfather, but anyway possibly not more than three or four degrees of separation. He described the virgin bush-land he grew up in, the kookaburras and their mad laughter, his poor sick mother and hard-working father and the estrangement he felt from his brothers, his own interest in photography, and how, during his architectural studies, he had earned his living as a barman. He planned to have a birthday party at his home the following weekend, he told her, and invited her to come along. He asked if she would like to bring her guitar.

It was a beautiful summer's Sunday. Under the trees in the side courtyard, they were a gathering of about fifty. She said she thought his home was beautiful. She liked his friends, had the feeling he was showing her off. He wanted to make a good impression. The crowd loved her, and when she took out her guitar and played and sang so beautifully they loved her more.

Amazing Grace, darkly beautiful half-Indian, drove an old

Chevy when she was twelve, broke in horses when she was fifteen, and now with a simple picking of chords she could accompany herself in just about every American folk song ever written, her voice mellow and beautiful. Woody Guthrie, Pete Seeger, Bob Dylan – she knew them all. Bill told Jim later that Grace said he had made a good impression and felt that something good might come of it.

They began a courtship, seeing one another more often, and before long they were living together, loving together. They became part of one another's lives. *One day someone will come along,* he remembered, her voice and her smile.

Grace finished her course and worked towards having an exhibition. She made the curtains out of old lace bedspreads and the cushion covers out of dark green velvet. Then, incredibly, they had a daughter, another cause for great celebration. She was born at about four in the morning. Was she going to be dark like her mother or fair like him, he was dying to know? The nurse behind the glass held her to him. She was fair. She waved her arms at him. He thought she mouthed, "Hi Dad, here I am, I made it – let's get it on." They called her Ingrid.

Now he had everything, he was on top of the world.

But wait. There was also Tom.

Jim liked Tom from the start. It was in a crowded pub in Kings Cross where they first met. He had not long ago arrived from Northumbria, in England. He spoke with a thick Geordie accent and his laugh lit up his face and flashed his white teeth. After his father died, and fed up with the weather, Tom decided to come to Sydney to make a new start. He was a homely, handsome guy in his mid thirties, slim, lightly tanned and with shaggy hippy-length hair. A carpenter by trade, he was seeking employment. He also needed a place to stay. Jim was able the next day to arrange work for him on one of his jobs, and for his accommodation showed him to the vacant house he had just renovated down the end of the lane. Tom couldn't believe his luck.

Sometimes on his way home Tom rapped on their gate. He would be in his work clothes, wearing his piratic red headband around his long hair. "Are you good for a cold one?" he would say, offering a six-pack. He liked Bob Dylan and Van Morrison, drank his beer straight from the bottle and sometimes rolled some weed. He sat and talked of the comings and goings on the job – small things, like him making good another chippy's work that had not been up to scratch, a bit of friction with the brickies, a late delivery of timber, or some rain stoppage, small things. His tan was getting darker. Once he came in with a nasty cut on the back of his hand, which Grace washed, disinfected and carefully bandaged. Occasionally he was invited to stay for dinner. He was good company, a happy, salt-of-the earth kind of guy. During the following months their friendship grew, and Tom became a regular presence in their home. Ingrid adored him, said one day she was going to marry him, and Toffee yapped and wagged his tail at him.

Others, too, were invited for dinner. Grace loved cooking and she loved experimenting with all the ingredients their vegetarian regime allowed.

On one chilly autumn evening in 1979, Jim and Grace invited four guests for dinner, including one of her classmates, Rakesh, a talented Bangladeshi sculptor of human and animal forms in logs of wood. He was taller than average, broad-shouldered and handsome; his white muslin shirt breathed out a raw scent of sweat and musk oil; his voice was loud and direct, his manner a little pushy, but not without humour. His hair, tied at the back, was like a brigand's ponytail, and on his forehead was a small tattoo that protected against the Evil Eye, so he said. While working in a timber mill he had lost two of his fingers. Their other guests were two good friends from the neighbourhood – Alan and Susan – and Tom. Jim was seated at the head of the table, Rakesh on his left – à *la sinistra* – and Grace on his right. Toffee seemed a bit wary of Rakesh.

The forged chandelier suspended by a heavy chain hung low over the table and bore five candles – the only lighting – and the warmth came from logs crackling in the fireplace. The background mood was Bach's Sonatas.

Delicious baked mushroom casserole with pastry and vegetables was laid on. For a while Jim talked about the architect, Frank Lloyd Wright. It was the twentieth anniversary of his Guggenheim Museum. It was also the tenth anniversary of the first moon landing. Who would ever have believed that one day we would be able to see, live in our own homes, the first man walking on the moon – his robotic movements, the crackling walkie-talkie, *one giant step for mankind*? The USSR had just invaded Afghanistan and Kashmir was topical still – the warfare of folly and the folly of warfare. Rakesh, knowledgeable about that subject, rather wanted to tell anecdotes of his own making, that ended up carrying much of the rest of the evening. He was engaging and charismatic. When he talked about life after death and said that he communicated with members of his family no one believed him. Grace said that even if true it would be an invasion of their sanctity. Cheeses and sweet delicacies were served, halva and Indian tea imbued with cardamom and ginger.

After tea Rakesh produced some strong hashish, or it could have been opium. He prepared it and it was then partaken around the table. He then asked for quiet. The recording had finished. The logs subsided for him into embers and soft grey ash. One lively candle flame took it upon itself to perform a curious dance. It flickered mischievously in Rakesh's eyes, the black eyes of a black-hearted brigand. The candle guttered and its flame extinguished. The smoke from its smouldering tip rose like a writhing serpent; it turned and bowed obsequiously in Rakesh's direction, then died. It was a game of deception he seemed to be playing. Now there was stark silence, four candles, and the surrounding darkness. He then created a mood by running his stub finger around the rim of his goblet, producing at first a low, hollow hum and then an eerie, high-pitched, resonating ring. Alan and Susan looked intrigued (or maybe terrified, difficult to tell), Tom looked stunned, and Grace, who never smoked anything, looked concerned. Rakesh seemed calm and relaxed.

He poured some wine, handed his goblet to Jim as he might a chalice, and asked him to take a sip. He took back the glass and leaned to Jim. He uttered in a sombre tone, "And now has come the moment." His eyes bored into Jim's. He took control of his mind. The sensation was very unsettling. Jim fell into a vertiginous swoon.

"Don't be afraid," Rakesh whispered, "I am with you. Together we shall enter the Kingdom of Mescal."

Rakesh's eyes held him captive, but Jim's mind was now floating into another realm, out there in rarefied space, adrift, fantastic. His dreadful fear was that, cut too far adrift, he might never find his way back. He would be forever lost to the world, and might be certified as insane and have to spend the rest of his life in a madhouse. His heart was pounding and he needed water. Grace put a reassuring arm around him and told him that the effect would wear off. "Everything will be alright," she said. She turned to Rakesh and told him he was being evil and asked him to leave, which he did. Alan and Susan and Tom shuffled away as well without a word. With melted wings Jim fell back to Earth and Grace was there to help break his fall.

After dinners Grace usually sang songs, or sometimes they played cards, or if a babysitter had been arranged they might go to Martin's Bar, or a late-night coffee shop. On some evenings when work was pressing, after Ingrid's bedtime stories, Jim stayed home while Tom and Grace went out walking.

One evening, during a dinner with a few drinks, Tom and Grace confessed that they were in love. They spoke of their desire to live together. Grace was abashed, and Tom had the look of someone who had been caught stealing a best friend's wife. Tom wanted to say something but like most of his type, when it came to matters of the heart, he stumbled over his words in embarrassment, awkward in trying to explain himself. He need not have tried.

Why had she not said something before? It was not like her not to have, she and Jim shared all their thoughts. They trusted one another. In his role now of cuckold he had to struggle with a sense of disbelief and of betrayal. He would not attempt to force them apart and take possession, though Grace might have seen some gallantry in that, to be fought over. No, there would be no chagrin. He reasoned to himself that if she preferred to be in the arms of another then that was where she was free to be. People don't belong to one another. They can't. That's the first rule of freedom. Obviously, there was lot to talk about, however, Ingrid in particular. She, only five at the time, when the sun shone out of her, would be shared, of course. Finally, what else could he do but give them his blessing.

Jim was baffled. He had disappointed her in some way, though for the life of him he could not see how. There should have been the signs, and probably there were, but he was too otherwise occupied to notice them. He still felt the same fire of passion as at first, but she, no longer did. That can happen with time. In marriage, like in any apprenticeship, one is bound to make mistakes, but they get worked out, adjustments made. Don't they? And when a child comes along then further adjustments. He had always been faithful and a good provider, and always loving. Ingrid was a strong and healthy child, happy in school and playful with her neighbourhood friends; Grace had all the freedom to do what she liked, but lately there had been a lack resolve. There was that time recently when after making love he sensed that things had changed. A space had come between them. They should have talked about it, but they didn't. He shook his head. Love can be fickle and selfish and go where it feels best.

For some, life without the love of a good woman can seem pointless. In his journals John Cheever, in similar circumstances, wrote, *In middle age there is mystery, there is mystification. The most I can make out of this hour is a kind of loneliness. Even the beauty of the visible world seems to crumble, yes, even love. I feel that there has been some miscarriage, some wrong turning, but I do not know when it took place and I have no hope of finding it.*

In Cheever's case, however, there were the added complications of excessive alcohol and his confused sexuality.

Tom had bought some scrubland up in Cooktown, the northernmost town in Queensland, a thousand miles away, and it was there they would go to build their new home and settle. There was that song she sang that kept coming back to Jim:

Are you going away with no word of farewell?
Will there be not a trace left behind?
Well, I could have loved you better,
Didn't mean to be unkind,
You know that was the last thing on my mind.

He wrote letters to Grace without a shadow of reproof or self-pity, to tell her he thought he knew where he might have gone wrong, and he could make amends if she were to give him another chance. He hoped one day there would be her key in the door and her voice calling out to him saying she was back … but no. It broke his heart and for the first time he entered a period of almost unbearable loneliness. He felt hollowed out with a bruised heart. Simple everyday life was difficult and his work was falling behind. And it was deeply hurtful that now, when he needed her love and understanding more than ever, she never wrote back, she denied him everything, even sympathy. He needed to be hugged. His only consolation was the belief that Ingrid would grow up in a loving home, better with them, he thought, than with him in his singular state of despair. For shared custody there was the usual arrangement – she would be dropped off each Friday at 5. Jim asked Tom in for a coffee but he always had to go. He seemed bothered. And then she would be delivered back on Sundays at 5. His last words to Ingrid before they drove away on that awful last day were that he would never forget her, he would always be in communication with her, and she would always know where he was. Then they left and he felt totally bereft. He couldn't hold back his tears.

He kept his promise and wrote regularly. Some twenty years later, in 2001, when Ingrid was in her mid twenties, in one of the letters she wrote from Queensland she told him Tom died of cancer. It was a particularly unhappy time for her. She told of her painful separation from her boyfriend. She had believed him when he told her he was going to marry her but he left her for another. Jim's response was to show that he understood exactly what she was going through because he, too, had suffered the same heartbreak. He described for her how during his own period of depression he sought peace of mind by finding sanctuary in the wilds of Queensland. That letter is here now and can be reread:

Dearest Ingrid,

My first impressions of Queensland came to me when you were only seven, when I was not much older than you are now. I went there to try to heal myself after our separation. It was in the summertime when the weather was almost unbearably hot.

The State Premier at the time was a hard-nosed conservative born of a Danish Lutheran family, his father a parish priest. He started off as a peanut farmer and then became the State Premier. He lasted twenty years as Premier, not because he was a great statesman but because he was a shrewd politician. In speeches he would often make gaffes that made him an embarrassment to his fellow ministers and a laughing stock to the nation; he was a moving target for satirical magazines. They say, in politics you get the leader you deserve.

Bjelke-Petersen wanted to make Queensland the richest state by exploiting and selling off its natural resources. He favoured oil mining in the Great Barrier Reef can you believe, and granted rights to overseas companies to mine the northern beaches for titanium. The royalties and kickbacks would be enormous. He approved the logging of the Daintree Forest, an ecosystem a million years old. The removal of this forest would eventually cause erosion of the land and the land would slump into the rivers and swamps, killing off the mangroves and consequently the insect and marine life that depended on them, and in turn the bird life that depended on them, as well, of course, as death by slow suffocation of one of the great wonders of the world, the Great Barrier Reef. Reducing, in other words, one of the few remaining thriving rainforests in the world to ultimately resembling the Sahara Desert because that, too, is the result of a similar process of degradation. The Brazilian rainforests are headed that way. It didn't matter a damn to most Queenslanders, even though the facts were made plain by ecologists – they wanted their share in his financial bonanza, forget about tomorrow. No worries mate.

A youthful environmentalist group formed and rose up in protest. It was mostly people from Sydney who confronted the bulldozers that were there to cut the roads through. Bjelke-Petersen sent his strong-armed police in to deal with the 'hippy bastards'; and there were fights and many arrests. The Premier made Queensland a law-and-order police state. He appointed as his Commissioner of Police a fat, corrupt punter who looked like a thug, a real redneck. He took bribes, and when he tried to cover his tracks he left more scratch marks than a broody hen. The courts did get him in the end. The state roads were patrolled and every young, long-haired bloke was searched for drugs because possession of marijuana was made a criminal offence. Some of your best friends today would have been put away. Tom was classified as a 'long-haired weirdo'.

At the time Tom was doing the unconventional thing of living on some remote beach near Cairns, building a boat for himself. Some of the young guys from a nearby military base would visit him and there was talk of happy smoking parties, which were dutifully reported to the police by some 'respectable' locals. The police came and ransacked his hut. They found no dope, but only, in his fridge, a jar of honey preserving a few magic mushrooms. They arrested him for that, kept him in jail for a week without a trial, then, while on parole, he was ordered to report every day at a certain hour to a particular police station. It was while they were trying to arrange his deportation back to England that I found out about it. It was very fortunate that a client/friend of mine, who was then an eminent barrister in Sydney and who later became the Commissioner for Civil Liberties, was able to arrange fair representation. It got Tom his freedom and saved him from deportation. They became the best of friends and sometimes went sailing together.

Tom rang me one day to tell me once again how sorry he was for my suffering and said he thought I needed a break from what I was going through. He suggested that I accompany him on his new boat he was about to sail from Cairns to Cooktown. He was going there to work the land he'd bought and build the new home. We needed to talk about the future anyway – our future, your future. I rang him back and said I would go. I made it to the Royal Hotel in Cairns the following Thursday at the appointed hour.

The sea voyage took only a couple of days and I will never forget how good it was for me. I got pretty sunburned but otherwise it was just what I needed. We left early with a good tailwind and on the first afternoon we entered the bay of Cape Tribulation, anchored, and went ashore. It looked like Paradise. We placed our bags on the beach, stripped down, and plunged in. Never before had the ocean felt so wonderfully refreshing and cleansing. I combed the full length of the beach for shells and driftwood and it was there we met old Mrs Reicher. She appeared from the forest to see who we were. She invited us to the house she and her son had built some thirty years before, when they migrated from Germany. We approached the house through their garden of mango trees, banana palms and vegetable rows, past strutting peacocks who seemed to resent the intrusion. We met the son and I remember he was slim and very handsome with dark, tanned skin and silken white hair just like his mother. He resembled the wise old transcendental Indian philosopher I was studying at the time, Krishnamurti. Over tea they described the reclusive life they had lived. There had been only a few explorers like us who had landed on their shore. They showed us the government's proposal of cutting a roadway through their yard for the trucking that would transport the logging from the north. We signed their visitors book and finally left them to go and sleep down on the beach. The night sky was marvellous: reconciled inside the plenitude were Orion the hunter aiming away from Leo and Taurus, Scorpius immersed in the white powder spray of the Milky Way, the four Pointers forming the Southern Cross, and most prominent of all was the taut white bow of the moon. The ocean was calm, the air was cool and there was absolute peace.

The next day we got off early. With Tom showing me how to read the navigation charts, we zigzagged our way north between shallow reefs, some of which we could plainly see just below. As we got near the open water a sudden strong wind picked us up and we got whipped along all the way to Cooktown. We struggled to make our way into the bay, then tied up at the jetty. I walked to the town pub to order a couple of nice cold beers while Tom went to the post office to pick up his mail. In the pub he opened his bunch of letters, most of them from your mother in Sydney. It was clear now that she was still in love with Tom, and Tom, I knew, felt the same. It was at that point I realised it probably really was all over for me. Could love wither like any other living thing? We talked about what we had to talk about and managed to find a reasonable arrangement – you would come up here and settle with them and you and I would see each other whenever we could; school holidays, at least.

The next day I bade farewell to Tom and Cooktown and began hiking my way south back to Sydney. I would take my time, there was no hurry – I wanted to explore this part of the world I had never seen before. I walked many miles the first two days without meeting a soul and slept on remote beaches. The night skies were more brilliant than I could ever have imagined. The salt-sea swimming and fresh air were making me feel good and strong again. I fed on nuts and picked bananas and mangoes. I was beginning to think more clearly about the recent years, about where I might have gone wrong, though I honestly could not think of a single reproach from either of us. There really was no blame as far as I could see. I was writing it all down as a letter I would send to your mother on my return. There is nothing that can equal the joy of having been young and wildly in love together, and the belief that because it was pure it would last forever.

I arrived back in Cairns. It seemed to me a flat characterless town without a centre, sprawling away from the sea. Instead of the vernacular timber-boarded-and-latticed houses common to the north, the architecture here, with one or two exceptions, was brash and artless. There was no sign of any professionalism or expression of a developed culture. I had to leave.

Tom had told me if I got to Cairns and caught the slow narrow-gauge train up into the hills, I could get off after about a half-hour at a small town next to a rainforest called Kuranda. He told me there were two pubs there, known as the Upper and the Lower. If I wanted to meet the straight townspeople I should go to the Upper one; the other was for Aborigines and hippies. In the Lower pub Tom said I could ask for a mate of his who was a regular there. Well, he wasn't there but somebody who knew him was. It was about midday. We talked, and shouting beers for one another, as is the custom, I got slowly and dreamily inebriated. Aborigines were in another room at the rear.

I had always wanted to know the ways of the Aborigine, the ways they could read the land, their rituals and sacred sites, and their stories of the Dreamtime. I'd never met them before because I'd never had an opportunity like this. I was warned not to go in there, but I went anyway. In the room were about twenty, a bit of shouting but not noisy. The nearest person, seated alone on a bench, was a dejected-looking woman. She was wearing a light cotton dress and no shoes. I told her I was up from Sydney and asked if she would mind if I talked with her. She said she s'posed so. I sat. I saw she was a bit drunk. I saw, too, the characteristic opacity of cataracts in both eyes. Before I could say anymore two guys came over and one, the biggest one, said, "Ay... you not gonna f••k our women....gedouda 'ere." I stood and tried to explain myself. I had the same right to be there, I said, and had the woman's permission to talk and meant no harm. Others came and started shoving me around. They came at me from behind and then were all around me, punching me. They pulled me outside, punched me to the ground and one kept kicking me, the kind of thing that wakes you in a sweat on a bad night. Everything was blurred and I struggled to get up. Blood from my mouth was all over my torn shirt. The boys at the front of the pub heard the commotion and came running to my rescue. The fight escalated to *a full-on fracas, involving about a dozen blokes, and three or four Aboriginal women who seemed to have taken my side. Finally the two groups broke apart and the aggressors went snarling back into their den. They could keep their bloody snakes and witchetty grubs, I thought spitefully.*

In a clearer frame of mind, I was more sympathetic. I was, after all, the last in a long history of white subjugation. Some of their worst memories go back two hundred years to colonisation. For aeons their race had lived content, and now it was ruptured and impoverished and at risk of losing its very identity. I lay on the grass for a while recovering my senses. When I did manage to get my way back to the bar I was jeered at, told to piss off, get out of town, because I was nothing but a bloody troublemaker. I got my bag and staggered away with my tail between my legs. But I needed to wash myself, so I went to the other pub, not far away, to use a washbasin.

The people there noticed me enter, coloured with blood. I washed up, and back in the bar they wanted to know what happened to me. This was a much different pub than the one down there – quiet old folks mostly, stout and bald senior citizens in old-fashioned cardigans. In one corner I saw a man-sized boy with chopped hair and thick lips clapping loudly and rocking with empty laughter. Someone offered to drive me to a local doctor. I said I thought it was not necessary. I was offered a beer. I'd had enough to drink but I was happy to talk to these good townspeople, a young guy in particular, Nick, who was most sympathetic. He had long, ropy, fire-resistant hair and a pleasing smile, complicated, unfortunately, by a row of bad teeth. He'd been living up here for two years, he told me, in an A-frame house he designed and built in the forest. When I told him I was an architect he wanted to show it off to me. They were having a party that same evening, he said, and I should come along. If I had nowhere to stay he could put me up for the night with some other friends who were coming up from Cairns. Sure, that would be great, I said, though, after the bashing, I wasn't really sure I was up to it.

We drove through forest in light falling rain. It was very dense and there were dark caves of undergrowth. The house was set in a man-made clearing; two barefooted nymphs came running to greet us. They seemed pleased that Nick had brought a guest. The interior was a simple triangular volume made rich with hippy-coloured drapes and stained-glass windows, the smell of sandalwood incense, and from the kitchen shelves I could see they were subsisting off the contents of lidded jars. On the table were two jars of bunched wildflowers. Their offering of tea and cake made me realise how hungry I was. One of the girls, so sweet and innocent and so full of love, dressed my wounds. Sitting at the fire, we smoked a few joints together and talked quietly about the city lives we'd left behind.I went for a walk outside in the moist, cool air to discover where I was. Their herb garden was about the size of a prayer rug and nearby was a patch of thriving tomatoes and beans. The thin ribbon of milk-blue smoke from their chimney was dissolving in the mist. Deeper in the forest, the sky became restricted by towering trees tangled in thick rope vines; the ground underfoot was soft. The rain was gently patting the palm leaves and everything was glistening, everything pristine and sacred, as old as the Garden of Eden. I felt, in a way, that I was trespassing. When the sun did manage to break through, just for me it seemed, all the wet-painted greens of the undergrowth became exaggerated in their intensity, palm fronds were swelling almost perceptibly, orchids intensified, grasshoppers spurted from everywhere, and a curious butterfly skipped nonchalantly by. Friendly birds secluded in the canopy above chirped and sang to one another. I remembered Yehudi Menuhin, the world-famous violinist, saying once that the birds of northern Australia made some of the most beautiful, musical sounds he had ever heard.

The party, with all the dope and booze, was a fairly quiet and mellow occasion, and went on through the night. Because of my appearance I had to explain my mishap a few times. I looked terrible.

I woke up the next morning on the floor, cold and still a bit damp, with my face wedged in the kickboard of the kitchen cupboards, feeling that jittery, seedy feeling that accompanies a hangover. And injuries are always worse the day after. My face was blotched and swollen and beginning to peel from the sunburn I got on the boat. I splashed my face and, after a cup of tea, was soon winding down and round the hills in a bouncing truck on my way back to Cairns. From Cairns I was lucky enough to get some good lifts along the coastal road down to Brisbane.

The coast road was knotted with small settlements, and the best beaches, with few exceptions like Byron Bay and Mullumbimby, were overrun by characterless, sometimes ugly, three-storey apartment blocks and holiday homes, all seeming to have been designed and built by the same real estate agent. The worst stretches were Surfers Paradise and all along the Gold Coast: illuminated hotels with flashing neon Miami Beach names, shopping malls blinking FAST FOOD, candy-coloured strip joints winking SEX, noisy pubs clattering poker machines, and leaping out from news stands, headlines like BABY EATEN ALIVE BY WILD DINGO, and I WAS A VICTIM OF GANG RAPE. In a mall the air was sweetened by the saccharine sounds of Mantovani and his thousand strings; outside a juice bar a stunted banana palm in its tub defiled with cigarette butts was cringing like a caged animal. Under a scorching sun the main streets were snarling traffic jams, and along crowded footpaths, young and old tourists clad in shorts and singlets and rubber thongs, nose cream and sunglasses, eating hot dogs and ice cream, wandered aimlessly in a surfers' paradise. I was reminded of Jack Kerouac's description of the American version.

Australia, as a nation, is a good place, youthful and forward-looking. There is some feeling of guilt now about our colonial past and amends have been made to help restore the Aboriginal culture. According to the OECD, Australia has the best standard of living in the world. It took coming to Europe and travelling as much as I have to realise how lucky we are. The Europeans I have met that have visited our shores think so too – they loved it because the air is so fresh, the skies so blue, the vastness and natural beauty, the backslapping friendliness, and the spaciousness of living accommodation. They envy us for our 'no worries' lifestyle and are amused by our parochial naiveté. Down there we are away from all the religious, territorial and political strife that seems to be disfiguring much of the rest of the world. Many of the great cities of Europe look back on the glories of their long historical pasts whereas the cities of Australia look forward to a bright and prosperous future. It's up to you Ingrid, dear, and your generation, and our foreign guests who want to work hard, to make it so.

Truckloads of love,

Dad

On his return to Sydney with a clearer mind Jim resumed life with renewed vigour. But it still played on his mind. Was he to blame, his dysfunctional family upbringing in a home of a sad, loveless marriage? Had all that could be said been said? After seven years had their marriage just simply run its course? Was it right, anyway that two people should make a life-long commitment to one another? That is always a risk. What if you are not cut out for it? And at that point he wondered if they really had been in love, if it wasn't just a very close friendship.

How grudging memory can be – Tom could laugh out loud, which Jim could never seem to do, and see how good they looked together, a pair of rustic-looking, dark-skinned infidels.

They say that divorcees make the best spouses and there may be some truth in that, but he thought he would not want to marry again. Love them all but marry none was his philosophy.

Not sour grapes, but eventually he came to think that his separation may even have been for the better – a blessing in disguise? In time he found his way back. He was sleeping soundly again, saving money, mixing with and making new friends. He dressed in ways that made him feel better about him self, he lived his life according to his moods. And he enjoyed the peace and quiet of being alone again, with Toffee, his one devoted and ever-faithful friend. Dogs make wonderful friends – their love is uncomplicated and unconditional. How often on those summer afternoons Toffee yapped with mad excitement, endlessly retrieving a ball in the park, and how contented they both were on winter evenings curled up together before the hearth of glowing, crackling, pinewood logs. Of course he missed his darling daughter, they both did.

In 1981 the challenge for the planners and architects in Hong Kong was how to cope with and provide for the astonishing growth of commerce and population. A new programme of high-rise housing outside the city in the New Territories was under way. For a temporary change, Jim applied for and was accepted into a firm located in Causeway Bay on Hong Kong Island. He'd had little experience in planning high-rise apartment buildings, so it was a new challenge. He would awake some mornings from dreams of towers with hanging gardens newly printed on vacant hillsides. The hours were long but the pay was good, and his new colleagues were friendly and helpful, some of them expatriate Australians.

Jackie, a South African traveller whom Jim had befriended in Sydney, was now living in Hong Kong. She was pleased to hear from him. They met in a hotel lounge and she introduced him to Denis, her young Canadian friend, unkempt and scruffy, drank and smoked heavily, but otherwise pleasant enough. On parting, Jim and Denis agreed they would meet again on some future arrangement.

It was during a Christmas break from Jim's office when they next met. It was in a popular bar on Nathan Road. They chatted and after a while Jim noticed a little guy was eyeing them. Why, he wondered, and so he asked him. He was Nepalese and wanted to know if they had ever been to Kathmandu. Jim said he had. "Would you like to go again," he asked, "you and your friend, with return airfares and $500 cash in the hand?" After more discussion they told him the offer sounded interesting, as long as they could check the bags before leaving the airport (they were supposed to be packed with cheap Hong Kong watches, but maybe other more serious contraband as well). A customs officer at the Kathmandu end, with a wink and a nod, would see them through. It was risky, of course, but the odds seemed OK, and it was twenty years since Jim had last visited Kathmandu.

Everything went as arranged: the described customs officer waved them through, a car was waiting outside and they were driven to a farmhouse. There they were offered cups of tea, chit-chat, then a man entered and backhanded them each $500. Accommodation was arranged in the city centre. They stayed for five days … but that is another story. Denis bought a quantity of hashish and Jim, after a long search, found a bronze casting of a standing Gupta Buddha. Denis surprised Jim when he divulged that smuggling was his way of life. He had been doing it for some years. He invited Jim to join him with another movement of goods from Hong Kong, by boat this time. He couldn't, he said, he had his job to go back to, and anyway he felt he had taken enough risk. It was some days later when Jackie informed Jim that Denis got caught in a typhoon in Hong Kong harbour, his boat capsized and he was drowned. *C'est la vie.*

After six months Jim returned to his home and office in Sydney.

Years later, in 1989, he arranged a meeting in a coffee shop with a client and the builder of a job just finished. He needed to get an agreement on what the final payment to the builder should be. They agreed, shook hands and walked out. Sitting there, feeling good about another job well done, he realised that for the first time in thirty years he didn't have any work to go on with – the restoration of the inner city was complete. Literally on a paper serviette, he did a rough calculation of how much his assets were worth. He decided right there and then that it was enough – enough to satisfy his longing to venture out, to discover the world through the lens of his camera.

During my own expatriation I have thought about this thing of Jim's leaving and never returning. He had never really felt at home in the Australia he grew up in. Why? Because it wasn't where he belonged. It seemed like an accident of birth. It was the dark-skinned, indigenous people, rather, he thought, who had evolved there that belonged. His skin was the wrong colour for a subequatorial island continent of predominantly flat, empty uninhabitable desert with long scorching summer heat, and so isolated from the rest of the world. He was pale. He hated the surf, getting knocked around by breakers, and the sunburn. Most Australians live in the costal regions, but there is still the scorching long summer heat. For the hedonists there is one long beach along the whole east coast and ice-cold beer. For the xenophobes there was a rich mix of many cultures. The mentality was parochial still. No worries, mate, she'll be right; fair enough is good enough. These are the reasons Jim gives to justify him leaving his birthplace. A northern, more seasonal climate would suit him better, he thought, somewhere in sultry Europe closer to his ancestral home, where he could trace his long history – ancient cities with ruins scattered by the Roman conquerors, ancient cities still with open marketplaces and cobbled laneways, different seasons, more developed cultures, home of Baroque and Classical music.

One day, during another heatwave, in the heat of a moment, Jim realised that if the world were to ever change it would have to be him who would bring it about. He rang Ingrid and told her he was going to New York and London and Paris and Rome. He set out for London. At the airport, when he thanked his friendly Aussie taxi driver for the ride, his enduring and endearing parting words were, "No worries mate."

In London he got a good job in an architects' office in a Dickensian part called Gray's Inn. He found meagre accommodation in Earls Court, where in crowded noisy pubs Australian barmen served pints of Guinness; and on his walk along Brompton Road, the Brompton Cemetery – pathways through wild unkempt grassland, graves with beautiful stone-carved angels and tombstones engraved with the poetry of love and sorrow. Nearby was a fish-and-chip shop that served the best North Sea cod. On Charing Cross Road, off Leicester Square, and down on the river on bench tables was where you could find the best range of second-hand books. Also on the river was the hourly reminder of the city's great, solemn patriarch, Big Ben.

Commuting in overcrowded trains each day, though, through smoke-blackened suburbs of rubbish-strewn backyards, was a cheerless experience, for everyone it seemed, especially during the dark, bleak, months of winter. It was the constant drizzle that finally got him down. After a year he left London and went to Paris. To inform her of his new whereabouts, he sent a postcard to Ingrid of the Eiffel Tower.

3

Paris

For as long as he could remember he had had so many fanciful imaginings of what France was like. When he was a boy he saw on the map it was just across the Channel from his grandmother England; a proud, sophisticated nation that spoke a foreign language and, let it be said, loved dogs and snails and frogs' legs, which further flavoured his curiosity. The beautiful, heroic Marianne, symbol of the French Republic in wanton déshabillé with long flowing hair, was also the image most depicted in his stamp collection. He could never have dreamed that in the future he would spend half of his life in Paris. It was the beautiful spring of 1990.

One thing that surprised him during those first days in perhaps the world's most beautiful city was how nonchalant everyone seemed to be, going about their business as usual, window-shopping, walking dogs, catching buses, sweeping streets, sipping coffee, etc., seeming not to notice, except him. He was the wide-eyed little boy with his nose pressed to the window, his mouth agape.

The city's facades of smooth stone were carved with vines and flower motifs. The townscape comprised five-storey apartment buildings huddled together with meandering narrow alleyways that led into public squares or civic spaces; the skyline was of domes and spires and jagged rooftops staccatoed with thousands of terracotta chimney pots; grand boulevards were lined with blossoming chestnut trees and manicured gardens with clipped hedgerows; open marketplaces displayed a cornucopia of fruits and flowers in the true colours of spring; lamp-lit black-cobbled streets bathed in soft yellow glow. Through the city centre flowed the beguiling River Seine with its two elongated islands like large ocean cruisers moored by bridges to each bank. The night's northern constellation was a different universe. Women were chic. There was a mosaic of moments and dozens of minute impressions, from rumpling tyres over cobblestones and foreign vowel sounds at side-street cafés to the plaintive tolling sounds of faraway bells.

It had not always been like this, of course. Paris in the eighteenth century was a squalid, rat-infested slum. Houses decayed with rot and mould were falling in ruin; without sanitation the streets breathed a foul and sickening stench of human waste and the putrid smell of river mud. So endemic was the pestilence, corpses by the dozens each day were carted and dumped into long ditches in the Cimitière des Innocents. Conditions couldn't have been worse.

The French Revolution in 1789 inspired new hope and new visions. In 1848 Louis-Napoleon Bonaparte became France's first President, and in 1851, its first Emperor. He had the greatest vision of all and the power to realise it. He appointed as his chief planner Baron Haussmann, to transform the city into one that would surpass all others, a chef-d'oeuvre. Thus it was that, in accordance with a covenant, all would be built in stone with cast-iron balconies; all roofs would be tones of grey – slate, lead, or oxidised zinc, so that in that northern light they would blend with the sodden slate-coloured skies, or leaden skies, or skies of grey-lilac glow. There would be generous parks and gardens, tree-lined boulevards, town squares and marketplaces, a new underground transport system, a new sewerage and drainage system, and along the river, five new bridges; it would have human scale. Significant historic buildings such as Le Louvre and Sainte-Chapelle, and, of course, the city's crown jewel of Notre Dame, would all be preserved. So let's give a clap for benevolent dictatorship.

What you see now as you walk around is the fait accompli: the city enshrined as a great work of art, a grand museum of architectural styles, including remnants of Medieval, and Belle Époque, Art Nouveau, Art Deco and Modern. The stone edifices are so massively heavy the city looks indestructible. Notre Dame has lasted 850 years, and the new Paris would last at least as long.

It is hard to believe what was achieved during those forty years between 1860 and 1900. Just consider: first of all the gradual demolition and removal of the old city; the mountains of sandstone quarried, transported, carved, then laid in place; hundreds of tons of roofing slates transported by steamers from the small Welsh mining town of Slodonia (to faraway Australia, too, useful as ballast probably); forests of hardwood felled for carpentry, and oak machined for staircases and flooring; iron ore mined, smelted and cast into so many elegant balustrades; the best Italian marble for fireplaces; plaster for ornate ceilings; glass for windows; underground service pipes and electricity; and remember, the machinery used was not much more than cogs and levers, and the transport horses and wagons. The whole nation was set to work. Who were all these tradesmen? How was it possible, during all those years of demolition and removal, excavation and then rebuilding, that normal life of baking bread and getting children safely off to school could be carried on as usual? Added to these difficulties was the Siege of Paris during the Franco-Prussian War in 1870–71. A new civilisation emerged, a belle époque.

And four distinct seasons, too, each beautiful in its own way – not so far north as to be smitten by the Gulf Stream's bitter freeze and excessive rainfall, not so far south as to suffer the

Mediterranean heat and humidity; in springtime the alchemy of spring, in autumn the colours and gentle rain. And far enough inland, too, not to be bothered by fierce coastal winds that cities such as Chicago and New York are exposed to. The skies... well, skies are beautiful everywhere. Here, Jim decided, was where he would live for the next hundred years. He would settle and see the world from here.

But where exactly? Up on the hill of Montmartre among the bohemians, or down in Le Marais, the Old Quarter, among the artisans? Somewhere central? He became an assiduous walker and cyclist. The Latin Quarter on the Left Bank was overcrowded and too noisy. If you look on the map, on the Right Bank opposite Notre Dame, where the river bends, that is Le Marais. It was once prone to flooding before the walls along the river were built – *le marais* means 'the marshland'. He loved the river, and Le Marais. With its stepped and splayed facades and geometrical shadows; its cobbled side lanes from which, around a corner, you could suddenly discover a public square with perhaps an old church and a splashing fountain, and from that square, intricate, winding passages that led you to others that also opened and converged – the whole quarter had an organic quality that gave it a distinctly medieval character. So yes, Le Marais.

A personable English barman named Edmond had worked for some years in Le Petit Fer à Cheval in the Marais and had gotten to know his regular customers fairly well. No, he hadn't heard of any vacancies or of anybody moving out. But, as luck would have it, an Irishman seated nearby heard Jim's enquiry and said he would be leaving his studio within a few days and would be happy to show it to him. From a third floor it looked onto a spacious, quiet, treed courtyard; it was airy and light with a high ceiling and, facing south it caught the whole arc of the southern sun. It was quiet as a church. There were good shopping and neighbourhood amenities with the Hotel de Ville Métro station nearby. It was easily affordable, and in the heart of the Marais, in the centre of the universe. Yes.

Jim felt now that he had arrived at the destination to where all along, without knowing it, he was bound – those juvenile daydreams he'd had about Paris were not dreams at all, he realised, but premonitions. Within a month of settling in he bought a laptop computer and taught himself to type. He enrolled in a language class to learn how to say properly, *Bonjour, mademoiselle,* and *Comment allez vouz?* and, with a smile, *Voulez vous dancer avec moi, si'il vous plait?* He could hear the cries of *"Couteaux! Couteaux!"* – the knife grinder wheeling through the streets; the glass cutter ringing his bell, and the wandering gypsy accordionist serenading women in upper windows. He soon got to know the denizens of his neighbourhood and quiet places where he could sit and read. This would be his very own belle époque.

April is the cruellest month, T.S. Eliot wrote, *breeding lilacs out of the dead land, mixing memory and desire, stirring dull roots with spring rain.*

Spring's rejoicing became summer's plenitude; autumn's desuetude sank into dispiriting cold and darkness. But soon enough there would be quickening expectation and things would begin to stir again. He described it all in detail in long letters to Ingrid.

It was in the summer of 1991, when Jim had just begun his employment with an American firm of architects that he first met Rudi. They each joined the firm in the same week and were placed in the same cell documenting the construction of the twin towers for IBM at La Défense – the new commercial zone beyond the Arc de Triomphe. Rudi was in his early forties, slim, with German good looks, and his trademark appearance was his wild, curly blond hair and his slim-fitting white linen suit. He had recently arrived with his family from Berlin. It turned out that he was also living in the Marais, just a hundred metres or so from Jim. He had married early in life and was the father of two grown-up daughters. The youngest, Hannah, was studying architecture at l'École des Beaux-Arts. Over the next couple of years they all got to know one another as good friends. Jim was given the honour of being invited to Hannah's wedding, a beautiful, quiet occasion in the Château de Noirieux in the small village of Briollay in the Loire.

They made frequent excursions together into the world of popular entertainment, Rudi and Jim. After drinks in the Cheval they sometimes went to a nearby noisy restaurant, drank some more, and once, Jim remembers – it was his idea – they hopped in a cab up to Montmartre, to Le Moulin Rouge, where he found himself swigging a bottle and indulging in some ribaldry with a dancer on the stage from which, in more sober mood he would have refrained.

Or sometimes he was invited into their home for dinner. It was old and spacious and had much character – exposed heavy-timber posts and beams; white plastered walls with hangings of famous art; book-walled rooms filled with volumes of Klimt, Poussin and Ingres; architecture by Hundertwasser, Palladio and Le Corbusier; novels printed in German, French and English; Ottoman rugs scattered about. Sylvie, Rudi's wife, also German, was an English teacher. She was delightful company, so much in love with life, and loved cooking.

After dinner, in the lounge room the two men talked casually over drinks and pleasant music, a choice of cheeses and sweet delicacies usually laid on. Rudi had a scholarly interest in Chinese civilisation. He could read and write both Chinese and Mongolian. One of his favourite books was Needham's

Science and Civilisation in China, a pirated edition he bought in Taiwan for 110 marks. Talk was light and sometimes serious. Jim answered questions about the youthful, easy-going life style he had lived in Australia, its unfettered history and so on, but he preferred to steer the subject away to historical and recent events in Europe – he wanted to learn about the Second World War and its aftermath. The number of those who could still remember was dwindling.

It was the year Jim was born when Hitler's tanks entered Paris, rumbled down the Champs-Élysées, along rue de Rivoli, and then camped in front of the mayoral office, just across from where he was now living. Here they were met with the sniper fire of La Résistance positioned along the upper windows. The tanks returned fire. On the stone facade there are still the same pockmarks, and inside, carved in perpetuity, the list of those heroes who died in vain.

The best way would be to show rather than try to describe the horrors. From a shelf Rudi lifted a heavy book, then placed it on the table next to Jim. He hadn't looked at this for years. Once more he would be visited by his nightmares. It showed maps and black-and-white war photos of the extent of the destruction, horrific scenes in Berlin, Hamburg, Frankfurt and Bremen. Jim saw photos of Dresden – what had been Germany's jewel city – just after the Allied bombing in 1945: it looked like a coral reef covered in ashen white dust, destruction total. Because Berlin was a mostly nineteenth-century-built city of sturdy brick buildings and wide boulevards, it didn't burn as readily as older cities with narrow medieval quarters, whose wood-framed houses caught fire quickly and spread. It took almost two years of bombardment to annihilate Berlin – the British by night, the Americans by day and the Soviets firing off their large guns as well.

The music stopped, so there came a heavy silence.

"So you really want to know, do you? I will tell you."

Rudi described the horrors of what it must have been like to be occupying a dark cellar in Hamburg or Bremen, gasping on carbon monoxide and other gases.

"Gradually the fires outside turned the cellars into ovens, so those who were not already asphyxiated had to face the firestorms raging with the force of a typhoon outside. Firestorms suck the oxygen out of the air, so you could not breathe or, if you did, the heat would scorch your lungs, or you might die in burning asphalt, or drown and be boiled in the steaming river. Then the aftermath, when concentration camp inmates were forced to dig out the charred remains of people in the air-raid shelters, whose floors were slippery with finger-sized maggots."

Rudi took down a second book.

"This is by Hans Erich Nossack, one of the few German writers to describe such scenes." He turned to a page and ran his fingers over the words:

'Rats and flies ruled the city. The rats, bold and fat, frolicked in the streets, but even more disgusting were the flies, huge and iridescent green, flies such as had never been seen before. They swarmed in great clusters on the roads, settled in heaps to copulate on ruined walls, and basked, weary and satiated, on the splinters of windowpanes. When they could no longer fly they crawled after us through the tiniest cracks, and their buzzing and whirring was the first thing we heard on awakening.'

There was a knock on the door. Mr Kowalski was escorted in with loud good cheer. He was an old Ashkenazi émigré whose roots were in Poland. He ran a kosher delicatessen in the nearby Jewish Quarter and lived just around the corner. He dropped in now and then to be sociable. He shook Jim's hand then took out a bottle of vodka. He liked Stolichnaya – it made him feel nostalgic. He sat and joined in the conversation.

"We have the Americans to thank," Mr Kowalski said disingenuously. "And the Australians," he added. His memories went back to the years of Nikita Khrushchev's showdown with President Kennedy over Cuba, and even as far back as the pact Stalin made with Nazi Germany, and Stalin's death in 1953. It all seemed like a replay of a scratchy old black-and-white movie. A baker he knew during the German occupation in a town near Rennes helped blow up an electricity substation, and in reprisal the Germans shot twenty-five of the town's citizens.

Rudi settled back in his soft leather chair with his cognac in one hand, and his Cohiba cigar – Castro's brand – in the other. He exhaled, ashed his cigar, took another sip and cleared his throat. There were only the three of them now: cognac, vodka and whisky, or if you counted the blind-eyed marble bust of Emperor Hadrian on the pedestal next to Rudi, there were four.

"It's crazy," he said with some emotion; he was quite under the influence.

"There have been epochs of history when for centuries races unknown to others had lived content – digging, hunting, begetting, doing what was requisite for survival and nothing else. Then one day, when confronted by a tribal culture of different appearance, with different customs and different gods, they got frightened. Out of fear all manner of crimes have been committed – the history of civilisation, still, today. If only they had sat down and talked they would have found they had much more in common than their differences – their common humanity, for one thing."

He sighed, sat back in his chair with eyes closed and a look of sadness and mild disgust. Mr Kowalski, looking baleful, just nodded. The silence now was filled with regret and recognition; there was nothing more to say. Jim couldn't ask Rudi what role he might have played. The darkness outside seemed strangely grim and complete; to the east there was a grumble of thunder. From the bathroom came the flush of the toilet.

Out of frustration Jim had to say, "But when in the history of mankind has there ever been a period of no wars?"

At precisely midday on the first Wednesday of each month, ever since the War, siren sounds rise up and howl over the whole city to check the alarm system in case Paris should ever become a target again, making that day the most strategic time for attack – a cry of wolf.

By chance Jim first met Cecily one Sunday afternoon, upstairs in Shakespeare and Company, the bookshop. She took down from a shelf in the shop's private collection a book she had written. It was about the history of the Second World War. She had been in Paris during the four-year occupation, working as a journalist for the Scottish *Times*. She was one of the few journalists who had managed to escape internment.

It was some few weeks later when they met again on a street in his neighbourhood, again purely by chance. She lived nearby, she said, and invited him to her home for a cup of tea. Her ground-floor apartment was luxurious and spacious, her walls thick with books, some signed to her by some of the famous writers of the time – Hemingway, Miller, Sartre, Durrell, et al. Jim admired Durrell's signature in the first book of *The Alexandria Quartet*. He told her it was one of his favourite novels. She entered with the tray of crockery. She poured his tea, added some cream and sat down to join him. She looked tired. She said that she was dying of cancer. In the silence he could hear a clock ticking away the seconds. Should he ask, he wondered, if she would mind telling him about what she remembered of those years? It was a rare opportunity and one too hard to miss. Yes, she said, she hoped he would want them to talk about it.

From her archives she drew some newspaper clippings: a front-page headline in January 1933 – *Germany Holds Its Breath as Hitler Sworn In as Chancellor* – and another from May 1939: *Adolf Hitler and Benito Mussolini Sign the Pact of Steel.*

"Well, those are the facts," she said, "but truths can only be known from experience. There was hostile opposition from French patriots to President Pétain entering into official cooperation with the German occupier, the communists mainly, but there were some collaborators too. There seemed to be a general apathy among the citizenry, but for many, to try to live normal lives in such abnormal times, not to relent, not to despair, not give up, but to retain their dignity, was a form of defiance. Sartre wrote that since the Nazi venom was poisoning their very own thinking, their every free thought was a victory. Meanwhile the Parisian Jews were being rounded up by Parisian police and murdered in Nazi death camps. Some citizens volunteered as nurses, and there were those not so noble who strayed into Germans' arms. Entertainment such as cabarets or film houses served as small distractions.

"The German occupiers wanted life in Paris to be easier (as long as you weren't Jewish or Communist) than in Warsaw, say, or Minsk. Parisians felt safer from bombing while the Germans were in occupation. There were German assaults on communist hideouts. Some of them were put up against a wall and shot. It was commonplace for the Germans in full Nazi uniform to be seen sitting among the French on the Champs-Élysées, smoking, drinking coffee and laughing out loud. On any evening there could be a knock on the door of a well-to-do French couple during mealtime and two young German officers – good-looking, blond, blue-eyed, dressed in swastikas and jackboots – would apologise for their intrusion and politely explain that because the apartment had been allocated to some officers, the couple would have to be out by the following week.

People could hear the wild parties that went on all night, the breaking of glass and tinkling of the chandeliers, wine cellars plundered. They took only the best. Even the clocks were set to German time. Meanwhile, most Parisians lived in penury. The darkness of the streets put a depressing pall over everything; a common smell was cabbage soup."

Cecily remembered some German officers spoke of how ashamed they felt to be in uniform on seeing Jewish girls in the street compulsorily wearing yellow stars for identification, when the trains even then were running from Paris to Auschwitz.

Young German officers, too, were being executed for desertion, like those found to be sheltering with a family of French farmers. In translation there was the meticulous recording in a supervisor's diary of the description at the execution of one such man. She opened it and read for him:

"He remembered the clearing in the woods and noted the spring foliage glistening after the rain; the ash tree, its trunk riddled with bullet holes – each one for the head and for the heart. He entered these notes on one young officer's arrival and his execution:

"Two military vehicles; Officer in Charge; Medical Officer; Pastor; four guards; two gravediggers; the victim; a wooden box coffin.

"Officer in Charge – agreeable face, attractive to women; expensive suit, grey silk shirt; handcuffs glinting; white cording. Something in his eyes, dancing, exuberant, childlike.

"'Does he want a band over his eyes?'

"'Yes.'

"'A crucifix?'

"'Yes.'

"Medical Officer pins red card over heart – size of a playing card.

"Soldiers in line… Fire!… Salvo one explosion.
"Five small black holes on red card like drops of rain.
"Body twitching; change of pallor.
"Guard wipes handcuffs clean.

"He remembered, too, there was a fly dancing around in a shaft of sunlight."

Cecily tried hard to remember more, searching for more detail, still with the same sense of urgency, fully aware, too, that there were only few people still alive who could tell what she knew. She talked more, and Jim listened with held breath.

"It was such a humiliating defeat for the Germans. With such a general feeling of deep and utter shame, the German people had, until recently, lived in a state of denial – kept quiet and looked the other way, didn't want even to think about it. Now there are some writers whose task it is to keep the nation's collective memory alive. The silence was broken with the publication of *Der Brand* (The Fire) by Jörg Friedrich."

She pointed to it there on her shelf. This exhaustive and harrowing account, city by city, month by month, of Germany's destruction became a bestseller in Germany and provoked an endless round of TV discussions, controversy in magazines and newspapers, radio debates, and books taking one position or another. It was as if Germans, having been mute for so long, needed now to talk and talk and talk.

Now she felt tired out. She asked to be excused. As Jim was leaving she presented as a gift the signed copy of *The Alexandria Quartet.*

After nearly three years in Paris, Jim felt that he too was floating in the same stream of history. On its banks so many wars had been fought – the destruction of thousand-year-old cities, of palaces, cathedrals, museums and libraries, and so many souls lost forever, some returning to see the horrors and starting over again. The world seems indestructible because we so desperately want to live.

Jim can't help it – he loves to discover the things about people that make them special, things that make them who they are. Everybody, he thinks, is a walking novel.

The occasion this time was a birthday celebration in the home of an American professor living in Montparnasse, about thirty guests, well-nourished, middle class of all ages, all shapes and sizes, Americans, mostly. Auden wrote somewhere that no matter what age the company, he was always convinced he was the youngest in the room. Or as Nabakov put it, 'If I live to be one hundred, my spirit will still go around in short trousers.' Jim too. He had been concentrated with work and so was pleased for the break to socialise. He was in a frivolous mood. The room was sunny and everyone was being sociable. A tango was playing. On the lounge seat with a glass, he found himself seated beside a young woman he had never met before. She was checking her phone messages. On her plain red coat were a dolphin brooch and another of the Eiffel Tower. She looked up, and with a friendly smile Jim asked if he could be her friend.

"Sure," she said cheerily, "I'll be your friend if you be my friend."

"That's fair."

She said her name was Beverly, Beverly Baker, from San Diego

"Hm, baker, eh, I'm Jim Turner, English wood turners."

She was here to study French, she said.

She had read *Madame Bovary* and *Les Liaisons Dangereuses*. Jim had also read *Madame Bovary*. Neither had read Balzac.

"*Fossette*," he said, touching her on the cheek; "that's the French word for dimple."

"Faucet?"

"No, that's a tap, no, fossette – f-o-s-s-e-double t-e – *une fossette,* feminine."

She lifted her hand to touch it. She blushed, a blush of embarrassed shyness.

He likes to learn about things others can teach him, and talk about things he can sometimes teach them. He asked what her special talent was, the one she was born with, the thing she could do better than anyone else in the whole wide world. After a few moments she said she didn't know, hadn't really thought about it.

"I'm good around people," she murmured, trying to be helpful.

She said she taught children how to draw.

How do you do that, he wondered?

"And you, what do you do?" she asked.

Eagerly, Jim said he was good on the tightrope, which, surprisingly, didn't surprise her, as it was meant to. Half an hour spent on the high wire, he said, transformed him from a shy and diffident man into a cool-headed hero, not merely in the affairs of high risk, but in the affairs of life as well. Pole vault gave him a similar thrill, he said.

She thought, how strange.

He asked her to tell him her life story.

"Oh, Jim," she said, "you wouldn't want to know my life story, it has been so boring."

"But … but how could it have been? What, twenty-five, thirty years on this wonderful planet Earth with everything around you changing every moment – how could it possibly have been boring? Life's so generous, so frightful and exquisite, we live in such a sad and beautiful world."

Was he being serious or just having fun?

She looked him in the eye suspiciously – she had to decide. Yes, there was something a bit strange.

He himself had to admit that at times he felt as if his life belonged to someone else, his story one that had not yet been written, a character who had not yet been fully imagined, making it up as he went along.

She began twisting her silver ring with its turquoise stone round and round her finger.

She reached for her glass and took the last sip.

With the conversation becoming precarious and the sense of feeling ridiculous he wanted to cut her some slack, give her a break, so he steered to the safer shore of French cuisine. She was vegetarian, she said, one preference being white goat's cheese.

"So how do you feel about vivisection?" he asked.

She seemed puzzled as to the word's meaning.

"Dissection of live animals for experiments," Jim said.

She straightened her back, restive. She was going to get another drink, she said, and asked if she could get him one as well.

"No, thank you, I'm fine."

She got up and walked away and didn't come back.

Humph, he thought, *the story of my life.*

Though it didn't matter; there were plenty of other fascinating novels to pry into. Another came and sat by his side – pert little breasts, funny jug ears, body slim and taut as an acrobat, and, wearing gypsy reds and blues gave an impression of East European provenance. Maybe her story would include travels in a gypsy caravan, her father a tinker, or her part in a circus, an acrobat, or maybe another high wire daredevil, a kindred spirit? Find out.

"*Bonjour*, my name's Jim. Can I be your friend?" he asked.

With all the time in the world Jim developed a mad desire to venture out. Sailors go to sea, soldiers go to war, adventurers venture out. The best way to see Europe, he soon discovered, was to go by train. Everywhere was so close – Helsinki, Stockholm,

Copenhagen, Prague, Vienna, Budapest, Barcelona, etc. – and other cities more exotic, like Cairo, Istanbul, Marrakech and Jerusalem. The medieval towns of Italy had always held a fascination for him – Venice, Ravenna, Perugia, Sienna – all rich with fantastic legends of martyrs and saints and princes. Florence, *la bella cita*, birthplace of the Renaissance, was where he studied Italian at the Scuola Lorenzo de Medici for a month, and where, on the Ponte Vecchio, before the bust of Benvenuto Cellini, he met the beautiful Gabriella. They both loved cannelloni with *vino rosso* and she was good for his Italian. The southern regions of France are where you go to live the good life, to enjoy the bliss of red wine and total denial. In New York he caught the first Obama election. In Mumbai he attended an international film festival and afterwards roamed Maharashtra to photograph traditional farm and village life; he picked his way through the slums of Calcutta, after which he caught clattering mountainside trains to the Nepalese border, then hitch-hiked to Kathmandu. In Cuba he learned what living under communism was like; in Japan he learned more about the aesthetics of the traditional home and the ways of Zen. He developed a passion for photography.

Back now to Paris, 1993, when his first venture began. Stupendous events were taking place in Russia and all over Eastern Europe. On 9th November 1989 the world saw the fall of the Berlin Wall and on 3rd November 1990, *Einheit* – the reunification of East and West Germany. On 25th December 1991, Soviet President Mikhail Gorbachev resigned, declaring his office closed, and handed over the nuclear missile launching codes to the new President, Boris Yeltsin. On that same evening at 7.32pm, the Soviet flag was lowered from the Kremlin for the last time and replaced with the Russian tricolour. The Iron Curtain, rusty by now, creaked its way open and twelve former Soviet republics scurried like mice to freedom, and the world rejoiced.

The big question now was would the new Russia turn to embrace the West and its ways, or would it remain bogged down in antiquated, bureaucratic bungling? Marxist-Leninist socialism had failed so change seemed likely, especially when the world witnessed on television a drunken President Yeltsin and a buoyant President Clinton hugging and laughing together like two unlikely-looking schoolboy chums. There was much reportage of the struggles taking place in Russia. Jim decided to go and see for himself.

4

Moscow and St. Petersburg

What a grim entry into Moscow that bleak September afternoon of 1993. The plane dipped beneath cloud into a sudden thrashing of fierce sleet. Passengers groaned. Nothing was visible below until they made their landing and even then it was only the tarmac. Their arrival was one and a half hours late so there was some discontent anyway. When their cabin door finally opened they saw the corridor link to the terminal was deluged with rain – incredibly, its roof had been blown off. There was no other choice but to run for it. Wet and cold then, they queued at the passport checkpoint. The queue was not moving. Officials up ahead were idly chatting to one another. Twenty minutes passed and no announcements had been made. Jim was beginning to worry that he would not be able to reach Nicholas in time before he left his office at the French Embassy. The arrangement was that Jim would confirm his arrival and Nicholas would inform him how to get to his apartment, where he would stay as his guest for the next six days.

He left the queue to enquire as to the cause of the delay. The official, in a shapeless suit, with gold teeth, looked like Brezhnev. "Computer kaput," he said mechanically. Complaints were flying about. The officials finally stepped aside to let the passengers through unchecked.

There was chaos at the luggage collection lounge. Finally, with his bags at around 6.30pm – though the clock was stopped on 11.21 – Jim was able to change money for the phone call.

The phone took the change but otherwise was not functioning. He reminded himself, once again, that he knew things were not going to be easy in Russia and that he was to remain calm and try to accept the inconveniences as part of the travel experience – smile, be nice. It worked. The sweet lady at the information counter – pretty, in colourful dress – offered the use of her phone. He caught Nicholas just in time. He warned against taking a taxi. "Most are illegal," he said, "some dangerous", and directed him instead to the number five bus that would transport him directly to Nicholas' home in Kievskaya, about twenty kilometres away. Squelching through the mud and rain of what seemed to be the backyard of the terminal, the darkness made gloomy by tired old street lamps, Jim found the dark form of a dead number four bus slumped at the kerbside. A little further on he found a small crowd huddled and waiting.

"Moscow?" "*Da.*"

That poor old number five rattled and squeaked and complained every inch of the way. The streets were gloomy; housing blocks with dark enclaves were hunched together like weather-worn drunks; the grim-faced passengers were hunched together like weather-worn drunks; a big, boxy warehouse that advertised household hardware and cheap clothing had beside it an acre of vacant asphalt car park, and next to it a bakery shop with a long queue of hunched grandmothers. Ministry buildings looked like blind and soulless mausoleums. There were no trees or colour, just the monotone of socialist austerity. Only few people were out. The snow by now had melted into sludge. But the number five did manage to get him there, right to Nicholas' front door.

Introduction to Nicholas had been through a friend they had in common in Paris, and although they had only ever spoken once on the telephone, Nicholas greeted him heartily and welcomed him in. He was still wearing his office suit, his shirt released at the collar, perspiration on his brow, and his breath smelled of tobacco and vodka. He had been based in the embassy for nearly two years now, mainly interviewing and processing visa applications. Young and single, he probably would have jumped at any overseas post. Jim dropped his bags beside the couch, and then was invited to join Nicholas in a drink. Yes, OK, he would try their vodka – when in Russia, do as the Russians do. Nicholas left him and went to the kitchen.

Jim observed that exposed lamp bulbs lit the room. French newspapers and magazines lay scattered on a crumpled rug, on a low table a game of backgammon in disarray, on a shelf Russian bric-a-brac: a souvenir samovar, a Byzantine cross on a chain, and some framed miniature iconic paintings. Parked in one corner was an exercise bike. The air was warm and stale. From the kitchen came a clatter of glasses, the clunky disposal of an empty bottle and then the opening of a full one.

Nicholas returned with a tray. He offered a tall glass like his own. Jim thanked him – *"Non, je ne fume pas, merci"* – for his offer of a cigarette. And no, Nicholas had not received the letter Jim had sent from Paris five weeks earlier, confirming that he was coming. It didn't matter, Nicholas said. He was anxious to know all about Paris, the Paris he had left behind, his own Eighteenth Arrondissement, Montmartre, in particular. He was excitedly happy, firing one question after another, clutching his glass and drawing deeply on his cigarette, flicking it at the ashtray. It was difficult to keep up with him. He was obviously homesick, and you could tell, too, by the pouches and pallor of his face, that he was probably on his way to becoming a sad and lonely closet alcoholic.

Nicholas apologised that in the bathroom water was gushing continuously from the basin's tap into an overflowing plastic bucket into the basin. The tap's thread was stripped and couldn't be turned off. The water supply to the WC cistern was turned off because its valve was broken. The bucket in the basin was meant to flush the toilet. He explained that he had rung the property's owner – the government – to no avail, and then three plumbers over the following six months, again nyet, and now he had given up. Cracks in the wall tiles showed the building was slowly failing.

After a half hour or so he asked Jim if he would like to play backgammon. Jim was too tired and Nicholas too drunk, so eventually they said goodnight and slept.

Nicholas had gone by the time Jim awakened the next morning. Standing at the third-floor window sipping Earl Grey tea, the outside darkness was thinning and there was a sprinkle of rain. He could see the large expanse of an open marketplace below, gloomily lit, just a few people here and there. Caravan-sized steel boxes in rows served as kiosks from which goods were sold. Smudging the scene were trails of light smoke drifting from piles of smouldering market garbage. Now he could see a row of women in heavy coats and headscarves selling small things on the footpath from cardboard boxes and spread-out newspapers. The marketplace was contained by five-storey walls of perfunctory-looking apartment blocks constructed during the latter part of the communist era. They all appeared to be in the same sorry state of deterioration; the neighbourhood seemed to be morphing into a characterless kind of modern slum.

Jim cleared the table from the night before, rinsed the glasses and emptied the ashtray. He tied the garbage bag slumped heavily against a kitchen cupboard. He left with the bag and locked the door behind him. On his way down the stairs he found an old lady, who might even have been living there, scrounging in the darkness, scavenging for bottles. She smiled kindly and indicated that he should leave the garbage bag with the others.

The wintry grey air had a crisp early morning freshness. He filled his lungs with his first deep breath. The gentle prickle on his face was refreshing.

Along the footpath that led to the open marketplace, laid out on the cardboard boxes were basic foodstuffs such as sausage; cheese; freshly pulled carrots; potatoes; piled cabbages; small, anaemic-looking tomatoes; small, brown-spotted green apples; kiwi fruit; and firm green bananas. Bananas (a much sought-after luxury) used to come from Cuba before the demise of the Soviet Union but now were being imported from Guatemala; the kiwi fruit from New Zealand. The sellers, women mostly, pulled into their coat collars, seemed depersonalised. Some had their own *dacha* – a small parcel of government-allocated land in the outer districts, on which there are private gardens and lock-up sheds. At about six each morning as many goods as can be barrowed are emptied onto the footpath market. Displayed also were dried sturgeon, cakes, boiled sweets, cups and saucers, home appliances with parts missing, drill bits, showerheads, twenty-five-watt bulbs, old spectacles and, inside some cardboard boxes, tiny puppies and kittens. A shrivelled old woman with appealing eyes was offering for sale handfuls of wilting, weedy flowers she had probably pulled from somewhere along the roadside. It was quiet; there were no trees. The smoke rising from the smouldering garbage was becoming more prominent now, creating something of an apocalyptic pall.

Drawing large crowds in the open marketplace were stalls of new and second-hand shoes and boots, as well as, the illegal money exchange booths. Last year the rate had been 250 roubles for the US dollar; now it was 1,300, and by Christmas it was predicted to go to over 2,000 – the rouble steadily being reduced to rubble. The rate of inflation in 1992 reached 2,500 per cent (bread went up nearly four hundred per cent in one week, from 40 roubles to 150). But this was still not expensive considering the average pension was about 35,000 roubles each month and rent for a government-provided apartment was only about 2,500. A lot of old people, who had always been controlled and protected by the government, didn't understand these changes and were confused and afraid. Each kiosk was a rusting steel lock-up cargo container, and each seller's face could barely be seen through a hole crudely cut by an acetylene torch. Fancy new advertising terms, like *Consumer Goods*, *Discount Price* and *Limited Offer* were shouting for buyers. Long queues formed for counterfeit Marlboro cigarettes and the cheaper American brand of Smirnoff vodka. Alcohol and nicotine were now the stultifying opiates of the people. Babushkas formed a long silent queue outside a nearby bakery, waiting. Queuing seemed to be one of their most common pastimes – it did, at least, give them something to do. In a single shop one may queue three times: firstly to get a receipt for the article you want to buy, secondly to present your receipt to a cashier and pay, and then finally to go and collect your purchase.

This was the withering end of an era that had dragged on for more than seventy years, an experiment in social idealism – a tottering Russian bear. The system was meant to have been organised and managed by the common people, but was instead seized upon by a corrupt and ruthless class of bureaucrats. Since, under communism, it was the dictates of the state's central authority – the Politburo – that determined what you could and could not do, the books and thoughts you could and could not have, there would have been no point in thinking seriously about how different things could be – any kind of initiative would have been spied on as a heresay, and rebels locked away in dark cells. Individualism was a form of heresy. And so daily life was reduced to the boredom of routine and despair. These days, with an easing of certain restrictions, new opportunities were opening up to allow a new kind of mafia – the oligarchs – to enter.

Boris Yeltsin was the new President. He was pushing ahead with the market-led reforms introduced by Mikhail Gorbachev in 1989 – Perestroika. Hard-line communists, led by Vice President Rutskoy and senior minister Khasbulatov, were opposed to these changes and defied Yeltsin's demands that they quit the government. These rebels and their sympathisers, about 150 in all, had in defiance now barricaded themselves inside the House of Parliament. Yeltsin gave them a fifteen-day ultimatum, till 3rd October, to get out. Otherwise he would force them out. This day was 30th September. Their electricity had been cut off – the two upper floors were each night lit with candles. They had enough food to last and a cache of firearms and hand grenades. The Russian people Jim spoke to about this said they didn't care – they were fed up with politics and didn't want to talk about it.

Jim had Nicholas' dinner prepared for him when he arrived home each evening. After dinner they would sometimes play a bit of backgammon or drive for half an hour to a bar called Bieli Tarakan (White Cockroach), where Nicholas met with friends. After parking, the approach was by foot from a dark side street then across timber planks laid over somebody's flooded backyard. There was a door check. Because the bar was illegal it was supposed to be secret but the police came each week anyway to get paid off. The place was a series of crowded underground caverns lit by candles, like a dungeon, like a place where dissident students might choose to meet.

The word got around that there was an Australian amongst them. Some came out of curiosity, and some inspected Jim and gave him welcoming smiles, making sure he had a drink in front of him. A big man, probably in his fifties – stubble-bearded, barrel-chested – emerged like a chieftain with three or four of his acolytes. He nodded and grunted a hello, nudged the person opposite Jim aside and sat. He studied Jim's face. The others stood around and watched.

"Why have you come here?" he wanted to know. His accented English was gruff. Jim said he was an Australian living in Paris and was visiting to see the changes taking place. He said everyone now was looking with special interest at the dissolution of the Soviet Union, Gorbachev and Yeltsin. When asked what he did, Jim said he was an architect.

Jim asked the man some questions. He had been banned from his post at the university for not conforming, he said, and now lived off the charity of others and gave some private tuition on political philosophy. He scoffed at the idea of imprisonment.

"Opposition from people like me is no longer taken seriously," he said wryly. "Thought is no longer a crime. Communism is a spent force; you must have noticed, everywhere it's a failure."

"Does it still have the support of the priests and bishops?" Jim asked.

"Very little, not like before. Christian Orthodoxy across Russia is old and slowly dying, like the congregations. It will one day become obsolete. There seems to be a bit of revival in some cities. It is tolerated as a conservative moral force, but it doesn't mean much. You can see the party's desperation in the new advertising, attempting to equate the sentiment of motherland – nationalism – with communism. There is a feeling of sentimental and subliminal patriotism in the hearts of most Russians. In an attempt to replace the less dependable churches there is a resurgence now of new war memorials all through the countryside – the new national altars. The Tomb of the Unknown Soldier, recently built beside the Kremlin Wall, now regularly attracts brides and grooms after their weddings to have ritualistic photographs taken, as if it confers some kind of sanctity on them, or the hope perhaps that the state's support and protection will see them through difficult times. Not Big Brother," he chuckled, "but Big Uncle. There is a long tradition in Russia. The people are satisfied to have anyone as their

President, it doesn't really matter who, and then wait for him to take care of them without doing for themselves.

"Most communists are lethargic and disillusioned, and even the average party members are cynical. They stay on because it is a job that pays them a wage. But there are still a few hardliners left," he said, reminding Jim of those still holed up in the House of Parliament. He hailed the Polish revolution that began in the Gdańsk Shipyard under Lech Wałęsa in 1989 – *Solidarność* – as the beginning of the end of communism.

"We are all fed up," he said. "Free-market capitalism is coming, as it has in China." The onlookers who had gathered closer now seemed fascinated, even though they couldn't understand a word of English. Nicholas, sitting beside Jim, seemed proud, as if it was he who had invented him.

It was a Friday night and at closing time a group invited them both to come with them to a party in the countryside. As Jim followed them outside he looked back and the big man glanced at him and nodded and grunted.

It was Peta's car, and when they were piling in she insisted that Jim sit beside her. He was glad she was not as drunk as they were.

It was a long drive. The party was in a large manor house in the countryside. It was in a state of partial ruin with no electricity. It was lantern-lit, packed and noisy with talk and laughter. Jim mingled and had a good time, though he found nobody who could speak conversational English.

Coming home Peta pulled into a dark and empty all-night petrol station. A shiny black limousine tailed them in. It circled them slowly without a sound, getting closer and closer, eerily, like a big black shark circling its prey. It eased to a stop some fifteen feet away. Peta cursed because she had been through this before. There were two of them, both in dark uniforms – the driver, and the other much older and bigger with statuesque good looks, a wooden face looking blankly in front of him as if he were blind. They were waiting for Peta to wind down her window. She did so and was then instructed over a small microphone to get out and come to their car, which she did. After some moments the chief's window slid down about an inch. His lips moved but his gaze remained fixed. Peta had to lean to the window to hear. She knew she had to be polite. Nobody in her car was saying a word. The conversation lasted about a minute. He never once turned to Peta. She came back and asked if they could help her with some money. The sum was scraped together, given to her then she went back. It was the driver who leaned across to take it. They pulled away as slowly and quietly as they came, found the road then vanished into the darkness. Peta got in her car, sat for a moment then let out a scream of anguished frustration.

The city underground train system is truly amazing, built as one of the Communist Party's first projects in the 1920s. To protect it from any future wartime bombing it is so deeply underground you have to descend on some of the world's longest escalators. Many station interiors are so grand and opulent in design they include huge crystal chandeliers and walls of marble, some carved in relief depicting the proletarian masses in toil: men working steel furnaces in zigzag-roofed factories and smoke billowing from tall brick chimneys; men and women working side by side in the fields reaping grain, tractors gathering the harvest; young, euphoric couples close up with blooming cheeks, turned, gazing at the horizon, beyond which was the soft glow of a fresh new day, a prosperous future, a brave new world.

On a station platform men were drunk, and inside the crowded carriages others were as well. The young emaciated-looking man leaning against Jim, and then another, reeked of stale sweat and vodka. Jim got out at Okhotny Ryad Station to walk to the Kremlin, the fifteenth-century walled fortress built on a loop of the Moskva River. This forms the nucleus of the city. All roads lead to, or radiate from, the Kremlin. Inside the Wall was the Lenin Mausoleum. Embalmed, wax-faced, lying prostrate in a glass casket, under guard, was the founder of the former Soviet state. The queue to see him was a hundreds long. He looked unreal. There are those who suspect it is not his body at all, but an effigy.

Just outside the Wall is a one hundred-year-old glass-roofed shopping mall where Jim went for lunch. It had once been the headquarters of Singer sewing machines. After lunch he began the long walk back towards his apartment and was blocked by busy six-lane roads he could not traverse. Office buildings – bureaucratic citadels of the 1930s, heavy forms of strict monumental symmetry, facades rigidly geometric – expressed the central government's similarly technocratic expectations of the new social order. Nearer to home he found himself walking through an open-air flea market. Taking some nice portrait photos, he thought he could feel the ground tremble beneath him, like the slight tremors of an earthquake. He noticed the people around had stopped what they were doing and were all looking in the same direction. He followed their gaze and couldn't believe what he was seeing. About half a kilometre away, conspicuous to all, was the fifteen-storey parliament building, the "White House," its façade being bombarded with missiles. He had forgotten that today, 3rd October, was the day of the ultimatum. Yeltsin was making good his threat. Tanks were now gathered around the main square.

During the past week the international media had focused their attention on this situation because more than one hundred communist supporters had been killed, including the sixty-two attempting the seizure of the state-run television station. Now, at this moment, the eyes of the world were in sharper focus. Jim felt an almost lemming-like compulsion to join the mainstream of people who were beginning to head towards the scene at the White House. Clutching his camera, he found himself picking up speed then breaking into a run. At the end of the street that led onto the parliamentary square, tanks had formed a barricade by bulldozing a burned-out bus and two burned-out trucks. On top were armed militia keeping the gathering crowd at bay. Jim climbed a nearby tree to get a view across the square. From a branch high up he broke away some leaves and could see everything. Over on the bridge to his left, amongst a lot of black debris, lying on its back like a large dead cockroach, was a black burned-out trolleybus; to the left of the White House, in hiding and waiting for their orders, were several tanks and hundreds of soldiers; and gathering below him maybe two or three hundred onlookers. From around a corner to his right, missiles were still being fired.

At about 2pm smoke began discharging from the White House and its occupants had moved down into its basement. At three o'clock they telephoned Yeltsin's office to make a declaration of surrender. The surrender was refused because there was still sniper fire coming from the rooftop. At four o'clock, indications from mid level were that the fire had taken hold: dozens of windows were simultaneously exploding outwards and belching black smoke. The occupants were still inside. The crowd of rebel supporters jeered and threw stones at the soldiers. There was a rattle of Kalashnikovs around the corner and a sudden dispersal of the crowd, some ducking and weaving and others, in panic, falling over as if they'd been shot. Some had. Still perched aghast in his tree, for some moments Jim forgot that he was supposed to be taking photos.

The climax came when a dozen tanks, followed by troop reinforcements, were suddenly mobilised and charged across the square, the one at the front smashing through the building's main entrance, then disappearing into the foyer. More rifle fire rattled from the roof. Shortly after the firing stopped the first buses quickly entered the scene. The rebel subordinates with their hands on their heads filed out first, and then were goaded into the buses. Then Rutskoy and Kasbulatov appeared. Cheers went up from parts of the crowd. The buses with their windows papered over speedily transported them all away. Down from the tree, Jim found himself covered with the black of the soot from the incineration of the rubber tires of the night before.

The final casualty count was 187 dead, more than 550 injured, and a modern building worth billions of roubles destroyed along with all its parliamentary and archival records. Jim recalled later that on exactly the same day three years earlier he had witnessed another historic occasion in Berlin, somewhere between the Reichstag building and the Brandenburg Gate – *Einheit*: the celebration of the reunification of East and West Germany.

On the night before Jim was due to leave Moscow he told Nicholas he wanted to treat him to dinner in a restaurant of his choice. He chose the Metropole, an international five-star hotel in the city centre, just opposite the Bolshoi Theatre. Nicholas wore his office suit and tie. They were escorted downstairs into a large, noisy, over-lit dining room. It was obviously a popular place to be. Of all the dishes Nicholas could have chosen he ordered spaghetti, possibly his first one for years. By sheer coincidence at a nearby table was a group of his friends from Paris, all in high spirits. He jumped up, rushed over, and they all embraced. When he came back he said they were a film crew here to shoot the famous French singer, Jean-Jacques Goldman, to be accompanied by a Russian choir. They had finished eating and now were drinking vodka and laughing drunk. On leaving they invited Nicholas and Jim to come with them to the first-night opening of Moscow's latest, glitziest disco nightclub called **MANHATTAN**.

Well, it was glitzy all right: slick, polished and high-tech, it occupied the whole first floor of a new office building with a view through floor-to-ceiling glass onto the floodlit Red Square, and just beyond, lit up majestically like a big-production stage set, was the Kremlin. **MANHATTAN** looked expensive. They were glad they had free tickets. This particular venture, it seemed, was betting on the 'new democracy' and was, therefore, maybe a mid- to long-term investment. When they arrived at around midnight nobody was there. The lighting concealed below and around the sweep of a long bar was a bright, rosy pink Perspex glow. Where guests were meant to sit in far corners it was a subdued rosy pink cosy glow. The central dance floor was besieged by a barrage of frenetic laser beams ricocheting off a large, suspended, rotating mirror-faceted ball. The air had been sanitised and had the cool, fresh smell of mafia. The music was… well, what can you say about disco other than that it is thumpingly loud?

Gathered around the bar were several beautiful Russian models in black leotards, the type you only see in James Bond movies. When they saw the group enter they broke off from their conversation and shuffled to designated bar stools. The French boys, in high spirits, ordered vodka and 'Sex on the Beach'. Being stone-cold sober, Jim felt a little excluded, but then, hey, it was meant to be exclusive, wasn't it? You had only to look at the prices and how few people were there, if you needed any persuasion of that. A very sexy girl, sleek as a black panther, came and sat practically on Nicholas' lap. During the next hour or so, three young couples arrived and sat cosily in the far corner. One of them, a thin teenager with bad skin and a stoned look of abandonment, came onto the dance floor and began to squirm among the laser bars like a caged serpent.

Jim went to talk with one of the models. She was Russian and beautiful but not, as it turned out, a model at all, nor had she played roles in any James Bond films. She smiled and leaned to Jim and told him he wasn't obliged to buy her a drink, that she was happy just to have his company. She introduced herself as Olga, and her accented English was delightful. Her grandfather, she told him, was a well-known portrait artist, still painting, and her mother and father, too, were painters, and now she herself had completed her first four years at art school. The barman served Jim a 'Manhattan Screwball' and for Olga a 'Manhattan Martini'. Jim asked who her favourite painter was. Because of his passion for sun, earth, sky and the stars, she said Vincent van Gogh. She had seen, as Jim had, his early paintings displayed in the Rijksmuseum in Amsterdam. He was a grey-suited office clerk then; his paintings were feeble, in tones of insipid grey. It was later, in the south of France, that the Mediterranean sunlight opened Vincent's eyes to the luxury of colour. She loved to work with strong colours, too, she said. She asked where Jim was from. She said she had a passion to visit Paris and visit van Gogh's grave at Auvers-sur-Oise. Had he seen Monet's home at Giverny? Yes, he had, and he described it for her, and Monet's Japanese collection. He told her he was an architect, and that he planned to go to St. Petersburg in the morning. She said he could ignore the *papiere mâché* architecture of the Hermitage Museum, but inside he must see the works of the mid-nineteenth- century painter A. A. Ivanov, and the Poussins. And did he know that Rostropovich was going to be in St. Petersburg to perform the Bach cello suites this week? She was very interested in architecture and agreed that, whilst she loved Moscow, it did need something to lift it out of its grumpy malaise – some good American or Italian designers, she thought, could add some flavour and exuberance.

"What is Australia like?" she asked.

She loved the sound of the free, easy-going way of life there. Fed up with Russian politics, she preferred not to talk about that, but she would be pleased, she said, if he would like to dance with her. They danced to their own time and she was as graceful as a gull.

The boys were laughing out loud and ordered more cigarettes. At around four o'clock Nicholas indicated it was time to leave. At the exit door Jim looked back. Olga kissed the card he had given her and waved him goodbye.

Outside, a string of taxis were parked in soft rain. The evening had been a curious mix. In the taxi, with Nicholas asleep and snoring on Jim's shoulder, spaghetti sauce still down his front, he thought again about the reference by William Burroughs on the T shirt of the young guy who was dancing with himself:

NOTHING IS TRUE
EVERYTHING IS PERMITTED

The taxi driver was pulled over by the police and had to fork out some money. He was used to it, he said.

St. Petersburg was much nicer. If Moscow were to be thought of as a lumpish *enfant terrible*, then St. Petersburg, with her frilled, elegant nineteenth-century architecture and her love for theatre and music, could be admired as its bluestocking distant cousin. Adding to her charm were her the pleasant neighbourhood canals and gardens. Here the people were courteous and dignified and cheerfully welcoming, once again demonstrating how much the character of a place determines the way its people behave. Where in Moscow the sky was a heavy, metallic tank-grey, here it was soft pearl, but still with the glass-sharp edge of numbing winter cold.

The city lies on what was once the flat swampland on the northern coast in the Gulf of Finland, and is embraced by a large loop of the Neva River. A canal system, like in Amsterdam, was created long ago to save the city from flooding. There are walkways along the tree-lined canals and more than sixty stone and iron footbridges.

Jim arrived by train on 10th October when the early-morning mist was just beginning to stir. In 1917 the Bolsheviks repudiated the name of Petrograd (St. Petersburg) as their capital city. On Lenin's death in 1924, the citizens changed it to Leningrad, and although three years ago they had changed it back to Petrograd, *LENINGRAD* was still displayed on the train station wall.

Jim was welcomed at the station by his host, Yuri Konenko. He helped with his bags and they walked together to his third-floor apartment not far away on the main central street, Nevsky Prospekt. His wife, Tatania, greeted Jim warmly. She was wearing a satin Japanese kimono. The apartment was shambolic and smelled strongly of cigarette smoke, but colourful and homey. They sat with Jim on big floor cushions breakfasting on coffee and toast. They were a pair of Bolshie bohemians. Yuri had an impressive collection of jazz recordings and archival films, liked strong coffee and strong tobacco, and laughed a lot. His sense of humour seemed to lie somewhere between Salvador Dali and Frank Zappa – thin, unshaved and with wild hair, he even looked a bit like Frank Zappa. Tatania was a tall, thin blonde, quick and personable, and also a heavy smoker. She, I would say, made most of their decisions. They ran the Leningrad Association Film Club together. Tatania spoke excitedly about this because they were preparing to go to Germany next month to present the Russian entry in the East European Film Festival. This was to be their first time out of Russia. After Germany they would go to New York for a few weeks. They had arranged for Jim to stay in Tatania's old room at her mother's place nearby, where her grandmother was also staying. In their company he was sure he would learn a lot about Russian life in the last fifty years, and, if they liked, he could tell them some things about the outside world as well.

After breakfast, Yuri and Tatania offered to take Jim on their favourite walk. It was a Sunday, zero degrees outside, and in the arctic sky the sun looked like a small white blister. It was snowing lightly. Their footsteps crunched and creaked. Yuri was wearing his sheepskin coat lined with thick wool. There was nobody else out at this time, and in that quietness they seemed to have entered a large museum, the city's museum of architecture: such fine examples of Russian Orthodox churches and onion-domed cathedrals, the Summer Palace set in the Summer Garden, Belle Époque theatres, statues and fountains in public squares, Art Nouveau and communist period shops, and, placed at the intersection of the city's three main town-planning axes, what was once the fifteenth century palace of Catherine the Great and now the third largest museum in the world, the Hermitage Museum. To enjoy the water amenity, one had to look down into the canals, so there was not the same immediacy of pleasure you get, say, in Venice, where the water laps right up to the threshold of your door. Jim was shown the houses of where some famous people had lived: Igor Stravinsky, Vladimir Nabokov – one of his favourite writers – and Joseph Brodsky, the then American Poet Laureate.

They stopped in at Radko's restaurant on Nevsky Prospect for lunch. This is a popular tourist restaurant. They accept payment in US dollars only. If you have only roubles they exchange them for you at their inflated rate, so that you can then pay for your meal. Any change you receive would be in roubles, again exchanged at a rate favourable to their business. To buy reasonable-quality fruit and vegetables in the tourists' supermarkets, one has the same advantage of choice with US dollars.

A building that had once been the head office of the Singer sewing machine company was now the city's largest bookshop. Among rows of scientific textbooks were war memoirs and many works by Marx, Lenin and Brezhnev, but practically none by the great classic authors. Where were Dostoevsky, Tolstoy, Chekhov or Pushkin? The official reason was the paper shortage, but millions of unread books on politics are printed every week. There was a small English section with a few tame American authors.

On another day he took a motorboat ride around the canals. The water-reflected palaces are of eighteenth-century refinement, and behind groves of trees many grand homes of Palladian elegance and warehouses of Georgian simplicity. Some bridges are forged with winged beasts and coats of arms, and on their balustrades, resting peacefully, were men with fishing rods, smoking pipes. There was not the presence of dire politics here, only neighbourhood calm.

Jim liked Tatania's sixty-year-old mother the moment they met. She seemed delighted to meet him too, and welcomed him with a kiss on each cheek. Her name was Nina. She was tall with a straight back, and beautiful in every way. She had too much pride to ever let herself become like the typical babushkas he had seen in the shopping queues in Moscow, in grey, knitted berets, roundly overweight with pale, desiccated faces and downturned mouths. She was sharp and intelligent, her eyes brightly intent, every movement efficient, purposeful, business-like. She kept the books a few days each week at the local police station, which earned a little money on top of her pension. She had his room nicely prepared with folds of blankets. There was no heating. She showed him the kitchen and bathroom that she and her mother were sharing with four other single, elderly tenants on the same floor, which was their cupboard in the kitchen, and their part of the refrigerator. She could speak little English, enough, however, to get by.

It was Nina's mother, Tatania's grandmother, who was the real prize. Madam Borisnova must have been in her eighties. She, poor darling, was wheelchair-bound, beset with the leg she had broken in a fall some four years earlier. The casting had been badly done and the bone never properly mended. Unable to leave the apartment she only ever wore her blue peignoir and a woollen shawl and slippers. When Nina had to be away during the day, Madam Borisnova was left alone in her own room. When Jim was at home he knew she pined for his company.

She had once been a schoolteacher of Russian literature, and had learned schoolgirl French, but no English. Jim's French was fraught with conjugational errors and jumbled syntax; hers, largely forgotten. They struggled, but found, with some amusement, they could manage.

On some days before venturing out Jim knocked on her door to ask if she needed help in any way, did she need something from the shops? It was a small room that had mellowed with age. There was no covering on the floorboards and the stains and cracks in the ceiling gave it character. On her mantel was a clutter of small keepsakes such as seashells, beads, silver trinkets, a porcelain cup, and a crucifix made from coral. On another shelf was her small collection of books. Taped to one wall were scraps of paper showing her godchild's brash drawings of Russian astronauts floating in space, umbilically connected to a spaceship blasting violent-coloured gases. Stacked in one corner were recent purchases of tins of biscuits and nuts and chocolates – durable goods that might have to see them through difficult times. Stored on shelves in the cavity between the double windows, in the same freezing temperature as outside, were jars of sauerkraut and marmalade and a jug of milk.

One morning Jim found her sitting in her chair beside the window, reading a book. With the sun making its rare appearance, filtering through the fine lace curtain and lying gently in her lap, she reminded him of a painting by Vermeer. The silence was silvern. She reached for him as usual and gently kissed each cheek. A strand of hair, so fine, hung lightly about her face. She liked to talk about the book she happened to be reading. On this occasion it was *Speak, Memory*, the autobiography of Vladimir Nabokov, which Jim had also read. Nabokov had once lived nearby, she reminded him.

On another morning he saw her deftly thread a needle – still at her age she had no need for glasses – and then go on with some darning, quite content just knowing he was there reading his *International Herald Tribune*. Something he asked took her mind back to when she was young, and the years of two world wars, the rise and now the fall of communism. She and her husband had escaped Russia during the Second World War to live in the Crimean coastal town of Sebastopol. She asked Jim to bring the shoebox of photos out from under her bed. Postcards in exaggerated colours showed the flat, pebbly beach of Sebastopol; its war memorial and plain public buildings. And there was Nina, on the same beach, with her dress tucked in, a little girl wading in the water. She showed him in fading, sepia tones her parents dressed in the finery of the period of the tsars. She found the one she was looking for, the one taken in 1942 of the house, their home in Sebastopol, bombed and in ruins. Sitting amongst the rubble one could just make out the figure of Madam Borisnova, and standing hunched beside her was her husband, Mr Borisnova, who, just minutes after this photo was taken, shot himself through the head.

On the afternoon of Jim's return from the Hermitage he found, to his surprise, dozens of cabbages piled high in the hall in front of their doorway. They spent much of the next day, the two of them, Nina and him, finely shredding them on cutting boards, compressing them firmly into storage jars, filling the jars with brine, sealing them tightly and stacking them away in a cupboard: preserved sauerkraut.

To take evening coffee and read newspapers, Jim began to frequent the lounge of the Nevsky Palace Hotel on Nevsky Prospekt, very close to where he was staying. He went also in the hope of finding someone who could speak normal English. One evening he was lucky to find an American freelance journalist. She also seemed to have the same need to talk. Her name was Patty. She was lovely and filled with exuberance. She admitted to having once been a young revolutionary – a Maoist, Fidelist, and political science student all at the same time. Now she was a journalist, passionate about her mission, charged with the responsibility of being the eyes of America. She was caught in the flow of history and wasn't going to spill a drop. These were interesting times. She also, of course, had been in Moscow the week before and witnessed the burning of the White House. There was so much to talk about: his meetings in the underground cave of the White Cockroach in Moscow, his night on the town with Nicholas, the photos he took, similar experiences she and he had had and, together, tried to make sense of. Too soon it was one o'clock and he remembered Nina's warning about not being out too late. She had heard rumours of new crimes being committed on some of the side streets. Patty was staying in the hotel, so they exchanged cards and promised to meet again.

It was freezing out, and sure enough, about five minutes into his walk, as he was approaching home, in the dim, deserted street a young thug who passed him wheeled around and suddenly sent a flying kick that just missed his face. Instinctively Jim clutched his shoulder bag, turned to run and then found, behind him, two others crouched and ready. He dodged sideways, jumped between two parked cars and onto the street. As he fled back towards the hotel he heard the aggressor shouting abuse at the other two for letting him slip away. They were obviously new at this game. The next day, Nina was shocked and insisted that they go together to report the incident to the police. Waiting, questioning and filling in forms lasted more than two hours. I am reminded now of the similar ordeal Jim will experience later in Havana.

Yuri and Tatania arranged with some friends to take Jim by car to Pushkin, about an hour's drive away from St. Petersburg. They were to see Aleksandr Pushkin's house and visit the Winter Palace. Just as they eased their way out of St. Petersburg they came upon sad flatland with barren fields; dark, desolate churches; fenced-in transformers; and clusters of old dachas with fenced-in gardens. Only about four kilometres from the city they came upon a large public sculpture in an open field. It was the Leninsky War Memorial. This was the site of the St. Petersburg blockade, the nine-hundred-day blockade that resisted the German invasion of Leningrad in 1941–42. That was during one of the most severe winters, when half a million Russians in the field perished from fatal wounds, starvation and exposure. The resistance refused to accept defeat. Jim asked if they could stop the car for a while. The museum is an underground mausoleum, a concrete bunker, and down there were displayed hundreds of the relics of that war, including many handwritten letters. There were also some handwritten compositions by Shostakovich.

Palaces are large by definition and are usually in proportion to how distinguished the personage is who is paying the architect his fees. In this case, for the Winter Palace, the distinguished person was the monarch, Catherine the Great, and the architect a Florentine, Carlo Rastrelli, who had also designed the Summer Palace in St. Petersburg. Both palaces were large and designed with the same verve of unrestrained ornamentation and vulgar ostentation, symbolic of what was at that time stirring the French masses into revolt. The Winter Palace had been almost completely destroyed during the Second World War. In 1980, it was restored to its former pristine state. Few, if any, other nations in the world have spent so much care and expertise in preserving their aristocratic heritage and prestige. It was difficult to see how the palace could function as a residence since all rooms seemed to open directly from one to the other – suitable for grand banquets, perhaps, but as private rooms? Standing at a window of one of the enormous upper rooms, one could see far into the palace garden. It was covered in snow. It was informal except for a few freezing statues clad in flimsy cotton garments and a path of hedgerows that led down to a pond where ducks had come to settle; beyond that, a white-layered dark forest, It was a snowfield of wild, unkempt grasses, each blade like a calligraphic pen stroke. The picture was frozen still, quiet as a picture. Jim wondered if he had ever seen a painting in winter light quite so beautiful with such fineness of detail. Monet?

By the time teas with scones were taken, if they were to return to St. Petersburg in time for that evening's orchestral performance, the inspection of Pushkin's house, unfortunately, had to be brief. They drove at a safe speed and arrived in good time. The Tchaikovsky performance was all pomp and glitter.

On a Sunday morning Jim walked to the end of Nevsky Prospekt to the Monastery of Alexander Nevsky where, surprisingly, eleven other churches and four small cemeteries also exist. A congregation was gathering there, and old women begged for alms. In its interior dimness, in a pleasant mist of incense, the firelight from silver-lustred candelabras flickered onto gilded framed paintings of venerable, bearded prophets illumined in blues and burgundy and gold; above, on the ceiling, Byzantine angels hovered. The bearded, long-haired priest in faded green-and-gold robes looked like a wizard, and over his congregation, with his mellifluous voice and acts of wizardry, he cast a spell.

Outside, walking among some graves, Jim discovered Tchaikovsky, Borodin, Mussorgsky, Gounod, Glinka and Rimsky-Korsakov, and, in a bed beneath a canopy of crimson begonias, Fyodor Dostoevsky. Scattered under unkempt grasses were the many unknown and forgotten.

The days passed slowly. The sunshine was feeble, the twilight sombre and the wind bitterly cold, but it was the muddy slosh of old snow mainly that made Jim reluctant to leave home each day. He rather preferred to spend his time in the company of his dear friend Madam Borisnova, making small meals for her, sipping tea together, and finding what they could to talk about. They were becoming very close.

Finally, inevitably, the day arrived when he would have to say goodbye – *dosvidanya*. A loaf of bread for just the two ladies would be stale by the end of the week, so Jim gifted them with a toaster, as well as a modern flint gun to save the frustration at the stove of all those inferior matches, and his last kangaroo badge as a souvenir.

They both knew they would never meet again. This time when Madam Borisnova kissed him, she turned away to hide a tear. Nina, in her embarrassed shyness, gave an awkward farewell hug. Yuri and Tatania were confident they would meet again, the next time in Paris.

"Write us a postcard," they intoned.

"Yes, of course."

Walking down Nevsky Prospekt to catch the evening bus that would transport him to his ship bound for Helsinki, Jim's two bags were heavy, his feet wet and numb. Snowflakes were fluttering down, light and soft as duck's down. He was feeling sad, still in the throes of the farewell. The shops were closed so there weren't many people around. He came upon a group of people huddled together, families with their children mostly, glued to a department store window, laughing. He wanted to rest his bags anyway, so he went to stand at the fringe to see for himself what the attraction was. They were watching *Tom and Jerry* cartoons on a display television set. Every time that little mouse outsmarted Tom, sending him flying through a door, into a wall, over a cliff, under a steamroller or some other such place, the crowd broke into hilarious laughter. It was easy to see whose side they were on. After a while, huddling closer to get warm, Jim found himself laughing along too, just like all the rest of them.

5

Havana

For most basically sound Western economies the 1960s and '70s were a period of boom and prosperity, a period of avid consumerism. Global share markets were wild with speculation, transactions dispatched through transnational media. Corporations mushroomed. Funding grew, and by the '80s manufacturing capitalism gave way to financial capitalism. With currency exchange fluctuations money itself became a commodity for trade and investment, as did priceless works of art. For those clever with numbers and who were in the know, it was easy to make big bucks. Thus began a new culture of greed. A rising cost of living was creating a new and larger privileged upper class. They slept between silk sheets; there was a strong smell of eau de cologne in the air.

During those years Jim frequented a small all-night coffee shop in a quiet side street of Sydney's night district, called Picolo Cafe. It was a meeting place for regulars, all kinds – some theatricals on their breaks from Les Girls; a few smelly bohemian outcasts who scribbled poems, one who always had his cat on his lap; and those who were Jim's friends – a disparate bunch of longhaired pot-smoking political animals who talked a lot, mostly about the injustices of capitalism. On one wall were stuck-on signed photographs of theatre personalities, and the jukebox choice was mostly The Beatles, stage musicals or Italian opera. Vittorio, the lovable, gay, aristocratic-looking Roman who served the coffees loved opera. He moved with operatic grace. This evening was his sixtieth birthday. Pavarotti was singing *Nessun Dorma*. 'Vito' couldn't hit the high notes, but with the same passion and theatrics, he joined in.

Bunched at one table were Jim and his friends: long-haired Chris, a quietly spoken maths teacher; Andy, who chalked up the bids on the floor of the Sydney Stock Exchange; Bill a long-haired proof-reader for the Murdoch press; Elias, a long-haired numismatist who had done his stint in the Israeli Army; Jacques, a long-haired Palestinian who, when he closed his vegetarian shop next door, came to join in; John, older, in his sixties, ugliest person you could ever meet, with teeth like raisins, smelly, and a mind with a memory like an archive; and long-haired Black Alan, a pinko on the dole, the one who talked loudest. And squeezed at the end was Jim. Vito brought slices of birthday cake to go around.

They usually talked about topical issues, but everything seemed to have political undercurrents and overtones. The American government's anti-communist wars in El Salvador, Guatemala, Nicaragua, Angola and Vietnam were most topical then. In the US, too, there were purges of suspected communists by the FBI and the CIA and a fanatical, paranoid Senator named Joe McCarthy, who uncovered 'reds in beds'; conspiracy theories still flurried around President Kennedy's assassination; Israel's pre-eminence in the Middle East after its victory in the Six-Day War. Economic systems were brought into question. Jim felt he didn't quite fit in. His hair was only mid-length; he had been schooled a bit in basic supply-and-demand economics and knew scant about politics, but was eager to learn.

Black Alan, because he was always dressed in black with a silver dog chain around his neck, was the most outspoken. He thumped the table as he railed against the injustices of capitalism. Arguments critical of the rich bastards were so heated they sometimes boiled over. Vito tolerated him. A self-proclaimed communist, though never a card-carrier, Alan knew the names of Kropotkin and Bakunin but nothing of their writings. One of a young generation sufficiently well off and far enough apart, he could romanticise about communism, especially when he was stoned on pot. He harped on about an alternative system where, according to a utopian theory, at least, people would come together in a common cause for freedom and equality. They would give according to their abilities and take only according to their needs, cooperate with one another rather than compete, and achievement of the highest standards of healthcare, education and housing would be their first priorities. Everybody would have enough. Politicians could be trusted because they would be of the people, Alan said. Peace would lie like a warm blanket. Nothing could be more alluring to a young idealistic hippy. He sang the praises of the 'great revolutionaries' like Mao, who led the Long March; and Che Guevara and Fidel Castro, who had just led their people out from under the yoke of US imperialism into their own socialist experiment, one that would build a model for sustainable human development and preserve their independence and social justice; one that would be a model for their Latin American neighbours, if not the world. He didn't talk about Mao's megalomania or his madness during the Cultural Revolution, or Stalin's Siberian gulags. So, what were the flaws in his reasoning for communism to have gone so terribly wrong? Jim thought probably a basic misunderstanding of human nature. Everybody is naturally out for them selves.

"But people are not like that," Jim put in; "people are selfish and competitive by nature; some want more than enough, they want to be allowed their liberties and maintain their individuality, not be reduced to a cog or a numbered badge. Coercion can only lead to rebellion."

"You're not listening," Alan said. "But for Lenin there probably would not have been the Bolshevik Revolution."

"Yes, and a new dictatorship by a powerful elite and another cycle of repression and corruption," Jim hurled back.

"A functioning, just society relies on moral choices made on behalf of its citizens by a qualified body politic," Alan, the sage, said; "an educated, benevolent meritocracy, like the Chinese have. Of course there will always be the spoilers, which is why there would be need for regulations, a security force and a proper judicial system."

"Under capitalism, regardless of whether or not there is any real need for much of what consumers are demanding," he went on, "all things – from flash cars to Barbie dolls, from prestige to full employment, non-degradable plastic garbage, etc., etc., – you have to produce, something, anything that will make a maximum profit, and if there is no need for those things then you create it virtually with a new fashion and shrewd advertising. It exploits the finite supply of the world's natural resources as if there were no tomorrow, destroying the land, polluting the rivers and the atmosphere. Capitalism is evil."

"Yes, well what about Chinese capitalism?" Bill said. "The Chinese are progressing under their new capitalist economy; great improvements in housing and service infrastructure have been achieved through capital investment."

"Yes, and it is mining mountains of coal and building dozens of new coal-fired generating plants every week," Jim persisted.

"Yes, maybe," Alan said, "and they have introduced a new family planning programme too to help stabilise the world's population growth. Quality of life was improving under Mao."

"Malnutrition of starvation in China is slowly being replaced by malnutrition of obesity," Andy said. "Those who once rode bicycles are now driving carbon-fuelled motor cars."

Alan admitted free-market capitalism allowed some freedom and was dynamic and efficient in its rate of production, but – and this was the point – it was also ruthless and greedy in its pursuit of profit and inequitable in its distribution of wealth, causing an ever-widening disparity between rich and poor, and social issues to be side-lined. Taxation was a system full of loopholes.

So then, Jim wondered, was the best solution a combination of both: a political system of a trusted self-elected meritocracy transparent to all, and an economic system based on capitalist principles, like China has become? The bad apple, of course, in even the most regulated societies, will always be corruption.

"And if you want to look at Cuba," Elias said, "it's not doing very well."

Alan ignored him.

It was after 2am. John Lennon came on with his new song, *Money (That's What I Want).* There was the flushing sound of the toilet. It was time to go.

If Alan had been asked then to choose between Manhattan and Moscow as a place to smoke pot and remonstrate publicly, I believe he would have been much safer and happier in Greenwich Village – just another radical crackpot, hardly noticed. The socialists had Karl Marx where we in the free-market world had Groucho; they had Lenin, we had Lennon.

If the disbandment of the defunct USSR in the 1990s meant that those former socialist countries, now free to choose for themselves, would turn away from socialism to capitalism, Jim wondered how this would affect the tiny faraway island state of Cuba, one of the few outsiders in the world who, for so long, had been the Soviets' ally and dependable partner, and who was still clinging to those values.

It was in the Cuban spring of 1998, nearly forty years after their change from dictatorship to socialism, that Jim went to make his own assessment of their experiment. I will tell it as it seemed to him then, through his observations on the streets and by talking with the people.

The stewardess on the Cuban Airlines flight from Guadeloupe to Havana looked as if she didn't care about anything, least of all her job. Certainly she had not tried to beautify with make-up, or trim down her waist, but she had at least attempted to restrain with clips her wild, frizzy hair that was worrying her face. As soon as they were airborne the usual treat of in-flight theatre began where, according to regulations, the crew had to show all the steps the passengers should calmly take in the event of an emergency, like plunging into the Caribbean Sea. All the while during her demonstration, the stewardess' gaze was fixed upon that mirror she had rehearsed before so many times, her lips pursed, her cheeks dimpled, not in the hope that something cute might come of it, but because she was sucking a gumball. Jim felt that he was not alone in wondering why the airline had not chosen a more attractive person for this kind of job, where looks normally count. But, as he was soon to learn, values in Cuba are different. Really, though, she might have been about to begin a frumpy striptease.

The passengers were mostly French, some Spanish, and one, distinguished by his lookalike, dress-a-like Fidel Castro appearance, could have been Cuban. Four black girls at the rear, dressed in electric Lycra body stockings were Cuban; they were the most conspicuous. They were in fits of laughter realising that they were giggling at one another giggling at one another. The French around them glowered and pursed their lips. They were typical of the young Cubans Jim would meet in many a dark and lonely street for the next few weeks; some of whom would try everything to lure him into the bounty of their charms.

A long downward slide, a bit of cloud buffeting, a gentle bump-bump, and then they were taxiing towards the terminal of Havana Airport. As Jim was leaving the plane the captain told him the aircraft was Russian designed but assembled in Italy, and just for the record, he noticed on the packet that the coffee milk was produced in Canada. The sugar, of course, was home-grown.

All the passengers rushed from the plane and hurried across the tarmac to be first in the queues for passport check-in and baggage collection. It is in their nature. On the roof deck of the terminal, strung out along the railing, was a small welcoming crowd for the four girls, all giggling and screaming with excitement. Jim stopped to register his photographic impressions. To remind him he was entering a highly politicised country, painted over the entry doors were the words:

POR LA SOLIDARIDAD ANTI-IMERIALISTA,
LA PAZ Y LA AMISTAD
(in the name of anti-imperialist solidarity, peace and friendship).

Standing at the tail of the queue inside, he could see the black-painted underside of the concrete roof structure and, partly concealed by a suspended ceiling of white slats, the dim white fluorescent tubes spaced far apart to save energy. It was gloomy but sufficient. His queue inched its way towards a light timber-framed box counter that had the look of a candy seller's stand. The comptroller, in jungle camouflage, with a nice face, was quiet and gentle as a farmer. He checked that Jim was not from the US, gave him a stamp, welcomed him to his country and, with a smile, indicated where he could go to get a taxi. Nice fellow.

The taxi, a 1959 Pontiac, smelled of fresh lacquer – the dashboard or the upholstery, or maybe both – and the driver, young and bearded, smelled of cigar. These many brands of big '50s American cars were the last to be imported from the US. As they drove through ramshackle suburbs Jim was astonished to see how many others still survived. Street bulbs feeble as glow-worms and stretched so far apart made the houses appear like dark forms with black holes for windows. Here and there was a light in a window.

He had read about the '50s years under the dictatorship of General Batista. The real power, though, was in the hands of the US capitalists who, especially after the Second World War, came to the island to do business. The island's natural resources were extracted for the benefit of the US manufacturing, and the working population was exploited. The city of Havana expanded quickly, the rural areas were neglected, and scant consideration was given to the social welfare of the Cuban people. In the 1950s, out of six million inhabitants nearly one million were totally illiterate and more than half a million of potential workers were unemployed. It was a period of corruption and repression. The International Mafia became part of the private enterprise system.

In the rich-class hotels, like the Hotel Nacional set high up on a coastal site overlooking the Caribbean Sea, or the Sevilla Hotel in the heart of Havana, embellished with exquisite Spanish mosaics, you can see in their halls of fame photos of many Hollywood stars who visited in the '50s, some basking beside the swimming pools taking the cool, fresh wind in their hair; some smoking the world's best cigars, and drinking the world's best rum adulterated with Coca-Cola; others dancing the nights away. Al Capone was a guest, as were Lucky Luciano, Meyer Lansky and the rest when they weren't too busy running the extortion rackets in the US.

The ordinary Cuban people, who have a strong nationalistic heritage and egalitarian values, began to mass together to resist this takeover. Their war of independence was a guerrilla war fought under the strategic leadership of Che Guevara and Fidel Castro. In 1959 Castro gained control. The new socialist government expropriated the casinos and land from the largest landowners (mostly US companies) to bring about a more equitable distribution to the farmers. Thousands of well-off Cubans – business managers and the educated classes, mostly

– transferred their funds and fled for the US, taking across the tarmac as much as they could carry, many settling just across the sea in Miami.

The US government, of course, was furious. In 1961 the CIA plotted the assassination of Castro. They set out to destabilise Cuba by beginning a comprehensive programme of subversion, which continues today. The US blockade prevents Cuba from seeking credit funding from lending corporations for its own development, and the embargo on goods and penalising anybody doing business with Cuba have very adverse effects on living standards. The US uses all possible means to monitor and track every trade and investment deal. For example, the taxi driver told Jim he knows a visiting Mexican businessman who sells soap and other toiletries from Mexico and had made a deal with Cuba to send two full containers. Soon afterwards he was invited out to breakfast with somebody who turned out to be an official with the US Embassy in Mexico. The official showed him the documents proving the transaction and said, in effect, "Look, we know that you recently sold stuff to Cuba for $40,000. And we also know that you've sold $1.5 million worth of goods to the US. Now you have all the right in the world to choose who you do business with and to decide who is the better friend to have, us or them." The US policy puts the Cuban people at a disadvantage, as it is meant to. It is aimed at punishing them for supporting their government. Some observers think that if the Cuban people are deprived long enough they will rise up against Castro and do the US' job for them.

Cuba came to rely on its socialist partner, the Soviet Union, for its trade deals. Since 1989, however, when the Soviet Bloc began its collapse, Cuba has been hit by severe economic crises. With that collapse eighty-five per cent of their import market disappeared. In 1989 Cuba imported thirteen million tons of oil from the USSR; in 1992 only six million. In 1992 around US$8.4

billion worth of other imported goods plunged to $2.2 billion, and by that year Cuba had only thirty per cent of the resources for the sugar harvest they had in 1989, so production of sugar their major export, fell to its the lowest level in thirty years. And then, too, in 1993, there was the worst storm on record. It destroyed forty thousand homes and many of the crops, and hotels that had been bringing much-needed hard currency were severely damaged.

Jim's taxi driver turned to him.

"There are two main Russian brands of cars imported into Cuba now," he said, "Lada and Moskvitch. When they go kaput, which is often because the quality is poor, no spare parts are available locally." He said the euphemism for 'shit' in Cuba is 'Moskvitch'. "The inside handles are the first to break, and before long, below both pairs of doors, rust-spotting appears. It is partly the reason why the '50s American cars are pampered and doctored and lacquered and kept going for so long. Many of them in immaculate appearance have become valuable collectors' items. My father sold his Ford Custom five years ago to a dealer from America for US$15,000, which, considering his wage was only U.S.$11 a month, was like winning the lottery."

After twenty minutes of driving and educating Jim, his driver dropped him at the door of his host family in the Old Quarter. He had gotten the family's name from a Canadian photographer friend who had stayed with them when she was in Cuba to take photographs for her book. They were up waiting for him. He heard their excitement when he slammed shut the car door. Before he had time to knock, five eager ladies appeared: Galia and Caterina (two grandmothers), Estrella and Hanny (a mother and her daughter), and Maura, their friend. When he entered he saw they occupied the whole ground floor of a spacious two-storey house that surrounded an internal palmed courtyard, a planning concept not uncommon in hot-climate cities like Havana. He was fussed over and taken to his room, and shown that there was no hot water in the bathroom. After being excused for his tiredness he retired to a large, comfortable bed.

The next morning he went to take his coffee. It was a ten-minute walk along an open mall to the city centre. On the way, dressed in a suit with a red tie, sitting alone on a bench and leaning forward with both hands clasped on his walking stick, was an old man. He looked sad and empty. On the wall behind him, painted boldly in uniform letters, was a government proclamation:

EVELIO FECHENAR NO TE OLVIDAMOS JAMAS
(Evilio Fechenar [a hero of the revolution]
we never forget you.)

Spaced along the mall, painted in 'happy' colours, were large concrete tubs meant for planting. Only leafless palm stumps that looked like they had been pecked to death cowered there. Some vacant shops were dark and dirty. The paving was swept clean. There was a queue for ice cream; $3 a scoop seemed expensive. A young man asked him if he wanted to buy cheap cigars; a pretty young woman asked if she could come with him to buy her a drink; a limping clump of a man in filthy clothes turned to Jim and continued his conversation with himself in Spanish; a strong, bare-chested man, for something to do, was teasing a large steel drum, spinning it on its rim, slapping it more whenever it tried to right itself. A small crowd was attracted by the noise it was making; a policeman looked on, half amused.

Somebody on the flight over had recommended breakfasts in the Hotel Inglaterra. On its front terrace a family of English-looking tourists was being served eggs on toast with quince marmalade and tea in pots with crockery cups and saucers; a French woman was complaining that her eggs were cold. It was stately with Doric columns, chessboard floor tiling, potted palms and caged parrots, and through reed curtains one could see interior arches and richly coloured mosaic walls with peacock motifs. Jim got the feeling of English Colonial. The waiters wore white tuxedos. A dark-skinned youth in white hotel uniform smilingly opened and closed doors for guests as their taxis arrived. This remnant of colonialism seems more a tourist ornament now, like the attendants in the toilets, hoping to be tipped for turning on the taps and smiling courteously. Jim wanted to ask them why they weren't doing something useful. He ordered tea and toast and two boiled eggs.

At the street kerb, two Americans, their heads under the bonnet of a polished 1958 Chevrolet, were inspecting and discussing the motor with its proud Cuban owner. Dozens of cars of the same vintage, as if parading themselves, were passing by. Cross-parked in the centre of the road, facing the hotel, were rows of them, like an all-American football team, heavy as tanks, their chrome grilles and bumper bars glinting in the sun. The Plymouths and Dodges, and Cadillacs with sweeping tail fins, and the Chevrolets with spread wings, seemed as quaint as wide-lapel suits. But with all those curves they could be seen as elegant next to the black Russian models, Moskviches and Ladas, austere as the lead-heavy Russian black-box cameras you see displayed in shop windows.

Made-up teenage Cuban girls on the footpath outside hissed through the palms to get Jim's attention, hoping to be invited in for a drink. Across the road was the central park, one block in size, well treed and with a fountain. On a fine day like this many people were sitting on benches. Under a tree, before a crowd, someone was speaking publicly. Was it politics, Jim wondered? Weren't political rallies supposed to be illegal? Curious, he got up, dodged some tricycle rickshaws, and went over to find out.

Whenever Fidel Castro gives radio speeches, sometimes lasting several hours, everybody stops and listens. Issues like US policies against Fidelism, and the US insistence that their naval base at Guantánamo Bay will not be dismantled and removed, naturally cause bitter resentment. Somewhere Jim had heard that public discussion, even dissent, about Cuban government policies is considered normal and the system allows it, but criticism of the system itself, however, is considered to be counter-revolutionary and is forbidden. To be against the system could seem to be allying oneself with the capitalist values of the US, under whose domination Cuba had been for over a hundred years. Well, that was the official reason, and a rather convenient one. One could go to prison for that. Some people think that Fidel is getting too dictatorial. So arguments at public meetings like this sometimes spill over and police step in to stop dissidents from being abused or, in extreme cases, to arrest them. On this day, however, the meeting seemed relaxed with good-natured jibing, sometimes raising some laughs. Unable to understand Spanish, Jim asked a young cigar seller if he could explain. It was about the big play-off that weekend between the nation's two most popular baseball teams.

Old Havana, *Habana Vieja*, which extends from the original seventeenth-century Spanish settlements around the shipping ports of Havana Bay to the city centre, is a conglomeration of worn two-storey terraced houses, all crammed together. They provide shade to the narrow streets from a sun that travels along the same latitude as the Sahara Desert; continuous overhanging wrought-iron balconies provide space for potted plants and for drying clothing, as well as providing shade to the footpaths and their doorways below.

Nearly every street is a fascinating hybrid of architectural styles – arched colonnades give support to heavy masonry walls made elegant with motifs and cornices that were typical in the rich European cities of the nineteenth century – La Belle Époque – and Havana's turn-of-the-century buildings were some of the finest examples of Art Nouveau Jim had ever photographed, as well as many in the Art Deco style of the 1930s. All the buildings in state of dilapidation looked older than they were. If some of the thousands of original owners who fled the island forty years ago were to come back today they would weep. Not that many of them would have lived in this poor neighbourhood, however. Their homes would have been in the modern style, beautiful, stately, architect-designed houses set in palmed gardens further out in Vedado or Miramar – that is where they would go and weep. Some roofs had been blown off and consequently the ceilings had fallen in. Jim's next-door neighbour's house was like that. On a few streets, for a whole block sometimes, there were only facades with boarded-up windows, nothing behind them. Where some of these walls had tumbled across footpaths and onto the streets, cars had to drive around. It looked like what I imagine war-torn Beirut was like, without the bullet holes. Judging by the weeds and saplings that were growing inside the houses amongst the rubble of interior walls, the damage had probably been done by the 1993 cyclone. Sites that had been cleared of their debris were where children go with sticks to play baseball.

During the last fifty years or so, three or four layers of different-coloured wall paint have been flaking away, revealing in patches and speckles the ones beneath, making suggestions, sometimes, of the fields and lakes and skies of faded impressionist paintings. Sometimes the colours were neutralised by that same mouse-grey mould that thrives on walls everywhere in humid, temperate climates. Where the layers had flaked away altogether to expose the bare cement walls, kids had chalked faces with big-eyed surprise, and boys' names that loved girls' names, and scratches that ran up and down in long curves; where the render had broken away, red callow bricks were revealed.

The April sun weighed heavily on the thick, humid air; the midday heat made the bitumen shimmer. On this day a second farmer in the city for some reason went bobbing by on a tractor. A brand-new Mexican refrigerator was being coaxed nervously along the rough surface on a rattling wheelbarrow, the delivery boy pushing from behind and the two purchasers, one on each side to stop it falling over. A frail old street-sweeper, his shirt loosened, gathered dirt into a small pile. His hand-forged cart he himself might even have made was frail and old as well – they seemed married to one another. He swept and shovelled the dust, tipped it into his bin, placed the shovel inside and then moved on. Jim liked him and went to him. Smiling, he patted him on the back and complimented him on the good work he was doing. The sweeper smiled shyly back. All he had collected was the handful of dirt that had blown into the streets. Indeed, no litter was anywhere to be seen; hardly any during the whole month Jim spent in Havana. He took a photo of the sweeper, posed and relaxed, one hand round the pole of his broom, the other resting lightly, almost affectionately, on the handle of his cart. He walked away, trailing his cart behind him – Don Quixote and Sancho Panza. No electricity wires were strung overhead and there were no advertising signs.

At a corner Jim leaned under the shade of a balcony to check how many shots he had left on his spool and waited for something to happen. Opposite, a young man sitting on the threshold of his doorway was chatting with a friend. He had laid out before him on newspaper, like a pyramid of snooker balls, bright red tomatoes, next to them bunches of tiny bananas, and hanging from his door, bunches of garlic – all for sale. Oh, and fixed to the wall above him was a large, amateurish drawing he probably did himself of that same graphic image you see everywhere: the

Alberto Korda photo taken in 1961 of the dashing young Che Guevara gazing off into the future. A fat man nearby, dressed only in shorts and sitting on a child's chair, almost squashing it, was repairing his motorbike. Tools, motor parts and a back wheel were scattered all around him. A few people walked by. As Jim pulled in his lens to see if it was possible to get all these elements in a single picture, a boy suddenly ran into his frame, calling out excitedly; a warning, something urgent. The fruit was quickly gathered up, thrown into boxes and about to be rushed inside but ... too late, a policeman entered the scene. Instead of doing something the policeman looked away and kept walking. This way, I suppose, if questioned as to why he didn't check the seller for his permit, he could with clear conscience say he didn't see anything, even though he knew.

In 1968, all forms of private enterprise, even those as small as this, were made illegal. The government's rationale was that only if the economy were to be run totally under their control could they guarantee the basics to everyone. Traditionally, and by definition, socialism has been characterised by a centrally planned economy. It doesn't believe that the market forces of supply and demand should determine whether or not you have access to proper food and shelter, can see a doctor, or have a good education. The Cuban government admits, though, that it has made mistakes. Goods became scarce and inflation resulted because although people had money, supply was insufficient. The problem of poor services still exists today, but because the system is meant to be an evolving one, corrections are being made along the way. So now, instead of small businesses (like selling tomatoes on the footpath) being illegal, they are regulated. In recent years people have been able to leave their state-run jobs and receive permits to work independently. Somebody with a car, like Estrella's brother, for example, is now permitted to drive it as a taxi, and these days, probably, he would be paid in US dollars. Estrella, herself, a lawyer, and Maura, an engineer, who both used to work for the government years ago, found they preferred working from home in their own time. They enjoyed making by hand quality boots for Spanish dancers. Four or five pairs each week earned them about ten times more each month than they were being paid as professional government employees. The US$15 cash rent Jim was paying each day for their spare room was the equivalent of the monthly government salaries they had been receiving. After his first few days in their home, choice sausage meat and ham began to appear on the dinner table. One day, in the apartment, a small gas leak from a pipe that needed replacing was reported to the owner (the government), and straight away, an employee came by and stopped the leak. To wait for the problem to be fixed, however, could take months, so Estrella engaged a local handyman to do it for a negotiated fee. One arm of Jim's spectacles broke, so he went to a fellow known to be working from his home nearby. He fitted two new arms in a few minutes for US$2.

Jim managed to engage Estrella in conversation. She explained that those with US dollars have access to imported goods that are sold only in dollars, such as tools and raw materials to start their own small businesses. It was estimated that US$100 million cash had been circulating in the black market. The decriminalisation of the dollar in 1993 was an attempt to bring these dollars into the legal economy. This change caused social tension and economic inequalities which some saw as a sign that the socialist experiment was failing, if it had not already done so. But whatever the social cost, Cuba needs hard currency to sustain its successes in other areas. Everyone has, at least, equal access to the most basic of necessities – food, healthcare and education. Jim shopped around with some pesos in the people's open-air food market where fruit and vegetables came from local farms. The choice was good and the quality excellent, everything sun-ripened, nothing that had been refrigerated like the supermarket imports. Healthcare falters only because of restrictions on supplies to doctors and pharmacies caused by the US embargos. In each of the four pharmacies he visited Jim asked the same question and was told that the most common complaint was stomach disorder due to the poor quality of drinking water. Water purification is a top priority, if any of those countries sympathetic to the Cubans' needs are listening.

Estrella continued. "To get as much hard currency as possible in the shortest time, Cuba has to develop tourism. In many ways Cuba is well endowed for this kind of development. It has miles and miles of clean beaches and uncontaminated sea. In the city centre and along the coast outside Havana, you can see dozens of hotels, nightclubs and restaurants being built as joint ventures with countries such as Canada, Spain, Italy and Brazil. It has a healthier atmosphere than many other places in the Caribbean, with no drugs and almost no street crime."

Even though rum was as readily available and as inexpensive in Cuba as vodka was in Russia, one rarely saw alcoholism, which was everywhere in Moscow.

And the people themselves, wonderfully welcoming with their love for dance and music, is Cuba's greatest boon for tourism. The tourist sector is doubling its income each year but, like tourism in most places, this does have its negative side effects: prostitution and black-marketeering.

Walking the streets, he saw a schoolroom through an open window. They were seated at their desks, and some showed their excitement and pointed at him. Their teacher invited him in to meet them and look at their work. Unfortunately Jim couldn't understand the lessons because of his lack of Spanish, but their handwriting in cursive script was elegant without exception. From a number of sources he heard that the literacy rate in Cuba is now around ninety-five per cent. The kids all looked happy and were well behaved. It was lunchtime and they were being served hot, healthy meals on compartmentalised trays. He took a group photo of the class and after he returned to Paris sent copies to the school, one for the teacher and one for each child. He hoped they arrived safely.

He wanted to see what reading matter was available in the main city-centre bookshop. The books – old, second-hand, some yellowed with age, dog-eared, cheaply printed and spattered with typographical errors – were mostly about Socialism. There were two shelves on psychology, the few poetry books were by only South American writers, practically no fiction from anywhere (Hemingway was an exception), and piles of building and engineering journals featuring articles on concrete design theory and steel frame construction in Russia in the '50s. Riveting stuff.

One day, walking around near the town centre, he discovered a four-storey building, a hundred years old but with no great architectural merit. It had functioned as the Capitol Theatre but now was so run-down it appeared abandoned. Its last performance must have been before the revolution. Upper windows were missing, small plants were growing out of cracks in its facade and a small tree, clearly visible, was growing behind its parapet, probably from the roof gutter. As he stood back across the street to view the whole building he noticed a strangely incongruous baby pram parked on an upper balcony. A door slowly opened onto the footpath. From the dark interior an equally dark elderly woman emerged. She was stooped and fat with long, bedraggled grey hair, holding a bucket that trickled with blue paint, the same colour as her knee-high woollen socks. She turned around, put her bucket down, hammer-gripped her thick tar brush, dipped it in the bucket and painted four short lines of odd-looking letters and numbers on the bleached grey wall. It was done in such a crude manner that each brushstroke trickled down the rough surface, making them practically illegible. When she finished, she picked up her bucket and then shuffled back into the interior darkness. The door closed behind her, then … end of scene. How curious. Samuel Beckett came to mind. When he looked around to see if anyone else had witnessed this, the streets were deserted, as if something had kept them away, as if the message in these words, whatever it was, was meant only for him. But none of it made any sense.

In another street he found people were being served ice-cream scoops in hand-folded paper cups. When his turn came he proffered US$3 to the sweet lady serving them. "Oh, no," she said, and showed him that without the 'US' prefix the dollar sign meant pesos, about one twentieth the value of the US dollar. Suddenly the cost of all the small things he had seen displayed for sale on footpath boxes – roll-on deodorant $15, twelve plastic clothes pegs $5, ice cream $3, etc. – were as cheap as everything else.

He liked the design of a particular three-peso bill that was still circulating around Cuba. It was in red print and was last issued around 1989. Its design included an oval-framed engraved image of Che Guevara, the famous Korda photograph again. He decided to collect some to bring back with him as gifts and souvenirs. Looking for them he soon realised that they were rare. The modern green three-peso bill that is replacing it, also with Che's image, is common but, for Jim, not as appealing. The two red ones he did manage to find were limp, torn and disfigured, as you would expect after so many years of street use. Unless one had an unusual interest like his, one would never go to the bank to buy pesos with US dollars. It wouldn't make sense considering the inflation of the dollar on the black market and its purchasing power over the peso. But that's where he went, to the Codeca Bank, the people's bank, where he had been told he would most likely find these bills and be able to buy them.

As soon as he entered, he realised that, due to its run-down condition, the darkness and long queues, this bank was where those who subsisted basically on state salary payments in pesos came. The peso could purchase only products rationed and subsidised by the state. A uniformed security guard, surprised to see a tourist among the customers, smiled at him and asked if he needed any assistance. She seemed amused by his interest in the old three-peso bill, then graciously took him to the front of a queue and asked a teller to find six bills for him as he requested. He could see stacks of green 3 peso bills on a shelf behind the teller bundled in lots with elastic bands. As she riffled through each lot, finding only one red bill, or more often, none, he became conscious of having jumped the queue, and that he was taking up so much of her time, and being a nuisance. Nobody in the queue showed any annoyance, however, only curiosity. Jim shrugged an apology to all and told the guard she was being too kind and, to please not bother any more. But she was determined to find them for him and went from the first teller to others, and they obligingly searched through their stock. Finally, only five notes were found. The guard apologised and said she would try to find others – could he come back the following afternoon? Leaving the bank he remembered he still had some packets of Cashmere soap he'd been giving away to the people he had been photographing. He went back inside and handed one to the kind assistant and one to each of the tellers. They were all delighted – nice-smelling soap was a fairly rare commodity in Cuba.

Six men in overalls, sitting in an open, well-equipped joinery workshop, were playing dominoes. Jim thought maybe they were having a break, but for six days, they told him, there had been no electricity supply to run their machines. Oil, needed to generate the country's electricity was still in short supply. To rectify this problem the Cuban government entered into agreements with

Canadian oil companies whereby the companies would put up all the capital costs for exploration. If they struck it rich the two parties would share the benefits fifty-fifty. If the Canadian companies did not find oil, the Cubans would not incur a single peso of expense.

In a shadow of a hot afternoon kids with plastic containers were queued along a footpath. Parked at the kerb was a trailer with a stone wedged against one wheel, and on the trailer lay a huge steel drum with a tap. As the children came forward one man filled the containers while the other received a few coins in payment. Amused by Jim's curiosity, the first man offered him a sample to taste. It was the Cuban version of Coca-Cola, paler in colour, not as strong in flavour but just as sweet. So even Coca-Cola could not be imported.

He was surprised, one day, to notice that Estrella, on her way out to do the shopping, had a page of ration coupons for sugar. How could sugar be rationed in Cuba if it was their main product? She explained that the government exported most of the sugar in exchange for the items Cuba cannot produce for itself, as well as getting funds to help maintain the education and healthcare systems and other social services.

One morning, in the week before he was due to leave his host family to return to Paris, Jim was given a finger-pointing reprimand for coming home so late each night. Just the night before, Estrella told him, a well-liked local restaurateur, locking up for the night, was knocked over the head, robbed of all his dollars and left on the street, where he was later found bled to death. This sort of thing is such a rare occurrence the news sent shockwaves throughout the whole neighbourhood.

He walked into a poor neighbourhood he was warned could be risky – the poorest part of the city. The streets were dusty, the footpath slabs were broken and dislocated, an emaciated three-legged dog hobbled by, shifty eyes watched him with interest, and mothers, sitting on their doorsteps, gave him the same finger sign he remembered from Naples, warning him to watch out for thieves. He tightened his grip on his camera. The hit-and-grab is usually calculated to come at you from behind. They approach you quietly, you hear their quickened steps at the last moment, and then they strike and your heart jumps nearly out of its cage. The strap around your neck can be slashed and the camera wrenched away. A boy grabbed the strap with a handful of Jim's shirt but all he managed to achieve was a long tear down his back. He turned and saw the boy in a green T-shirt hop on the back of his mate's bike as it was speeding away. A few concerned people gathered around. One said she knew who the boys were and they would be punished. And someone must have rung the police because within a minute three of them sped up in a car. One jumped out, had Jim verify himself, and he was then ordered to get in. They drove around the neighbourhood for the next ten minutes, asking questions and looking for the boy in the green shirt but to no avail. Jim was taken to a police station to make a report. He was left alone in an empty reception for about half an hour. He asked how much longer he might have to wait. They said they were having trouble finding a typist. Could he type, by any chance? Eventually he was taken to a hospital where a doctor typed the police report and then, after a check-up, he filed his own report, certifying that Jim had received no injury, which, of course, he already knew. It was raining heavily by then, so the police offered to drive him home, some fifteen minutes away, for which he was most grateful.

Two days later, near the same area, some fool of a man pulled Jim to the ground and wouldn't let go of his shoulder bag. Jim had to fight him. As they wrestled on the ground, people suddenly came rushing from everywhere, including a cyclist who threw down his bike, pulled out a gun and fired two shots into the air. The assailant fled. Jim dusted himself off, then walked away before the police could arrive. Needless to say, he never went back into that part of Havana.

The best time to photograph the people of Old Havana with black-and-white film was in the twilight of evening, when the day's heat has abated and everybody is out to enjoy the sea breeze. Half the people appeared to have African provenance, and the others Spanish. The kids were home from school then, so there was skipping and hopscotch in the streets, and on vacant blocks where houses once stood, games of baseball. Women holding babies stood in their doorways; others rested on their elbows in open windows to chat with those passing by. A child sitting on a step cuddled her puppy; another, a shy little black girl closed the door across her face when Jim stopped and smiled and said hello to her; children delivered home from a joyride around town clambered down from a pony-drawn, four-wheeled waggon. Through open doorways, families in small rooms watched TV at high volume; Jim got views past wrought-iron staircases into common courtyards, catching more glimpses of typical daily life. One young man on the street was giving his tricycle rickshaw a fresh coat of paint; another, with newspaper spread beneath it to catch drops of oil, was probing into the gearbox of his Russian-made sidecar motorbike. And, of course, they paid great attention to the maintenance of their big American cars parked in the streets. If one was up on blocks then in all likelihood somebody was working underneath; if the bonnet was up then three or four men might be involved in a motor transplant. A clapped-out 50s Chevrolet motor could be being replaced by a 50s Pontiac motor or, as Jim saw, a 1988 Toyota HiAce two-litre motor being mounted in a '55 Plymouth body as a replacement of a '58 Chevrolet motor. Hard to know how much putty and how many spray coats these bodies have had, but they still managed to look as reasonably youthful as the ageing Hollywood stars who may have had as many facelifts.

The streets were lined with people selling small things laid out on cardboard boxes, like in Moscow: shoes, glasses, potatoes, deodorant, flowers etc. The one-legged man in his wheelchair repaired, refilled and resold cigarette lighters; the shoeshine man who worked under the footpath colonnade in the city centre is a well-known storyteller – of truth and lies; a barber swung around his seated customer, whose face was only half shaved, half lathered, to smile at the camera, while a blown-up photo of the same long-haired, bushy-bearded Che gazed out from the wall where a mirror would normally be. Most liked to have their photo taken. Young men came often to sell cigars 'cheap'. In other countries it was "Psst, feelthy postcards" or "Ay, you wanna buy my muvver?" or "Smack?" but here it was just cigars.

It was normally quiet at night in the district where Jim was staying, but one night a dog in somebody's home nearby barked incessantly till well after two o'clock. It must have kept everybody awake. No one did anything to stop it, no shouts of complaints, which, of course, would only have made things worse. Nothing could be done except to wait for its owners to return which, finally, they must have done. But he was restless anyway – unfamiliar surroundings, a different bed, odd sounds during the day half heard, unusual things half understood. Turning over in his bed after the barking finally ceased, he could not stop thinking about the things he'd seen. He'd found out, by going back, that the blue words and numbers painted on the Capitol Theatre by the old woman were parking rates – like other run-down buildings in the city centre, the theatre had been gutted and stripped and converted into a car park. It was a strange sight from the doorway into this old theatre: in the dimness, no longer the rows of seats but rows of dozing old cars, like a vintage car museum, the stage was cluttered with bicycles. Stalwart columns supported a mezzanine floor with loops of dress-circle balconies faced with plaster relief designs where dust was sleeping, and in that semi-darkness thick, diagonal shafts of dust-filled sunlight like bright gold bars leaning against broken windows shone down. The same old woman, sitting on a box in the dark, was collecting fees in a tin can. And the other things he saw: that man in the plaza off Obispo, whose whole face and body were covered in a chain mail of steel ring piercings; the shy, colourful girlfriend couples on the streets, who laughed and hissed for attention; and the legless man who refilled cigarette lighters on the tray of his wheelchair. He saw again gentle old Rafael, who delivered their eggs each week and who, it was said confidentially, carried a gun; the children's squeals of happiness when Jim photographed them in their classroom that afternoon; the frustration and thrust of a hustler's obscenities in the dark when he was too tired to listen to his insistent pleading and so told him to please go away; the thin old lady with sagging leather skin dancing to the music on the street outside the salsa bar she was forbidden to enter; and inside the bar – which also played cha-cha, bolero, tango, tumbao, son, merengue, and biguine from Haiti – the tourists in palm beach shirts in that carnival atmosphere of loud trumpets and maracas getting drunk on rum and smoking cigars for the first time with Cuban girls who couldn't believe how easy they could make it for them to throw so much money around; bellicose propaganda exclaimed on concrete walls in defiant language:

PATRIA O MUERTE, VENCEREMOS!
(The homeland or death, we shall win!) and
SOCIALISMO O MUERTE!
(Socialism or death!)

All these images just outside the edge of sleep, then going over the edge into the nothingness of sleep, then jolted out again by something else extraordinary – a dream was it, another recollection, or another noise? Not sure which – to and fro, to and fro until the light of dawn, with the weird, strangled cry from a distant farm of a cock's crow, and Galia at the stove preparing eggs for breakfast.

The bar and restaurant called El Floridita on Calle Obispo owes its reputation to the boast that Ernest Hemingway used to drink there – though it was not the only one. Apparently, he invented the *mojito* there. It is another expensive restaurant where many Americans used to live it up in the '50s. Photographs of people of that period adorn the wall around the long, sweeping bar. There is the one of Hemingway and Castro standing together, another chummy one of them close-up, the novelist Graham Greene, the Australian actor Errol Flynn, and others not so famous. These days glamorous women frequent the bar with men with cigar-coloured faces who smoke cigars, and tanned bald men in white suits who look like Picasso. Jim happened to be there as the invited guest of two Canadian women who were travel agents.

A waiter in a red tuxedo escorted them to a table in the Oval Room. The room had been made sumptuous with primary colours of flower arrangements and modern paintings. Those at other tables, Americans or Canadians, conversed in loud, rum-drunk laughter, the arresting smell again of cigars. The fish Jim was served was export quality, though cold. He discovered, pencilled on the back of a WC cubicle door, the words:

> *Freed from your economic whip*
> *We will not ride your bloody ship.*

And:

Our will is strong
Your won't is wrong

Near the end of his stay, Jim asked a number of people he had befriended if, honestly, they still believed in the revolution. "Believe in the revolution?" vivacious young actress Esther said, "I *am* the revolution!" She was running an acting school free of charge for anybody who wanted to come along. She made her income renting a couple of spare rooms in her home to travellers, and also from performances her group gave in other Latin American countries. She had just returned from Costa Rica. Others he asked looked down thoughtfully; others looked over their shoulder.

It is a serious question Cubans are often confronted with, and the answer, for different reasons, may best be left unspoken. Some say that to give up now would be a betrayal to the heroes of the revolution, those who forty years ago gave their lives in the struggle. Giving in to capitalism now would mean giving up on the commitment of trying to achieve a free and just society. Many are still willing to make sacrifices.

"But it has been forty years," Jim said to one, "and standards of living are still poor, social values are slipping."

"The problem," he replied, "is the American embargo; it has made the experiment practically impossible. But we believe that one day the shackles will be broken. It is absurd, especially since the break-up of the Soviet Union, for the US to think that our tiny island state could possibly pose any threat to its security, the most powerful country in the world. If the US does not agree with our system and believes it can only self-destruct then it should stand back and let it do so. If Cuba should fail, the U.S. could then come, if they wanted to, to help pick up the pieces and enter into fair trade agreements that would be to our mutual benefit."

In the opinion of another, if the Cuban people worked for the ideal of a just society as an alternative to an unjust capitalist system, and it should fail, the world should, at least, give Cuba credit for the courage and dignity of having tried. Others – the ones who look over their shoulders – say that Castro has become too much of a repressive dictator and that the cause is lost anyway.

Most, though, Jim was pleased to find, still have the revolutionary spirit, and the courage and the willingness to make the sacrifices that come with it. Many still admire 'el Che' and have great respect for Fidel. But there does seem to be a growing feeling that when Fidel goes, which could be any day, things may move rapidly in another direction.

Estrella expressed a sentiment in a very private joke:

An old man, drunk, lurching home late at night, leans against a lamp post and yells to the rooftops, "Fidel, you are a lousy old son of a bitch!"

He then lurches on to the next lamp post and shouts the same thing: "Fidel, you old son of a bitch!"

A policeman is across the road. He goes to the man and says, "I'm sorry, comrade, you can't say things like that about Fidel, I'm going to have to take you in."

"What do you mean?" says the old man, indignant, "there are a lot of people in Cuba called Fidel."

"Ah, yes," says the policeman, "but there is only one Fidel who is an old son of a bitch."

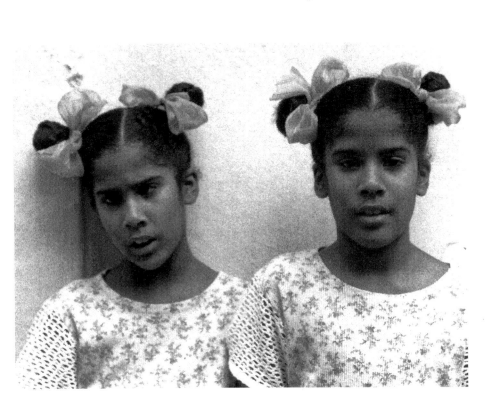

6

A Town Called Sablet

Recently, Jim was roused from his bed by the cries of a thousand migrating gulls. It was a spectacular sight. Bathed in moonlight they were all ghostly white. Their aching cries seemed to be for one another, urging one another on for their arduous voyage south to the coast of Nigeria. Jim felt he wanted to be gathered up with them. "Take me with you!" he almost cried. Strung out at the end were a few stragglers, the least able, they who probably wouldn't make it. It is part of the world in which we live.

Next morning it was snowing. The world had turned white overnight. The silence was snow. In the glow of street lamps it was like a landfall of alien moths. Jim's old, kind-hearted Senegalese friend, dressed in regulation street-sweeper green, tipped his cap and smiled. "*Bonjour, monsieur, ouais, ça va.*" he said. With his broom – a binding of willow twigs – he had depicted in the snow's black ink tussocks of grass and thistles and gusts of wind. And then Madame Berdeshevski – "*Bonjour, madame.*" She is old and didn't hear. A woman clutching her dressing gown stepped onto her balcony to see. The first little kids, bundled and bright-eyed, embellishing the silence with gleeful squeals hurried up the steps and through the brick archway of l'École Maternelle – *LIBERTÉ, ÉGALITÉ, FRATERNITÉ.* Newspaper delivery trucks slammed shut roller-shutter doors. In the dimly lit café Le Fontenoy, puffy-eyed workers in heavy coats, wet-haired and sleepy still, hunched at the zinc counters, were reading in *L'Equipe* the write-up of the game they saw on TV the night before. One sipped his espresso then from deep down, got his first big tobacco hit of the day. "*C'est la merde*," he sighed. The only other shops with any visible activity were *la Boucherie* and *la Poissonnerie*.

In the gym, Bruce Springsteen was giving an overweight woman the loud encouragement she needed with *Born in the USA*.

"This is bloody hard work," she said, puffing.

She reached for her towel and mopped her brow. There were only four more minutes to go, and having expended nearly three hundred calories she was pleased with that. This was the third time Jim had seen her, but the first time they actually met. She was on the treadmill next to his, her weakness being raspberry-and-honey-cream chocolates and chocolate mousse. Having his own work to do, he just smiled and didn't say anything.

Shortly afterwards, at the nearby Café Le Parvis, where Jim goes each time to catch the first edition of *Le Monde*, they found themselves sitting on opposite sides, then, before he knew it, at the same table.

"Do you mind?" she said, unloading herself. "That was a great workout, I feel like Superman."

She was wearing Superman colours: a blue-and-green silk scarf, colours that matched her navy-blue coat with large red buttons, bright lipstick matching pendant earrings, Nike joggers for the snow, and now, on the chair beside him, her Nike shoulder bag.

Sonia is taller than average, a little plump, Renoir proportions, which to some added to her desirability, and at fifty-three she is still fairly good-looking. In Italy men she didn't know gave her second looks, and here too she gets looks, but not with the same excitement as before. Half Indian, she grew up in Hong Kong, then moved to England, on to the US, and now she lives in Paris. The Indian darkness she inherited from her father, as well as his estate. She was born with a silver scalpel in her mouth – he was an eminent surgeon. Her sickly English mother, however, a devout, hapless Catholic, was born and died under a dark cloud. Sonia herself was schooled in a strict convent, but was never taken in by it. She preferred to live it up. Men offered her gifts and she accepted them – sweetheart deals. She married well and divorced three times. Her third husband, a wealthy, elderly doctor whom she used to take to the opera in a wheelchair, and to whom she had been previously married for six months, she remarried. Then he passed away. "I have that effect on husbands," she joked. She had once run a surgical supply business, sold it for a good profit, did well in a top-end Parisian boutique, and now, with some of her father's estate and assistance from her son high up in the loans department of Société Génerale, she is involved in the lucrative real estate business. Her own apartment, from the sweeping first-floor terrace, has a view almost into the atrium of the Eiffel Tower.

"*Bonjour, Philippe, ça va?*"

Sonia asked for *café crème*, Jim *café-noisette*.

Charles Aznavour was in the air, and there was another well-known person reading *Le Monde* Jim was sure he recognised.

"Laurent Dupasquier," Philippe whispered.

"Ah, I thought so."

Sonia recalled that a cat she had never seen before walked into her apartment that morning, and commented on the new, sparkling lighting of the Eiffel Tower that makes her apartment bristle. They talked about other favourite cafés and what they do outside the gym. Her father's family were originally from Bombay, she said. Jim told her he had recently returned from a film festival there. He told her he was an architect.

"Ah, *bon,* that's interesting. I have a house in mind," she said over a chocolate mousse; "it's in the south of France. It's rather large and I need to know if it can be divided into three apartments; one for me for a few weeks in the summer, and two to rent out. It's a deceased estate and no one has lived in it for sixteen years. The sale has been delayed because of messy title deeds, and apparently there is no will. In the meantime I've taken out an option to buy."

"Great," she said when, after she asked if he would be interested in looking at it, he replied, "I'm sure I could." He gave her his card.

The men in suits were leaving, and Sonia, too, needed to go. She paid, picked up her bags, and then bade him goodbye. "I will call you," she said.

Light rain had melted most of the snow now, making slush and puddles; the darkness thinning, the air fresh and cool with wafts of familiar smells – pizza, fresh fish, flowers, dog urine. Reflected traffic lights looked like flashing pools of blood and poison; black birds strung out along wires looked like crotchets on a musical score; skeletal trees were snared with abandoned nests; brass plaques for doctors and psychotherapists were highly polished. Cars swished by.

Jim shouldered his massive wooden carriage door that has dutifully resisted entry for hundreds of years. He checked for letters and found two and a package: an electricity bill, a postcard from friends in the Costa Brava, and on a bulky foolscap envelope, an array of Indian stamps and his name written across it in blue ink. It felt like a book. On the back it said it was from Carmel in Bombay.

He crossed the courtyard. It is symmetrically arranged in the French style; a central path, low clipped hedgerows each side and beds of gravel, two tall elms. The hedgerows looked freshly painted in green gloss; overjoyed grasshoppers frolicked and flicked about, blissfully unaware of the interest they aroused in the hungry insectivores above. Brown-spotted, mustard-coloured leaves lay about. A rush of wind swooped down and picked up two, then sent them skipping off together.

"Bonjour, Monsieur James."

"Bonjour, Maria."

She was struggling with an umbrella that wouldn't open.

He bounced up each step to the third floor. In the corridor he was met with the nice, homey smell of warm toast. His door was the last on the left. The tumblers shouldered the lock. When he entered something in the air moved – less than a draught, more than thoughts – sighs and whispers, the revenants, the demigods who supervise sleep. They were alerted by the sound of his key. It was warm inside, the light dim, white paper milky grey, the red rose black.

Jim has lived here now for more than twenty-five years, the same studio apartment in the heart of Paris – in the centre of the universe, as he likes to think of it, in his 'chateau'. Well, *un petit château* – a man's home is his castle. Sometimes it is his Palace of Sighs. It is, in fact, only one room with an en-suite, but it is spacious and all he ever wished for. It has a high ceiling, and the pair of tall French windows that allow the full arc of the southern sun and offer a view down onto the treed courtyard. The furnishing is simple: a few pieces mismatching and second-hand, his drawing board, bookshelves and a few lampshades. It is quiet as a church – so quiet he is sure he can hear the whispers.

He placed his letters on the table, hung his coat on the chair, changed out of his wet shoes, washed his hands, and peeled for himself an apple. He put on the kettle for a mug of tea. The kettle boiled. He took his tea and sat in his window seat. He was in a pensive mood. Don't forget John Banville's talk at the Irish Cultural Centre on Thursday, he reminded himself. Looking around, he wondered about those who had lived here before him, since before the revolution, solitary boarders like him probably, most of them long dead by now – students, painters, firemen, barmen, zoo keepers … who knows? Sometimes he had a feeling that the ghost of Baudelaire was looking over his shoulder, scrutinising his writing. There were no discernible clues as to who they might have been, the whisperers. At the time of stripping the worn old carpet he found no old newspapers or a secret trapdoor with hidden van Goghs or Monets, only a fish bone wedged between floorboards and a few dead matches. On one wall, though, beside his bed, were four downward-slanting lines of a poem – too recent to be Baudelaire, but Baudelaire nevertheless:

Je veux, pour composer chastement mes églogues,
Coucher auprès du ciel, comme les astrologues,
Et, voisin des clocher écouter en rêvant,
Leurs hymnes solonnels emportés par le vent.

"To compose my poems," he says, "I want to have my bed beside the sky, as astrologers do; I want to lodge beside the belfries, and dreamily listen to their solemn songs being borne away on the wind." How poetic.

Judging by the number of chimney pots outside, there would probably once have been a fireplace with a mantel.

He took a sip then put down his mug.

As if for the first time, he muses idly upon his collection of small ornaments on his shelf: the painted chalk pasha he found in Istanbul, the small wooden red owl from Kyoto, a black-stained elephant from Marrakech, votive objects left at an abandoned Hindu temple, and a furry little koala Ingrid sent from Sydney. His bedspread is the Lomblen cloth he bought in Bali, and hung on the wall above, alongside the map of the world, are three long scrolls of Chinese calligraphy from Shanghai – *Happiness, Providence, and Good Health*. There are several framed photographs: one of a village scene he took inside Maharashtra, one of slum dwellers in Calcutta, and another in garish colours of a Hindu deity. In Rembrandt lighting, an old, bearded tailor he shot in Istanbul; a pretty geisha in Kyoto; a costumed prince in Venice; and the sepia portrait of his dear mother. Some of Ingrid too, when she was young, when the sun shone out of her. Beneath the wall lamp is a page of illumination from the Book of Kells. On a shelf where dust is sleeping, trinkets of worldly provenance lay: a small white stone, for example, from Jerusalem's most sacred site, the same site, it is said, of the Garden of Eden. His eyes rest on the standing bronze Buddha he acquired in Kathmandu in 1981, an example from the Gupta period, beautifully etched with floral motif. It reminds him of Denis, the Canadian he was introduced to in Hong Kong, who went with him on that trip to Kathmandu, and whose boat later capsized in a typhoon coming into Hong Kong harbour, drowning him. To Jim's right is a book wall of sleeping bedfellows, famous authors mostly, some not altogether happy with their alphabetical arrangement: Thomas Mann between Mailer and Miller feels misplaced; Nabokov next to Nietzsche feels perturbed; Styron in the company of Tolstoy probably feels it a great honour. Covering the seagrass matting floor, dyed with dark mountain browns and blues, is an antique Baluchi prayer rug. The wallpaper has yellowed like pages of old books, and, mysteriously, cracks in the brown-stained ceiling show the coastal outline of some undiscovered continent. Up there, too, crouching in a corner snagged with carapace and wings, waiting with unending patience, is the same tiny spider. Sometimes, fascinated by the sleeping giant, a meek little mouse ventures out, twitching its whiskers. Over there, under the sink, shivering and quietly mumbling to itself, is his refrigerator.

To sweeten his day, he reached for the radio. Ha – Mahler's *Adagio*: not sweet, sublime. Standing at his window now, it was sprinkling still. Across the courtyard, slate roofs were shiny black like sealskin; in window boxes, potted red geraniums, and in his were mint, chives and parsley, bejewelled with beads of raindrops. His ivy vine, leafless now, has spread like arteries over the entire back wall. As if by trick of magic, a pigeon visible for only a second wheeled and scribed a small arc above the roof opposite. He wondered if it was the same one that had alighted in his window box last spring. Its mate came and he heard their affectionate cooing. They stayed nestling for a while, then flew off. The next day he discovered a small white egg. How wonderful. Next day the egg was gone. Yes, unaccountably, unbelievably, gone. Not smashed down on the ground below, gone. Jim was crestfallen. Then on the next day, a single white feather lay there.

Beyond the rooftop chimneys, not visible but well within earshot, is a school playground. Freed from their classrooms, infant children run amok – innocent, perfectly beautiful, lovable children go mad and run amok. The little girls scream their heads off as if a hump-backed madman is running round with a big carving knife, the boys kick and yell, and then the bell. Each Wednesday afternoon, strung out along the footpath in toy colours with their satchels, holding hands and full of good cheer, the little people go off to splash about in the local swimming pool.

Each day over the last several weeks, Jim walked the streets to photograph stains on walls and cracks in footpaths – strange, you might say. But, really, it is amazing what you see when you are looking, some of the things that so often go unnoticed: salt efflorescence and water stains on the city's stone-faced walls that depict landscapes and seascapes, for example; cliffs and rock-falls; lagoons and folded dunes spiked with single blades of salt grass; a winter vineyard in a stony desert; the sun in morning mist; a solar eclipse and sunset skies. Cracks in one footpath resembled a medieval townscape with great stone walls and a castle tower. Cracks in Montmartre, a mount where swallows fly, depicted tall rock formations where eagles fly, a smudge suggesting rising smoke; black skid marks on white bitumen-coated pedestrian strips were like spontaneous brushstrokes, smudges like vignettes. The world of appearances is only a manifestation of an infinitely subtler other reality. Oscar Wilde himself once wrote, *There is some spirit hidden of which the painted forms and shapes are but modes of manifestation.* Garcia Lorca called it Duende and Lao Tzu, Tao. These forms and shapes are not art, of course, because no artist was involved, no dilettante or bearded rebel with creative spirit, no volition, no meaning, nothing more than a mere presence. Without them there would simply have been nothing to ponder. Or perhaps it was that mischievous elfin sprite playing games of Serendipity and Chance. Jim will sort through them and make a final selection in the hope of an exhibition. *PARIS JAMAIS VU*, he will call the series. He will include them on his website.

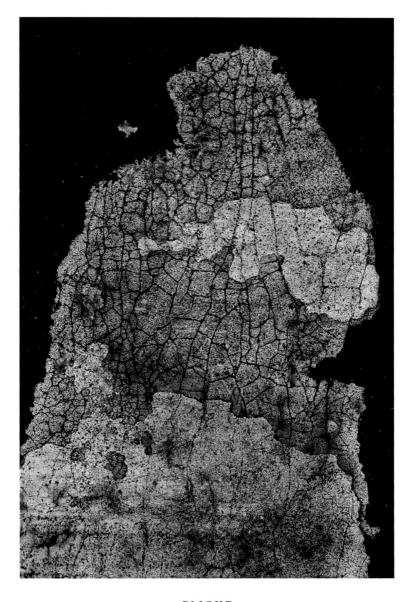

FLIGHT

I CALL TO REMEMBRANCE MY SONG IN THE NIGHT

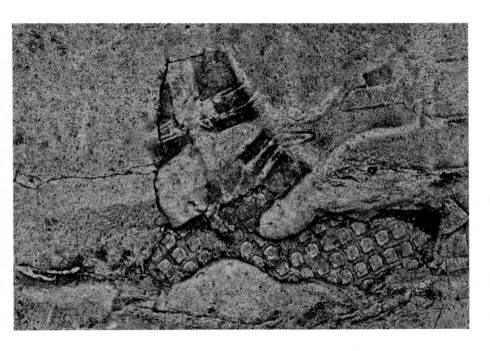

PLATYPUS

CRAYFISH

MOTHER AND CHILD

WILD BOAR

SEA AND SKY

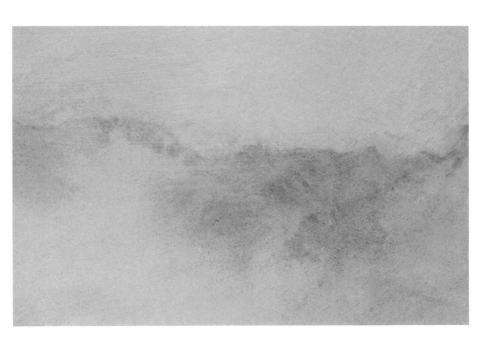

HILLS

MISTY VALLEY

RISING MIST

DUNES, SUNSET

MOUNTAINOUS REGION

DUSK 1

LANDSCAPE 1

BREAKING DAWN

LAKESIDE

LANDSCAPE 2

DUSK 2

TUNDRA SNOWFIELD

ICE FLOW OFF COAST OF FINLAND

FROZEN NORTH

SAFE ANCHORAGE (COAST OF DOVER)

ROCKY LANDSCAPE

MEDIEVAL TOWN, CASTLE, VINEYARDS

THE KINGDOM OF MESCAL

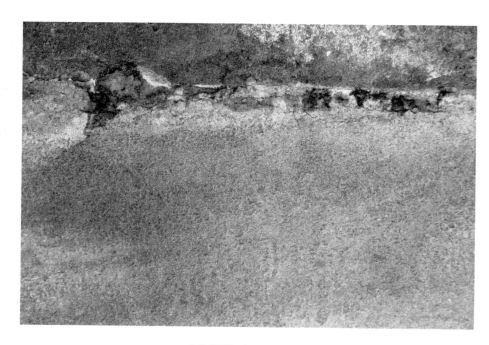

ROCKY OUTCROP

LANDFORM 1

LANDFORM 2

SAND DUNES 1

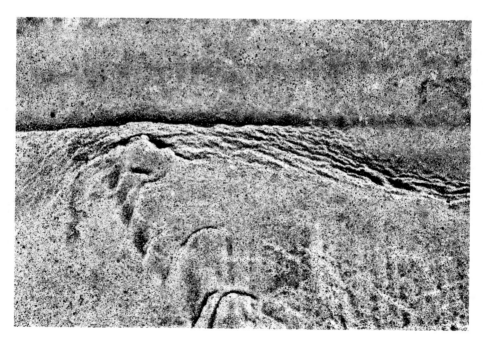

SAND DUNES 2

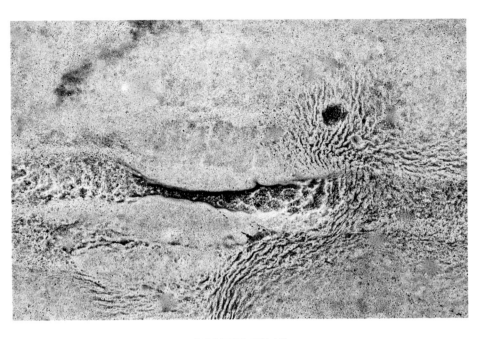

DESERT HEAT

GUELIN – CHINA

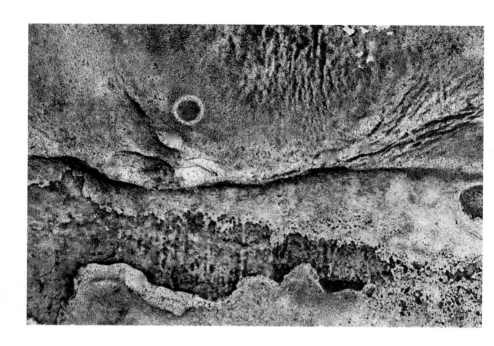

SOLAR ECLIPSE

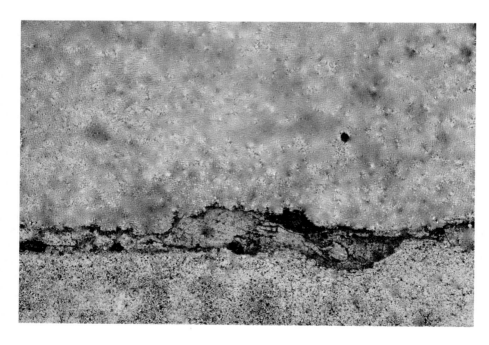

SMALL TOWN

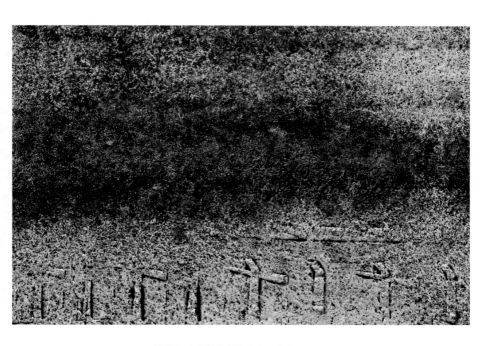

THE ALMOST FORGOTTEN

MOUNTAIN WHERE EAGLES FLY, RISING SMOKE

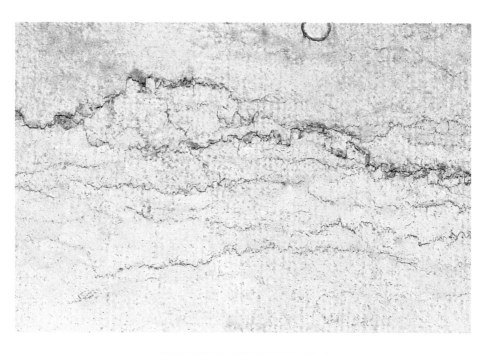

MEDIEVAL TOWNSCAPE 1

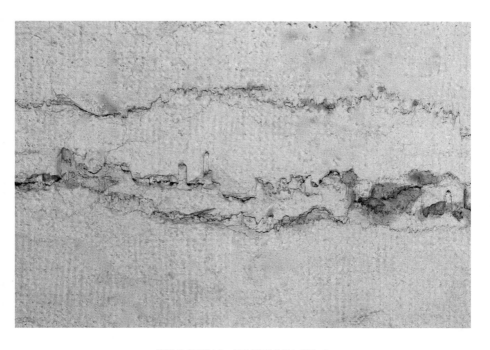

MEDIEVAL TOWNSCAPE 2

VENUS RISING

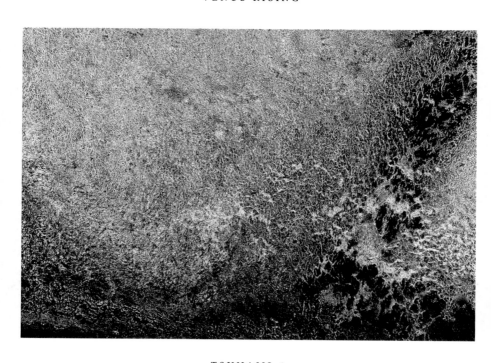

TSUNAMI 1

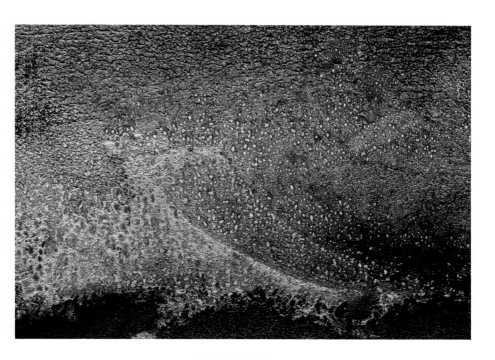

NIGHT WAVE

TSUNAMI 2

COAST OF ALMERIA

CAPE TRIBULATION

MOONLIT SEA COAST

HEADLAND ON SEA COAST

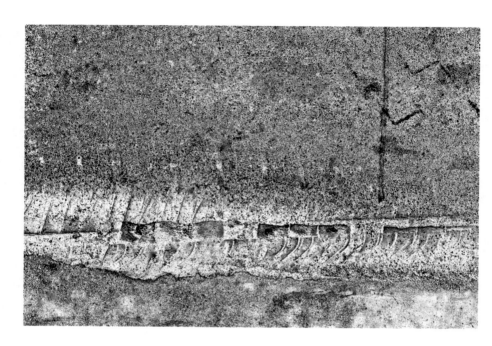

FLOODGATES

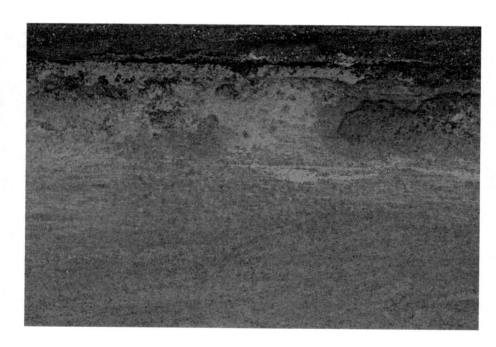

STARLIT BEACH

ISLAND MONASTERY

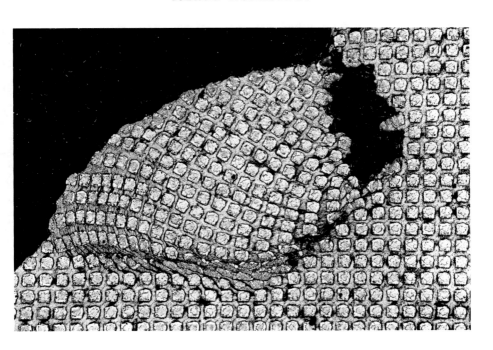

RUPTURE

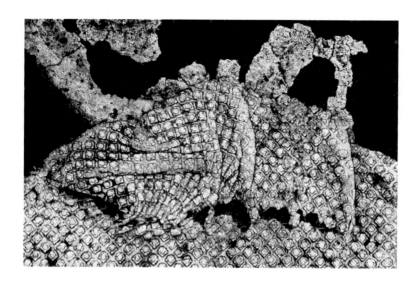

REPTILE

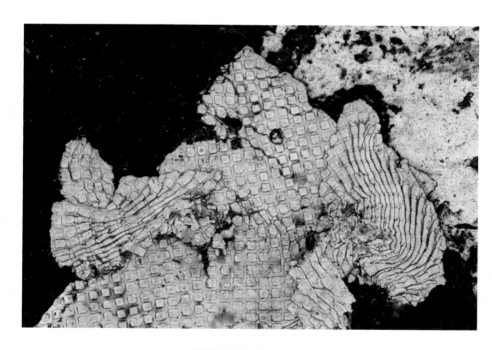

METAMORPHOSE

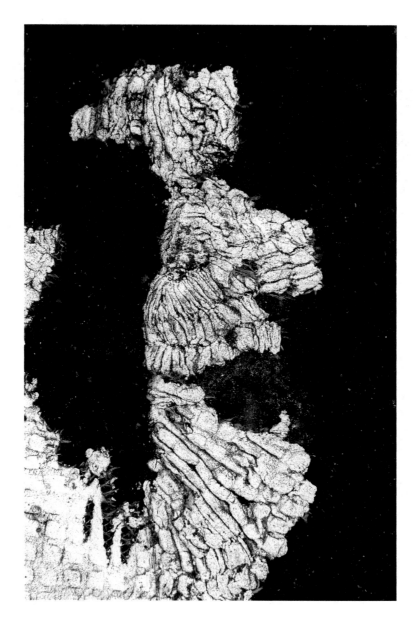

AUNT BESS

LEAVING HOME

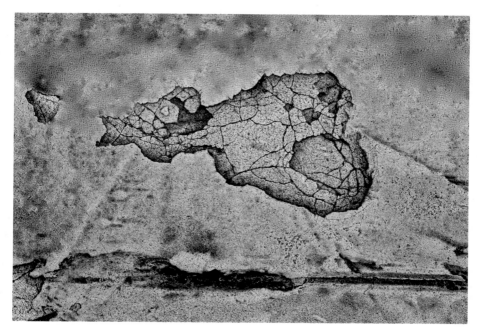

DISCONNECTED FLOATING WORLD

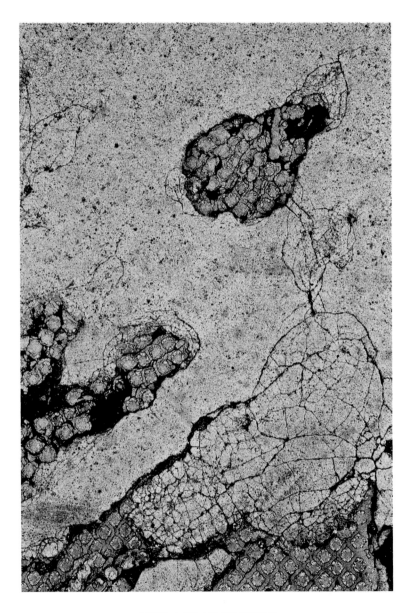

THE ARRANGEMENT

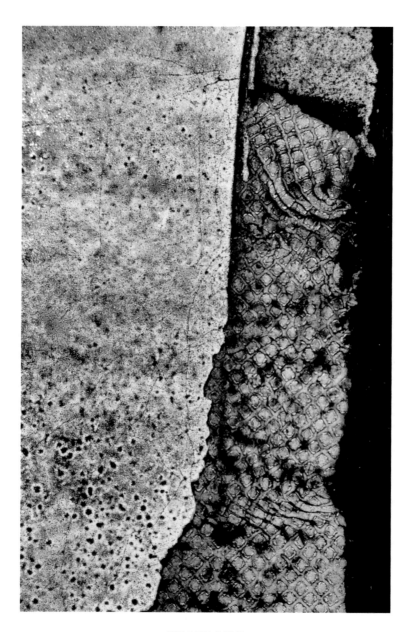

MELTDOWN

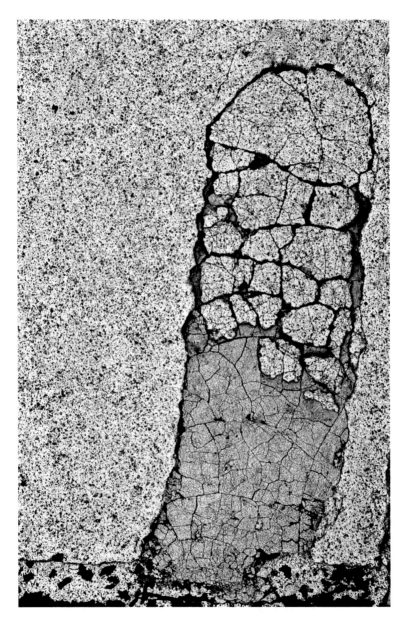

LEANING TOWER OF PENIS

RITE OF SPRING

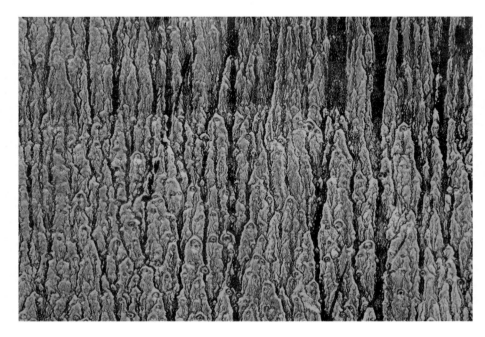

FOREST PEOPLE

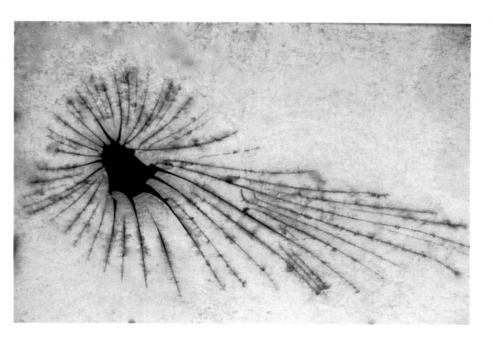

SPARK

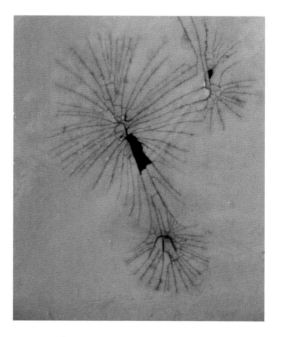

MICROSCOPIC

CABLE STRUCTURE

DECONSTRUCTION

SUMMER BREEZE

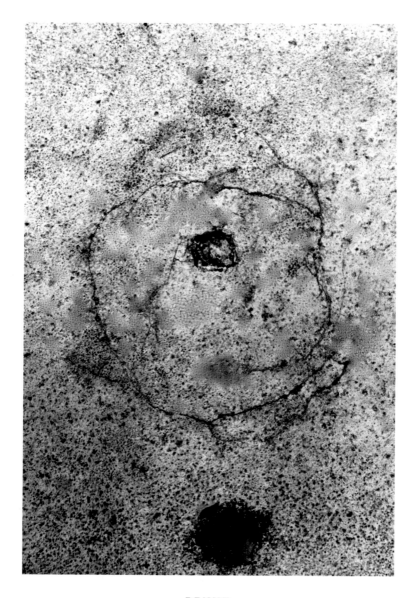

BENNY

BATHER

He sat to check his email. The one he was hoping for had arrived:

You lucky dog, Dad, it said. *How I envy you all your freedom to travel wherever. I loved your descriptions of Istanbul and was amused by the barber who played the song by Bing Crosby. What about India – you still haven't told me anything yet about farm and village life and the people you met? You said you would. Please, otherwise I won't love you any more.*
Love,
Ingrid."

'Love, Ingrid' – words he'd come to cherish. He had hoped she would go on with her studies, but she wanted to see the world instead, and so got a job as a flight attendant with Arab Emirates. He had inspired her, she said. She sent postcards from stopover cities he had never been to. She stopped over in Paris, where they met and dined together. After four years in Dubai, she returned home to marry and settle down with the man she met there, an Australian fingerprint expert, about whom she has said very little, only that his name is Steve, that he is bigger and stronger than Jim and just as gorgeous. Jim will get round to writing to her about his last trip to India. And it was a book in his letterbox: *The Life of Form in Indian Sculpture,* the one Carmel was working on when they met in Mumbai. She signed a warm dedication to him on the inside page.

Don't forget Yoko and Mitsuyo, he reminded himself. He had their English lesson to prepare – prepositions this time, the smallest and, for some, the trickiest of words.

Like most northerners during these colder, darker months, Jim tends to go into a squirrelly kind of hibernation. He stocks his freezer with bowls of vegetable soup of a special recipe –

pumpkin, sweet potato, broccoli and puree of chestnut with a variety herbs and chicken stock being his favourite. His life takes on a rather monastic simplicity, staying in more, listening to radio plays or music, reading, writing letters, or enjoying the involvement of inventing another story. He sometimes attends first-night gallery openings, bookshop presentations, or sometimes a restaurant dinner with a promising French *femme*. An occasional architectural job comes his way, and teaching English is a good standby. He volunteers time to the Red Cross in winter, handing out meals to the homeless. His winter walks are like sleepwalks in soft, sky-less fog, down to where the mists float blindly above the mercurial river among branches –*la grisaille*, it is called. Chaste as a monk, too – he misses the warm embrace of a good woman, someone who would call him her Lordship, who would stare at him with intolerable tenderness over a bowl of muesli, then take his bowl to the sink and wash it up for him. Not many around like that these days.

It is so good to be able to live your life according to your moods. Some days go by and he hasn't spoken a word to anyone, not even sure sometimes what day it is. To write he needs to be alone. In silence there is peace.

Some months passed before he saw Sonia again. She called and arranged a meeting at her home for dinner and discussion. Her other guest was Tony, Italian American. Sonia had met him recently at the Cannes Film Festival. She had a thing about Italians. She found him interesting: a part-time movie cameraman, a part-time private detective, a sometimes school sports teacher, and his lizard-skin boots. He was broad-shouldered, affable, had a great laugh, and was a good drinker. He was now living in Paris. He liked Jim and asked for his card, said someday he might need a stills photographer.

The job sounded very interesting: six storeys, built of rubble stone, and in the heart of Sablet, one of the several twelfth century towns of *la Région de Vaucluse*. It had remained empty for the last sixteen years. Jim's brief stipulated a conversion into three apartments. With the legal matters now settled, it was ready for his inspection. He reckoned he would need about two days to measure up and a few more to explore the region famous for its *Côtes du Rhône* vineyards and Gigondas wines.

In the vaulted gloom of the great Gare de Lyon Station he could see on the walls the soot blemishes from the Steam Age; through its skylight windows the summer sun's brightness was blinding, and resounding in its huge volume were the quiet noises of talk and the bustle of arrivals and departures.

At Platform 10 the bullet train looked magnificent – sleek and polished like a streamlined Superjet. It was patiently awaiting its complement of passengers, conserving its energy for its next marathon dash to Avignon.

Jim loves train travel, most of all the dog carriages that rattle and squeak and clackety-clack between small towns in poor countries. They are like big toys. They give you time to think about what you are seeing; you can wave to farmers and children through open windows. One day on a slow ascent to Darjeeling, he remembers, he jumped off to snatch up a bunch of bananas, threw down some change, and then jumped back on. Mind you, on any hot afternoon in open countryside the dog-carriage trains can sometimes, for no apparent reason, begin to slow down, come to a long, creaking, grinding halt, then like an old man on a park bench, just quietly nod off to sleep. The passengers look at one another and shrug, and after a considerable while wonder if someone should go and look to see if the driver is OK. A tree has been blown down onto the track, or an errant goat won't budge, or they have stopped at a filling station, or some other such thing. In these that fly so quickly between modern cities you get only blurred vision. You can't even focus and register something just there before it's gone. *Cheeeeeeee-ew*, gone, what was that?

A giant's voice announcing their imminent departure bellowed and echoed unintelligibly over the whole station. The scheduled arrival time was 4.50pm – north to south in a mere two hours and forty minutes.

"*Vite, madame, vite, vite!*"

With the luggage racks full and everyone seated, the doors hissed closed; hermetically sealed. It was fresh and cool. He leaned back against the antimacassar and felt relieved that he had made it on time. To his right was a French businessman with his computer.

"*Bonjour, monsieur.*"

Jim had reserved the window seat.

Almost imperceptibly they moved. A sad little girl on the platform holding her mother's hand was waving farewell, a loved relative by the look of it, her tearful eyes reaching out. Watching her passing by, a vague sense of déjà struck Jim – a film noir scene, another dream memory, a real memory but of something that had not yet transpired – a premonition? What was it?

Still searching his mind, dirty grey embankment walls appeared just a few feet away, graffitied with precocious-looking words in languages of invented alphabets (or perhaps it was Arabic?), and down there in the grime among the weeds, miraculously it seemed, little white flowers were waving cheerfully in the breeze. The train clanked over terminal points; a thinning mess of poles and wires and tracks were diverging to other parts of France. The train crawled like planes do when taxiing to their runways, past shopping malls and office blocks, just warming up. The inner suburbs were a mix of high-rise apartment blocks giving way to low-rise, and then warehouses and used-car lots with high wire fences, then brownstone houses with chimney pots and TV antennae and rubbish-strewn backyards. In the factory zone it began to accelerate; on entering the countryside it raced at full speed, like the wind. It was so quiet inside it inhibited conversation. People spoke in whispers.

The land, mostly agricultural now, was decked out in summer's dense colours; gently undulating hills combed smooth, approximated mounds of cinnamon. Ploughed in furrows, they were like brown corduroy, and those planted with mustard seed, in that bright afternoon sun, were carpets of glaring primary van Gogh yellow. Cows and sheep, standing still in a field like paper cut-outs in a child's colouring book, were ruminating or muttering into grass-green grass (complaining about the prices of cheese and wool, he imagined); cuttings of steep-sided embankments exposed the land's raw flesh and bones. A naked strip of tarmac raced by, and up there, in loops just outside the window, wires seemed to be prancing along with them, sometimes whipping away in a dramatic change of direction; in the mid-distance, small, picturesque towns set amongst trees – a parish spire characteristically in their midst – floated by like flotsam, Jim turning and craning his neck to quickly verify some uncertainty. Everyone got a sudden fright from the loud whack of a train, only inches away, hurtling in the opposite direction. A polite moustachioed conductor passing down the aisle punched everyone's tickets. In the dining carriage for a coffee, Jim met a friendly, engaging couple from Tunisia. The train entered a region the Romans had occupied two thousand years ago. Eventually it slid to a halt at Avignon Station spot on time, fresh as a daisy.

It was on his walk to the car rental office that he felt the first pleasure of change. He could smell it – the oxygen of clean, fresh, country air. It was noticeably warmer, too, and the sky was cloudless, dense enamel blue. He hadn't been down in this part of the world since the Avignon Festival of six years ago.

Driving north, sprinkled along the roadside verge were wild poppies gaily nodding in the breeze, two little gypsy girls selling them on the way; in his wake, two ducks flared up in the rear-view mirror, a rabbit scurried to safety, a farmer on his tractor trundled by, in his trailer a bouncing pig. It really was a glorious day.

Jim found the right-hand turn at the crossroads, followed three miles of winding road, then over the brow of a hill a signpost that directed him to the steel gates that stood open, and up a long, curving driveway to a traditional cream-coloured house with blue-painted shutters. He let himself into the small porch. He then rang the bell of the inner door. She would know who it was – Sonia had phoned that morning to confirm his arrival time.

"*Bonjour, Monsieur James, comment allez-vous? Je m'appelle Cybèle, bienvenu.*" And she held out her hand and pressed it in his like a little gift. Dressed plainly in jeans, white blouse and a headscarf, she was fresh and fair as a milkmaid, the touch of her hand so beautifully feminine. There was a kind of innocent wantonness about her. She gladly accepted the bunch of poppies.

Leading Jim up the creaking stairs from the entry, Cybèle told him how beautiful the last few days had been, the marvellous sunsets and cool evenings. She turned to him with a smile and said, in her lovely meridional accent, "*Sonia m'a dit que je dois être accueillante et très gentil avec vous*" – in Sonia's words, probably, that she was to spoil him rotten. She became even prettier when she smiled.

The room was old and spacious with a low ceiling and small windows. It smelled of jasmine. Whitewashed walls contrasted with hand-hewn beams and dark heavy furniture: a chaise longue with plumped-up cushions and antimacassars; an escritoire and chair; bookshelves with Proust and Flaubert, a Nabokov and a few Grishams. On one wall was Cézanne's *La*

Montagne Sainte-Victoire, which Jim had also seen from the car, and folded neatly on the duvet were soft white towels. The jasmine was displayed in a majolica jug sitting on a washstand, beside it the soft yellow light of a lamp, and also fresh from the garden, still in their pods, a bowl of ripe brown almonds. His presence in such a large house seemed spare. He opened a window slightly to set free a buzzing wasp, letting in a little fresh air and the faint chiming of six o'clock. He could see beyond a plain of verdant pastures an escarpment clustered with medieval stone dwellings – a postcard picture of Sablet.

Cybèle called to ask if he would like tea or coffee.

"Coffee would be nice, *j'arrive, merci.*"

There was an openness and sweetness about her that made her immediately likeable, lovable even. Ah, zee French girls.

From the kitchen the softening light and coolness outside was the afternoon waning into dusk. While Cybèle was busily preparing their meal Jim took a broom and swept up the leaves that had accumulated over the rear terrace, where a heavy outdoor table beneath a great, still oak was set for dinner. From there a trimmed lawn stretched beyond to where a few apple and almond trees stood, and beyond those, a wall of hedge. As the sun sank slowly behind the oak its shadow crept across the table and settled on the terrace; a soft breeze gently stirred the bower of jasmine and carried its fragrance to merge with the rich smell of bouillabaisse from the kitchen, a favourite regional dish.

With some local wine, dinner was delicious, conversation jovial. Cybèle's impulsive laughter was a sudden delight. She reminded him of his cousin.

"Very smooth and pleasant," Jim replied when asked about the journey down, and that there had been no difficulty in finding the house. He spoke of the conversation with the Tunisian couple in the dining car about the peaceful coup and ousting of their President. He told her how he and Sonia had first met – on treadmills in the gym, of all places, her struggling to keep up with Bruce Springsteen, which made her laugh. He told her the kind of photos he took. She was expansive in her description of her home city of Toulouse; and her years in Paris, in Montmartre, where she once rented an apartment from Sonia, which was how they first met, and her irresistible passion there for vaudeville. She had studied at L'École Internationale de Théâtre Jacques Lecoq and was now rehearsing the role of the playful and flirtatious Célimène in *Le Misanthrope*. She insisted that Jim come to see the show next month in Montpelier. On the stage, she said, is where she feels improvement and self-fulfilment. What was happening in Paris, she wanted to know – the changes to the Bastille neighbourhood where she had also briefly lived? She complimented Jim on his French, but she preferred to hear the sound of English. She was curious about Australia – the beaches and rainforests, the central desert and Aboriginal culture. She didn't know Australia became an English colony in the same year as the French Revolution. Cybèle liked the sounds of 'upstairs' and 'downstairs' and wanting to practise her English, she repeated them.

As the meal came to an end she asked what he thought of the French, and French cuisine.

"Snags and baked beans, *qu'est-ce que c'est que ça?*" she asked.

She laughed at this being a traditional English pub breakfast.

"And chops, what's chops?"

'Feeling a bit peckish', she found amusing. She giggled at 'being a little bit tiddly'.

"Eet ees my dhyeam for going in Austchalie," she said.

Faint-sounding bells concluded the day. The air became suddenly chilly; one by one stars appeared, intimate sounds of crickets, a bat flitted by. Beyond the plain and to their left could be seen the small lights of Sablet, where tomorrow Jim would begin his first day of work. The table was cleared and then they took their glasses up to her room, which had heating and a DVD player, to watch a 1946 film, *It's a Wonderful Life*, starring James Stewart, Jim's namesake.

Cybèle told Jim there are about seven or eight medieval towns in the region. On the road map they look like tiny knots in threads of cotton, and fewer than a thousand people live in most of them. They were established typically on hilltops to have good surveillance against marauding invaders, and to give the church a dominant position. So to visit them these days, one has to spiral up by road to finally arrive in the main square.

Surrounding the square you will find mature plane trees giving shade to a mayoral office, a bank or two, a pharmacy, a *boulangerie*, possibly an antique shop, a provincial wine shop, and cafés with outside tables where, each afternoon, old black-bereted townsmen come to play cards and partake of *pastis*. You may find a darkened stone church with tilting tombstones in an unkempt graveyard. You will likely find a fountain with perpetually flowing water, and to one side, brushed with sunshine and dappling leaves, a stone memorial to the young and valiant who fought and fell in the First World War. They are depicted in carved relief with their faces blown away, not by the battle of that war but by the battle with the raging seasonal winds that seem determined to reduce everything in this region to dust. It is known as *le Mistral*. In its rush down through the Rhône Valley and over the plains, picking off these small towns, it permanently disfigures all the windbreak cypresses in the direction of the sea. Once a week the village square becomes a marketplace where on trestle tables local produce is sold: fruits, either fresh from farms or as marmalade; a variety of cheeses; small sachets of fresh lavender and mixed herbs; embroidered doilies; lacework; and bits and pieces of memorabilia. A walk away from the square along narrow, cobbled laneways you may even find the ivy-covered ruins of the original castle. A town clock tolls the hour as it has done each day since the Middle Age.

Sablet is just like this, except that part of the village fountain is roofed over for the benefit of the wives who come with plastic buckets to wash and talk. For communities of townspeople like these, who don't read very much, whose lives are built on oral tradition and common gossip (*Two things spread quickly: a forest fire and gossip* being a local proverb), spying on friends and ne'er-do-wells, but especially strangers, is common. Many of them, colourfully dressed and with dark leather faces, appeared to be North African Arabs or Eastern European gypsies.

Jim went to the realtor's office and picked up the keys of the house. He was anxious to see what was in store for him. "The last one on the left, Number 67," the agent indicated, pointing up into the sun, a freestanding house on top of the hill. Walking past the silent houses with potted flowers and ferns, their doors closed tightly against the world, he glimpsed faces hidden in lace curtains. One woman sweeping her doorstep secretly looked up, or was it the women at the fountain who stopped talking, who didn't look up, who gave the signal?

The house presented itself with an ordinary grey-rendered facade with two steps up to a front door of desiccated grey timber with flaking blue paint. The lock yielded and the door needed a bit of a shove. The hinges squawked an alert for whatever was inside. The air that had been imprisoned for so many years escaped past in a rush – it smelled boxy and salty, the odour of stone cellars and decay. It seemed like an awakening from a long somnolence: a creak from the staircase, a stir of dust on the hearth, and a shuffle that sounded like feathers. He went to a window to let in some light. The shutters' hinges groaned, and with the sudden splash of sunlight the faded wall colours rose up in alarm; the suddenly opened empty cupboards blinked with surprise; shadows crept slowly in and hid in corners.

It was when he entered the house, apparently, that the word was passed around. In the first hour of measuring up and taking notes, the owner, Madame Guillon, appeared and politely wanted to know who he was and how he had gained entry. Having accepted his explanation, she walked away.

The floorboards protested as he went from room to room. His shoes left footprints in the dust. Upstairs, in one bedroom, words of love painted on a wall from a boy to a girl appeared to be still as fresh as they themselves must then have been. One could see vague traces of where pictures had once hung.

The lowest of the six floors, the basement, opening onto a lower back laneway, with small ventilation windows grown over with ivy, was a brick-floored wine cellar, dusty bottles concealed in cobwebs and darkness; walls more than five feet thick were remnants of the town's original ramparts. It was like a dungeon. There was no dampness, which was a relief. Beside the two large carriage doors his lamplight picked up a fine-looking horse wagon tilted back on its haunches and a few wrought iron bed frames. From the next floor level, looking from the rear terrace down onto the neighbour's, children were playing; the muddle of typical sun-bleached terracotta roofs on the opposite side of the lane stepped down to the right and spilled into the town far below. Up on the top floor, in the attic, where he disturbed a few roosting doves, the plaster ceiling in one part was darkly water-stained – a missing or broken tile, probably. A softly breathing silence filled the house. He opened a dormer window and felt a thrilling flush of wind. The view looking directly south offered a mid-distance hillside covered with vineyards, and on top was an old stone homestead with three small grey-boarded outhouses, all protected on their windward sides by a steadfast regiment of cypresses. In the far distance were faint dove-grey forms of other hills tinged with a pale lavender colour, or, where there was cloud cover, daubed with mauve, rather like a Cézanne. A voice, a girl singing, barely audible, gave a certain sweetness to the air; higher up, in the clear stillness, swallows circled.

Jim could see how this empty, soulless place could be brought back to life. Its structure was strong and massive, so all it basically needed for its conversion was some re-planning with new amenities, wiring throughout, repainting, curtains, cooking pots and plates, a bit of a scrub, and some laughter. Just like a violin needs to be bowed regularly if it is to retain its roundness of tonality, a home, too, needs to resonate with gaiety.

It took two whole days to get all the measurements. All the rooms were out of square and some boundary lines had to be guessed at.

Off with early starts, in sunny weather, their next days were spent discovering, one then another, the villages in *la Région de Vaucluse*, all with enticing names – Séguret, Vaison-la-Romaine, Beaumes-de-Venise, Roaix, Rasteau, Gigondas, Carpentras, Vacqueyras. The region was mostly planted with vineyards. Lupins, lavender and poppies were in bloom, and oranges were more plentiful than usual. It was hard to see how the vines could grow in such stony, anaemic-looking soil. But the grape is a tough, tenacious plant – sinewy, not muscular – and it can take the extreme heat, though, evidently, not the wet. There had been some recent flooding which was to blame for the scraggy end of harvest, most evident on the plains where the fruit was left to wither and rot. On higher ground they stopped to pick a bunch missed by the new mechanical harvesters. The vines' leaves had turned their summer colours, most of them the same alizarin as the wine they produced. Sometimes at a roadside approach Jim could take a photo view of a whole village profile, usually culminating at its summit with a church spire or castle tower.

More and more foreigners, Americans and Germans mostly, are buying into these hilltop towns and restoring them with good taste. The houses and even the paving of the winding lanes are consistently of the same local bone-white stone. The only colour relief you get are the walls covered in ivy vines – crimsons, yellows, greens and browns, sometimes blue wisteria, in window boxes bright red geraniums, and along clothes lines billowing sheets and towels and rows of upside-down socks. And, of course, the ever-changing skies.

It was as if their time together exploring this region, on this their final day, must conclude with an occasion that would make it the most remarkable. From a window high up in Séguret, sipping wine – how long was it, maybe ten minutes? – they witnessed a spectacle that perhaps would best be described by J. M. W. Turner, or Beethoven. It was a sunset.

The view was of a clear sky of enormous preternatural glow, a plain that stretched as far as the eye could see, and a great, suspended ball of sun. Laid along the horizon was a thick rug of dark grey cloud; entrapped within it was red earth dust caught in the turmoil of a fierce windstorm. The sun descending was at first burning bright, then as it penetrated the cloud layer, it changed to a golden-brown disc, flat and dull in the likeness of a Roman coin; the eddying and colour transformations of the dust were comparable to tinctures of chemical crystals slowly dissolving in a beaker. Fully submerged then, the sun suddenly flared up like a match, igniting everything around it. New forms appeared, block forms resembling buildings, and it seemed as if some great city – Rome again, or Paris, was it? – was being engulfed by fire with gases exploding in slow motion. As the intensity died down, the forms, like lumps of coal encrusted with glowing red jewels, slumped and shifted and lay in ruins. Jim caught himself with his mouth agape, wondering if anybody else in the village was looking at this most amazing spectacle, or if it was just for them. When all was settled as glowing embers, the sun was reduced to just a speck on the horizon, not unlike a magical, radiant, golden chariot. It waned, flickered, as if bidding them farewell .... then was gone. Emptied of its fire and gold, now in tattered robes of purple and blue and yellow, the day began to slowly die, to sink into darkness in such glorious splendour it could have been the last day on Earth, more beautiful, he thought, than anything he had ever seen.

One day he drove alone all the way to the port of Marseilles, 2,600 years old, the oldest city in France, though most of what you see today is eighteenth and nineteenth century. It was a pleasant change to stroll along wharves: in the clear water tiny nautical creatures fed off the algae; a lingering salty mist smelled of fish and seaweed and scraps of wrack, the lapping and gulping sounds of water, wooden bumping sounds of hulls, hawsers straining at their bollards, metallic sounds of halyards slapping against masts, somewhere an engine sobbing, and the shrill cries of gulls circling overhead. He pulled in another deep breath of air.

He walked and sat at an outside café for coffee and a croissant. A wary, scavenging three-legged dog hobbled up and glowered at him. A wild-eyed passer-by flashed some hashish at him.

Turning off the city road and winding his way up, Jim found, in a pine-shaded hilltop village, a generational community from the Comoros, the small island group north of Madagascar. He got out of the car and climbed the narrow streets. They lived and dressed as their ancestors had – the old women's dark faces showed vague markings of tattoos. They were surly and suspicious. They made it clear that no photos should be taken. He bought a colourful hand-printed scarf and a punnet of strawberries and walked on. At the end of a broken, deserted lane of ruined houses, where errant newspapers shifted about in a pungent reek of surface drainage and urine, he came upon a rebarbative derelict sprawled like a sprayed insect propped against a wall. He was in a dark suit, his trousers smeared with mud, no shoes. He was in a state of utter despair, half his face egregiously scarred. He was an alcoholic with festering hatred, probably infecting others with his malignant nightmares – Goya in a vile mood. He needed some kindness. Jim approached him and offered him some strawberries. He gave a virulent sneer and broke into coughing. He grunted as he tried to raise himself to strike out, but he couldn't, he waved his fist and snarled and barked at Jim to go away, then withdrew back into his misery. There was nothing left for the poor man to say. The vocabulary of despair is so limited – it is the end of language. Those without hope are those who have exhausted all the possibilities of the only life they think they have, instead of trying elsewhere with other possibilities. Yes, I know, it's easy to say. I think he might have accepted a cigarette if Jim had had one. When he wasn't looking Jim photographed him curled like a leaf on the ground. He had the thought that one day this poor fellow might die crying in the rain.

The thing about life is you can always expect the unexpected. After walking through some pine groves and alder shrubs, Jim came upon a trout stream with marshy grass and dabbling ducks, buttercups and daisies, fidgeting bees, skipping butterflies and seething motes of pollen. Sitting cross-legged on a neatly laid-out mat and shelling peanuts was a bushy-bearded, orange-turbaned sadhu. He had before him some incense and simple offerings to his god. Jim smiled and greeted him with "*Namaste.*" He told him India was one of his favourite countries, and that he had been there five times. The sadhu seemed unimpressed. As Jim raised his camera he looked at him nonchalantly.

"I am thinking you are coming from Amrica," he said.

"No, I am not coming from Amrica."

Click.

"I am thinking you are coming from Germany."

"No, I am not coming from Germany."

Click.

"Have one more guess."

"Japon."

"No, I am not coming from Japon."

"From which country are you coming, sir?"

"Australia."

Click.

"Ah, Australia. Three for 234."

"What do you mean?"

Click.

"Australia three for 234," he repeated, referring to a small black radio among his few possessions.

"Ricky Ponting out for twenty-seven."

He was keeping a ball-by-ball account of the Second Cricket Test between India and Australia. Why, Jim wondered, had he chosen this spot?

His name was Raj. He said he had once managed a mini-market in Bangalore and was now the owner of a small pea farm about two hours' bus ride away. He came here three days each week to meditate, smoke grass, and listen to Test cricket. Not a bad life, Jim thought. For a while, sharing peanuts and a joint, they both listened to the match. Australia was winning easily. The summer heat was bearing down; a Red Admiral butterfly fluttered by; far off, you could hear the dull, plodding sound of a village bell. Before Jim left, Raj drew a diagram of where to find a bus and a bush track so that one day Jim could come to visit him and his family.

Returning to his car through a whispering, watchful copse of birches and melodic bird calls, there on the ground was a small grave: a mound covered with a blanket of leaves and withered wildflowers, a twig crucifix leaning a little in soft ground. Scratched on a stone was *Colette*, and beside it, ex-voto, a seashell and a string of coloured beads – a small creature, a bird perhaps, or a pet rabbit. The thought that it might be a bird took Jim back to that day in his childhood, in the churchyard next door, when he found the dead pigeon. He and Eunice had given it a proper burial, too, under a mound of soft earth, and Eunice for her part placed a decorated piece of broken crockery and her mermaid clip and Jim, his rare Connie Agate marble.

It was getting hot. He was feeling good. In his car he turned on the air conditioning.

For a lunchtime, *le Mistral* was quiet. Happily whistling *Toreador*, an unusually tall, thin barman in a white apron was arranging a rack of picture postcards; waiting for customers were chairs crouched in orderly fashion beside tables set with paper tablecloths and menus sandwiched between salt and pepper shakers. Jim ordered a beer, then went and refreshed himself with a splash of water. When he came back he noticed at a table near a window a man dressed as a travelling salesman. He had before him a trout, the *plat du jour*. Over in the window seat, quite remarkable for how long and thin he appeared – a real-life, pimply-spotted Giacometti – was a downy youth dressed in shorts and long grasshopper-green socks, a Black Sabbath T-shirt and a baseball cap pinned with several badges. Before him were a draughts set and a fizzy fruit drink with a straw, and sprawled on the floor beside him, flat as a tiger-skin rug, asleep, was a fat indolent dog. He seemed to be happy – big, round eager eyes. Jim gave him a wink, and with some help from his jaw he tried to wink back.

Jim went to him.

"*Ça va?*"

"*Oui, ça va,*" he replied.

'Guillaume', I think, he said his name was.

Jim sat and challenged him to a game.

The view outside, beyond the car park, was of small white cottages floating on a sea of vivid green; masts of dark, pointed cypresses; a sky of cloudless postcard blue. There was the needling buzz of a distant tractor.

Guillaume set up the board. Sitting opposite him, with his glass of beer, Jim wondered how he fitted in – probably part of the establishment. Guillaume sucked his drink with subdued snorkelling sounds. Jim had to cheat to let him win. On a winning streak Guillaume clapped and giggled. Jim complimented him. Guillaume began to arrange the pieces for another game, but Jim said he had to go. He awarded him fresh lemonade and a kangaroo badge and ruffled his dog.

Jim found the barman sharpening a pencil this time, still whistling *Toreador*. He asked if there were any flea markets in the region, *marché au puce*.

"About twenty kilometres away," he said. "Today, every Saturday, mostly locals."

From a shelf below a trout in a glass case, he lifted two small silver trophies to let them be inspected, one engraved for golf in 1968, the other for javelin in 1969.

"*Je les ai trouvê la-bas la semaine dernière*," he said; found them there last week.

So with time to fill, Jim decided that as this was his last day he would go there. Before leaving he washed dog off his hands, combed his hair, and on his way out remembered to buy a few postcards.

"*Merci, monsieur*," he said for the tip, and "*bonne journée*."

He waved farewell to Guillaume.

Guillaume waved back and garbled something.

In the acid sunlight, Guillaume's dog with his tongue out, grinning at him, was peeing on the tyre of his car.

He turned on the air-conditioning. He drove the countryside whistling *Toreador*.

The town was small and typical for the region with a Sunday kind of quietness – a drowsy yellow somnolence, baking bricks and sleeping cats, too early for siesta. Walking towards the main square market, he caught the first sounds of impassioned wailing and the strumming of flamenco.

It was a gathering of townspeople mostly, those with simple tastes, modest expectations and time to waste, because in small, provincial towns like this, drained of youth and vitality, time doesn't seem to matter very much. They all dine at seven and are in bed by nine. Each evening the streets are dim, forlorn and dead to the world.

Most things displayed on benches were typical bric-a-brac: unusual-shaped bottles; mismatched plates; plastic toys; chipped picture frames; vintage magazines; coins on saucers; piled, post-marked postcards; axe-handles; an abacus (which tempted him); a chamber pot; rusted things, such as animal traps and garden tools; what looked to be the last relics of embroidered tablecloths and lace; and perhaps from the same homes, old family Bibles. A young, bearded hippy in a palm beach shirt was selling spices for headaches, leaves for insomnia, herbs for constipation, a green Indian concoction for removing warts, and OptiMystic cards which, according to him, one shuffles to avoid bad luck; a Senegalese, his leather belts and blackened tribal masks. On the bare ground were the children and pots and pans of a nomadic-looking tinker family. Jim bought the abacus and was lucky with a most unlikely find of an ikat-woven cloth from the Indonesian island of Lomblen. In a marketplace in Bali in 1972, he learned of the different styles of these cloths from the various surrounding islands – Savu, Sumba, Flores, Timor, Lombok and Lomblen. Since a disastrous tsunami struck Lomblen in 1951 and wiped away most of the population, their cloths have become fairly rare. The price he paid for it clearly indicated the seller didn't know. Some of the sellers had laid out lunches of chicken or cheeses with baguette and the local wine. There was a smell of frying merguez sausages. Most people were quietly browsing and chatting.

It was amusing to find that the source of the music, which was still pouring out and seeping away into the streets, was two ridiculously small black speaker boxes at the feet of a cross-legged, dusty-looking Rastafarian bookseller, his hair like potting mulch, and he was rolling a family-size joint. A girl next to him, dressed in blue denim, was dark too – burnt sienna, night-black eyes, straight black hair pulled tightly into a plait, a sheen to it. Her face looked carved: a beaked nose, features that could have been part native American, and she radiated a pleasing, contrasting white smile. Jim moved in to look through the faded hardbacks, and in the glimpse of a glance caught a white gleam, a star in her eyes. The writers were mostly unknown, some hippy comics – *The Fabulous Furry Freak Brothers* (Freewheelin' Franklin's life philosophy: *Dope will get you through times of no money better than money will get you through times of no dope*) – and to his surprise, in the paperbacks, poems by W.H. Auden and Baudelaire, and an Elmore Leonard novel he hadn't read.

"One of my favourite crime writers," Jim said as he handed her the €4.

"That was my book," she said, nodding, "I like him, too."

"Clever with dialogue. He must be in his eighties now. Did you know he served as a marine in the US Navy during the Second World War?"

She didn't.

He asked if she'd seen *Get Shorty*.

She hadn't, or *Out of Sight*.

She'd not heard of Raymond Carver or Paul Theroux. Jim thanked her and was moving away.

"You were watching me, weren't you?" she interposed with her pleasing smile, the star beginning to twinkle.

A bit taken aback, Jim admitted that he had noticed her.

"You come from England, don't you?" she said.

"You're close, Australia, but I left a long time ago."

"Why did you leave?"

"Because I couldn't bear the isolation any more, and that extreme summer heat is enough to bake potatoes. My ancestral home is London and I lived there for a while but it rained too much. Now I'm in Paris. Paris is beautiful, and I love her four seasons."

On her jacket was a finely embroidered scorpion, and round her neck a Mexican Indian charm.

"I have an uncle in Australia," she said. "In Perth, he's a mining engineer. He likes it, says everybody is so friendly."

Her accent was Spanish.

"Well, I'm glad to hear that. And you, I think you are South American?"

"Mexico," she said, "Mexico City."

"Really? I saw it once from a helicopter, it's enormous, it seemed to go on forever, like a conglomeration of four or five cities. What's your name?"

"Tequila," she said, and with a delightful smile, "Tequila Sunrise."

She was watching him, the gleam in her eye unwavering.

Jim smiled back.

"Why are you called that?"

"Because it's my name."

Tequita, her real name, made her feel small.

"Jim, *mucho gusto.*" And she offered him her hand. It was like a soft leather purse.

She had nursed in a hospital in Mexico City, she said, and served in a Mexican restaurant in Manhattan, set up a vegetarian stall there on Union Square and started a radio chat show. Afterwards she broke up with a Peruvian guy in Marrakech, then came to live in France. Now she was just letting days happen. They were distant as people but Jim felt drawn to her – her smile, or perhaps it was because of the vagabond freedom of his situation. Her dark, carved features sparked memories of the woman he once loved, the Canadian Indian woman he married.

There was a pause.

She asked about the Lomblen cloth. She asked his star sign (Aries: courageous, optimistic, honest, passionate); then she told him hers (Scorpio: brave, sensual, stubborn, passionate). He said he hoped the two signs get on, and she said they do. There was a whiff of musk oil on her clothing and cigarette on her breath.

Looking over her shoulder, Jim asked with a smile and a nod at the Rastafarian if he was her brother, and she laughed.

"He's sort of my boss," she said, and looked back to see that he was quietly happy. Bob Marley was singing now. She poked her tongue at him. He didn't take any notice. He had the casual, sleepy look of a camel.

"He has a second-hand bookshop."

She worked for him part-time, just weekends.

An English couple in white summer clothes approached with *A Year in Provence*, a bestseller. Wishing her a lovely day, Jim said goodbye and walked away, thinking the twinkle might have indicated she was pregnant.

Jim exchanged his return bullet-train ticket to Paris for the one that departed at 8am, dog carriages that crawl for ten hours through farms and small towns and rugged ranges with waterfalls. It was a beautiful day and he had his book. He thought he might even get out his pencil and do a bit of sketching on the plans. He loves slow train travel.

On the opposite seat of an otherwise empty compartment was a quiet, respectable-looking old gentleman in a dark brown, old-fashioned three-piece suit, in its breast pocket a folded handkerchief, no tie, just a worn, clean shirt buttoned up to the collar, a light sprinkle of dandruff on his shoulders. He had forgotten to button up his fly. Beside him were a brown paper parcel tied with string, and what appeared to be a small plastic lunch box. His hands were clasped on his lap – worker's hands, gnarled like vine roots. His hair was ragged and grey, his face unshaved and weathered.

"*Bonjour, monsieur, oui, pas mal,*" he said in reply, a rustic simplicity and shyness in his faint smile, a southern accent. Jim could see by the way he looked at his words that he must have been blind, and yes, there was also his white stick.

He could speak no English. It transpired that he was a farmer from the region of Cotaux Lyonais – pears and apples, mostly, and also a brood of turkeys he fattened each year for Christmas. His brother had left the farm at an early age to take on a city job and find a wife. Seventy-six-years-old now, he was in a Paris hospital recovering from a second, more serious, heart attack. The parcel contained a set of warm pyjamas wrapped around a flask of whisky, both of which had been requested. He said he hadn't seen his brother for thirty-eight years, and wondered if they would have anything to talk about.

"That's if I get there on time," he said.

They talked some more. The farmer did attend church services, but only on ceremonial occasions like marriages and Christmas. It wasn't until recently, during his wife's dying and now his brother's illness, that he first took seriously the notion of a God. He seemed to think that the closer you got to death, the nearer you came to God. Death, he thought, provided an exit for the soul, or what they call the spirit, which would then likely find its place in Heaven, or possibly inhabit some new incarnation.

"The most frightening thing when you know you're going," he said, "is the darkness afterwards; your friends not being there any more, not knowing which way to go, just drifting, lost in some huge, totally unfamiliar place."

"You mean the soul finding its way to Heaven?" Jim said.

Yes, he thought so.

Jim told him he found it hard to believe in such things.

"For me there is no life hereafter, nothing – it ends with finality, the fire of life is extinguished like a flame, or spent like a withered leaf on the ground. An American poet once said fancifully that we turn into leaves of grass. It is incredible what the church preaches; that if you believe in God and bow down to his commandments, your soul – call it what you will – will find eternal happiness in Heaven, whereas those sullied by sin, without absolution, will suffer forever the flames of Purgatory."

He said further that he thought Heaven and Hell is the greatest hoax ever perpetrated on mankind. It was the medieval theologians who made up those stories. And it was an example of man's arrogance to personalise God in man's image. He suggested that one could think of God not as the patriarch invented in the image of man but rather as the infinite universe; and Heaven, or Paradise, as being this place here on Earth, rich with such abundance and variety of life. The old man was staring at him, then he blinked. Jim could have said, but didn't, that he thinks those who pray are those in hope and need, many seeking help from the suffering that the church itself induces through fear and guilt. James Joyce said it was the nuns who invented barbed wire. Misinforming the masses with biblical miracles and holding them subservient has been the power and deceit of the church, and being charitable and a patron and custodian of great works of art has been its virtue.

The farmer and his wife had had no children. In their late seventies they had lived from day to day with only small ailments. He was at her bedside on the night she passed away. Just moments before, he said, he sensed a strong presence in the room, something both beautiful and frightening; it seemed that angels like white apparitions were assembled, and then, on her last breath, they ascended, taking her life with them. He knelt by her body, as if in some way it was still hers, and prayed for a safe delivery. He vowed to her that one day they would meet again. He said he had wanted her to go first because he knew she wouldn't be able to bear the suffering and loneliness. Now it was he who was suffering, in the chest, he said, like a big bruise. Struggling with that promise, he pursed his lips and frowned; he seemed to have lost a dimension, shrunk a little.

In quiet desperation, and seemingly in hope of a rescue, he said in a voice strangely hoarse, "*Mais, l'âme doit bien aller quelque part.*" (But, the soul has to go somewhere).

The farmer felt for his stick. His mouth was dry, poor fellow – he needed some water, which Jim was able to give him.

They then let the subject drop.

The clacking noise was relentless.

Soon after their departure from Avignon, Jim had a good view of the vineyards of the Rhône Valley. Then they climbed slowly up to the Massif Central. He described for the farmer the pine-covered mountains up to the snowline, the clear water cascading over ledges and down rocky cliffs, gorges with white-water rapids and rising mists. Rounding a bend, the old man felt the sun suddenly light up his face. And he knew by the sound that they were in the long, dark mountain tunnel to Clermont-Ferrand, when Jim had only his reflection to look at – darkness visible, and when they came out of the tunnel there was again a sheer drop to the waters below. Then down once again, into the sunshine-brightness of Burgundy, past rolling hills of sheep and cattle and vineyards, and fields of sunflowers all facing the same direction of the southern sun.

The stops and starts along the way were clean and tidy stations with cantilevered cast-iron roofs, colourful flower tubs, hanging baskets and bench seating; no advertising slogans, just the names of each station. One person got on, another got off. A stationmaster in dark blue uniform with gold buttons looked both ways, raised an arm to the driver, then blew a loud shrill on his whistle. Then the train moved slowly on again.

At one station they stopped for a thirty-minute refreshment.

"*Est ce que vous voullez quelque chose, monsieur?*" Jim asked.

He shook his head and said, "*Non, ça va*", unwrapped a salami sandwich and uncorked a half-bottle of wine. Jim could see he wanted to be left alone, probably to think about finding a cheap room somewhere near the hospital, and what he might be able to say to his brother. The farm was up for sale – that was one thing. He would have wanted his wife to know, and guessed that she probably did. Jim told him he was sorry if he had said something wrong. The farmer said he didn't think he had.

And Jim did get out the measured plans and tracing paper and sketched for a while. It resolved itself quite nicely. With a new external stair up to a first-floor lobby, and from there, an internal one continuing to the next floor, and with some new doorways and extra amenities, the house could be converted neatly into three spacious apartments. It probably wouldn't need planning approval. It was nice job for him and a nice way to earn a living.

After six days of fresh air, and now after so many hours of the incessant beat of the train, the carriage rocking like a cradle, and the soporific effect of the lunchtime wine, Jim began to feel drowsy. He read another page of Elmore Leonard, placed the bookmark and closed it. He let himself float into a reverie. His thoughts found their way back to Sonia, and how if they hadn't met that day in the gym he wouldn't be here now; and then

Cybèle, how she had so happily 'spoiled him rotten', her French accent: *Eet ees my dhyeam for going in Austchalie.* Tequila, too, her brazenness, poking her tongue out like that… then he drifted into sleep.

He dreamt he was in a hospital and in the hospital he had a dream about his daughter and chocolate, "a dream within a dream:"

"Hi, Dad," she said. "Sorry I'm late. How are you?"

"How long have you been there? Why didn't you wake me up?"

"You looked so peaceful I didn't want to disturb you."

"You are wet, is it raining?"

"Yes. Are you feeling better today? I brought you your favourite chocolates."

" I am remembering now – I was just having a dream about you."

"Really? I hope it was a nice dream."

"It was a strange dream. We were on a bus. I was standing next to you, but for some strange reason you weren't aware of me, as if I were a ghost. I didn't say anything, I just watched you. Your hair was different. You were wearing it in a different style. Then you moved to get off and I followed you. On the street you stood and looked both ways, not sure which way to go. You stopped someone and asked for directions. You thanked him and then walked across the road towards the park. There was some loud thunder and then it began to rain. You ran to take shelter under a tree. You had a worried look on your face. You looked at your watch. After a minute or so you decided to make a dash for it. The rain got heavier. You took shelter under the awning of Spalding's for a while then you went in and bought an umbrella and a box of chocolates. I don't know what happened after that."

"I rushed to the hospital," she said.

Then doors banging, bags bumping, the real world nervously coming back. A throng of people rushing by on a platform outside, and the old man vanished without a trace, as if he had been part of another dream.

When Jim arrived home, Ingrid's email said, *I don't think you love me any more, Dad*; her way of teasing him. She was appealing to him, once again, to tell her about his latest trip to India.

7

Inside Maharashtra

It was in the warmth and quietness of his home one cold autumn morning in 2008, at around 3am, with a steaming mug of tea beside him, Jim sat with his notes to recollect his experiences during the recent weeks he spent in India.

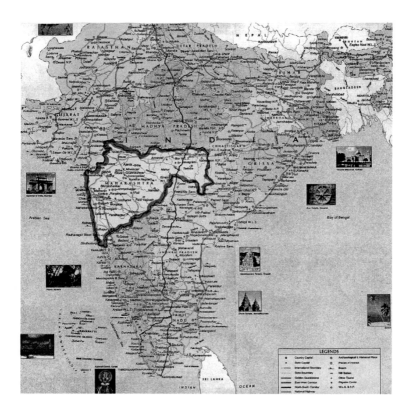

Dear Ingrid,

I had been in that room before, he began…

It was a morning long ago, more than forty years now, when Mumbai was still known as Bombay. We were university students who had arrived by ship the day before. It was the dining room of the Salvation Army hostel and we were assembled on our first day to begin the biggest adventure of our lives, a three-month odyssey into the exotic, mystical world of India. For the first two weeks each of us would be assigned to a family and then we would be on our own. I was billeted to Benares, the sacred Hindu capital some thirty hours train ride away. Benares is where many of the sick and old go to die and have their cremated remains ceremoniously sprinkled into the Ganges. My train, I remember, was packed. There was no chance of me being able to occupy the sleeper I had reserved. We had on board a regiment of Indian troops who were on some routine transfer to Kashmir. On arrival I had the good fortune of being welcomed by a kind family of sari merchants. After my stay with them I hitched to Kathmandu, then proceeded to the pristine summits of Darjeeling. With a Sherpa boy as my guide, I set out on a two-day trek to a small outpost from where I was told I would see the sun rise over Mount Everest. We arrived exhausted and famished. Two American college students were huddled in a corner listening to a transistor radio. President Kennedy had just been shot and was being rushed to a hospital. When the news of his death came a few minutes later they quietly packed their things, left us some chocolate and raisins, and then went to mourn with the rest of their nation. So that must have been November 1963.

But I digress … that same room, some forty-five years later – more a canteen really than a dining room. It had barely changed: a high ceiling with heavy beams; slow-moving fans; four pairs of French doors opening onto a closed-in balcony (an Internet space now); and there, still on the same wall, the large framed photo of a tired, bearded William Booth, founder of the Salvation Army, dated 1906; the same framed portrait of Jesus Christ; the Pilgrims' Map of the Holy Land, circa 1942, showing the paths of Christ's travels in Samaria, Judea, Galilee and Capernaum; and, because it was the month of December, cut-outs in festive colours of a jolly Santa Claus and Christmas bells. All around me were the same tables cluttered with the same breakfast plates that had served these same thousands of hungry, scruffy-looking young travellers lured by the fascination of this ancient, god-drunk place called India.

It was about 9.30. The last person got up and left. Or so I thought. There was another down near the front, hunched over a book. It was a woman. I could see she was plainly dressed in a shirt, slacks and sandals; her hair grizzled and grey, cut short like a boy's; an old face, serious, India-worn. Who could she possibly be? On my way out, I paused to say hello and asked what she was reading. Slightly taken aback, she said, "Oh, the journeys of Marco Polo and his meeting with Kublai Khan, I am very interested in that period of history." Given my age I think she quickly guessed we might have enough in common to not be a waste of her time, so she invited me to sit with her.

"That would have been late thirteenth century China," I said.

"Yes, on his return from there by boat he stopped briefly in southern India. I want to research his travel diaries to see if he made mention of the Jain temples I am interested in."

Normally, the maximum stay in the Salvation Army hostel is six days but Carmel had occupied a room on the top floor for the last thirty-seven years. She had left behind a husband and a Manhattan apartment. From time to time she would go back there for visits, or travel to her house in the Negev Desert south of Jerusalem, but most of her time she spent here in India, deeply involved in classical Hindu sculptures. She had made pilgrimages to the most important caves and temples, taking with her a Hasselblad camera, tripod, lanterns, and even candles to study and record details of forms. She has published five books, including studies of the cave temples of Elephanta, Aurangabad and Ellora, as well as a recent analysis of the Mamyamardini myth. She knew Hindi and Marathi well, the principal languages of Maharashtra.

I showed her what I was reading: the latest book by Paul Theroux, The Elephanta Suite, *set in the Taj Mahal Hotel in Mumbai, just across the road in fact. I told her I had come for three months, firstly to attend the Mumbai Film Festival, then to go out and photograph the traditional farm, village and town life of Maharashtra. If successful, I would compile the images into a book. I thought I would call it,* Inside Maharashtra.

"Well," she said, "if you need any information about Bombay you couldn't do better than see Mahindra, he is honest and knows the city better than anyone."

She knew him when he was a shoeshine boy on the streets, and had helped and cared for him over the years. I was eager to meet him. Looking at her watch, Carmel got up to leave. She kindly invited me to accompany her the next day to the opening exhibition of the Brâncusi sculptures. I gladly accepted. As she walked away, I noticed her limp.

I liked Colaba, the district around the Salvation Army hostel on Mumbai's southern peninsula. It is residential, of domestic scale, where many streets of fine houses in the Victorian style are shaded with jacarandas and banyans. Colaba's marketplace is rich in variety, and the main street is busy till late with retail shops, clean restaurants, footpath stalls, and a good barista coffee shop with Internet. There are few public gardens, but there are pleasant walks – the evening one, for example, from the giant stone arch of the Gateway Monument along the stone curve of the lamplit seaside wall. I would stand there sipping from an earthenware cup, feeling and smelling the evening breeze, gazing at the lights of the fishing boats bobbing up and down drunkenly in the black ink of the Arabian Sea.

On one such evening a young boy approached me, maybe ten or twelve, in dirty shorts and bare feet. He had a beautiful face with gleaming white teeth. He politely wished me a good evening.

"From which country are you coming, sir?"

I told him.

"You play cricket in your country."

"Yes, indeed we do."

Another trolley came by and the boy fetched for me another small clay cup of tea. He asked where I was staying. When I told him he said he would meet me the next morning to be my guide. I said I didn't need him, I preferred to discover on my own. His name, he said, was Janki, Janki Balap. I asked if he was attending school. He said he did when he could – two, sometimes three days a week – but he had to make money to help provide for his family. Reading was his favourite subject, he said. I asked him to read for me a few lines from my book, which he did very well. He was a bright little kid. I asked him what he would like to be when he grows up and he said an airline pilot, like his uncle.

We walked together and he took me to a nearby street where many sellers had second-hand books laid out along footpaths. After some discussion he chose A Tale Of Two Cities *by Charles* Dickens *and* Oscar and Lucinda *by the Australian author, Peter Carey. I chose a poor-quality pirated copy of a long story I had already begun back home called* Shantaram, *written by an Australian prison escapee about his life in a Bombay slum. Janki then led me to shops where I got for him two bars of soap and an ice cream.*

After the film festival I did arrange to meet Mahindra. We met at Leopold's for lunch. He was plump and personable, his hair crew-cut and his upper dentures conspicuously new. In his mid thirties, he was married with two children. He spoke English well enough and laughed a lot, unconcerned about how his dentures moved. I took a liking to him straight away. We ordered chicken salad. To give him an idea of the kind of photos I was after, I showed him some I had taken a few years before in Calcutta. Yes, he said, wobbling his head, a gesture that is characteristically Indian, he knew places where very few foreigners had been, certainly no tourists. With him I would be safe. I explained that my first plan was to explore the hinterland for a couple of months, and then I would return to Mumbai. He abruptly remembered that his best friend, a taxi driver, was about to drive north to visit his family. He rang him on his mobile, and sure enough, within minutes, he arrived.

Kishore and Mahindra first met as fourteen-year-old runaways shining shoes on trains. They fell in with some riff-raff who stole from warehouses and slept on train-station floors. They all smoked two packs of cigarettes a day and sniffed amyl nitrate. Despite his rough edges, Kishore was a lovely guy who laughed a lot. My Australian accent amused him. It reminded him, he said, of an Australian he once met. He asked him how long he'd been in India and what was his purpose there, and the Australian replied that he "jest came 'ere t' die" (today), which had Kishore rolling about laughing once again. He said he was going to visit his parents on their cotton farm up near the northern border. The drive would normally take a couple of days, but he could stretch it out with a longer route, and, yes, he said, laughing, he would be 'tickled pink' if I came with him. I would pay for the petrol and a small commission. Looking back now, I try to speculate as to how different my time in India would have been if I had not met Carmel. Was it chance, or was it fate?

Before we left Mumbai, Kishore invited me to his home for dinner and to meet his wife and family. They lived in a nearby slum on the peninsula's eastern seaboard. Kishore came to walk me there. A shoal of fishing boats were moored in the foul-smelling low-tide mud; the rocks are where the inhabitants, noticeably the kids, go to relieve themselves; and there was a small strip of sandy beach where boys kicked a ball, mangroves further out. I could make out, not far in the distance, the approach of new high-rise office buildings that would someday transform this place into a prime site for development. Across the road, in stark contrast, was the World Trade Centre, a huge, modern, air-conditioned building with three levels of shops selling jewels, silks, intricate crafts and expensive antique rugs.

The slum was ten acres of wretched poverty with several thousand tiny shacks coated with the city's grey dust, housing the lowest caste – Dalits – all crammed together along winding corridors. There was some electricity, no running water, and no toilets. Sometimes there were cases of cholera and typhoid. I was impressed by the sense of community, how content everyone seemed to be, all seeming to know one another, their front doors open and kids running everywhere, squealing, playing games. Near Kishore's home was the sickening smell of an open latrine concealed by screens made from reed matting. Elsewhere, that smell was dispersed by the sea breeze, and it was rather the smells of spices, cooking and incense that predominated. Music playing on a radio somewhere was the shrill soprano voice of Lata Mangeshkar – a love song from an Indian movie.

Kishore, his wife Alka and their two kids lived happily in two small rooms. Alka gave me a friendly nod of greeting, modestly holding her cotton sari to hide her face; his boys looked at me with astonishment. The walls were painted a dense blue, the concrete floor was covered with cracked linoleum, and the fitful lighting consisted of a dim overhead bulb, and on a shelf, two flickering candles. The shelf also supported a TV, a DVD player and a framed brown photo of Kishore's older brother, who some years ago was killed in a car accident. Next to the brother was another *photo: Dr Bhimrao Ambedkar, the only way you ever saw him – a rather plump man in suit and tie wearing round, thick-rimmed glasses on an otherwise characterless face. India's first Untouchable to be educated abroad, he completed postgraduate studies at Columbia University in New York, then, in 1916, qualified as a barrister in London. Dr Ambedkar was elected Minister of Justice in Nehru's government, and he drafted the 1950 constitution of the newly independent India. He became the Untouchables' great leader, more important than Gandhi. He encouraged them – the Harijans (the children of God, as Gandhi called them), or Dalits (in Sanskrit, 'the broken or shattered'), as they now call themselves – to abandon Hinduism, which had enslaved them, and turn to Buddhism, which could enlighten and liberate them. The slum was named after him: Ambedkar Nagar*

The dinner of stewed dried fish, called 'Bombay duck', was spicy, of course, and delicious. I had my own bottled water. As is the custom, Alka remained out of sight in the kitchen space. She would eat alone when we were done. She had cooked the meal over a gas flame supplied from a cylinder. I shuddered at the thought of what might happen to the community in the case of a fire outbreak.

Another photo flickering in its frame was of Saptashrungi Devi, the family's chosen deity – a deviation from the more common choices of Brahma, Vishnu or Shiva. "She is my second mother," Kishore said, smiling lovingly. He saw no conflict in his conversion a few years ago to Buddhism. "Buddha was a human being," he said, "not a god, but it wouldn't have mattered anyway; you can have more than one god." Out of the vast pantheon, she was his favourite.

Saptashrungi Devi, too, was once an ordinary human being. One fine morning about two hundred years ago whilst crossing the Ghads – the seven hills that form part of the Sahyadri range in Maharashtra – she was suddenly turned into stone. When the stone was discovered it became an object of devotion. A white temple clinging, to the cliff side, was built around her. She is visited all year round but on holy days thousands come and climb to worship her, the sick and elderly carried on chairs. We would go there in a few days time. In Kishore's photo, Saptashrungi Devi was depicted as a smooth, slightly conical lump of stone about three feet tall, smeared with red paint, her only features a large pair of astonished eyes – round painted yellow spots circled with white bands, like a pair of fried eggs – the shock, I guess, of suddenly being petrified. I suggested to Kishore that this event was not possible because it was not natural. His wide-eyed reply was that that was the amazing thing about it: it was impossible, and so it must have been a miracle.

But even if one believes in miracles, why, I asked, had this ordinary mortal turned into stone become an object of worship and for so many? He didn't know exactly, hadn't really thought about it, but she did answer his prayers – sometimes. "We prayed for two boys," he said, "and now we are blessed." When our meal was finished the electricity cut out, so we talked by candlelight.

This irrational way of thinking floats over much of India. Encapsulated all round – east, west and south by oceans, and in the north by an insurmountable wall of mountains – Indian culture evolved in isolation, uninfluenced by outside traditions. Their education for a thousand years has been based on myths. Each myth, according to the Source Book of Hindu Myths translated from Sanskrit, celebrates the belief that "the world is boundlessly various, that everything occurs simultaneously, that all possibilities may exist without excluding one another". *Since ancient times only the Brahmin priests, the highest caste, were permitted to read and write. Their duty was to control the social and religious order of society. They led the lower castes around like lambs and told them what to believe, not how to read and think for themselves. The Brahmins institutionalised religion* and erected innumerable temples, all the while bleeding the lower castes of the little they had and lining their own pockets. Religion truly became the opiate of the people.

Many people who visit India today are struck by the squalor of the urban slums that assault their senses almost immediately after they leave the airport. I asked Kishore why he chose the struggle of this urban life when he could be with his family working on the cotton farm up north.

"I left my family village when I was fourteen," he said, "because I didn't want to be poor and lonely any more. The village was very small and had no school; my mother and father had three children and no land then. We often went hungry."

Villages tend to be traps for the lower castes. There is no healthcare and schools are few and far between, jobs hard to find. Agricultural reform will eventually introduce mechanised farming, which will result in even fewer jobs. Then, like Kishore, they will drift into the cities.

"As a taxi driver I can support my family here, where it's cheap, and the kids can go to school. Besides, we all like the community life in this part of the city."

I realised then that it had not been Kishore's intention to drive up to see his parents. Mahindra had called him from Leopold's to hand him a new job.

Kishore arrived on time the next morning with a full tank of petrol. I felt refreshed after my cold shower and simple breakfast and was happy to be finally on our way. January weather is the best for travel in India. My rucksack was on the back seat and my camera on my lap.

We set off in a north-easterly direction towards central India, not along the highway but on a double-lane back road. How exciting it was to see typical life in medium-sized towns with rivers and ancient temples, but mostly it was village life and flat *farmland. Life in these parts is the same as it has been for hundreds of years: families working their own fields, cutting and gathering twelve-foot-high sugar cane by hand, and then transporting the harvest by bullock wagons to the mills; harvesting and winnowing vast fields of maize, and like in biblical times washing clothes beside waterholes and pulling up buckets of water from wells. Rajasthani cane cutters come down each season and set up their own communities with shelters that resemble the tepee tents of nomadic American Indians. For the first time I saw cotton fields – shoulder-height thorny shrubs, the fluff of snow-white buds bursting from their pods, and nimble pickers reaching over their shoulders to add to bags slung on their backs, earning about 150 rupees a day (less than €3). Another example of how resistant the rural people are to change was the age-old tradition of the sari, even here, picking cotton. Imagine: a loose flowing garment in a field of thorns. Ironically, the sari fabric of today is more likely to be not cotton, but polyester. I visited a cotton mill to see how seeds were separated and how the cotton was baled. We passed brickyards with smoking slope-sided kilns and long neat rows of stacked mud bricks curing in the sun.*

Our first stop around midday was at a site on the Godavari River where, along its banks, the ancient city of Nashik had been established, now the fourth largest city in Maharashtra. Devout Hindus believe this is where Lord Rama lived during his fourteen years in exile. Wide stone quays along each side of the river provide for congregation of its people and the hundreds of thousands of devotees who come during each year, as well as the tens of millions who descend every twelve years for Kumbh Mela – the most religious of all Hindu festivals. Many stone temples, eroded and blackened by floods and time, some subsiding towards the river, some actually consumed by it, provide places each day for spiritual cleansing and small sacrificial offerings; the wide steps down into the river allow full immersion for bathing and praying. 'Ram nam sate hai' *was the repeated chant of mourners carrying a body wrapped in muslin cloth sprinkled with coloured powders and marigolds. The body would be cremated on a funeral pyre at the water's edge. It reminded me of Benares, but as I would discover, this occurrence is common in most river towns all over India. Water everywhere is sacred.*

Market stalls were strewn along Nashik's many crowded, narrow streets. Kishore accompanied me on my walk. As well as stalls selling daily requirements such as foodstuffs, artisans of all kinds worked their stalls – cloth merchants and tailors, coppersmiths and goldsmiths, and even a barber who told fortunes and removed wax from your ears. The products ranged from handcrafted brooms and combs to scented powders and perfumes, Ayurvedic remedies, religious paraphernalia, flower garlands and home-made fireworks. To add to the excitement and congestion, wandering bands of musicians, goatherds, and rickshaws managed to manoeuvre their ways through. From a street bench, sipping ginger-flavoured tea with sweet cakes, I marvelled at this fascinating flow of humanity.

At around mid-afternoon the riverside was crowded. A sadhu in full beard and turban talking with a dhoti-clad farmer beckoned me to come and sit with them. Scriptures and smouldering incense were laid out before them. It appeared that the sadhu had been giving the farmer a lesson. Large, thick, black-framed glasses distorted his eyes and he was wearing a Casio watch similar to mine. He asked about my purpose in India. He knew Australia only by name, and asked about religion there. It was touching to hear him retell the fantastic story of Hanuman, the ubiquitous monkey god, son of the wind god, omniscient, virtuous, destroyer of all demons. My fascination was not so much for his fanciful story – I had heard it told before as it is always told – but his theatrical air of authority. He was a pedant rather than a poet, a scholar rather than a sage. I asked to take his photo. With straightened back and proudly raised chin his pose was statuesque. I felt compelled to stay here for the day so Kishore arranged our overnight accommodation.

That night the lanes were full of bustling crowds, the stalls now lit by kerosene lamps and dancing candle flames. Kishore suggested we order a meal of dahl. We sat on a bench and scooped hot, ginger-flavoured lentils with chapatti. Hot chickpeas roasted on a brazier were handed to me wrapped in a cone of newspaper – they were overcooked, so brittle I broke a lower molar tooth.

At the riverside where I came the next morning at dawn, all others wading in, shrouded in mist, appeared like ghostly apparitions – men fully dressed in white dhotis, women in beautifully coloured saris, children joyfully ducking and splashing; bathing, washing clothes, worshipping, offering marigolds to their gods that bobbed and floated off in the current. Saris were spread out in the sun to dry. After a cup of chai we drove off on another day of great expectations.

Surprisingly, lush vineyards surrounded the city. As the region became more arid we began to spot rustic villages camouflaged in earthy landscapes. They were built out of what was available – tree trunks as posts, stick-reinforced mud for walls, tamped mud floors, and grass-thatching for roofs. Again, at the nearest river or well or water hole there was the early morning routine of women washing clothes. The vivid colours of their saris contrasted markedly with the neutral ochres of parched background. The occasional muddy waterhole provided a place for black leathery water buffaloes. Smoke rose from the tall chimneys of distant sugar mills.

Along the hot, pebbled roads Kishore drove at the moderate pace I asked for and took no risks. Big trucks drove at reckless speeds and their bulk forced other drivers to the sides of the roads. We sometimes came upon small bands of pilgrims, the eager young and bearded old, some barefooted, tinkling bells and cymbals, skipping and chanting; some dressed in the cloth customary for their sect – string-stitched, ink-printed hessian bagging. We stopped and talked with some. They were in high spirits, their faces alight with hope and longing. They were on their way to Shirdi, another earthly paradise, which happened to be on our route as well. They travelled like this for hundreds of miles, merrily skipping and singing, from one religious festival to another. Sometimes in the early afternoons, on the back roads alongside cane fields, miles from anywhere, uniformed school kids coming home with their satchels were pacing together. They wouldn't accept offers of lifts.

Shirdi is a small, burgeoning town, best known as the late-nineteenth-century home of guru Shri Sai Baba. He has a large following across the country and even in parts of the Western world. He didn't preach religion. Like Christ, he was a simple man with a simple life philosophy: 'Only serve humanity with true heart' was his message. Money gathered by the Brahmin fraternity was used to build a temple in Shri Sai Baba's honour. It was faced with marble, and inside, thanks to a particular donor, a life-size effigy and a throne were made, it was said, of solid gold. He was depicted with a trimmed beard, garlanded and robed, wearing a gold crown, one leg crossed over the other, his face drawn. If he hadn't been cremated, I'm sure with this kind of extravagance he would have turned over in his grave.

It happened to be a day of a religious occasion when a huge juggernaut was making its way through the intensely crowded main street. Near me a loud cry went up, "Pickpocket! Pickpocket!" The crowd seized upon the alleged miscreant and he was brutally punched about the head and face, forced to the ground and repeatedly kicked and stamped on. There was no way out for him; he couldn't possibly have survived. That same mob mentality is what sparks religious riots and caste warfare. I was not brave or foolhardy enough to try to intervene. If in similar circumstances one sees a foe he wants disposed of he need only cry out the same thing.

On our third day, Kishore said he would like to visit his idol, his second mother, his beloved Saptashrungi Devi. He did this at least once each year. It would mean a full-day diversion, which was fine with me: everywhere was as good as anywhere. We drove the last three hours through bare, sunburned mountain ranges where the monsoon rains never reach, winding our way along brittle, precipitous roads, finally arriving at the site.

We managed to park close to the base of the temple mount, where many other cars were parked and where a lot of religious paraphernalia was for sale. High up, clinging to the cliff face, was the small, white speck of the Temple of Saptashrungi, and leading to it was a covered pathway. An endless ant-like stream of pilgrims made their way up, the disabled being carried aloft on chairs. We walked in that direction. At the base of the mount some of the devout had come to exorcise spirits, women mostly. Some got carried away in torrents of religious hysteria. Fast beats of a sorcerer's drum accompanied by a tambourine's rattle led one woman through ritual steps until she fell into a trance. Then in a wild frenzy she beat her breast and pulled at her hair until overcome completely by a fit of mad, orgiastic shaking. Nobody seemed to notice me taking photos. When her ordeal was suddenly over she looked calm and relaxed, then walked away as if nothing had happened. Nearby was a grotesque spectacle I would have avoided if I had been able – goats were being ritually slaughtered, their throats slashed, larva of black blood spreading across the sand. Kishore asked if I would walk with him up to the temple. The sun was too hot, the climb very steep and I wasn't in the mood, so I let him go off alone. There were plenty of other roughly humanoid stones I could look at down here, if I wanted to. I took some photos of him with his temple high in the background, which filled him with even greater joy.

He was surprisingly knowledgeable about the road works under construction, probably learned to educate his tourist *passengers. After India's independence in 1947, the north-south road to Delhi was upgraded with the first use of asphalt. By now India had all but completed the three-thousand-mile Golden Quadrilateral Expressway linking the country's four largest cities – from Bombay (Mumbai) north up to Delhi, east across to Calcutta (Kolkata), south to Madras (Chennai), then diagonally north back up to Bombay. We found ourselves travelling beside the new roads under construction that would eventually link into this system, excavations through solid stone hills, and massive concrete bridges crossing valleys. We often had to make detours, or sometimes wait in long roadblocks, occasionally detained by herds of bleating goats. The interstate truck drivers with their feet up and sleeping were the worst hit. As well as seeing massive earth-moving equipment, we saw the army of India's labourers toiling at many small tasks: women and children breaking rocks with hammers, shovelling the rocks, and carrying them in metal dishes on their heads (whoever has heard of the Indian wheelbarrow?), some laying and spreading molten asphalt, others tying rods of reinforcing steel. On the roads you see cars manufactured in Japan, Italy, America and Germany. We were driving a Hyundai from South Korea. We passed trucks loaded with new John Deere tractors from Holland. The roadside billboards advertised mobile phones (last year India became the world's third largest user with eighty-three million new subscribers), iPods, modern apartments for sale and holiday villas in Spain, and there were shiny new gas stations with air-conditioned mini-supermarkets that sold cold drinks and frozen food. Behind these billboards was traditional rural India – brick kilns simmering with smoke, a yoked bullock ploughing a field, villagers cutting sugar cane or winnowing grain, or women gathered together drawing water from a well. Surprisingly there were very few new factories, which could provide much-needed employment for the unskilled and semi-skilled.*

We stopped for lunch under a large sun-shelter roof where there was a scattering of maybe twenty or so charpoys (traditional wooden-framed string beds). The truck drivers sat on them cross-legged, eating, scooping with their fingers, then lay down to take their afternoon siestas from two till four. There could be up to twenty big interstate haulage trucks parked outside. The toilets at the rear were just open ground.

Back on the road again, there were depots with little red onions piled high as houses.

After a lapse in our conversation, Kishore turned to me and asked if I had heard of a book called Shantaram. It was then a popular seller, a story about an Australian prison escapee who went to live where he thought nobody in the world would ever think of looking for him: amongst the poor in the dust-covered streets of a Bombay slum. Johnny Deppe had just bought the film rights; he would play the lead role and Mira Nair the famous Indian director, would direct. I told Kishore that back in Bombay I was reading it for the second time.

"Do you remember Prabakar?" he asked.

"Yes," I said, "wasn't he the taxi driver that Shantaram, or Lin Baba as he called himself then, first met on his arrival at the airport? During the ride into town they formed a friendship."

"Well, he was my brother," Kishore said.

"No! But in the story he was killed in a car accident."

"Yes, it is true, one night in pouring rain, out near the airport. His windscreen wiper wasn't working and he ran into a truck with an overhanging steel beam."

And then Kishore talked about that friendship, how his brother cared for Lin Baba, saved him from his heroin addiction by taking him away from the Bombay influence to be with his family up north, where we were now headed. He was welcomed into the village and stayed for six months. He came to love the simple way of life and the goodness of those around him. He wrote *most of his story there – about his experiences and the people he had met in the Bombay slums.*

"My mother loved him, and it was she who named him Shantaram. It means Man of Peace. You will be sleeping on the same charpoy he slept on."

After five days we finally did arrive at Kishore's village, home for about three hundred souls. They were native Marathi speakers, who don't speak Hindi very well and don't speak English at all. Kishore's mother and father lived in the only brick structure, paid for by Shantaram. Kishore's father, Kishan, dressed in the traditional white dhoti of the farmer caste, was a humble, likeable-enough old fellow, small and thin, stooped and frail, who hobbled on a leg that had never properly mended, and he hardly ever spoke a word. Kishore's mother, Rukhmabai, was the opposite – large and cumbersome, shrewd and domineering, always henpecking the old man, forbidding him to smoke bidis, his only remaining pleasure in life. I could feel no warmth from her. Kishore told me that with him and his two brothers she had always been very strict.

Their cotton farm, about half an acre, two miles away, employed six villagers. The harvest season was nearly finished and one room in the house was stuffed full to the ceiling – Rukhmabai was waiting till the market sales were over, when the price would rise. Four of the village's milking cows were tethered out front; the house's water, drawn from a nearby well, was contained in large earthenware pots on the front veranda. Rukhmabai cooked out under the stars over a twig fire with pots supported on stones. Sometimes for fuel she used dried pancakes of buffalo dung mixed with straw. She served spicy lentil dahl with roti or, now that the cotton was selling, spiced chicken with rice.

That evening Kishore took my arm to walk me round and show me off to all his neighbours. I was, after all, the only foreigner to visit the village since Shantaram, about twenty years before. The walls of the huts were either finely crafted thatched twigs or daubed with mud, and the roofs made of straw. Friends of Kishore invited us inside for tea, while many onlookers came and gathered outside. In the lamplight I could see the earthen floors were neatly swept. Everywhere was clean and tidy. Parents and grandparents looked healthy and bright-eyed, the children active and full of energy. The little girls were hopelessly shy – they hid their faces and ran away giggling, but would soon sneak back again, peeking out from dark corners to marvel at me through their marvellous, panther-like eyes. As Kishore had said I would, I slept on the same charpoy that Shantaram had slept on.

Early the next day I got some good shots of the people rising, sweeping and preparing fires, the children getting ready for the school bus. I then went into the cotton fields where there was still some picking. Deep down in a dry well young men were excavating while others hauled up buckets loaded with stones.

The moment finally arrived when I would have to leave my good friend, his mother and father, and the villagers who had been so hospitable. They all gathered to participate in my farewell, to smile and wave me on my way. I gave Rukhmabai two thousand rupees and, surreptitiously, to the old man some smuggled packets of bidis. To the children I gave out kangaroo lapel pins.

It was a fine morning. Kishore drove me to where I might hitch a ride. We hugged and agreed to meet again on my return to Bombay. He invited me to come again to his home to see a film on DVD by the famous director Satyajit Ray. My peregrinations now, for the next six weeks, would be as a lone vagabond.

Kishore had suggested an itinerary on my map that would take me to out-of- the-way places hardly ever visited. I began making my way south to see the frescoes and sculptures in the Buddhist caves at Ajanta. By the time of my arrival the caves were closed. In the reception of the guesthouse where I stayed that evening I saw for sale Carmel's book: The Life of Form in Indian Sculpture. The *next day the caves and the breakfast rooms were so packed with busloads of tourists I pushed on.*

With the vicissitudes of chance, or sometimes because of some local advice, or a change in direction of a breeze, or a whim, my course became erratic, sometimes trudging doggedly for hours, sometimes stopping buses and motorbikes and getting off wherever it seemed right to do so. It could be in a remote village of some obscure tribe to which no road led, where children ran to greet me, excited and fascinated. I was accepted and given kindness – a bowl to wash my face, a kerosene lamp to write up my day's notes and a mosquito net to sleep under. One day I took shelter from a downpour under a ruinous creeper-covered temple roof, where myriads of bats hung like dead seedpods. Farm-fresh food, the fresh country air, and the miles of walking each day kept me in good shape. I kept myself clean as best I could; my boots, though, were wearing thin.

Each village was built of locally found raw materials – piled stones, tree trunks for posts and beams, twigs and mud-lined walls – simple indigenous architecture. The women toiled hard in the fields, gathering and carrying heavy loads; they laundered on wet stones and kept their homes neat and tidy. Their faces – in my presence modestly half-veiled – were mostly exquisitely, unselfconsciously beautiful: clear dark-skinned, black eyes, teeth of dazzling whiteness, and their combed-back jet-black hair lustred with coconut oil. Their jewellery was beaded necklaces, many plastic arm bangles, silver anklets, earrings and nose rings, and even rings on their toes. Almost none of them could read or write. The children were always incredibly shy and beautiful and, because they were not mine, painfully lovable. This was the typical life of roughly eighty per cent of India's 1.1 billion people.

I came upon a lepers' colony administered by nuns and a very kind, bearded Dutch doctor, a real Samaritan, who had lived there for twenty years. He came forward to greet me and welcomed me in. He said he seldom saw people from the outside world any more. Whitewashed mud-brick row houses formed the compound, the walkways clean and tidy, and to one side garden rows of green vegetables. He had twenty-six patients under his care, men and women, some able to meet with me, others too sick. Some had no noses, and lips and ears were missing, stumps for fingers. I was provided with clean water and warm sustenance and shown to a cool place where I could lay down to rest. I sank into fathomless sleep for maybe three hours. I was awakened by the sound of someone digging nearby.

Sitting with the doctor at a bench table under a tree, we drank tea and on my map he located an isolated point in some ranges where a five-day-long mela (religious festival) had just begun. It was in honour of Lord Rama, as well as marking the beginning of a New Year. Many different tribes from all over India, all imbued with the same faith in the same gods, would be there. It would be a rough ride, he said, and could take a couple of days but he was sure that on such a special occasion I would see things that would astound me. I was convinced I should go. The next morning he packed some food for me from his garden, shook my hand, gave me God's blessing, and bade me farewell.

So it was that, feeling somewhat refreshed and with a lighter stride, I made my way back again into the noisy main traffic. It was a long, intermittent trek, stopping and starting, some dirt roads seeming to lead to nowhere, the dust clinging to my face, my throat parched. It was difficult to follow the route on my map because sometimes I had little idea of where I was. I managed one good lift and for the last twenty miles or so I was on the pilgrim trail. I was crammed in the back of an open truck with quiet families squatted together, and just next to me, in his little red coat and matching cap, was a docile, chained-up monkey. Red ochre-coloured, steep-sided ranges were bare and dry as bone. We wound our way up, sometimes around rockfalls that were perilously close to cliff edges – the only time I ever felt my life was in danger. I should have gotten out on some of those bends with sheer drops. Then, at around dusk, around another bend, we quite suddenly arrived.

The crumpled, reddish terrain was turning brown, shadows slowly creeping their ways in. On some slopes and the desert plateau a makeshift village had been set up. There could have been ten or twenty thousand or more, many who had reached here by foot, and many more still arriving. Encampments were formed with lean-to tarpaulins fixed to trucks, under the wagons blankets were laid out for children to sleep on, and spread out, were cotton cloths for sitting. Propped on small ground mats, surrounded by candles and incense, were garlanded picture frames containing colourful depictions of their beloved deities: Shiva, and Lakshmi, the wife of the god Vishnu. In the last daylight hour, in the fitful light of kerosene lamps, meals were being prepared; smoke rose from small wood fires. Here and there, camels too, with looks of detachment, were squatted on the sand. It reminded me of a similar occasion in 1963 at Jasilmer in the central Rajasthani desert. It was all wonderfully exotic, like illustrations from tales of The Arabian Nights. Walking among them, always a conspicuous foreigner, I feared being seen as an unwelcome intrusion but all I met was their friendly welcoming faces. They beckoned me to come and join them, to sit and eat with them. I had little to offer, and there could be no spoken communication, only gestures that were sometimes amusing. After praying, then eating, they ritually broke coconuts, drank from them, shared the white flesh, and then what was left they placed before their candle-lit pictures, with sprinklings of grain, coloured powders and sticks of smoking incense.

Around midnight seemed to be the hour for turning in. I was not yet ready for sleep – I still had my day's notes to write up. I sprawled on the sand with a lantern, next to a campfire with its flames licking the majestic, pharaonic-looking camels kneeled nearby. Why this place, I wrote, this remote, season-less provenance of long-dead desert? What auspice so long ago had placed it on the festival calendar? The surroundings resembled the moon, barren, everything so old: these tribal people old as fire and their rituals old as gods, their land old as time, and above, the dark, silent infinity of the universe – time beyond time. And in all of eternity, why now, and of all the billions of others, why me? If I had not left India back in 1963 and instead had settled here, I wondered what kind of life would I be living now? Would I have been happy living like these people, clad in dhoti and sandals, close to the earth, or would I have perished? A sweet little girl came and offered a cup of tea, such a beautiful child. She told me her name was Mira. She sat and watched me drink. On the back of her hand was a mehndi decoration, the stamp of a henna floral design that is popular with most young girls. I wondered about her future. It would almost certainly be the traditional village life with limited schooling, if any. But who knows, India is changing so dramatically, with a passionately ardent spirit, she may become a university graduate, a professor, or even a Bollywood film star. She took my cup from me and melted away. I packed my things, still under the sleepy gaze of the camels, put out the lantern, and then curled up beside the fire. I marvelled at the stars again, thinking, wondering, until sleep crept up slowly from behind and stole it all away.

The first light of dawn was a new awakening. The eyes of the same little girl holding a cup of tea surveyed my waking face. Pleasant notes of a flute floated among the unfolding sleepers; children's voices could be heard; fires were lit. The tea was good and hot and sweet, and the chapatti wrapped around a banana was still warm. I stood and stretched. In my sack I found a stick of sugar cane to take with me on my first full day of exploring the campsite. My camera, too, with its all-seeing eye, seemed anxious for some sightseeing.

All that day I wandered, enraptured and alert to every strange new experience. I felt again that I was the outsider looking in. I *walked slowly. I stopped for a while to take tea with a spiritual healer and listen to his fantastic story which I could understand but not believe; I was given a lucky talisman by a blind preacher who hurled oaths and imprecations at his small circle of listeners; women, mesmerised, were flailing to drumbeats and the tinny rattle of tambourines, some crawling about like scorpions, one who fell to her knees choking out the sounds of a dying animal. A long-haired fire-eater who drew a crowd of children blew long, explosive flames; a trainer, accompanied by his sluggish, smelly bear, made continuous rattling sounds; a garishly dressed transvestite goddess with matted hair carrying a trident passed through hardly noticed. A sacrificial goat was slaughtered, then skinned and sliced; a thin bearded holy man with yellow markings on his body wandered around naked; itinerant pedlars plied their wares of trinkets and religious paraphernalia; and turbaned elders sat together in a circle, quietly smoking hashish. There was one only tree, large and long dead but sturdy still, its branches and twigs tied with many small ribbons, giving the appearance of coloured leaves, and votive objects like strange fruit. Jubilant barefooted children skipped by my side, jostling one another to take turns at holding my hand, my camera an object of great fascination for them. Nobody minded my taking photos and some even allowed me their faces as individual portraits. The only other foreigner I saw all day was a semi-naked youth with long, ropy blond hair, sitting cross-legged, his eyes closed towards the rising sun.*

Then for two days I was sick as a dog and ate nothing. I felt wasted and needed to bathe.

The fifth and final day of the festival was the day of iconoclasm and totally unexpected. Shockingly, all the holy pictures were seized by their owners, smeared red in some cases, then smashed to the ground, trampled on, kicked away and left strewn in complete desuetude among dried blossoms in the dust; the worst kind of sacrilege imaginable, or so it seemed to me – another strange kind of exorcism? Still in their broken frames, behind broken glass, the pictures of saintly faces were quite beautiful, and nobody minded that I went round gathering some. I have the few here with me now, over there, displayed on my wall.

Each new day was like the beginning of another chapter, each one ending wherever I happened to be, not really knowing where I was or caring – such a wonderful sense of abandonment to be lost in India.

I saw wheat fields heavy with grain that swayed with each breeze like the rising and falling swells of deep ocean waves; once, at a day's end, when there was still the bright glow of sunlight, ox-drawn wagons stretched as far as my eyes could see passed me by, their cane stacked high to the sky, the families resting on top waving and holding my gaze, the oxen bent low under their heavy yokes, plodding wearily on to the smoking mills beyond. I saw biblical scenes of sari-ed women gathered around waterholes washing cloths and filling their urns from buckets then lifting them aloft, finding perfect balance before moving away – the apotheosis of elegance and grace. There were so many idyllic paintings I'd come all this way to photograph. Water was always a problem because it was scarce and often unsafe. There were few rivers and only sometimes wells. When the waterholes dried up in the summer heat, the parched mind saw only the mirage. And yet despite this isolation and this long sojourn in a strange land, my mind remained intact, knowing that soon enough I would be able extricate myself and return to my own normality.

Back in the Bombay bustle, with nearly two weeks to go, a phone call came for me from Bollywood Film Studios. The Salvation Army counter clerk, Abhi, who had gotten to know me each morning at breakfast, surreptitiously gave them my name. They were looking for a non-Indian who would play a role as an extra. When the scout asked me my age I said I was about the same as Bruce Willis and half the price. "Thank you, sir," was all he said. A pity, in a way – another novel Indian experience was there to be had. I imagined an episode of Bollywood soap, a love story perhaps, between a chubby billionaire shipping magnate and a well-nourished, wayward daughter of a Brahmin district judge, possibly a pretty tabloid celebrity, both in a hideaway retreat in some sumptuous palace. I imagined Kashmiri rugs scattered about, a palmed swimming pool, the lilting sounds of a sitar, and as the two converged to kiss they would dissolve into soft focus and puffs of pink mist, and then cut. I cannot imagine what they might have had in mind for me.

There are annual weeklong writers' festivals in the David Sassoon Library – authors interviewed on stage and then reading of extracts from their recent published works. Paul Theroux was the special guest this time. He read from Sir Vidia's Shadow *about V.S. Naipaul, the sour end of their lifelong friendship – revelations, transgressions and betrayals of trust that you expect more from celebrity divorcees. Questions were then asked by the audienc. "Just leave home," Theroux called out to one young aspirant at the back who asked how she could get started on a writing career. "Leave home, get as far away as you can, and read, read, read." Then he signed books. I went last in the queue so I could have him to myself. In my copy of* The Elephanta Suite *he scribbled a perfunctory,* To James with best wishes, Mumbai, 7 Feb 08, *signed* Paul Theroux. *I told him I had read twenty of his books and my favourite was* Picture Palace, (1978), *rarely seen now because it has long been out of print. I told him I knew some things about him: the year of his marriage break-up in England – he had written about it, it was the same year as mine; Theroux's birthdate was exactly the same day a year after mine, and his son Louis was the same age as you, Ingrid. I could have told him I knew about that evening in a boozy Singapore bar in the late 60's when he had his first encounter with Anthony Burgess, and of his earlier life* with the Peace Corps in Malawi and Uganda. Of the many other things about his life I knew very little. I wished we could have gone somewhere for dinner to talk some more.

Twice I met Kishore back in Bombay, and that was all. He was surprised, he said, at how much weight I had lost. I was still nursing the molar I broke crunching roasted chickpeas. I contacted Mahindra to arrange a meeting where he would tell me about the 'special places' he would take me, where 'few foreigners have ever been'. We met again at Leopold's, a large, lively, cheap restaurant that attracts many young travellers, and which was also a regular meeting place for the Bombay mafia in Shantaram's story. It was a crowded lunchtime, all hubbub.

The menu offered beef curry, mutton curry and chicken curry. I asked the waiter which one he could recommend.

"Mutton curry is mostly goot, sir," he said, wobbling his head.

"Well, if mutton curry is mostly good, I will have that."

"No, sir – mutton curry is mostly goot."

When Mahindra explained that mutton curry is mostly goat, I chose the chicken instead.

And who should be there, seated alone in the far corner, but Shantaram himself? Mahindra knew he was there when he recognised his vintage Enfield motorbike parked outside. He was tall and bald on top with a bleached, plaited ponytail down his back. I went to him, excused myself and told him how much I enjoyed his story, especially Chapter 6, where he describes his stay in Sunder village. I said I knew Kishore, and had just come from the village. He smiled, put a hand to his heart, then asked me to sit with him. I was chuffed. He was anxious to hear about some of the villagers, especially the old man, and if this year had been a good harvest for them. Suddenly his two friends arrived, so I left him. I regret that I didn't make more of the opportunity and ask if we could meet again to share our experiences and look through some photos.

I took a small, cheap room in the Carlton Hotel in Colaba, just opposite the rear of the five-star Taj Mahal Palace Hotel. Some days when I wanted a quiet read, I put on a tie and went there to sink into the cool armchair luxury of the reception lounge.

And Mahindra did take me to places very few 'normal foreigners' go: Dharavi, the biggest slum in all of Asia – a seething, dark grey shamble of commerce, everything traded, from gems to clocks to earthenware pots, and where smells of poverty mix with heady, meretricious smells of counterfeit famous-brand perfumes; and Chor Bazaar, known as the 'thieves' market' because it is full of stolen goods and squabbling bargain hunters. Mahindra's uncle, Rafik – a sandbag paunch and deep, croaking voice; a pipe smoker and a rat-catcher; a polished black stone on his thick ring finger; and not without a certain charm – dealt there, ostensibly in rugs but mostly in whisky.

Mahindra introduced me to some of his friends – some who smoked hashish, scavenged in bins, and slept on train-station floors; others who smoked hashish, dressed in pinstripe business suits and slept between soft silk sheets. We got invited to an expensive, kitschy nightclub, which I declined. In the Muslim quarters, always crowded and industrious, were small back-lane rooms with young apprentices sitting cross-legged, single-mindedly hammering metal for machine parts all day, welding bike frames or sharpening knives. In the lane, men wore traditional kaftan robes and topis – the beaded cap, or the white lace cap of the haji, those who had made the pilgrimage to Mecca; off the lane, where bearers bustled with enormous bundles on their heads, we sat at a Muslim vegetarian shop with white marble tabletops to take refreshment of cardamom-and-ginger flavoured chai; schoolchildren could be heard reciting verses from the Koran. Nearby was a large, public outdoor laundry festooned with drying bright cottons. Mahindra took me to the seaside to see the dyeing and drying of large red floor coverings used for marriage tents, and how they billowed in the seaside winds. We drove about fifty miles south to a fishing village lush with palm trees called Alibag, where large catches of prawns were spread out on the ground to dry in the sun, and where a large wooden hull, rolled on logs from a dry dock across a shore, was hauled into the sea.

I got my more than one thousand photos contact-printed. I selected what I thought were my best fifty and had them blown up by a recommended freelance printer. He did a good job. I was eager for Carmel to see them. I wanted to see her again anyway. "Yes," she said, when I phoned, "I have been waiting for you."

We met over a cup of tea in her usual tea room on Mahatma Ghandhi Road. She held the photos, studied each one very carefully, took her time remembering some of the villages, stroked some, and her first words after seeing them all were that she thought they were beautiful – a nice compliment. Then she did something quite unexpected: she placed her hand gently on mine and said quietly that she thought that I too had reached into and discovered the heart of India.

We dined a few times at the same Muslim vegetarian restaurant she frequented, and though she had read widely her conversation was not esoteric; rather it was more about the things and places she and I had seen, and people we'd met. She was one of those rare people who had created a philosophy to live by, and whose life was earnestly spent trying to live it. The true source of her feelings was to be found in her books of the gods. She hardly spoke to anyone else. She invited me to a gallery nearby where her bronze and stone sculptures were on display: an enormous amount of work. They were thirty-two depictions of Indian deities, classical in form but not in style, each about sixty centimetres high, waiting to be shipped to a gallery in New York. I thought I could detect some influences of Picasso or Henry Moore – she was of that period.

I was missing my BBC radio, so most nights in my small balcony room, lying on my back till well after twelve, my eyes *closed against the bright white street lamps, I took my mind off the day to meditate on what was happening around me now, in the immediate present. Most pressing were the sounds of traffic below, in fact there was nothing else: a motor accelerating; the horns – some attenuated, some just short honking, tooting, beeping sounds – accompanied by the quacking of motor rickshaws; a bike's trilling ring; rattle sounds; an occasional vocal cry or a loud piercing whistle; and for a short while, even, like the beat of tabla, the hollow, percussive sounds of horses' hoofs. Sometimes there was a discord of simultaneous similar sounds, like an orchestra tuning up. It seemed yin sounds were metered with yang silences. I came to think of them not as random sounds at all, but rather as a composition of sounds, common sounds making, as it were, original music – acrobatic antics of musical chance whose structure was the complex geometry of chance. This was how I would count sheep before sinking into deep sleep.*

I worked it so that, leaving for the airport, I had rupees enough to pay Kishore's cab fare and a generous tip. At check-in they told me I was sixteen kilos overweight and would have to pay a shocking sum for excess baggage, nearly the price of my ticket. Baksheesh was out of the question, because, well, firstly, I had no baksheesh to give. I had no choice but to sort which things I could dispose of. I stepped aside, opened one of my bags on the floor and began selecting and stacking the framed pictures of deities. I was overcome with despair, exasperation and deep disappointment that, because of this last-minute nuisance, I had to give back these treasures that so briefly had been mine. Well, did this cause consternation! The Indians behind me glowered and staff came from everywhere in reproach; it was a frightful sacrilege to spread their gods over the floor like that, they said. I wanted to tell them that I found them smashed in the desert but instead apologised for my indiscretion. I looked at the clock. One dear English lady came forward and said if I was going to London she could take some for me. I asked for help. The staff got into a huddle, called a senior officer, and decided finally that if I liked them that much, and because I really was broke, I should be considered as an exceptional case, and be allowed to repack them and take them on through. Hallelujah, praise the Lord(s).

I took a fine collection of photos, about thirty spools in all. When I eventually returned to Paris and exhibited my best in the Indian Embassy I was rewarded with some fair acclaim, wonderment and shared experiences. One gallery owner asked if I would make a retrospective showing of my Calcutta photos that I took back in 2006. I was proud of them, too. Yes, I said, I could be interested in that.

So now dear Ingrid, I hope that for answering your request, I have earned your undying love.

Truckloads of love,
Dad.

Then he went to sleep.

8

Calcutta

The Calcutta series Jim took in 2006 when he attended the twelfth International Calcutta Film Festival. After the festival, when most people had left, he remained to meet the photo challenge – always to capture a hoped-for unexpected moment, the essential character of place and peculiarities of its people, common people in their normal daily lives, sometimes in unusual circumstances, sometimes the very poor. He had considered the risk to his health by having hepatitis and typhoid vaccinations before he left home, and brought with him anti-malaria pills. He also had with him his faithful old workhorse Olympus camera, as well as twenty rolls of black-and-white film.

For his lodging during the festival he booked into the Fairlawn Hotel in Sudder Street, central Calcutta. Originally it was a large two-storey bungalow built in the 1780s by one William Ford, and since its conversion to a guesthouse during Victorian times it is still run in the British manner. Breakfasts are served on spotless pressed linen, usually cereal or boiled eggs, warm toast with butter and marmalade, teapots that have cosy covers, and bone china cups and saucers. Perennial old waiters in white uniforms with cummerbunds and turbans address you as 'sahib', bow, smile, ease your chair in for you, then melt away. Framed on the walls were photos of the royal family (favouring Diana), clippings of newspaper write-ups, and letters expressing gratitude and praise by some well-known English writers, including Graham Greene; ceiling fans fluttered.

On the wall of his room were lithographs of Chitapore Road and *A View of Chandpal Ghat* as they were back then; and in his drawer an old, well-thumbed print of Gideon's Bible. He liked the place for the way the large, high-ceilinged dining room gave onto a wide stone terrace with a lush jungle of palms and a giant banyan tree, whose mass of vines, like tentacles, wormed their way down its trunk to suckle the damp earth below. Cane chairs and tables were arranged so that in the half-light shading, maybe catching a bit of breeze, one had the opportunity of meeting other guests, or just relaxing with a book and ale. An inconvenience was the crows above. He came to detest the intrusion of these ravenous carnivores that roamed all over the city as if they owned it; cruel; black as sin; black-beaded inspectorial eyes; ugly accusatory squawking. One evening, in conversation, he was besmirched – vindictively, he thought – on his shoulder. The tourist he was talking with laughed and said she believed it was a sign of good luck. He wasn't in the mood, so he excused himself and went to bed.

Seeing three, sometimes four festival films each day, was exhausting, mainly because of the difficulty of getting not more than three or four hours' sleep each night. There was too much agitation in the city, and his nerves were excited.

What was immediately striking was the pressure of overcrowding; the manic blowing of horns; the air – an asphyxiating mix of methane gases and black dust; the grey, monsoon-stained walls and the smell of monsoon mould; and along the footpaths, especially in the dim night lighting, so many dark forms of families huddled together, living there. Standing in the middle of it, there was such visual overload it was difficult to know which way to turn – at 1/250th of a second you can grab it in only small doses. Yet the challenge, in the end, is to try to get it all, to capture what makes this extraordinary city what it is. Now, to try to describe in words what he saw and felt, that is an even greater challenge.

After the festival he needed to find another, cheaper and quieter, place. There was one nearby for about a quarter of the tariff of the Fairlawn, a room in a newly renovated hotel with a polished stone floor and a white-tiled bathroom, matching lacquered furniture, a clean and comfortable hard mattress, and breakfast delivered to your door. It was on the third floor at the back, away from the street noise.

Calcutta is the capital of Bengal. The first big influx into the city was from Bihar next door, in 1937 when there was a devastating earthquake. Six years later, a famine that killed 3.5 in Bengal had many seek respite in Calcutta; in 1965, with the partition of Pakistan, millions of Hindus fled the riots and many chose Calcutta. A cyclone and the dreadful drought in Bihar sent millions into Bengal; hundreds of thousands of Bengali farmers too, because of crop failures and unemployment, came to Calcutta in the desperate hope for a better life, and still do. Farmland is now being sold off for new factory buildings; that week, for example, just outside Calcutta to Tata Motors, which provoked violent opposition in Parliament (tables and chairs were thrown about) and street protests, but the deal had already been pretty well finalised. The city needs foreign investment, but only few foreigners would be enticed into a place like this that has only a short-term future. People are still pouring in and the city can't cope. It is an urban disaster. When the polar ice caps have melted, Calcutta, because it is built on a low-lying swamp, will, mercifully, be one of the first cities to go under the sea.

Along footpaths, sheets of plastic or reed matting tied to walls and propped with bamboo poles give cover for families who do all the things publicly that we do in privacy – bathe, cook, wash pots and dishes, eat, sleep and die.

"Hello Uncle," the kids cry out, "give money."

A cotton sheet might be laid out on the footpath to sit on and to define a patch of ownership, and a bit of curtain might give some privacy but nobody pays them much attention anyway. It is mostly the mothers there with their kids whilst the fathers are out working, or, more likely, looking for work – rickshaw puller, factory hand, labourer, hustling tourists that might earn them a commission; anything at all. She scours pots or gets a coal or kerosene fire going, or is slicing food or boiling rice for the evening meal. The kids laugh a lot and, like kids everywhere, play games – the girls, hopscotch or skipping, at the same time caring lovingly for their little sisters and brothers; and the boys play marbles or cricket, or sometimes fly kites from the rooftops. The young men, most of them seeming bored, sit around playing cards.

Jim got to know some of the street families by sitting and talking with them. Most had come from villages and many asked for help. He gave food each morning to some, the breakfast left at his door that morning – slices of toast and a couple of boiled eggs, small packets of jam and butter. In the afternoons, on his way home through the market, he sometimes picked up some rice, or lentils for *dahl* soup, about the only source of protein they get. The mothers always distributed the food to those most in need – the elderly or the sick, usually. The law of the slum is that you help one another. The trouble, when you give on the streets, is that little kids come in swarms and follow you as if you are the Pied Piper, begging and touching but never aggressively.

There was Mara, a strikingly good-looking woman who wore glasses and spoke English nicely. Her husband had died from alcoholism three years ago. She had six children, four of them in school, she proudly boasted; the other two sleeping by her side. The scraps of rag she scavenged she made into patchwork quilts to sell on the street. She showed how pressing the needle had cut into her thumb and forefinger. Asking around the market, Jim managed to find some thimbles.

On the other side of the street were a mum and her beautiful teenage daughter. One day, on his way home the girl said, "You pass us every day and you never talk to me." He said that he had said hello to her, and that on one occasion he gave some food. "Yes," she said, "but you don't talk to me like you do the others". Her English was good. He apologised and asked what it was she wanted to talk about. She said she watched him every day and wanted him to have sex with her. She didn't like black men, she said. She tugged at his arm and said he should come with her now, to a room she knew around the corner, where she would give him sex like he had never known – probably at a heavy price. A passer-by, an old man in a suit stopped near them, looking and listening. She lashed out at him – "You f*** off!" He slinked away.

What would life be like for them in the winter, I wonder, when the freezing Himalayan winds sweep down; and in summer during the monsoons when the temperature reaches more than a hundred, the humidity about the same, and when the city gets inundated with floodwater? The real tragedy for the poor would be if they lost hope and fell into despair. It is their visceral religious faith, I think, that binds them, not in hope so much as acceptance. For those born in poverty, those who have never known any different, it is, they believe, their fate. Their lives seem as normal as the seasons are extreme.

Throughout the day there is a maelstrom of traffic of every kind flooding in all directions – buses, cars, taxis, trucks, scooters, rickshaws, fully laden hand-pulled barrows, sometimes even herds of goats – the incessant noise of horns that could eventually drive you crazy. Calcutta is built on a black silt delta, its grain fine as powder, and when dried it swirls into the air as dust and clings to you. By about ten in the morning there is a black rug hanging over the city. On the streets there are the cloying smells of urine and excrement from open latrines, and sickening breath from drains. James felt so sorry for the poor traffic policemen, barely visible in the flurry of it all.

There was a health report in the Times Of India with the headline: *Kolcata Tops Lung Cancer Chart.* Besides lung cancer and haematological abnormalities, the article stated, genetic disorders and neural-behavioural problems are on the rise. Seventy per cent of Calcutta residents, rich and poor, suffer from respiratory problems. Another problem the government is trying to deal with is that of sewage and drainage disposal. On the city map, blue spots, like sores, showing the locations of the swamps, were where Jim saw the worst: shelters constructed on the mud with sticks and clad with matting or plastic sheeting. The swamps smelled of defecation, but above all was the ubiquitous, overpowering smell of methane. He saw a woman, her baby on her back, scouring cooking pots with the mud. How incredible the armour-plate immunity these people have developed and survived where no other form of life could. That they managed to make it even through infancy seemed miraculous. Why, of all places, did they choose to settle here, around the swamps? These images are scarred in his memory.

Many rivers from the mountainous north of India, including the Ganges, Brahmaputra and Jumna, flow down through hundreds of towns and villages, picking up all their outflows, then flood down into the many channels in this delta region of Calcutta. The untreated or partially treated sewage and waste water of Calcutta itself also seep into the rivers, swamps and ground water. After passing through Calcutta they discharge into the Bay of Bengal, where fishing boats go.

Most in the urban region now have access to water for bathing and cooking in their homes or from street pumps. The trouble with the pump water is that it comes from deep down in the ground, and although there are trace elements of arsenic (not enough, they say, to be dangerous), the lower the water table – and it is getting lower – the more traces there are to be found.

One day, Jim saw a young man in the city area spraying some green chemical named BETEX into pooled gutters to prevent the mosquito-spread of malaria. He told Jim he was part of a team that did every street systematically each week.

I am sorry about this, but I will go on. In his third week Jim was feeling the symptoms of a virus – stomach pain, lethargy, vomiting and headaches. Even that boiled egg – innocuous, he thought – made him sickeningly bilious for two days. He had to be very careful with everything. He restricted himself to imported foods such as packaged English porridge with boiled milk for breakfast, hermetically sealed New Zealand cheese, foreign biscuits and fruit. Then he lost the desire to eat anything at all and was feeling weak. He bought pills that didn't seem to be doing him much good. But he was getting some good photos of life on the streets.

He still wasn't getting his proper sleep. Thank God for the mercy of sleep for all those others, he thought, the city lying exhausted in the darkness of night, bandaged by dreams of better times. After midnight it was all so quiet. On approximately each hour there was the faint din from the city's timekeeper – the same tune as Big Ben, but flat as a frying pan – and sometimes the clacking of a distant freight train. A dog's sudden ghastly yelping, sounding like it was being disembowelled, would set off a chain of neighbourhood dogs but that racket would soon die down. At five o'clock, flowing from the minarets, was the call to prayer; at around 5.30 the crows that filled the trees would begin their ugly squawking; and then at six it was time for Jim to drag himself up again, splash his face, take his camera, lock his door, then descend into the cool air, the dawning light, the city unfolding.

At this time the footpaths were still covered with sleeping bodies tightly wrapped in mosquito-proof and rat-proof cotton gauze, looking like corpses ready for cremation. The footpath sweepers working around them with their whisk brooms brushed the debris into the gutters, foraging rats scuttled along the walls. Then would come the gutter sweepers with their shovels and barrows. They wheeled away the rubbish to a local dumping site, one of which was the end of Jim's street, creating a hill from one side to the other. The scavengers of the city would descend on these dumps; crows; sniffing wretched dogs; rats; and soiled women on bent knees – the 'rag-pickers', plucking bits of rag. The lowest form of life – often hairless grey skin with scabs, and God knows what writhing around inside them – were the dogs. The female dog was the hardest hit. She can be seen in the streets, wearily trailing three or four males, snarling, snapping, gnashing at them because they won't leave her alone. You can see by her condition that she has been through this most of her life. She can find refuge crouched under a parked car, while the others, tongues hanging out, sit and wait patiently for her to emerge. Thousands bitten by dogs die of rabies each year. The rats are corpulent. You see a lot of them in the rubbish pile too, dead, because there is a green powder spread around.

It is still early, and Jim is making his way towards the central food market. He stops to take tea with a small crowd on the footpath. A tea master (*chai wallah*) has everyone's respect. A small hand-thrown clay cup of tea costs two rupees (the new paper-thin plastic cups, cheaper to produce, are replacing the earthenware). The tea is white, very sweet, and gets its distinctive flavour from added cardamom and crushed ginger. The milk and water are mixed and heated over an open flame. Care is taken not to burn the milk whilst bringing the mixture to broil. It involves constant swirling of the pot, and after it broils and foams for a few seconds, the tea, sugar, etc. is added. The mixture then is poured into a large teapot for serving. The cooking pot is then replenished with water and put on the flame for the next serving. The tea is drunk as soon as it is made, the clay cups then thrown to the ground and smashed (a strict Hindu will never drink or eat from a vessel that somebody has already used). Jim salvaged some as souvenirs.

Further along the footpath around a street pump, semi-naked men are bathing with lots of lathering and scrubbing and snorting and brushing of teeth. Many people now are heading for the marketplace and the sky is spattered with the black of crows. In the middle of all this melee of pushing and shoving and honking of horns, it is hard to believe, three farmers with sticks are goading and keeping together a herd of maybe sixty goats on their way to the abattoir; hundreds of chickens in baskets are headed for the slaughterhouse or to the street market to be sold live, trussed and hung on handlebars, and wheeled away. At the market itself all the goods are passing from hand to hand: trucks are offloading bags or boxes of all the goods that the city needs – cereals and sugar grown locally, a big variety of fruit from Bihar, eggs from Kashmir, poultry from Bangladesh, meat from Andra, fish from Orissa, tobacco and betel from Patna, cheeses from Nepal, rice, flour, potatoes, etc. Sacks are carried away on backs or pushed on wheelbarrows or motor rickshaws, or piled high on trucks and buses, whatever, which is the main reason for the whirling black dust, the entanglements, and the deafening noise of honking horns. At its peak, at about midday, when the taxis and hand rickshaws are also participating, it is a collective madness and sends your head reeling.

Jim is caught up in it, getting good shots of all that is typical, but other extraordinary sights as well. He is having a field day. On footpaths some men are cooking vegetables in big pots over gas flames; others are rolling *bidis* (the dried-leaf cigarettes tied with cotton string); another is making *paan* (crushed betel nut mixed with ground dates and lime paste, all wrapped in a green leaf, which the Indians masticate and spit the ubiquitous red spit);

or cutting *khainee* (a revolting, rotten-smelling brown tobacco leaf mixed with lime powder, which is tucked under the tongue to taste its juice all day, causing permanent teeth discolouration and eventually mouth cancer. There are bearded old men wearing thick glasses, sitting cross-legged on neatly laid-out cotton sheets, tapping out translations and business letters on antique Remington typewriters (Jim is amused by what he read – pedantic in the British manner); a hunchbacked barber, who will also swab out your ears; men in singlets covered in black dust weighing and selling bags of coal; and another, because it's Friday, filling containers with rationed kerosene – 2 litres per family each week. A few deft chops with a machete and you have a coconut to drink from.

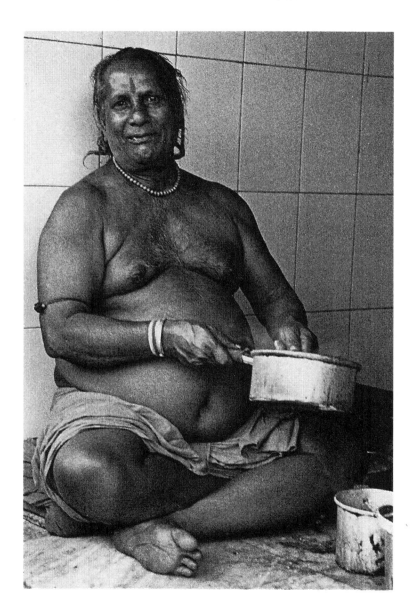

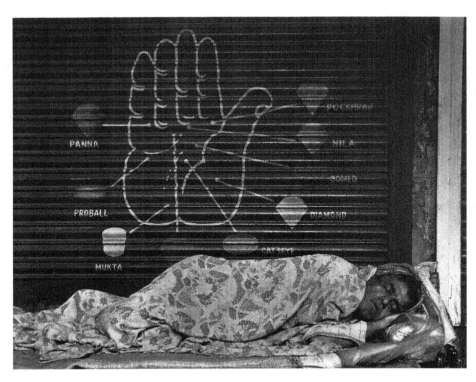

Along Banerjeee Road, skilled tradesmen – carpenters, painters, masons – sitting in the pale morning light, their tools of trade neatly arranged before them, are waiting to be hired. God knows, there is so much restoration and new building work that needs to be done (grand Victorian buildings have trees growing from their facades and their roofs falling in), but they wait there all day, most of them.

From one in a crowd, then another, Jim gets excited cries of "Hello sir, take photo, take photo!" each holding an imaginary box to his face and simultaneously pressing two shutter buttons, or another viewing him through simulated binoculars. "Take photo! Take photo!" they cry. He smiles and sometimes pretends to take some. The photo results don't seem to be of interest to them; it's the taking that delights them. Or the tinkle of a rickshaw bell --"Rickshaw sir? Mothers?" meaning the shrine to Mother Teresa, where a lot of Christian tourists want to go. "No, walking," Jim says, with a walking motion of his fingers, "Taking photos." He is conspicuous as a foreign visitor and so attracts beggars everywhere – you feel the gentle touch of an old woman on your sleeve and, with a furtive gesture, she whispers for help.

What is missing is the music he remembered years ago in Benares when the shrill sound of flutes and the thrilling girlish voice of Lata Mangeshkar drowned the streets. She was the Edith Piaf, the Maria Callas, and the Om Keltum of India. Maybe it was there, but he heard very little music in the streets of Calcutta.

Now, at around 11, with the sun so hot and casting dark shadows, he decides to take a break and go to where he usually does, Kalsa, the Sikh restaurant near where he is staying. A.P. Singh has gotten to know him, and likes him to sit next to him at the checkout so they can talk. His grandfather began the shop in 1937, and seven years ago it was left to him and his two brothers.

359

A.P., as he is known, has masculine good looks, dresses in Western clothing and a turban with a full beard going grey, and for such a burly man his voice is soft-spoken and educated. It is said that the family is one of the richest in Calcutta. To see him seated at the checkout reading an English newspaper, absent-mindedly signing vouchers or letters, nibbling a piece of chapatti, you wouldn't think so. He has a generous nature and seemed not to care about anything very much, not even his religion. In his friendly way, he talked about his two years of business school in San Francisco. He showed Jim places on his map he thinks he should visit, some to avoid, and if he wants shirts made to measure there is a tailor he knows who wouldn't cheat him. The shop is as clean as you'll get and provides Indian newspapers in English. On the breakfast menu is a tourist choice – cornflakes or porridge, peanut butter or baked beans on toast, fruit, Nescafe.

A.P. warns Jim of the health danger of staying too long in Calcutta. Jim goes to wash his hands and clear his nostrils.

One day, at lunchtime, like a sudden panic, a stream of excited street kids burst through his doorway and grabbed places around the bench tables. A big bloke wearing a blue *PEACE* T-shirt and a rucksack fell in behind them.

"Right," he shouted, "now I want yous all to sit down and behave your selves. Any mucking up and I'll have the owner chuck yous all out, OK, so settle down and keep quiet."

They didn't understand a word he was saying, of course. He came to A.P. and asked if he reckoned he could do a deal on twenty bowls of rice and dahl. Just then, for the word had got around, ten more streamed in and now the room was packed full. The guy rushed to the door and put up his arms to stop a further influx, shouting, "OK, that's it, that's enough, no more, finito!" He came back, exasperated and said, "You better make that thirty."

His girlfriend sitting near Jim said they'd just arrived a few days ago and Rob was appalled by how these people had to live. They were a couple from Sydney, he a parole officer. A blind old man and a haggard old woman walked in. "Better give them some too."

"Jeez," he sighed.

After breakfast Jim would go to his room, wipe the mask of black off his face and be horrified that, since that morning, it had again penetrated into all his fingernails. It was in his nose. God, he thought, what is happening to my lungs? He rinsed some clothing in the washbasin. He slept till two in the afternoon then got up to catch the light till four. After that hour the twilight suddenly became dingy and so the day's shoot was over. He returned to Kalsa for a Nescafe then back to his room, overcome with tiredness, to catch another couple of hours of sleep.

He decided he couldn't take the sleepless nights any more, so for the first time in his life he bought some sleeping pills. After a couple of days he was able to re-establish his normal pattern of nightly deep sleep from ten till five.

There was one Sunday morning, when he just couldn't get up to face another day, so he stayed in bed and watched Australia outclass England in the Third Cricket Test on TV.

From bamboo scaffolding high up a fellow with a tar brush was repainting a building white. James stood back to see how he was splashing the windows and the brass words in relief – *INDIAN MUSEUM* – as if he were drunk at a party. It was large and ornate, built during the reign of Victoria, quiet and soulless, as most museums are. In the foyer, larger-than-life and looking imperial was the statue of the Empress herself, dated 1878, and only few tourists.

It was pleasantly cooler inside. Entry was free. The biggest collection was in the geology section, where rocks and dirt from all over the world had been shovelled into hundreds of darkly lit glass cabinets, too high to properly see into. Pumice, the solidified froth of lava, is the only rock that floats on water. He was informed, too, that the difference between the radius of the Earth at each pole and the radius at the equator is only twenty-one kilometres. The small art room showed mostly works of some late twentieth century Indian painters attempting Modernism, very few of which, it seemed to Jim, showed much talent. Rabindranath Tagore, a Nobel laureate, no matter what talent he may have had as a poet, showed he had none for sketching and painting, or so it seemed. Jim was lethargic on that day too, so maybe it was just him.

After an evening nibble at Kalsa he sometimes joined a street crowd around the corner, all riveted to a TV watching cricket, urging India on, this time against South Africa live in Johannesburg. Cricket has enormous following in India, it is their second religion. In a narrow lane nearby he discovered the Juice Bar – pure juices blended while you waited by a pleasant young guy named Bijay. One evening, while sipping orange juice on the bench seat, watching swallows high in the updraught picking off insects, two lovely little girls he had gotten to know, Kiran and Sushi, came to sit and chat with him. They asked if he would buy them each a KitKat chocolate bar. After a while the man seated next to them politely excused himself and said he had been listening to the way Jim spoke English, and asked if he would be interested in doing an audition for a one-hour reading on national radio the following Wednesday. He said yes. The man would talk to the agent and let him know the next day.

He informed Jim the next day it was too late – the reading had already been arranged. Over the next few days, however, they got to know one another better. He said his name was Jack, and it turned out that he was the owner of the Juice Bar. He was young and handsome, suave, a flash kind of guy with longish, oily black hair, and one who obviously spent lavishly on clothes.

Being the owner of a small business and a new motorbike gave him status his friends looked up to. He had trained as a classical dancer and looked like it. His graceful movements suggested that he may have been homosexual, and also that he believed in efficiency. He invited Jim to his home to meet his quiet old mother, who invited him to sit and eat with them. Jack was supporting her, his brother, and his abandoned niece – a sweet, lively little girl. His father had been a factory owner but after his murder things went to pieces. They still had the big home, though, where the upper floors were rented out from time to time for marriage ceremonies. And there was the Juice Bar, which seemed to be doing pretty good business.

At the Goethe Institute, where there was a superb exhibition by a German portrait photographer, Jim received an invitation for two to a pop/rock concert to be given by a German quartet in the grounds of St. Xavier's College that same evening. He rang Jack and asked if he would like to come along. Jack turned up on his motorbike tastefully dressed in a flowing black-and-white silk shirt, flared black pants and matching black-and-white shoes, his shiny hair neatly held with two hair clips.

After the concert an English lady who was in the audience recognised Jim from the film festival and invited them both to come to the book launch that was happening right then at the British Council – a Ms Smith's *The Indian Diaspora*. They arrived late, unfortunately, when the last of the drinks were being served. Ms Smith's slim book with a thin paper cover, more like a bulletin, was an academic study full of statistics, diagrams, population flow charts, etc., so it wasn't surprising to see her appear as a straight-backed, middle-aged, spinsterish-looking lady who, for all Jim knew, might have been, though it seemed unlikely, one of the world's most charming people. The crowd was thinning and some were heading off to an informal gathering at the Bengal Club, the once-famous, unofficially exclusive non-Indian headquarters of the Raj. One member, a friendly Scotsman Jim had been talking with about the tribulations of the first convicts in Australia, and who was reddened with alcohol, invited them both to come along to the club as his guests.

Each with helmets then they headed off. They swung out into the churning traffic, winding and beeping their way through; they crossed a petrol station driveway; and at one point, at a bottleneck, even wove their way along a footpath. Jack was being foolhardy and showing off, having the time of his life, happy to be invited. But he rode with the sure control, anticipation and cunning he'd acquired over the years, though Jim came within an inch of his life when his elbow brushed a stationary car's just-opening passenger door.

They rode up the long, curved driveway to the lofty portico flanked with Doric columns. In the club's foyer, displayed in gilt lettering was the long list of names of all the past presidents going back to 1831, making it the oldest club in India. Up to 1967 the names were all British, then, mainly because of the riots in 1960, which sent a lot of the Brits packing, the names changed to Bengali.

Inside, in the main banquet room, was a quiet gathering of members and guests under glinting chandeliers. On one wall in ornate gilded frames were portraits of past presidents; on another, lithographs of famous Calcutta scenes such as Dalhousie Square, the Queen Victoria monument, people strolling in the botanical gardens, and an oil painting by Stubbs of a meeting at the Royal Calcutta Turf Club. The curtains were drawn over the large windows, candles shone softly upon the white napery of long tables, and laid out were stacks of plates, gleaming cutlery and four or five hot silver tureens. Liveried old servants offered drinks. Eventually Jim helped himself to a few slices of tender roast lamb and potato.

He found opportunities to introduce himself and Jack to a

few, but apart from the now happily inebriated Scot who had invited them, they seemed an unhappy lot, standing around in couples with pinched faces, buttoned up, not saying much, waiting, it seemed, till it was time to go home to their beds. Ms Smith was there. She had noticed Jim looking through her book at the British Council. He mentioned now the Indian coup that had taken place in Fiji ten days earlier, and she said yes, she'd heard something about that then turned away. The feeling Jim was getting was that he and Jack were not welcome; they were both being avoided.

When he returned from the toilet he saw that Jack was at the centre of the whole room's attention, everyone scowling. An official, who may even have been the club president himself, was castigating him. Jack had no right to be there, he was saying, and who had invited him, and if he wanted to dress like that he should go to a discotheque. The official was blushed with anger. Jack, apparently, wasn't the type that fitted the club's image, even on this one informal occasion. He wasn't British, for a start. Jim, it seemed, was acceptable. He hastened to Jack's rescue and explained that they had both just attended the British Council and had been invited here by a club member as his guests, a member who, when Jim looked around, was nowhere to be seen. He asked the official quietly if he didn't think it would have been more in keeping with the club's code of manners if he had taken his friend aside and explained quietly why he was being asked to leave, instead of creating this spectacle and causing such embarrassment. The man admitted his indiscretion and apologised. Jim and Jack left and went back to the Juice Bar, met some friends and had a good time.

Another recollection was the day Jim chose to venture into the Muslim Quarter. He could not tell with Muslim areas whether he was entering a minefield (for Moslems can get hostile even at the sight of a camera, due to a superstition that it has the power to steal one's soul), or a goldmine, because the Muslims are industrious and so the bazaars and workplaces could give some good photo opportunities.

To get there he needed to walk through a red-light area. The booths were dollhouse colours with bead-curtained doorways; the women, in chiffon and garish cosmetics, looked fierce and frumpy. He smiled a hello to some but they just glowered, as if it wasn't just him they hated, but all of mankind. One of them, with what looked like unruly coconut-fibre hair, if she'd poked out her tongue could have been Kali, Kali the Terrible. He feared if he attempted to take her photo she would have scratched out his eyes.

He then entered lanes of goldsmiths where, traditionally, they have always been, in tiny rooms with dim lighting, seated on floors, working molten gold with pipettes and tiny flames. In other rooms there were sparks flying from bike frames being welded and new knives being honed; from others came the repetitive noise of metal plate being pounded into machine parts. Young boys with crochet needles were painstakingly fixing sequins to embroidered saris. In a lane at an outdoor tap there was a long queue of women with earthenware pots; schoolchildren could be heard reciting verses from the Koran. A new Mosque of the most artless architecture covered in a mosaic of broken glazed tiles loomed, sandals strewn all around its shaded doorway. It was obvious now that he had arrived in the Muslim Quarter.

In the marketplace, laid out on a footpath bench, were freshly chopped goats' heads whose eyes looked like polished marbles, and next to them, hanging on hooks, goats' shanks and flesh being picked at by the same crows that had possibly been scavenging in rubbish dumps that morning. The butcher nonchalantly waved them away with his knife while he continued slicing. He was more insistent with Jim when he saw him across the street raise his camera. A goat tied up there to a post, the next in line, couldn't believe his luck as he munched juicy leaves being thrown his way by the cauliflower seller – his last supper. A loud cry that Allah is great rose up and was amplified across the city, across the whole Islamic world. Jim didn't know where he was on the city map.

"Hello, sir, where coming?" they asked.

They were concerned that he might be American.

"Ah, Australia – good country."

Some didn't mind that he took their photos while they were doing things. Some even allowed him their portraits.

The peculiar thing about some post office stamps is they have no glue on the backs of them. Jim said to the postmistress, "These stamps have no glue on them", and she said she knew. Well, could he have some?

"We don't have any," she said.

Did she know where he could get some nearby?

"No."

Indians still love Charlie Chaplin. A cinema in the heart of the city is called the Chaplin Cinema and beside it is a small park called Charlie Chaplin Park. The entry gates have two large, black cut-out Charlie Chaplins welded to them, and flanking each are Charlie's funny shoes, exaggerated to the size of a pair of sleeping Brahmin bulls; the roof over, his bowler hat. On underground station platforms there were suspended TV monitors, and during every day of Jim's stay there were continuous reruns of Charlie Chaplin films. Slapstick humour drives Indians mad with laughter.

The underground Metro line, which runs north to south through the city centre, provides a great service and, of course, each carriage is packed like bunched asparagus. There is a sign at every station entry saying, *PHOTOGRAPHY IS PROHIBITED.*

He was followed down the stairs by a railway official and told he could not take photos. It was OK, Jim said, he had read the sign and had no interest whatsoever in taking photos in the Metro. The official told him to remove the batteries from his camera, and Jim told him to get lost. He was on his way to Kalighat Station, way out near the southern extremity of the city, to see the temple of Kali, Kali the Terrible.

Between Kalighat Station and the temple there is a crowded bazaar that sells religious icons – Kali, mostly – and garish paraphernalia. Kali, or Durda, as she is more commonly known here in Bengal, or Kali the Terrible, as she is famously known, wife of Shiva the Destroyer, has devilish, staring eyes, her tongue dripping with blood, a cobra entwined around her neck and garlanded with a string of shrunken human skulls. She is a sight to behold, a real sweetie. Mythology has it that when Kali died, Shiva was both grief-stricken and angry. He placed her on his shoulders and went stamping around the world in a dervish dance of mourning, getting madder and madder. To stop him, Vishnu, another divinity, cut the corpse into fifty-two pieces and scattered them across the face of the Earth. The little toe of her right foot was discovered near the Bay of Bengal, and a temple was built there with an attendant village. The village was named Kalikata, later to be known as Calcutta, and now Kolkata.

Jim wanted a pilgrim's hand trident, the three branches representing the three main divinities – Brahma, Vishnu and Shiva. Instead of the kitschy new, polished-brass ones displayed, he wanted one that looked more authentic, one that had weathered the travel of pilgrimage. He asked around and a trail led him to a backroom where he found three steel relics that had been hand-forged. He bought all three.

Outside the walls of the temple was an enormous crowd, queued, shuffling, ordinary people in street dress, young men in suits, most garlanded in marigolds, and young women in embroidered saris and bangles. Once inside, each in turn came to face their goddess, a statuette ensconced in a small candlelit shrine, deathly white, glaring, her red, bloodied tongue protruding, the entwined cobra and shrunken skulls, and a veil of incense smoke which made her only half visible and all the more mysterious. Each devotee uttered a few words of prayer, laid offerings of sweets or spices on fresh palm leaves, tinkled a bell, then moved on. Jim had nothing to offer, and for a frightening moment he made eye contact with her. In the courtyard, as a sacrifice to Kali, he saw, to his horror, goats and sheep having their throats cut and their heads chopped off, disembowelled, their skins peeled back, their flesh sliced and then given to a bramble of outstretched hands. Once upon a time the sacrifices were humans. A Brahmin priest, supposedly, came to Jim for an 'offering' of money for maintenance. He showed his chagrin when he refused. Jim was glad to get out.

At the ghats nearby (wide steps that lead down to the river's edge for praying and bathing, and where cremations take place), again there was that putrid smell of swamp, black mud and excrement. Visible in the river were flotsam scum and humanoid forms wrapped in cloth. Kneeled on the steps at the water's edge, beautifully sari-ed women were wiping away the scum to cup some water to carry up the steps to sprinkle on the heads of their daughters or their mothers – a sacred blessing, an amazingly resilient faith in archaic spiritualism. Three large, rotting hulls were roped end to end to form a bridge to a village on the other side. Jim stepped carefully across onto the middle one to get some shots back at the *ghats*. He got one and was zooming in for a second when he was suddenly set upon by a man, not angry, but with fire in his eyes, who kept saying he was sorry, he was sorry, because I think he'd made up his mind he was going to have to push Jim in. He had a very firm grip on both Jim's camera and his shirt. Jim was terrified. He kept saying that *he* was sorry and, in panic, managed to break free, skip across to the first boat, off, up the steps and away.

He walked back to the railway station. Behind it, along a dirt track to where the city was thinning, there was a confluence of the Metro line and state lines. A dilemma. He decided to follow the latter. He stepped along its sleepers and eventually, to his amazement, found there was a community living in flimsy huts strung out along the tracks, so perilously close that each time a train came by, which was frequently, many had to press themselves against their walls. The trains gave a loud warning sound and then slowly passed by. He couldn't believe it. Why would anyone choose to live beside a train track? Children, laughing, excited, came running to see him; mothers, holding babies on their hips, curious about this stranger in their midst, stood timidly by; a tethered cow and some chickens didn't seem to notice anything unusual. To win the confidence of the kids he let some of them look through his lens while he zoomed in and out on their friends, their little hands clutching from everywhere. A youth came forward like a diminutive chieftain, bowed, and told Jim to follow him to where they would take tea. Jim walked just behind him – he was his trophy – and more and more people joined the throng, some of the children jostling one another to take turns at holding Jim's hand.

They arrived at a small, framed hut. Jim took off his shoes, bent down and entered. He sat where indicated on some reed matting. It was a family shrine, only big enough to accommodate six or seven at most. The air smelled of incense, and placed centrally on a small cupboard sprinkled with grains of rice was a statuette of Kali. On one wall were garish posters of Ganesh the elephant god, Hanuman the monkey god, David Beckham the football god, famous Indian cricket gods, and Bollywood film stars. On the floor in one corner, shouting for attention like a precocious brat, was a salesman advertising soap powder on a tiny black-and-white TV. Piercing through holes in the wall matting and resting on the floor were slanted rods of golden sunlight. Soon a little girl appeared carrying a tray of hot sweet tea in clay cups and a small packet of biscuits. Jim was thirsty.

They couldn't speak English. All Jim could do during tea, with many small faces peering in, was smile approvingly and feel embarrassed about the hole in the toe of his right sock. If only he'd had some gifts in his bag – some kangaroo pins, euro coins, or some other small souvenirs they probably would have cherished. The TV was quiet now, a misty love scene in an episode of Bollywood soap this time.

A youth entered, squeezed himself on the floor beside Jim, and nonchalantly began blending some hashish and tobacco.

"Hashish," Jim said knowingly, and smiled awkwardly.

Minutes after the smoke Jim thought he could hear the sound of a train. It was a train, a train coming in their direction, a train getting louder and louder, closer and closer, its horn blaring, the earth trembling. He showed his alarm. Everyone laughed. Where the children had been standing just seconds ago in sunshine, just a metre away, dark huge iron wheels went slowly racketing by. Surrounded by so many gods and urchins staring at him, teatime got more and more bizarre and claustrophobic. He got up to go out and walk. He was escorted around the village, meeting everyone's big eyes and cautious smiles.

Continuing his walk along the railway sleepers, much to his consternation he could see from the bridge he was crossing, between the sleepers, there was a busy roadway below. At about midway he stopped – I don't know why– looked back, and to one side saw something that made him gasp and nearly lose his balance. It was an image he knew he would one day want to show the world: on the top of a mound rising from a creek, some activity was taking place among the community of a small pottery village, and smoke that had just begun rising from the kilns was creating a thin hazy smudge across a background row of ancient, dark-stained Hindu temples. Like a charcoal sketch. To get the extra height he needed for his composition, he had to pull himself up the steel structure of the bridge and cling there like a monkey – the most dangerous of all his photos. The sun behind him was at just the right angle. Click, click.

One day he walked the mammoth Hooghly River Bridge, spanning the Ganges from Calcutta proper to Howrah city. The main interstate railway station terminates there and is always intensely crowded. Beside the station are a large tent-covered vegetable market, the city's biggest flower market, and more excruciatingly dire poverty. In front of the station, alone, was a thin young man whose filthy nakedness and dusty hair showed he never washed. He was calm and seemed to be in awe of everything around him, as if hallucinating on LSD. He slowly reached down and picked up a speck of dust, studied it closely, then put it into his mouth. Only the insane or holy men are ever seen publicly naked, most of them quite harmless.

Turning from him Jim found another interesting character standing by, an old bearded man, noticeable because he was gesturing to the sky, in communion with a god, it seemed; no words, just figments and gestures, totally absorbed in his own realm. He had a nice face. The cloth around his body was tied with string. Fascinated, Jim drew him close up with his lens and rattled off several shots. His physiognomy was oddly affecting in the way his mouth changed shapes in the thicket of his beard. The man turned and noticed Jim, and then brought him into *his* focus. He approached slowly, carefully, staring at Jim, and then gripped his arms so tightly he was in pain. And scared. An inch away from his face, he stared deeply into Jim's eyes and with great passion kept repeating the words, "Godfather, godfather."

He then released his grip, buried his head on Jim's chest and sobbed uncontrollably. What to do? People were watching with casual interest. With his arm around him and gently patting his back, Jim tried to reassure him that everything was OK.

Afterwards Jim asked a boy if he knew who the man was and he said he claimed he was Bin Laden.

It was the Chinese traders who introduced the hand-pulled rickshaw to Calcutta in the early twentieth century. It was the only city in India that had them. Mao banned them in China. The rickshaw *wallahs* are a humble, hard-working, trustworthy class of people. You wouldn't think, by how typically stringy they are and how old they look, they would be capable of such strenuous work every day in such difficult conditions. They have carried schoolchildren through flooded streets and lanes, the sick to hospital when no other form of transport could budge, and many, many tourists. For everybody the rickshaw has been an integral part of the city's transport system. And for the city itself it is, in a way, its symbol. Remember the scenes in Satyajit Ray's *Apu Trilogy* and *Parineeta* in the '60s, and more recently the slum scenes in *City of Joy*?

Since neither of his hands can be freed to sound a horn, every rickshaw puller has a small brass bell tied to his wrist or a thumb, so jogging along he jingles like Santa Claus. He also uses the bell when he is parked at the kerb to tap on the shaft to rouse a potential customer. They used to do it to Jim in his street until they got to know he lived there and that he was a walker everywhere he went. They would still wave to him, though, and cry "Hello, sir!" every time he passed. One night, late, when a group of them were sitting and smoking, waiting for business, Jim surprised one by saying he was going home and he wanted a rickshaw. The old man jumped to it.

"No, no, I pull you, " Jim said. He wanted to know what it was like.

The old man hesitated at first, not sure, then took Jim seriously and climbed on board. Jim asked to wear his bell, then off he trotted, jingling all the way up to the end of his street. The others were highly amused. Approaching his door, puffed, he realised, with such momentum and no brakes, it required much effort if one needed to suddenly come to a stop. He put the wallah down and said, "OK, that will be fifty rupees", which was extortionate. The old man's serious look was wiped away with the fifty-rupee note Jim handed him.

Now the government wants to abolish the rickshaw.

"We have to end once and for all this humiliating man-pulling-man beastliness," says the chief minister. It is expected they will be phased out over the next year. Then where will the wallahs find work? There is talk that electric ones could replace them, but they never could, not really.

Near the end of his sixth week, Jim was really at the end of his tether. Anything he ate only fed his vomiting and diarrhoea, so he stopped. He sat sprawled on the ground against a cartwheel, nursing his hunger, too weak to move. Two crows were taunting him to get up and leave. Home was where he needed to be.

Before leaving Calcutta, however, he was anxious to see the results of his photography. A long-established photo supply shop, Bourne & Shepherd, which was the only local supplier of quality black-and-white film, recommended a Mr Bikash Bose as a highly competent darkroom professional. Jim met him at his home laboratory, saw some of his work and gave him one roll to try him out. The result was excellent. He then gave him the whole twenty-seven rolls to develop and contact-print. A lot of the shots were good, some exceptional, enough to have made it all worthwhile.

Then he had to leave. He phoned Emirates and was told there was a flight that evening, and with his standby ticket there was a good chance he would get it, the only catch (there has to be a catch) being a seven-hour stopover wait in Dubai. He was out at the airport by mid-afternoon, waiting, desperate for home.

9

Yoko

Steaming along rue de Rivoli on roller skates, a full pack on her back, heading in the direction of Istanbul, a little old grey-haired granny. In the same afternoon sun, a leaf-green Department of Sanitation truck spraying the air with all the colours of a rainbow. Taped to drainpipes and pinned in *boulangeries* home-made notices, sometimes in the handwriting of a child (a lost cat or dog), and often students (*jeune femme, Polonaise, serieuse avec experience)* wanting some hours for house cleaning, ironing, looking after children, walking dogs, reading to old-age persons – anything at all. On a wall, a crayon drawing of a figure with long hair, full breasts and male genitals, and another, fiendishly cutting open his stomach. In the same afternoon sun, Yoko is on her way for her English lesson.

A funny thing about Yoko is that she learned French from a Scotsman while she was living in Edinburgh and so speaks it not very intelligibly with a Japanese/Scottish/French/English accent. Something else: she has proper nouns for each thumb – Thingamejig and Thingamebob – and she can sing *London Bridge is Falling Down*. She is one of Jim's students. She is very sweet, pretty as a geisha, lips like cherry petals, and, as he soon found out, has a sense of humour that is delightfully childish. She writes in English for a Japanese publisher. The book she was writing when they first met was entitled, *Simple Conversation with Your Dog*. Her English needed a bit of tidying up – well, a lot, actually. She asked Jim if he could help her with it. It had lines in it like *You are sleeping like a baby*, and *Wake up you are running in your dreams again*. They worked out together, instead of *You are a spoiled dog*, a good alternative would be *You are a pampered pooch*. She asked if he could give her and her friend Mitsuyo English lessons each Sunday. Jim suggested they meet in Café Beaubourg, next to the Pompidou Centre.

The café has a large floor area with big columns, a double-height ceiling and a wide stair that curves up to an open mezzanine; one glass wall opens onto a terrace. Its interior design has the hallmark of a well-known French designer: serving as a recurring theme throughout – a whim probably – there are small square holes in the walls, columns, and chairs; in the paved white floor and in some of the white marble table tops, black scalene triangles are inlaid; the chairs are of moulded timber, clunky and comfortable; the waiters serve in black suits and black bow ties.

On this Sunday afternoon only few are present, and a tinkling piano is playing *Sad Movies Always Make Me Cry*. Near the doorway a made-up transvestite has on her table an *omelette au fromage* and on her lap a sleeping, good-natured poodle; near the stairs a dapper man in a white linen suit, while perfunctorily feeding his mouth with a Caesar salad, gives his attention to Le Monde; a spectacled man sips his coffee, looks up to think for a moment, then continues his writing, and Jim, too, earlier than usual, is seated with his camera, reading the latest edition of The New York Review of Books. He circles the advertisement in the Personals column: *Scintillating, sexy, cerebral, seeks starry knight in battered armour living in Parisian chateau with good sound system.*

"*Bonjour, monsieur, ça va?*" Pascal, who knows his habit, smiling, places his *café noisette* and croissant.

"*Bonjour Pascal, oui, ça va, merci.*"

The tables and chairs outside look onto the large, cobbled square that serves as a public stage for buskers. On the Pompidou Centre's facade is draped a large photo portrait of Henri Cartier-Bresson, advertising a retrospective exhibition of his life's work. On the far side of the square is the Brancusi Museum, and on its exposed roof a large flock of pigeons every day huddle in wait for the whiskered old man who feeds them. He scatters a bagful of bread and is momentarily lost in the frantic mêlée; he snarls and throws curses at those with cameras.

Most customers on the terrace are watching the passing parade, so Jim too, this time, not really in a reading mood, goes outside. As two American women stand to leave, the one with a shoulder bag knocks a glass onto the ground. Everybody turns and looks. Jim slips into their place. Pleasant sounds of a Chinese lullaby can be heard drifting in the air. Someone is, or had been, smoking a cigar.

It is remarkable how tattooing has become such a fashionable art form, and how many have taken to roller-skating and fold-up scooters. There is a world of buskers – jugglers, musicians, mime artists, live statues, caricaturists, and a wild-eyed spray-can artist depicting Martian landscapes with gushing waterfalls and the moons of Phobos and Deimos. Monsieur L'Oiseau, selling bird whistles as usual, is being ignored by the birds because his chirping and cheeping sounds don't make sense; a magician in a white suit, white gloves, a panama hat and a curled moustache performs his white magic with a white rabbit; one wearing her clothes inside out, and with painted red cheeks and a cherry nose, recites poems by Baudelaire; a young man hobbles by with an exaggerated spastic walk – his way, perhaps, of getting attention, like the American woman who smashed her glass to the ground. Jim sneaks a sideways glance to his left onto pages 102 and 103 of *Mein Kampf*; on his right a young woman with a Mickey Mouse tattoo, writing a postcard, looks English; a telephone rings – *"Oui, allô"*. Just beyond, on the square, seated on his collapsible stool, a thin middle-aged Chinese man with a pained, stuck-on smile is bowing sweet, traditional lullabies – with eyes closed, one could almost imagine the serenity of countryside: misty hills, rice fields, and a boatman passing by. He has been playing there for at least an hour. Many of the bemused passers-by, too, want to join in the fun: one on roller skates, plugged into his Sony, shares publicly what is going on inside his head; two worried-looking Ashkenazim dressed in black, whiskered, pale as nuns, dodge through the crowd in haste.

Suddenly, a loud, explosive bang goes up and with it, like shrapnel, a flurry of pigeons. They circle twice – a tumult of leaves in a whirlwind – the whimpering sound of their wings overhead, their air-cushioning descent, the flutter of splashdown, then, on spindly pink legs, like little wind-up toys or typewriters they resume their normal nodding and strutting.

A couple and their daughter arrive and take the now-vacant table beside Jim. Aristocratic-looking, they could be Swedish – he, a count, perhaps, or a champion at polo; she, not so attractive, tight-lipped and in sunglasses, takes no interest in the surroundings; she takes out a cigarette. Not a word passes between them. There may be another woman. Their flaxen-haired daughter – seven, eight, maybe, very beautiful in her white-collared navy-blue dress, shiny black shoes and long white socks – has before her an iPhone, an orange juice with a straw and her own semicircular arrangement of sugar cubes. Jim makes wide-eyed, friendly faces at her, mouthing *"Bonjour"*, and *"Comment va tu?"*, and with more persistence and raised eyebrows, *"Ça va?"* Her father smiles but she, with that sophisticated, European, preadolescent maturity, probably wondering why a grown person should want to behave like this, ignores him. *Noblesse oblige.* She'll become just like her mother, he thinks – rich and stuck-up. As they get up to leave she slurps the last drops of her juice and reaches back and pockets the tip.

A thin, unshaved drunk staggers up to the Chinese musician, finds focus, bends down, picks up his bowl, empties the coins into his hand, gently puts it down, then staggers off. The Chinese man's face does not change – still the inscrutable smile – but his music does, to a racy version of *Frère Jacques*, then a very feisty *Jingle Bells*. Sitting there in his chair, Jim feels that he is the nucleus of all the forces orbiting around him. Idling time away like this is good relaxation and good for making notes.

And there is Yoko – she has arrived. He waves to her. She lights up, waves back and comes to him. They embrace. A little dragonfly clasp is nestled neatly in her hair.

"Well, Mr Scallywag, how are you?"

"I'm absolutely gorgeous, thank you. I might not look it, but I feel it.

And you? You look gorgeous."

"You too, you do look gorgeous," she says.

They go inside and sit.

"And what have you been up to this week?"

"All the mischief I could find," he says (this is all part of the fun), and that he had just spent the last hour people-watching and eavesdropping.

"Eavesdropping?"

He explains.

She presents him with her usual neatly wrapped gift for her teacher, not an apple this time but a punnet of the season's perfect strawberries.

"You are the milk of human kindness," he tells her, which is new and confuses her. He explains that it is an idiomatic expression. She then presents her just-published book of *Simple Conversations with Your Dog*, and shows that on the back page is a printed acknowledgement of him for his assistance.

When she asks Jim about his daughter, he says that she is over the moon with her new son.

"Over the moon with her new son?"

Mitsuyo could not come today, she says, because she had to go back to Japan for an emergency – her father's village was struck by an earthquake and, although his home was destroyed, he was OK, though rather shaken Yoko is unaware that she has just made a pun.

"A pun?"

Jim explains what a pun is, or in French, a *jeu de mot*. He gives examples of French puns: for the painter Ingres, his hobby was playing violin, and so one's hobby, any hobby, might be referred to as a *violon d'Ingres*. There is a particular restaurant in Paris called Le Violon Dingue, which sounds much the same and means 'The Crazy Violin'. Similarly, another restaurant called Le Coude Fou – The Crazy Elbow – is a play on *coup de foudre* – to be struck by lightning, or love at first sight.

He asks about her new accommodation. It is small, she says, but adequate. "Beggars can't be choosers," she says with a smile – an aphorism from last week's homework. Jim tells her briefly about his meeting in the gym with Sonia and the work he has just completed on her house down south in a town called Sablet. They order *deux boules de glace* to supplement their strawberries.

Yoko suddenly remembers and tells Jim excitedly that she contacted her best friend in Kyoto, Mori-san, a practising Buddhist monk. She told Mori-san about Jim, her English teacher, an Australian architect who has studied the traditional Japanese home but has never been to Japan. Guest accommodation in the monastery would normally not be permitted, but, yes, he said, because Jim is her good friend, he can come and stay for two months if he wished. He asked only that Jim bring two tubes of French-brand toothpaste and two large jars of Nutella – a plump monk, by the sound of it, and with shaved head probably resembling the Dalai Lama. It sounds too good to be true. Jim says he would love to go in the springtime, in cherry blossom time. It would be another photo challenge.

"*Voila, monsieur.*"

"And are you reading a good book at the moment?" she asks.

He happens to be rereading Nabokov's autobiography.

"As a child he developed an interest in Lepidoptera, winged insects, moths and butterflies particularly, and throughout his life searching for them became a passion, travelling far and wide to discover, capture and describe rare examples. Their protective mimicry fascinated him. The caterpillar of the lobster moth, for example, in infancy looks like bird's dung. When a butterfly is disguised to look like a leaf, not only are all the details of a leaf beautifully rendered, but sometimes markings resembling grub-bored holes are also part of its chicanery."

"Butterfly is a funny word," says Yoko.

"Yes, it is neither a fly attracted to butter, like a bee to honey, nor flying butter."

"Flutterby" would be better," Yoko suggests.

"What is the Japanese word for butterfly?" Jim asks. He wants to make comparisons of word sounds of the same thing in different languages.

"*Batafurai,*" she says.

"For Latin peoples the sounds of the names for things are usually soft and lyrical," Jim says.

"The word butterfly, for example, in French it is *papillon*, *farfalla* in Italian, *mariposa* in Spanish. In German, *die schmetterlinge* sounds more like the name of a mechanical wind-up toy."

They talk about prepositions, the words that express relations of one word with another – the smallest words and for some the most difficult to learn. He suggests they go and shop for prepositions.

"I would be delighted," she says, and, to show off, "what a jolly good idea", the Scottish coming through.

"L'addition, Pascal, s'il vous plâit."

They leave.

BHV nearby is the biggest department store in Paris. Among many other things, they got a guarantee *on* a non-stick fry pan, prices *on* a range of bathplugs, and in the lighting section, information *about* new energy-saving forty-watt light bulbs. With Jim's prompting, Yoko asked the salesman, "How many Frenchmen does it take to change a light bulb?" He didn't know. He actually didn't know what she was talking about. He looked questioningly at Jim.

Walking away, Jim estimated maybe three or four because of the red tape you have to go through, 'red tape' meaning bureaucratic procedure.

'Bureaucracy', he explained, "like 'bizarre', is one of the most French of the many words that have come into the English dictionary."

From BHV, Yoko had to leave to attend her Spanish lesson. He reminded her to please inform Mori san that he would love to be his guest and that he would like to go next springtime.

With his camera slung on his shoulder and in good humour, Jim decided he would take a stroll down to the river. Geneviève, a neighbour, dressed colourfully and holding a bunch of assorted flowers, was pleased to see him. She reminds him that next Tuesday will be the opening of her exhibition.

A favourite of Jim's is Rue du Pont Louis-Philippe, an always-quiet residential street with interesting shops, one with art papers – hand-pressed papers and Venetian marbled papers with exquisite designs and colours; another, calligraphic stationery; and two others display unusual old musical instruments. A Japanese arts and crafts shop is opposite. There is a good view from here of the Pantheon profiled high up on the distant hill, Mont du St. Etienne, in the Fifth Arrondissement.

Hanging from a bracket over a doorway was a red-painted back plate of a violin, advertising *LUTHIER – REPARATION ACHETERIE EXPERTISE,* a shop that makes lutes and sells and repairs stringed instruments. Over the years, the traditional lute-maker has learned to turn his hand to all the orchestral stringed instruments.

Two violins were displayed in the front window, one cut away to show the details of its construction, and the other, printed on water-stained paper an elaborate workshop drawing of a famous violin: the numeric geometry of its convex front and back plates, its internal structural details with dimensions, and doubled full-size details of its bridge, scroll and turning pegs – entitled *Antonio Stradivari, 1724.*

On entering there was a tinkle of the doorbell and an immediate rush of varnish. The door closed itself behind Jim with the same tinkle. The interior was deep and narrow. It was, in fact, a workshop.

Along one wall over a workbench was a tidy arrangement of chisels in ascending order, as well as an array of fret saws and wood files and, incongruously, hanging from a nail, a full complement of a white horse's tail. On the bench, just beneath the jaws of the vice, fine as pollen, was a small cone of sawdust; close by, glued and clamped and waiting to set, was a recuperating violin. Displayed on shelves along the opposite wall were the instruments awaiting adoption. Were they discards of untalented children, Jim wondered, or heritage, perhaps, disposed of by the beneficiaries of deceased estates? And, being members of the same string family, they all had the same ruddy complexion, large and small alike. The cellos, shapely maidens, hopeful as wallflowers, sat primly in line on a middle shelf, waiting; a whole orchestra of violins and violas peered down from above like well-disciplined children, quietly attentive to all the shoptalk about Paganini, Isaac Stern and Yehudi Menuhin, and of standing ovations in famous concert halls around the world. Lying about on the floor like hibernating bears were two grandfather double basses – because they are so big and clumsy and don't do much more than snore at the back of the orchestra they were the least likely to go. From a small radio tuned to Radio France Classique, between classical recitals, a musical voice advertised double-glazing, or proffered retirement homes for old-age pensioners.

Monsieur Arguence, an elderly Frenchman from the Auvergne, worked alone, has done so since his son left to play in l'Orchestre de Paris. Happy, he seemed to be, his amiable corpulence neatly wrapped in a dark blue cotton apron, his complexion also ruddy, his hair thinning, and white like his toothbrush moustache. A wooden pencil was visible in his breast pocket, and perched on his nose, a cursive double-O pair of spectacles, all of which gave him a resemblance of Geppetto, Pinocchio's father.

Monsieur Arguence was bent over a small, wet oilstone, expertly sharpening the blade of a chisel. Jim asked if it would disturb him if he talked with him about his family of musical instruments.

"Bien sûr Monsieur, avec plaisir."

He seemed happy that Jim was curious.

Incredulously, Jim said he thought the classic centuries-old form of the violin was invariable.

"Mais non, monsieur, pas du tout!"

To him they differed quite significantly, and to compare them he took two down from the shelf. Their proportions *were* obviously different, and in comparing the convexity of plates, both front and back, they were subtly different; and the neck of the baroque example did not bend away from the body like the modern example. What they had in common was that the front plate was nearly always made of spruce (the best grown in the Balkans), and the back plate, maple. The fingerplate on the neck was always ebony.

"Did the viola evolve as a different species from the violin?"

"What is it about the Stradivarius that makes it so special? If it was simply a matter of form then couldn't it be replicated exactly, measurement for measurement?"

"The form, yes, could be copied," Monsier Arguence explained, "with the same quality of craftsmanship, but the quality of the wood was imperative: the fact that the Spruce tree from which it came was more than two hundred years old, and coming from a freezing climate meant the wood was extremely dense; and then if you add another 250 years for the age of the violin itself, well, you have a very rare instrument indeed. The way the timber was seasoned was also important, of course, and frequent use over time improved its tonality. *Et voila.*"

And the best bowstrings, he said, are cut from the tails of Mongolian horses.

There was the tinkling sound of another customer. Jim thanked him, wished him a good day and bade him au revoir.

From a cobbled laneway Jim came upon the grey stone steps that lead up to the doors of Église St. Gervais, one of Paris' oldest Gothic churches. Sprawled there in her black dress and gypsy shawl was the same wretched fat woman who was always there, begging for alms, the same feigned forlorn and pinched pitiable look.

"*Une petite piece, s'il vous plaît, Monsieur.*"

The bells' chiming announced the beginning of the afternoon service. In fulfilling their daily sacramental duty an order of monks and nuns ascended the steps, passed through the portico and into the nave to occupy the front rows of seats. The young woman who entered just before Jim lit a fresh candle with a wax taper, dabbed the font of holy water, crossed herself from left to right before the crucifix, then found her own place among the small congregation. Jim entered unceremoniously. The height and volume were enormous. The light was dim and the air cool, the smell was of prayer books, smoke, candle wax and age-old mustiness sweetened by Abyssinian myrrh.

A stone tablet was fixed on the northern wall, and engraved in perpetuity the words:

LES ILLUSTRES SERVITEURS DE DIEU
PAROISSIENS DE ST. GERVAIS
Louise de Marillac
Fille de Charité
Décédé à L'âge de 65 ans
1649
DE PROFUNDIS

Beside the tablet hung the time-darkened painting of *The Adoration* by Claude Vignon. It was a depiction in dim lighting of Mary holding her baby child and an elderly woman dressed in black kneeled before her in prayer. On the floor before the painting, an elderly woman strikingly similar and dressed in black was also kneeled in prayer.

Jim found quiet seclusion in a pew in the side chapel of St. Jean-Baptiste. On the sunlit floor were shadows of the breeze-blown branches outside, stroking the flagstones with impossible softness; glass of exuberant reds and blues depicted fragments of biblical history – parables and saints in Galilee and Capernaum. A dark man burdened by some misgiving grumbled as he hobbled by; a young tourist couple spoke in whispers.

A tall, handsome, robed priest appeared. He took his place at the altar. Behind him two flames were flickering, and between them stood a golden crucifix. With affected magisterial voice, he solemnised the holy sacrament, invoked the word of God and intoned prayers. The congregation murmured confirmations. The voices of the choir rose in glorious psalmodic harmony, floated, and then softly died away.

Jim got up and left unnoticed.

Outside, the supplicant, the same forlorn look: *"Une petite piece, s'il vous plaît, monsieur."*

In daylight now, with a fresh breeze coming from the river, in the clear blue sky a speck smaller than a silver bullet scribed two parallel chalk lines in a long, perfect curve. Slowly, slowly, they dissipated into smudges and within a minute were gone. And more extraordinary and totally fascinating, high above the river in perfect instantaneous coordination, swooping and swirling, were the changing amoebic shapes of a myriad flock of starlings. Leaves of the plane trees along the riverbank, gone from green to brown-spotted yellow and now crisp brown, letting go and rocking and dipping like butterflies with melted wings.

With many Parisians away on their annual holiday and the flood of tourists not yet arrived, this was a practical time to carry out shop maintenance and street repairs, and also to seek permission to have streets closed for shooting films. Stories of love and intrigue often include scenes along the river, or couples on bridges, with a backdrop of beautifully embellished Belle Époque architecture.

On Pont Louis-Philippe, the bridge that spans from the right bank of the river to the island of Île Saint-Louis, a film shoot is under way:

"Lights ... Camera ... Action!"

A cab pulls up, a man in a hat and coat jumps out, runs down the steps to a woman standing under a tree at the riverside, takes her shoulder and turns her around to face him ..... Cut! They are to do it again, a bit more gently. On the bridge there is a background crowd scene, a typical gathering of people enjoying their Sunday outing, buskers among them – a harlequin with a mandolin; a red-nosed clown with a bunch of balloons; a bowler-hatted unicyclist juggling fire sticks; in a flared pink tutu and tap shoes, a fat lady leading her shadow on a merry dance; couples swaying arm in arm, singing with an accordionist a song Jim remembers from his youth:

"How would you like to be,
Down by the Seine with me?
Under the the bridges of Paris with you,
You'd make my dreams come true."

And maybe a pickpocket or two, like in the opening scene of *Les Enfants du Paradis*.

Below, a crowded pleasure boat passes from under the bridge. Upturned happy faces; one, beautiful as a film star, waves to Jim, then he to her; he blows her a kiss and she blows one back, they laugh and kiss, and continue this game of strange attraction till she has gone beyond reach. To Jim's left, around the corner, Notre Dame with her double flying buttresses is bowed like a prima ballerina before a busload of photo-flashing Chinese tourists. A cab pulls up again, a man in a hat and coat jumps out, runs down the steps to a woman standing at the riverside under a tree, takes her shoulder and gently this time, turns her around, a close-up:

"Cherie, ne me quittez pas, s'il vous plait." (Darling, please don't leave me.)

The music plays on. The film in Jim's mind, all around him, is called *La Vie Est Belle*.

Whilst leaning on the bridge with his camera the sun at times seemed reluctant, hiding behind a slow drift of cloud, providing that subtle light he wanted to take grey-wash photos of the jagged roofline receding down along the Left Bank. The bells of Notre Dame bonged loudly and the air above the rooftops and beyond reverberated. He heard his name being called from the quay below. It was Casquette, his alcoholic friend, beckoning him to come and join him and two others for a drink. Jim zoomed down and got his picture.

Now, Casquette is an interesting specimen, let me tell you. To enter his world you have to get down on your hands and knees and crawl.

10

Casquette

On most summer evenings between nine and ten, *entre chien et loup*, Jim likes to lock his door and go out on his animal walk.

His quarter, known as Le Marais, is normally quiet. The French sit at footpath tables sipping wine and smoking cigarettes; sometimes a drunk with his hand out lurches from one to another; the long-aproned waiter on a break for a smoke keeps an eye; a boy skates by on his skateboard, another scoots by on his scooter; a graffit-covered van thumps out loud rap music.

> He puzzles over graffiti,
> Sees landscapes on stained walls,
> Moon-reflected cobblestones,
> Almost never back-street brawls.
> He sees the same bearded mute
> Going round the shops,
> Searching through their garbage bins
> Collecting bottle tops.
> Walking slowly along the footpaths
> He wonders if it feels
> For the unattached young lover
> Like that chained-up bicycle wheel.
> The greeting of a couple
> From the same small town in Wales,

Smelling first their noses,
Then under both their tails.
Madame George, theatre owner,
After cheers and long applause,
Is taking in her doormat
And closing down her doors.
On his animal walk as well,
The snooping night-black cat.
On the particular evening I want to talk about, however,
We'll hear no more of that.

On this occasion a picnic crowd was gathered at the riverside of the island St. Louis, about fifty or sixty, Italians mostly, on holiday. It was a beautiful evening – the stars, the soft glow of lamp lighting, the pleasure boats passing by and their reflections shimmering off the black water, the passengers joyfully celebrating their presence in such a beautiful city, their singing carried on the breeze. In Jim's hand was a glass of sweet chilled wine, under his wing a sweet, warm Caroline. She had dressed herself tonight to look seductive.

Admiring the lighting of St. Gervais church on the opposite bank, he sensed that somebody was observing them from the peripheral darkness at the water's edge. And yes, he was right – he could make out a lone figure hiding behind a shrub, like some nocturnal creature that might scurry away if you got too close. Jim became more curious about him. What was he up to? He was looking at them. Caroline said he was probably one of the tramps living under the bridges, someone who may once have painted pictures or written poems, then fallen on hard times, and then into alcohol, one of the meek who had not inherited the Earth.

Jim went and saw it was an old man with a stubble beard. He was thin; his shirt hung from coat-hanger shoulders and his trousers by a tight-knotted tie; on his head a *casquette* – the peaked French beret. His eyes were sad, wet little monkey's eyes, each with a diamond sparkle; his movements slow and tentative. He was probably younger than he looked.

Jim said *Bonsoir* and asked if he would like to come and join them. He mumbled something that seemed to mean he preferred to stay where he was.

Jim offered to give him a drink, and quietly and politely he said, *"Oui, rouge."*

With his drink then, Jim asked if he could keep him company for a while.

"Oui, si tu veut," he said with a shrug.

While they spoke, the old man looked down at the ground. He raked his beard – it gave him something to do. Jim asked him his name and he said people called him Casquette. And it so happened that he *was* living on the river, had been for some time. The winters got a bit rough, he said, but otherwise, *ça va*. Others were down here as well and they all managed to get on. He accepted the offer of another drink and it seemed that he was beginning to accept Jim's friendship as well.

Jim was surprised to hear Casquette had formed a small theatre and that he was its only actor. He called it Le Théâtre de l'Abyss. He said it was close by and the next performance would begin at midnight, in about ten minutes – would Jim like to come along as his guest?

"Really? Can I bring my friend?"

"Ba oui, bien sûr monsieur," he said.

Jim took Caroline's hand and a bottle and off they went.

They followed Casquette's graceless form along the quay for only about fifty metres, as far as the big stone stairs that stepped up to the bridge. In the wall supporting the stairs there was a ventilation hole at window height and with its bars removed there was just enough room for a person to squeeze through.

Casquette stepped up onto a box and steadying himself on both knees said to follow him. He squeezed into the abyss. Caroline, wide-eyed, without hesitation whispered, "Yes, yes, definitely, let's go."

They crawled on planks along a short tunnel, turned right, along a bit more, then through a small curtained opening. Jim couldn't believe his eyes. It was a candlelit cave. But most surprising was that seated on two rows of scaffolding, eating baguette sandwiches and casually sipping drinks, were fifteen or maybe twenty college-age youths – a scene, it seemed, from a page of Harry Potter. The walls were stone, and the ceiling, which was the underside of the outside stairs, sloped downwards to a one-man stage, which was represented by a tattered oriental rug surrounded by several flickering candles. The strong smell of underground dankness was sweetened with incense. One could tell by other things lying around that this must also have been where Casquette was living. When he arrived on stage everyone applauded. He shrugged and nodded and smiled. He seemed now, on this stage of his own making to be a changed person – no longer an outsider but an insider; no longer one just to be seen but noticed; not one just to be heard but listened to, and applauded. In closed silence, then, with the flames still flickering, he began to tell us his story.

It was difficult to understand exactly what he was saying at first, but it became clear that it was a character story – a story about himself, recollections of what his life was once like on the cobbled slopes of Montmartre and Pigalle. He named and described the best street cafés of the time and the best croissants from a particular Viennoiserie; there was a blind boy outside the Métro Abbesses, who sold pencils and postcards and sang ballads, and another, a street musician who, with his barrel organ and red-costumed monkey, played vaudeville music. He brought shame one day when his monkey went berserk and seriously bit a precocious child. Gypsy Rose Lee hypnotised and told fortunes behind her glass-bead curtains. Casquette knew all the cabarets and nightclubs, the Charleston at Les Folies-Bergère and cancan in La Moulin Rouge. Edith Piaf, too, *La Môme* as she was known – the little sparrow – whose singing everybody loved. Casquette and she knew one another as waifs on the streets of Pigalle. At her funeral procession in 1963, more than a hundred thousand turned out. He spoke of the still-famous celebrities – Jean Cocteau, the mime artist, and Yves Montand and Charles Aznavour – and the secret affair between the black American jazz singer Josephine Baker and Maurice Chevalier.

He recounted how he himself had spent more than twenty years in the theatre. He once performed in Strasbourg in a play by Franz Kafka called *Nous les Héros*, and in a film with Catherine Deneuve called *Le Temps des Loups*, directed by an Austrian he admired named Hanquin. He talked about places he had visited: Brussels, once, where he stayed for a year; and Berlin, too, where on 3rd October 1990 he joined in the reunification celebration of *Einheit* at the Brandenburg Gate, during which he suffered an injury that landed him in hospital. He confessed that he had spent a night in a lock-up, too, for disorderly behaviour.

He settled finally in an outer Paris suburb as a responsible husband and a father of two. His small audience was listening to every word. After a pause that was not rehearsed, he spoke of how, on a winter's night on an icy road, coming home, there was the tragedy – his wife and both daughters. Still he hadn't gotten over the loss, if anyone ever could. Unable to do his work any more, he lost his home to the bank and became derelict. With nowhere else to go, he came down here to the shelter of the bridges, found companionship through sharing, and became an alcoholic; he found the mercy of deep sleep. "In sleep," he said, "you could cry out in silence." Some of his companions never uttered a single word. One day he realised that somehow he had to make something of his life. And so he created his theatre.

"I thank you all for coming," he said.

With these last word there was silence, then loud applause.

Each person on their way out dropped coins into a bowl; someone left some bread and cheese, someone else a bottle.

On the quay under the bridge, most stayed to talk and drink and dance to the music of a blond German saxophonist who was dressed to look like Mozart. The sound of the saxophone in that volume resonated with fortissimo. Jim and Caroline went to Casquette to thank him and talk about his story. Most of the others had experienced tragedies like his, he said, ruin in one form or other, always leaving irreparable damage to the heart and permanently sore eyes. He felt he was getting better.

He lived and performed in the 'Abyss' for about two years, until the year of the infamous flood, when the river came up to the level of the bridges and washed everything away. When it settled back to its normal level the river authorities reinstalled the bars to his entry to keep him out. He had gone, and maybe he'd returned, but when Jim asked around nobody knew where he was.

One day not long afterwards, in Café Beaubourg, he couldn't believe it. At the table next to his, Casquette's face, large as life, was looking at him from of a back page of *Le Monde*. He looked better than Jim remembered him, bristly-bearded still, wearing his *casquette*. According to the article he was performing in Berlin in some small theatre called Le Théâtre de l'Abyss, and, as far as I know, he still is.

11

Days of Spring in Kyoto

The job in England went well. It was one of those dream jobs – the weather had been kind, the builder was competent, and the clients were happy. Now, free once again, Jim was ready to undertake another new overseas adventure. He promised himself that in the spring he would go to Kyoto. He made a final check with Yoko that his stay with Mori-san was still assured, and it was. Mori-san was expecting him. Sandrine, next door, during his absence for two months, would receive his mail each day and water his plants.

It was in the clear, early-morning coolness when Jim arrived at the monastery. The heavy wooden gate was unlocked. He pushed and entered and found a garden sanctuary. Along the far side was a towering forest of bamboo. The path that divided a green lawn, still damp from a shower, led to the dormitory wing of the monastery, and beyond that, set amongst trees, was the four-hundred-year-old temple. The temple veranda looked onto a shallow fish pond surrounded by thriving ferns and moss-covered stones, and spread over the water were beautiful canopies of star-shaped maple leaves. Large red carp caught his eye. The silence was aroused by the rustling sounds of bamboo.

He knocked quietly at the door and waited. The door slid open.

"Hello!" the monk cried in greeting. "You must be Jim, I am Mori-san; Yoko called just a few minutes ago to see if you'd arrived. Welcome! Welcome! Come in, football boots outside."

He was dressed in dark blue robes. Slightly disconcerted,

Jim smiled at his informality. Mori-san took his bag and Jim took off his shoes.

In the lounge room was a low table strewn with coloured magazines and a bowl of half-eaten breakfast; an American baseball game was playing silently on the TV. Mori-san reached over and switched it off. He asked Jim if he would like breakfast. Jim thanked him and said his breakfast had been served on the plane.

"Aiko, come and say hello to Jim."

Aiko appeared. She came and leaned against him while he stroked her soft thick coat – she was a lovely white, pink-tongued Labrador.

"He's come all the way from Paris, so we have to be nice to him. He's Yoko's friend."

She looked up at Jim, and her smile said, *Well, if you're a friend of Yoko's, you're a friend of ours.*

Mori-san said he would have to leave soon to take Aiko for her walk. Jim told him the flight had tired him and asked to be excused to catch up on some sleep. He followed Mori-san up the stairs, past a bathroom and on to his small room. There was a bed and a hand basin. The window offered a view over the garden. Mori-san gave Jim a towel and a light cotton kimono and slippers for house use. Jim presented him with the two tubes of French toothpaste and two large jars of Nutella he had requested. He was delighted.

"Don't feel too formal here," he said. "Have a good sleep. Use any of the bikes if you want to. I should be back in about one hour."

Then he went back down.

On his second day, Jim woke at dawn to the faint, repetitive din of a bell coming from the house temple. It was Mori-san finishing his morning meditation. After prayers, it was his habit then to walk Aiko to the Shinto shrine situated on top of the nearby hill. Jim asked if he could join them. It was another beautiful, crisp morning.

'Shinto', Mori-san explained, "literally means 'the way of the gods'. It got its name in the sixth century in order to distinguish it from the Buddhism coming from China. In the eighth century, Shinto gods were enshrined in Buddhist temples as protectors of the Buddha. Shinto philosophy involved a loosely held set of pagan beliefs that all natural things are animated by supernatural beings and that those beings control them, together with the forces of nature. Shinto shrines were erected on sites considered particularly sacred and there the devotees worshipped natural phenomena such as the sun and the moon."

After twenty minutes or so they began their ascent on well-worn steppingstones. At the top was a small shrine set amongst trees. Mori-san was not a devotee, he said, but he took it upon himself to go each morning to sound the giant bronze gong, which first rang out some eleven centuries ago. A large, horizontally suspended log strikes the gong five times at equal intervals.

Soon after their return, Mori-san began the first of his daily chores. He perfunctorily swept up the leaves, trimmed some shrubs and raked the grounds, seemingly without much pleasure. Jim told him how much he loved the garden and asked if tending it could be his job each morning. Mori-san thought for a moment and then consented. To make it official he presented Jim with a suitable gardener's habit – a woven karate-style tunic with matching baggy pants and a tie-around belt. It made him feel special. Every kind of worker in Japan has his or her own apparel according to their occupation.

Each morning, then, at five, in the dawn half-light, Jim rose, stretched, doused his face with cold water, then began his two hours of loving, meditative service – gardening.

He swept up the leaves and with the rake he unearthed a lot of pebbles and piled them to one side, then raked smooth the ground. Along each dry base of meandering watercourse he simulated flow patterns of imaginary streams. The pebbles were wheeled away out of sight. As if to express indifference to his art, or maybe to embellish it, even before his back was turned the cherry trees, azaleas and camellias dropped their leaves and blossoms all over his work. In the distance Mori-san's tolling could be heard. On his return, the monk would set about preparing breakfast. Aiko, meanwhile, crouched like a sphinx and with calm curiosity watched Jim pile the leaves. Usually four or five bags were gathered and left bundled at the gate. With the tools stored away, he then went to bathe in a wooden tub.

For breakfast they sat together on woven cloth laid out on the veranda and enjoyed usually tea and toast, fruit with yoghurt, and now Nutella. The fish gathered in expectation of small offerings. The same white heron returned to its tree high up for its bird's eye view. After breakfast Jim would take his camera, hop on a bike and set out for a day's shoot. That was the plan, anyway. Unfortunately, days of clouds and rain too often intervened.

Kyoto is ideal for cycling. It is a flat, fertile basin and the inhabited part of the city is only about six kilometres in diameter. It is thinly divided by its river, the Kamo-gawa, and, except for a narrow breach on the southern side, is contained all around by steep, densely forested hills. Where Jim was staying was on the lower slope of the city's eastern range of hills, in Gion, its *kagai* or geisha quarter. The view, no matter where you stood, was arrested by steeply forested hills. This containment of the city, like the garden walls that contain a traditional Japanese house, gives its dwellers a strong sense of place and, therefore, belonging, unlike the feeling of anonymity one experiences in the nebulous sprawl of typical modern suburbs elsewhere.

It was an easy coast down to the river and across the Shijo Dori Bridge into the bustling city centre. To his dismay, this once-beautiful city was now showing the same desecration most old cities in the world have suffered during the last fifty years. There were the all-too-familiar rows of modern, characterless box forms of shopping centres, cinemas and office blocks, created with the same lack of feeling as most other products of that period, devoid of any philosophical core that once expressed mankind's faith in itself as a spiritual being. But occasionally, interspersed among the new, were some weathered remnants of two- to three-hundred year-old traditional houses, which gave some of the last opportunities to imagine the former character of these neighbourhoods. Kyoto was not bombed during the Second World War. It is estimated, though, that since then some forty thousand *kyo-machiya*, (traditional wooden-framed townhouses) have been razed.

Jim was given permission to visit the interior of a nearly four-hundred-year-old house built when Buddhism in Japan, like Christianity in Europe, was in its renaissance. The rooms here were the quintessence of austerity and simplicity. Through Zen, not simplicity itself but the aesthetics of simplicity were discovered. Floors were made of thick straw mats that yielded slightly underfoot – their fine texture and uniform colour diffused the natural light (the addition of carpets or rugs would detract from this simplicity). Walls were of rectangular modular units of white plaster or glass or, for privacy, sliding paper screens or panelled timber doors, obviating any need for curtains. The low table was designed for comfortable kneeling, hence no need for chairs, and the futon was rolled up and stored in a closet each day so there were no beds. There were only one or two shelves and the tokonoma – a small-room recess – for the placement of revered objects. The shrine to Buddha, however, wasn't in the light, airy part of the house but rather in the privacy of a subdued family room. The Buddha itself was contained in an ornate and elaborate dark red tabernacle with small sliding panels, and candlelit it gave the Buddha an air of mystery. Placed there were incense and flowers and also recent offerings of rice and leaves of tea. The lady of the house took memorial tablets from within the shrine to show in brown ageing photographs family members, mostly dressed in the robes of monks and priests.

Because of the grid layout of the city, it was easier for Jim to find his way to some of the 1,600 Buddhist temples and four hundred Shinto shrines. To visit some remote shrines, though, he had to leave his bike and climb steppingstones high up into the forests. He seldom met anyone on the way. How old everything seemed to be – the worn stones underfoot – how quiet, and how long dead the sounds of footsteps. He saw last tarnished leaves of autumn's multitude stuck to a stone, yellowing; blood-red petals on thick cushions of thriving, verdant moss. It was the fresh green grass, the leaves' rustling, the sun's rays and birdsong that kept him moored to the present. At one small shrine he saw rows of lichen-covered stone Buddhas whose faces had been worn featureless, stone posts with barely visible ancient markings, and a vase inside that contained three fresh white chrysanthemums arranged in formal style.

At sixty-one Mori san had a seemingly happy outward disposition. He looked different to how Jim had imagined him. He was handsome and slim, taller than average, calm and graceful; his hands were slim, like dancer's hands, his head shaved. He wore faded cobalt-blue prayer robes and thick, rimless glasses. He always looked impeccable – being tidy was part of his nature. It was slightly amusing to imagine him with his face lathered in shaving cream, or in a coffee shop chuckling into an iPhone. He was casual with Jim and playful with Aiko. Jim was careful to respect his privacy, keeping to himself unless encouraged to do otherwise, but Jim was away most of the time anyway. Mori-san had a little fit of existential despair one morning when he found the roof had sprung a small leak.

He did have an air of distinction about him and, Jim was pleased to discover, he also had a sense of humour. One evening while dining together he told Jim that years ago he had visited England. He stayed first of all on a pig farm in Surrey, his hosts aptly named Mr and Mrs Bacon – a lovely couple, he said. They took him to the Epsom Derby one day and it was one of the most exciting days of his life. He won a race, "Got it from the horse's mouth," he laughed. He said he felt a great affection for the English. One of their endearing qualities was how, for something to do, they would sit down to their own tea ceremony – "A chinwag over a cuppa," he chuckled, "adding milk and sugar and dunking sweet biscuits." After that he lived in Oxford for three years, studying comparative theology. His English was very good, with even a slightly Oxfordian accent.

"Are you religious?" Mori-san asked.

"No. I sometimes attend the masses at Notre Dame to enjoy the theatricality – the fabulous Gothic stage set with stained-glass windows, the priest in his costume and the solemnity of his delivery, the incense and candlelit darkness, and the subliminal sounds of the Vespers and Gregorian chant. Other times, when there are few tourists, I might go inside just to enjoy it as a place of peace and quiet."

Jim asked Mori-san to tell him about the design principles of the traditional Japanese house. He had done his own studies on the subject.

"Well," he began, "to try to understand the essential qualities of the traditional house and garden (human scale, the sense of proportion, simplicity, balance, rhythms, composition, harmony and contrast, the use and expression of materials that are natural to the site, the unity of house and garden), one must try to understand the philosophy of Japanese Buddhism. Buddhism has always been concerned not only with man's spiritual life but also very much with his practical everyday life, and with the morality of society as a whole. For somebody who has grown up in Western culture the philosophy may be difficult to understand clearly, because to 'live' Zen is to go against one's conventional schooling of valuing concepts or theories more important than experience. Also, to analyse and try to explain Zen in words means to descend to the realm of words and definitions with all their inherent limitations. In learning Zen one begins to grasp the idea that the life permeating oneself and the multitude of all other forms of life is the one and only life – it unifies all the different forms in which 'life' appears. This elicits compassion for all beings, inanimate as well as animate."

Mori-san poured another cup of tea.

"To have this knowledge," he continued, "is to have enlightenment, or, in Zen terminology, satori. One experiences a state of being one with the universe – the beholder and his object, the thinker and his subject, all merge into one. The single grass stalk contains the essence of the universe as much as the universe contains the essence of a single grass stalk. This accounts for the Japanese people's love of nature in all its forms and their concern for the relationship of 'oneness' between the house and the garden and the garden and the house. Zen, then, considers immediate experience the method of reaching wisdom. It considers expressions of art and intuition to be more basic than those of morality, because art, as creation, is an expression from within, from the heart, contrary to a code of morality, which is formed by the intellect and thus remains imposed from without. Zen, therefore, was particularly closely associated with art."

"Most art forms in Japan, including the martial arts of kendo (the way of the sword) and kyudo (the way of the arrow), karate, aikido, judo and sumo, as well as shodo (Japanese calligraphy), haiku (poetry), chado (the tea ceremony), ikebana (flower arrangement), kenchi ku (architecture), Noh (theatre), are expressions of seven-hundred-year old Buddhist traditions. It was especially so in feudal times that simplicity was the expression of lack of means and poverty. Zen's unsophisticated methods and its non-discriminative attitude found particular favour among the intellectually and materially less fortunate classes such as the warriors and farmers."

What simpler and more practical construction could there be, then, in a country endowed with forests and troubled by earthquakes, than houses with frames made out of wooden posts and beams? And for a country where its people have to try to assuage their discomfort in scorching, humid summers with fans and parasols (and these days, resting in parked cars with their air conditioners on), what could be more appropriate than a light-framed house that slides open to catch the evening breezes and welcomes into it the psychological and real coolness of a damp and lush moss-covered garden? Except that during brief winters, with only panes of rice paper between you and the snow outside, the house could be very cold. But winter is a preferable season for the Japanese and one can deal with it by stoking the fire and applying more layers of clothing and blankets.

"What appeals to me," Jim said, "is the aesthetic of simple rhythms in the house design, the ordered repetitions of its elements."

"Ah, yes, the rhythm is due to its construction using a modular system, which derives from the basic unit of the tatami, the two-inch-thick floor mat of compressed straw measuring approximately six feet by three feet, the size originally chosen for the space needed for two men facing one another to sit and talk. The standard-size mats covering the entire floor area of a Japanese room determine the standard sizes of rooms. Room sizes are expressed in terms of the number of mats it takes to cover them – two or three mats, for example, in a typical tea ceremony room. The mat dimensions determine the spacing of the timber posts, thereby establishing the primary horizontal module; the vertical module, between the floor and head beam over each doorway, is determined by human scale and also by the Japanese intuitive sense of proportion, as are all the minor rectangles that make up the panelling of the facade design. The external expression of the Japanese house is, as you say, one of repeating timber-made elements, such as the doors themselves and their timber panelling, or the finer intricacies of screens with blades of latticework – a play of solids and voids, if you like, the spacing of the solids giving proportion to the voids. In another example one could think of the Japanese calligrapher, whose bold brushstrokes give proper concern for the shapes and proportions of the white spaces they enclose."

"In a way, like baroque musical compositions," Jim suggested; "sound and no sound, where the spacing of notes (the determinant of the silences) gives the qualities of rhythm and harmony. And although there is repetition of the same elements, there are variations to the simple thematic expression. Intuitively, the overall composition feels unified and complete, resolved as neatly as a mathematical proof but without the use

of logic. It reminds me of the compositions of, say, Bach's cello suites with their simple variations of a theme, and the unity is such that if one were to add a single note to the composition it would be superfluous and incongruous, to say the least, or to take away would be to rob it of its perfect unity."

"Good," Mori-san said, "I think that is a good analogy."

He took another sip from his cup.

"Palladian architecture, too," Jim added, " with proportions based on the golden mean, is an expression of balance and unity."

"Another characteristic of the *kyo-machiya*, the traditional house" Mori-san continued, "is the *tokonoma,* and this again is closely associated with Buddhism. The *tokonoma* is a picture recess, an alcove of usually two mats, where three objects of beauty are normally placed. The sacred meaning of the *tokonoma* can be traced back to the houses of the Zen monasteries in thirteenth century China, where on one wall a sacred Buddhist picture scroll (kakemono) was hung, and below it, on the raised floor of one step, were, typically, an incense burner and flowers arranged in a vase. These items are still used. The Zen monks gathered in front of this space for spiritual exercise and meditation, and there, in a profound ritual, they drank tea ceremoniously from one bowl. The *tokonoma*, a place to meditate with pure thoughts on the beauty of creation, is still an essential part of the typical traditional house."

In the four-hundred-year-old-house, Jim recalled, the scroll in the *tokonoma* contained a poem, which described the serenity of an August moon in its fullness on a misty night. The full moon at the autumn equinox is the biggest and brightest of the year.

"And of the garden, could you talk to me about that?"

"Ah, yes. The garden of the *kyo-machiya* is an act of love and worship. Again, Buddhism is at the core. Buddhism conceives all physical forms upon the Earth to be the material expression of a single force. Whether it be man or a rock, the 'life' that creates and controls both is the same. While feeling one with nature, selfhood ceases to exist – 'self' and 'other' merge into one. To become one and feel one with the object without intellectual intervention of any kind is to grasp directly its reality. To respect nature is to love nature; it is to live nature's life.

"In its treatment, the garden, in a way, is a macrocosm of Japan's rugged geography. Japan is a fragmentation of islands with a mostly mountainous topographical nature, due to the region being prone to earthquakes. In the countryside (except for the planted timber forests), the plants have been allowed to take root wherever their seeds have fallen. Seasonal rainwater flows down its slopes through ravines and onto flat, fertile rice fields. Its distinctly seasonal climate produces changes to its flora that are breathtakingly beautiful, particularly in the forests on their steep slopes – maples in rustic colours, bamboo-covered hillsides that sway with the wind's breath, pink cedar forests touched with blue wisteria, and the imbrication of conifers so uniformly planted on the almost vertical ranges resembles the scales on the back of a large, sleeping dragon. Often one sees this scenery through veils of dusk or sprays of mist rising from ravines. The traditional garden can seem to be all of this, though it is not a natural garden. All the elements are designed in place, and often cultivated and modified to produce intended forms."

"A bit like a sculpture garden," Jim said; "man coercing nature to conform rather than letting her have her way."

Mori-san pursed his lips.

"Well, yes, to some degree. Trees are continually trimmed, otherwise their full natural growth would endanger human scale; mounds are covered with grasses, and small-leaf shrubs restricted in growth by the containment of their roots (bonsai) can represent forested hills. Stones with their ledges covered with moss can represent forested mountains seen many miles away, and water flowing down over them can seem to be miniature waterfalls. Flowers are normally excluded because their colours would be too dominant."

As a space strongly defined by perimeter walls, and with the house walls slid wide open, the Japanese garden can seem to be an extension of the house's interior. The use of a wide timber veranda and its overhanging roof as an extension of the white ceiling adds to this effect. The garden is built to be seen from the interior or to be meditated upon from the level of the veranda. It is never an afterthought as it often is in the Western house – a space left over that has to be dealt with – but an essential part of the architectural concept.

Mori-san explained that a significant element of the Japanese garden, too, is the form and placement of the main rock, for this will determine the encompassing order of form and scale of other elements, including other rocks.

"These elements are all brought into harmonious relationship between themselves as well as with the house. Like the French with their many different cheeses, and Eskimos with their many distinguishing names for snow, in Japan there are 138 distinguishing names for rocks. It is not uncommon for someone who wants to make a gift to a friend for a special occasion, such as a marriage, to arrange the delivery of a specially chosen garden rock."

Jim thanked Mori-san for his enlightenment.

There is a huge temple in the south-west of Kyoto called To-ji and in the north-west there is a shrine called Kitano Tenmangu. In the grounds of each there are large open-air marketplaces, flea markets, which attract mostly foreigners. The Japanese tend not to be interested in second-hand things. Wares on offer, a lot of them antique, include kimonos; ceramic pots, vases, bowls and sake cups; tools; furniture; books; cloths; scrolls; and junk.

What interested Jim most were the textiles, the kimonos in particular. The kimonos on offer were of fine-woven silks of many colours, the design of each unique unto itself. It is still common to see them being worn in the streets, especially in the geisha quarter where he was staying – women shuffling in small steps as if hobbled at the knees. Since early times this style of dress had been essentially two pieces of cloth back and front, sewn together and held in place with a cord or sash tied at the waist. Over time the kimono became a single garment with wide sleeves and flowing looseness to make it comfortable for the summer heat. To keep warm in the winter it was only necessary to put on more layers of kimono. Around the ninth century, conscious selection of designs and colours of these layers became an aspect of Japanese culture – ladies of the court wore several layers for ceremonial occasions. There are many rules and customs to learn in exercising one's taste, such as those that apply to the season or ceremonial occasion. No one, for example, would think of putting on a kimono with a cherry blossom motif in winter or autumn. It would be more appropriate to wear a design of bamboo leaves covered with snow, say, or rustic-coloured maple leaves, or plum blossoms. In the summer, ocean waves would be felicitous. Textiles in more subdued colours of pre-dyed threads were the cotton robes worn by priests; stencil-dyed cotton cloths were used as bedcovers. Of particular interest, too, were small pieces of old offcut cloths that could be used for patching, or just cherished as the beautiful things they were. Pieces of patch-worked cloths about one metre square were on display. One of faded blue patches looked antique.

"It is a *furoshki*," the seller told Jiim. "If you look in one corner on the small label you can see the handwriting shows it came from a family called Hada in Osaka. They are used mostly as wrappings to carry small possessions, the four corners tied diagonally and the two knots for holding. Peasants and road travellers used them mostly, including samurai warriors who used to carry the heads of their victims."

Jim bought it as a gift for Ingrid.

Blue-uniformed schoolchildren from all over Japan, involved in learning the history of the city as part of their cultural education, were everywhere in Kyoto. All the temples were open to the public, so it was difficult to experience them as places of solitude and contemplation. Children dropped coin offerings into grated boxes at temple doorways whilst Japanese tourists in temple gardens, often bent over their tripods with long lenses, photographed flowers close up. Old trees sometimes needed crutches to support their sagging main branches, and some were clad in coats of straw to protect them from winter frost. Some struck by typhoons needed bandaging for their wounds. Some temples had thickly thatched roofs resembling, in colour and texture, fur hats.

Jim liked going into the handicraft shops, old shops with low ceilings usually, to see the many uses of bamboo, from brooms to baskets to flower holders to combs of many different shapes; and black *tenmoku* vases, green celadon pots and raku tea-ceremony bowls, all hand-thrown. Second-hand bookshops were stacked floor to ceiling.

Pontocho is the name of a famous narrow lane that runs near and parallel to the river. It is a nightspot full of bars and restaurants where a lot of Japanese businessmen go to get laughing drunk with hostesses who help them to feel human. In the windows the sample range of meals displayed on plates are actually clever, convincing, rubberised plastic imitations. When you take your place at a counter or table you will firstly be given an *oshibori* (a small hot towel), a cup of tea and a menu. You will get all the help you may need in ordering your meal.

Although the dishes are standard there is enormous variety. Unadventurous by temperament, the Japanese would not dream of concocting new dishes or tampering with traditional ones. And unlike the Western custom of having all the plates and bowls uniformly round and matching, Japanese dinnerware consists of multifarious shapes and colours, depending on what is being served – presentation and atmosphere are as important as the flavours.

Jim was served at a counter where he could sit on a stool. There was much activity, noises of pots and pans clashing in the kitchen, and a great hubbub of talk and excited laughter. Three Japanese men over at a table were beckoning in his direction. "Me?", he mouthed, pointing to himself. They were insisting that he come and join them. Jim was more than happy to do so.

They were in business suits, architects, two who had worked in America and the other in Australia. There was a spillage of sake on their table and already they were at the laughing stage of their evening. They got to talking about and comparing languages. Jim learned, over a sake or three, that their writing system uses three different scripts, the most difficult being kanji – the ideographic brushstroke script you see everywhere in public places. The most extensive Japanese dictionary lists nearly fifty thousand different *kanji* characters. One character can consist of more than twenty separate brushstrokes so you have to be careful. You probably need to know only about two thousand of these characters to be able to make sense of a daily newspaper. To make sense of the menu one would need to know only forty-eight katakana characters. They asked Jim to speak the few words he had picked up –

Kombawa and *Konichywa*, and, with a smile and a nod, *Ita dakimas*, and, a little more assertively, *Doe dakimashta*.

They complimented him on his pronunciation.

The pronunciation was not difficult. The vowel sounds

don't change, unlike in English, but changing the length or intonation of a vowel can change completely the meaning of a word. Sometimes, in conversation, if the meaning is not clear, you may see the respondent person stop, frown, then, with his index finger write on his palm the kanji character to be able to 'see' the meaning. Similarly, in English, spelling out a word can sometimes help to clarify understanding.

Jim was beginning to feel a bit loose (or was it lost?), too, at this stage, so he didn't know if they were pulling his leg when one told him that the word '*seikan*', depending on how you sound it – *seikan, seikan, seikan* or *seikan*; he couldn't tell the differences – can mean 'sexual feeling', 'naval construction', 'can manufacturing' or 'serene contemplation'. The only examples he could think of to offer in return were from the French language: *cou, cul, cout, queue* and *coup*, pronounced approximately 'ku', 'ku', 'ku', 'ku' and 'ku', all sounding much the same to a Japanese ear but meaning, respectively, 'neck', 'arse', 'cost', 'tail' and 'strike, strike not as in walking off the job but as in a blow, and not blow like the wind but as in making a decisive impact, to the head, for example, or to a ruling government – a coup d'etat. Ah, the versatility of language. Then he learned that the word '*kamikaze*' the Japanese name accepted into the English language meaning the World War II suicide bombers of the Japanese Air Force, and literally meaning 'divine wind'. As a riposte to this, Jim was able to offer the etymology of 'typhoon', from Chinese *dai foong*, meaning 'big wind'. Eventually, after much food, spillage, laughter and confusion, it was time for a singsong. They bundled off to a crowded karaoke bar where each was given a microphone and more sake. Still, the spirit was one of uninhibited, carefree abandonment. Together, arms around one another, they harmonised atrociously with *Yesterday*, and with *My Way* they did it their way, sounding like four bulls stuck in mud. Sake does terrible things to you.

Then Jim had to try to find his way home. This can be a challenge even at the best of times. Many Japanese streets have no names, and houses have no consecutive numbers. The first house built in the district gets called Number 1, the next, maybe half a mile away, gets Number 2, and so on, hence a high number does not mean the house is situated near the end of a long street but that it is in a heavily built-up area. House numbers are not displayed anyway but exist only in documents. But there *is* a system. It is called *Banchi*. *Banchi* are the numbers of the lots on which houses stand, and often (not always), hundreds of houses in a big city have the same *Banchi* number, like a postcode, but no street name. It is a long time before a postman comes to have a fair grasp of who lives in the area he is assigned to.

At the time of this night of debauchery, Jim had recently changed his address. He showed the address card to his taxi driver who, at four in the morning, could not figure out where to go any more than Jim could. He finally got home by navigating their way around the streets he remembered near the Imperial Palace.

Jim's new address was the vacant upstairs apartment of a hairdressing salon. Yutetsu, the hairdresser, a friendly, hospitable young man he was introduced to, welcomed him there free of rent. On three weekends they went to the house Yutetsu was building in the countryside, a simple framed structure, one hour's drive from Kyoto. The construction was nearly finished, the landscaping still to be done. In some nearby grassland, looking for steppingstones, Jim encountered two small, venomous-looking green snakes poised in fear and ready to strike. The heavy stones he found he wheel-barrowed and, after some discussion, laid in place the stones that now lead to Yutetsu's front door. Jim took some photos with Yutetsu standing proudly on his threshold. He promised to send them to him. He asked him to write down his address in *kanji* on a piece of paper as it usually appeared on his mail. When Jim returned to Paris he photocopied it, stuck it on an envelope and only needed to add Japon for the benefit of the French postal service. They were nice photos. He hoped Yutetsu got them.

The riverside was a truly delightful location. On weekends, especially when it is hot, lots of the young came to meet one another. There were none so happy as the teenage girls when they got together, took off their shoes and socks, rolled up their dresses and paddled among the ducks. With one eye peeking, they laughed behind their hands at the boys' attention. They sang songs together, and in the evenings, letting off their own fireworks, they laughed and screamed with great excitement.

One rainy day, sitting in his coffee shop next to the river, Jim saw two ladies in kimonos with their umbrellas crossing the timber-framed Shoji-Dori Bridge. The image immediately reminded him of something he had seen before … yes, the famous woodblock print by the nineteenth century artisan, Utagawa Hiroshiga, set in Tokyo on a rainy night on a similar bridge with Mount Fujiyama in the background. Jim was able to capture with his camera a similar picture in modern Kyoto.

SHIJO DORI BRIDGE 2002

UTAGAWA HIROSHIGE

Each afternoon at around three, he would go to the same coffee shop to write up his notes; sometimes also to take refuge from the rain, and to meet people. The schoolgirls were always shy and giggly, and one who could barely speak English asked in her own delightful way if Jim had seen any "*maiko*" over where he was staying. He didn't know what a *maiko* was until she began her beautiful little sketch in his notebook of an apprentice geisha.

I have to tell you about an incident that was one of the most pathetically funny and remarkable things Jim has ever seen.

There he was in his usual window seat with that same view of the Kamo-gawa River outside and the Shoji-Dori Bridge, and beyond, the forested hills of Gion. The river was really more like a mountain stream – pebbled and crystal clear with grassy banks, little grassy islands and small skirmishes of white-water rapids. Further downstream, men with fishing rods were standing in the river. Long-legged birds, too – cranes, I think – high-stepping in the shallows, poking and picking at things to see if they were edible. Ducks came skidding in to paddle about and quack. In fact, *kamo-gawa* means, 'duck river'. There were seven sculptured stone tortoises arranged as steppingstones from one side to the other, their heads out of the water, lazily gazing upstream – another example of the many lovely human touches you find all over the city.

Now, each day, above, about sixty feet above, hovering and fluttering with his head down, his eyes scouring the river for fish, was the same big hungry hawk. Sometimes he stopped, pulled in his wings and dropped like a stone, made a grab, missed, and then rose again to make the big circle back to the same place. On this particular day, however, he dropped, slapped the water hard and grabbed a fish so big it was possibly more than his own weight. They ascended, both of them flapping like mad. Jim had to lean forward in his seat to see how far away they went. What a thrilling sight. The hawk then began circling back as usual, and just before reaching the bridge the fish broke free and fell. In a long, descending arc it fell, then it hit the roof of a car crossing the bridge, bounced off like a ball, and then skittled a cluster of schoolgirls. The girls exploded and screamed blue murder. In their panic they came running to Jim's end of the bridge, then into the coffee shop. One of them was bawling while the others were trying to pacify her. Everyone was looking at her with astonishment – she had a nasty red slap-mark on one side of her face.

12

A Song in Manhattan

"Hello James, this is Svetlana Blum, would you call me?" Then her number. "It is fairly urgent," she added.

Jim thought for a few seconds: serious-sounding, Russian, Jewish, woman with an American accent … he concluded that he didn't know any Svetlana Blums. He did, but he'd forgotten. He called her nevertheless.

"You don't remember me?" she said.

Her tone suggested more a statement than a question. Jim knew he could get caught telling a fib.

"You *have* forgotten me" Accusatory now.

"About four years ago," she prompted, "the fundraiser for American Democrats Abroad. We met that evening; you are an architect."

Jim remembered the occasion. It was 2008, just before the first Obama election – a luxurious apartment; an expensive dinner for about thirty guests; Catherine, the hostess, warm-hearted as she was dutiful; and afterwards him helping a ninety-two-year old man named John down the stairs and into a taxi. Jim must have given Madame Blum his card, and maybe she'd given him hers – though that he didn't remember. He had butterflied around to most of the ladies that evening.

"Ah, yes, of course."

Her voice sounded cultured, a touch arrogant, possibly a difficult personality. He visualised her as being bit younger than himself, well manicured, well off. It had been so long it was likely she was calling for advice, possibly of an architectural nature. He was right. She said she wanted some changes made to her apartment in the Sixteenth Arrondissement, the rich quarter. He began to tell her that he doesn't normally do work in Paris because administrative procedures are too complicated when she cut him short. She told him where and when they should meet to discuss the matter, at a bistro called Chekhov's, close to her home.

She was inside waiting for him. Her smile was perfunctory and uninviting, not even a thank-you for coming. Her hair, drawn tightly into a chignon and tinted blue, gave her pale Siamese-cat-blue eyes an arresting quality; her painted lips were cherry-coloured, matching her fingernails; her cheeks marshmallow pink; her teeth white and even, like her string of pearls that contrasted with her dark blue dress, décolleté, touched with a cameo brooch, suggesting a fashion of the past. Her white gloves lay neatly on her lap, her glasses neatly on the table. Her straight back, locked knees, raised chin and pursed lips gave her a sedate and dignified presence – she was starchy, old-fashioned bourgeois. And, as she had been with each of her husbands, with her airs and graces, she was also seductively persuasive. She asked for tea and brioche. He still didn't remember her.

Her youngest son, Dimitri, she had raised and he was now college age. His father, she said, in deciding it was time for him to learn some independence, bought the apartment below hers on the ground floor, and gave it to him. As well as providing new facilities – a kitchenette, a modernised bathroom, some extra heating and numerous new connections for Dimitri's electronic equipment – there would be the installation of a new internal spiral staircase linking the two floors.

The staircase was not what Dimitri wanted, of course.

"Don't let her do it," he pleaded, "she can come and knock on my door if she wants to see me."

He had just found a new girlfriend. In spite of this, or more likely because of it, Madame still wanted to keep an eye on him. Appeals to reason on Dimitri's behalf were stifled. She glared, she refused to discuss the matter; she was used to getting what she wanted. Talk of money – building cost and fees – she dismissed; she would pay whatever it took.

On the day of his inspection Jim sat while Madame Blum prepared cups of tea. Her apartment was as he had imagined it – a typical example of *la Belle Époque* with tall windows draped with heavy velvet curtains gathered with tasselled stays; ceilings of ornate plasterwork; gilt-framed dark portraits of bearded old men in the style of Rembrandt; bookshelves weighted with volumes of Complete Works; arranged on the mantel, delicate ceramic ornaments; and in glass-fronted cabinets, snuffboxes, ivory fans and china figurines. Near the unsullied marble fireplace, heavy upholstered chairs sat around a coffee table like a gathering of fat old dowagers. All was quiet and soulless as a museum, a lonely place. He took all the measurements he needed. He drew the plans to her approval, and work began.

On an upper floor of the same building lived Madame Dunayevsky, alone with her yappy little poodle. Her husband, a civil servant, had died some seven years ago. One day, with an eye out for her on the stairs carrying her shopping she met the plasterer.

"Lovely little dog," Mykola, who disliked dogs, said in Russian.

"Babka," she said when he asked his name.

Babka growled at Mykola's outstretched hand.

She mentioned the dusty footprints on the hallway carpet, and he assured her they would be cleaned up straight away. They were both about the same age and from the same district in Sebastopol. Mykola had come over recently with no particular qualification and took pretty well any odd job that came his way.

He was a serious man, not bad looking, decent. To his request of letting him use her jug during the period of interrupted electricity she said, *"Da"*, to his offer to fix her leaking cistern she said, *"Da"*, to her offer of a glass of sherry he said, *"Da"*, and to his appeal to let him move in and share his life with her she said, *"Nyet."*

Apart from the nuisance of noise and dust, and the inconvenience of being without hot water and electricity for a couple of days, the job went smoothly. The quality of workmanship was good and there were no extra costs.

On the day of the final inspection, Madame Blum, by way of gratitude, offered Jim the use of her Manhattan apartment. She knew of his intention to go there to catch the Presidential election. Her eldest son, doing his PhD at NYU, had just married and vacated the apartment. It was downtown, in the Lower East Side. This arrangement would suit him very well, he said, and he thanked her very much. He planned to leave the following Thursday.

"Fine," she said as she rose to lead him out. "You can come and pick up the keys on Saturday, and I expect you will stay for dinner."

Her smile barely exposed her dazzling, white teeth.

From the night sky, Manhattan was an elongated island set in the glitter and colours of a large pinball machine, a dark patch at its centre. Its scale is as big as it is ambitious, expensive as it is wealthy. Here, big money gets big money.

"Why do they call it the Big Apple?" the little girl in front of Jim asked her father.

He smiled. "Because, darling, it *is* Big."

Of course, everyone knows the sheer cliffs of glass casting long shadows, steel cages occupying the upper strata – the altitude of wealth and power, masters of the universe. Jim looked directly down into the live circuitry of the grid. It was waiting for him. Something Big was going to happen, he could feel it in the quickening of his pulse. He was sure Obama was going to be elected.

Just as Madame Blum had described it, her downtown apartment was spacious, very comfortable, and high up with a view across the river. He had been warned about the winter weather, not the sub-zero temperature so much as the arctic wind sweeping down and off the Atlantic Ocean, across the Hudson River, along the canyons of the city then, like a sword, straight through him. It howled like packs of wolves, it rattled his windows; they stiffened and fought back; it was ferocious. Fire engines, squad cars and ambulance sirens whined through the nights, helicopters fluttered overhead. He wanted to make it another photo shoot, but it was so cold he had to take refuge in coffee shops and cinemas for much of the time. He couldn't form the words, 'a hot cappuccino, please' because his mouth felt anaesthetised. He read two novels in coffee shops and sat through five films.

On the eve of the election, on Rockefeller Plaza everywhere you looked was festooned with bunting, and NBC News had a big screen reporting the votes as they were coming in. The Democrats were winning. A lone woman on the footpath was ranting and raving with a McCain banner while everyone looked at her as if she was a screwball on speed. Being New York, it was an even bet.

Most mornings Jim took the M14A bus to Union Square and then walked south through Washington Square to Greenwich Village, or north to midtown where all the skyscrapers are. One rainy day, the only person sitting in the bus shelter was a little black girl, her hair tied in many tiny plaits with different-coloured ribbons. She didn't look up when he came in.

"Hello."

"Mn."

"What are you drawing?"

She was left-handed, with a funny way of holding her pencil and her mouth. Two amorphous shapes were touching one another.

"A goldfish eating a cow," she said.

"A goldfish can't eat a cow."

"Yes it can."

"What about the bones?"

"What about the bones; it can spit them out."

The rain was light.

She said she was going to Madame Tussaud's wax museum to see Picasso.

"Aren't you a bit young to be travelling on a bus on your own?" he asked.

She attached a tail. *Why do people always have to ask such dumb questions?*

When he asked her name she said, "Look mister, if you're an alcoholic I'm not supposed to talk to you, and could you, like move along and make a bit more space for my friend?" Toki, her secret friend, accompanies her everywhere she goes.

"Sorry."

Chastened, he sat fascinated by the changing plumage of an oil slick.

The elderly, the disabled and the particularly heavy travel only by bus because the buses 'kneel' to let them on and off. The driver pushes a button and the steps fold down to make a platform at street level; they wheel on, or step on, and then he elevates them. A large black woman had to struggle.

"Thank you, Gus," she said when he gave her ticket.

"You're welcome, Lisa," the driver replied, in a pleasant, sing-song kind of way. He waited till she lowered her prodigious posterior; the seat gave a wheeze. All done he then moved slowly onwards. The place she found was next to another big black lady

433

with a little boy sitting on her lap. Straight away, they found they had parrots in common.

The thirty-minute ride to Union Square is pure, unrehearsed theatre, everybody a real-life character, talking loudly, being friendly. They are so jolly, and with the rocking and rhythm and beat of the bus, you could almost expect them to rise up in song to praise the Lord.

"Geronimo never stops yacking," Lisa said. "'Barack Obama, Barack Obama' – he never stops."

The other lady said hers eats anything – carrots, spaghetti …

"'N chicken bones," the little boy piped up.

"Hee-hee-hee, dat is so funny," said Lisa, pointing at Jim's *RECYCLED LOVER* T-shirt.

"Where's yo fom?" she asked.

"Australia!" she said with surprise.

"Welcome sir to Noo York city."

When they passed St. Mary's Church they crossed themselves.

Jim got down at Union Square.

"Take care," the driver called after him.

After five days of confinement and with a break in the weather, though still, of course, very chilly, people ventured back into Central Park. On the city map it is enormous – fifty blocks long, three blocks wide, more than eight hundred acres of wilderness with big boulders and wild grasses, grass-lined lakes for boating, and forests of deciduous trees that flame up in the autumn; bereft of all their foliage now.

An athletic black girl in shorts on roller skates, plugged into earphones, with one leg extended, glided gracefully as a swallow. Playfully circling and ensnaring Jim in her web of invisible thread, she called out,

"Hey honey, where's yo fom?"

"Australia! Welcome, sir, to Noo York City, you have a good day."

And with that she made an expansive bow, broke away, and then again was back up in the clouds.

At the western edge of the park near 72nd Street, some were singing. It was Strawberry Fields, a fairly large circular mosaic tile clearing, and around it about fifty people. At its centre, strewn with rose petals, was a plaque with the single word, *IMAGINE*. Every weekend they gather, some with guitars, to remember. Jim huddled with them and together they sang Beatles medleys. During *Imagine* he was overcome with emotion. When they finished with

We hope one day you'll join us,
and the wor-or-orld will be as one

his world was misty, and through his blurred vision the young man with the guitar opposite uncannily resembled John Lennon.

On the east side of the park is the Metropolitan Museum, and when Jim entered he was relieved to find a seat and some warmth. Above were three large domes; the supporting columns and motifs showed – once again, like many buildings built in the late 1800s – the profound influence of Classical Greek architecture. Rather tired now, he didn't want to endure further fatigue by visiting the interior museum, and besides, it was getting on for closing time.

Outside it was becoming dark, so he made his way over to the Whole Foods Market on 14th Street where those who are fussy about what they eat go. Over a hot soup of pumpkin, potato, sweet potato, broccoli, chicken stock and chestnut puree, he finished reading *Accordion Crimes* by Annie Proulx, a very well-researched, witty and enjoyable novel about the lives of immigrants coming into America between 1890 and the 1970s.

Reinvigorated, he then walked to the Strand Bookstore on 12th Street, near Broadway, where they boast of having eighteen miles of bookshelves. He looked under A for a book by Paul Auster.

"Oh no, you won't find him there," the assistant said; "that's his latest book, it'll be in New Editions. Come, I'll show you."

The black plastic badge on her blouse showed her name was Aretha. She was a short, dumpy Puerto Rican with spectacles, errant black tendrils playing around her face, and flawless skin with no make-up, just a very faintly shadowed moustache. And she was nice. Her favourite authors, she said, were Virginia Woolf and Toni Morrison; her favourite book, *The Bluest Eye*. She liked that Toni Morrison was making a cry for feminism and her concern for African Americans, retelling the black American story her way. Her enunciation was good and her voice pleasantly girlish.

"You know Toni Morrison is going to give a reading at the Union Square Barnes & Noble next Friday, don't you?" Jim said.

"Of course."

He said if she liked, if he got there early, he could keep a seat for her down front. Sure, she said, then was off serving another customer.

They were seated together down front. On stage Toni Morrison was statuesque, her face cut in brownstone; her hair – copious ripples of grey – had flint in it. She was a tough lady, a strong advocate, and very much of her own style. Her reading from *Beloved* won her a warm round of applause.

The coincidence was that Aretha and Jim were neighbours. They were both living in Madison Street in the Lower East Side, which meant that they could catch the 14A bus together. She lived in one of the municipal high-rise blocks occupied by elderly people, Hispanics mostly. She shared a ground floor apartment with her parents. They were from San Juan. She asked if Jim had any plans for the next day. She said her parents were 'real characters' and wanted him to come to meet them. They'd never met an Australian before. To use an Americanism, he said that sounded great. When she smiled goodnight he noticed she had the cutest pair of dimples.

Norma looked up. "You're the man for the oven, you said you were coming on Tuesday." She was on her knees weeding a garden of bulbs leading to the main entrance door. This was her garden. It included an arrangement of glazed ornaments – two conjoined swans, an elephant and a rabbit, but fish mostly. They formed a kind of proscenium arch around a central figure, a pretty blond boy wearing a crown and a blue cape, holding an orb, and dangling from a small branch over him was a cut-out plastic owl; behind him a small birdbath. He was the boy Christ. Norma was wearing a plastic raincoat and rubber boots, her face looked kind with friendly, slow-blinking eyes, like a saintly old tortoise. She was something of a talking point in the neighbourhood.

"No, no," Aretha cried, coming to his rescue, "Jim is the man I told you about last night, the Australian." But Norma didn't remember. She said it looked like rain, that she needed a bit more time, and to go on in.

There was a smell of Alpine freshener, and a loud television. Miguel, a betting man in a baseball cap and loose Miami palm-beach shirt, was glued to the TV. He served behind the counter in Stinson's hardware store. Aretha introduced him to Jim. He shook his hand, offered a beer and then turned back to the loud, excited racing commentary. Aretha directed Jim to the lounge room and then went to freshen herself.

Elephants, ornamental and toy species of every kind, shape and colour, jostled one another on shelves or were caged in glass-fronted cabinets – twenty-seven in all; Aretha had counted them. Rubber vines were taking over the apartment, which was slowly becoming a jungle like back home in Puerto Rico.

Perched on the mantelpiece among the leaves he could make out photographs; one, overexposed, of Miguel and Norma arm in arm, squinting at the hot Miami sun (*Honeymoon. Miami 1985*); an old one of a man in military uniform; one of Aretha when she was tiny; and a postcard of the Pope at the Vatican. There was a gently bubbling aquarium with two goldfish, on its sandy bottom a toy castle with a drawbridge, and on the drawbridge a boy sitting with a fishing rod. On a small table stood a statuette of the Holy Mother and a permanent votive glow of a red Sacred Heart.

Norma came in looking tired, closed the door behind her, removed her boots, then went to the kitchen. She handed Miguel his lunch tray while his eyes were still glued to the horses.

Friends started dropping in, paunchy men in baseball caps with six-packs. Beer cans hissed and dribbled. Talk over the racing commentary was loud, and tips like Momma's Boy and Magic Dream didn't have a chance. Shangri-La, apparently, was where the money was.

Being Australian made Jim an object of curiosity. "G'day, mate, 'ow ya goin', orright, mate?" Carlos said in a gruff voice not his own, then he laughed. He said, one day he will visit Australia. Jim made him promise he would travel the north-east coast and not miss out on Byron Bay and Mullumbimby. When more friends arrived and Norma brought out crisps and peanuts, there was the makings of a party.

Bernard, who was a teetotaller and had no interest whatsoever in horses, preferred tomato juice – he sold cars and was advising on the best car radio. Nelson, the next-door neighbour, married to Rita, though she wasn't there (they didn't want their women there), was from Venezuela. They'd been married eighteen months – she was his third, three times lucky, he reckoned. She didn't stop yapping, he said, so he was glad she spent most of her time out shopping. He confided that he thought she was going crazy, alluding to the day he found soap and a bottle of shampoo in the fridge, and another when she was standing in her raincoat and shower cap in the pouring rain, watering the plants. The gasman, who actually came to read the meter, before he knew it, he too was fizzing beer. Jim was on his third and having a great time. A captive herd of elephants now did seem a bit funny. Anybody else who might have noticed them wouldn't have found it so remarkable – it's what a house is for, after all. The cigarette smoke in the room was noticeable now, the Heineken ads on the ashtrays mostly covered, and the laughter was louder than it had been. When after the last race the horsemen changed to screaming redskins circling wagons, Ozzie's wife upstairs sent him down to tell them to turn it down and he got caught up as well. Norma didn't trust Ozzie; his thin moustache, the floozy she had heard about. She had a way of detecting trouble and was good at controlling her irritation. She wasn't happy with the beer cans next to her elephants.

"You feel all right?" she asked Miguel.

"A little tired."

"I told you not to get too excited. Remember what the doctor told you."

She went and found sanctuary in her immaculate kitchen.

While Norma was waiting for the kettle to boil, Jim found her at the window putting seeds in the budgerigar cage, and planted there were two potted cacti and a species of miniature elephants. On the wall over the fridge was a Stinson's hardware calendar showing a photo of the Brooklyn Bridge by night.

"It's far too noisy and smoky," she said.

Jim nodded, not really thinking it was. He was having a terrific time.

Passing him a cup of tea, Norma said, frowning, "He needs to watch his heart." She tried not to nag him. She knew how important his horses were.

"She's a good girl," she said about Aretha, "serious, a hard-working girl, never stops reading."

With her back pain, Norma said she didn't get out much any more. Sundays she went church for Mass and to sing in the choir, Monday nights to play bingo. The congregations were dwindling, she said sadly; "Everybody's getting old." He said he had never seen bingo and asked if he could come along.

"Oh, you wouldn't find it very interesting," she said, "only old people go."

He wanted to go, he said; some of his best friends were old people.

"OK," she said, "come next Monday if you like."

Outside the window on the amenities court, a foursome was slamming a ball at the walls. A rumble of thunder sent a reverberation through the building like a small earth tremor; the first big, slow raindrops began tapping on the window.

Aretha came in and said she thought it was time to leave. She suggested they go to the Whole Foods Market on 14th Street for a coffee, then, if it stopped raining, a walk around Union Square – a good idea. On his way out, Nelson asked Jim to come and join them for Thanksgiving dinner the following Thursday. Norma asked if they could pick up some birdseed.

"Have a great stay in New York," Miguel called after him. Jim thanked him.

Next to the ground-floor lift, taped to the wall, was a photocopy picture of a spectacled old lady in a cardigan and black beret sitting in a rocking chair, a blanket on her lap, sad, and under it was written:

With a heavy heart we Regret to Announce
the passing of our beloved Grandmother,
Carmen Rodriguez.

Funeral Mass: Monday November 18th, 2008.
St. Mary's Church
440 Grand Street.
Time: 9 am

Wake: Ortz Funeral Home
22 First Avenue.

The lift door opened and a whiskered old man in striped pyjamas and slippers shuffled out to go shopping in the rain.

They got off on 14th Street, passed through the sliding doors of the Whole Foods Market, caught the escalator up to the first floor then sat at a window counter with the best view over Union Square. On a clear day the square gathers a large crowd of people – stallholders selling fruit and vegetables, jams, watches, sunglasses, cheap French-brand perfumes, and on days like this, umbrellas. Chess-players challenge anyone passing by; a riddle: *Seven little copycats sitting on a fence, one jumps off, how many left?* Jim remembered this is where Tequila told him she had once set up her stall.

There was the usual lunchtime noise of talk and clatter and country and western music – Johnny Cash with his deep, sad voice singing *Don't Take Your Guns to Town*; on the walls were five large framed photos of coffee plantations in Guatemala and hessian bags opened wide to show roasted beans. Jim's sugar cube, floating on the foam, drank his brown coffee then disappeared; the shadow of Aretha's orange juice on the green plastic table top was neither orange nor green but a kind of orangey green.

Next to them were four giggly-silly teenagers in designer-torn jeans with mobile phones, talking enthusiastically, sounding like Disney ducks and chirpy chipmunks.

"Like she would be, like, two different people ..."

"Like, you know, they have, like, this stupid pitch ..."

"It was awesome, like totally".

It was difficult to make oneself heard, like, totally.

Jim leaned across the counter.

"Aretha," he said loudly, "why do Americans have to talk so loud?"

"It's part of our culture; another way, I think, of asserting our dominance in the world."

"Why is it that young people everywhere, especially the girls, have developed this silly habit in conversation of saying 'like' so often, not even making similes but useless conjunctions?"

"I think it might be a remake of the pre-feminist beatnik days," she said, "when for a girl to seem vague and stupid was an attractive quality to young guys."

"I do too," Aretha said, when he told her he liked her name.

"It reminds me of Aretha Franklin."

"My mother named me after her."

"Do you know Freewheelin' Franklin, one of the Fabulous Furry Freak Brothers?"

Nah, she was too young, another generation.

"I was named after James Stewart, one of my mother's favourite film stars. He won his Oscar for *The Philadelphia Story* in 1940, the year I was born. Humphrey Bogart won his Oscar two years later. Shit, I'm glad I didn't get Humphrey. It was common in the '40s and '50s to name your kids after film stars. Hollywood was all the go then. Ballroom dancing and cinema were about all they had. My sister got Lauren Bacall – she was married to Humphrey Bogart."

Aretha agreed Humphrey was not such a good name.

"My daughter got Ingrid Bergman."

"I loved my mother very much," Jim said. "You know where people go when they die? Walt Whitman said they turn into leaves of grass, but I say they go deep into the hearts of those who loved them. And then, when *they* die, they're lost in the graveyards of oblivion. Ah, the grandeur of human insignificance. Not Mozart or Beethoven or Shakespeare, of course; they will never die."

"She was great, wasn't she?" Aretha said, meaning Toni Morrison.

"How did you come to be working in a bookshop?" he asked.

"My mother wanted me to be a nun, but I didn't want to live in a convent all my life. I wanted to live a normal life in a house and have kids."

"So how did you come to be working in the bookshop?"

"I used to go often for second-hand books and one day I saw the job advertised and I got it. I just love being in a space surrounded by books. I love biographies, reading about other people. Can you imagine any place other than a library or a bookshop where you can tune in to so many wonderful life stories? "

"Hmm, on a crowded train," Jim suggested. "Everybody has a fascinating life story whether they realise it or not, we are all complex and surprising, we are all the sum of every moment of our lives – the difficulty is, you have to have the storyteller's gift to be able to share it, to be able to describe it, paint it, tell it as it really was."

"When I was a kid I loved having stories read to me. A life story," she said, "is like a long poem, and with a voice it becomes a song."

"That's nice."

Pause.

"And you, what do you do?" she asked.

When he told her, she said it must be very complicated designing buildings, getting all those ducts and pipes and wires and things in the right places.

"Don't you worry that things might go wrong and turn out to be a mess, that for the next hundred years people will think it's ugly?"

"Not really. They say doctors bury their mistakes; architects just grow ivy over theirs."

That made her chuckle.

"I suppose you will be following the big game this weekend?"

"Nah, not really into baseball."

"Did you ever read Don De Lillo's *Underworld*?"

"No."

"It begins in New York in 1951 with one of the biggest showdowns of the century, the Giants versus the Dodgers, and who should be sitting together in the VIP box but a very cool Frank Sinatra with his bulbous tie loosened to give him that Frank Sinatra look; a very drunk and miserable TV funny man, Jackie Gleason; and a very straight-faced, short and ugly J. Edgar Hoover – 'Jedgar', Sinatra called him – head of the FBI. Special agent enters, squats beside Hoover to whisper that the Soviets have just conducted a test at a secret location somewhere inside their border. It was the atomic bomb. Hoover, still looking ahead, purses his lips – otherwise his expression doesn't change."

They were both gazing at the outside world, the sky full of so many changing realities. It had been sullen during a light shower and then, with its greyness washed away, the sun came out. Swallows were slicing through the air, barely touching it.

"I hope there is a beggar's bowl at the end of that rainbow," Aretha said.

Pause.

"You see George Washington over there, Aretha Franklin?"

He was in the square, drenched and dark green on a dark green horse, larger than life, his sword by his side, his left hand cradling his three-cornered hat, his right arm extended pointing, pointing straight at them; hanging from his finger, a brassiere.

"He's got a brassiere hanging from his finger," Aretha remarked, her lips blindly searching for the tip of her straw.

"Yes – you know what he is saying?"

"What is he saying, James Stewart?"

"He's saying, 'You, sir, are the harbinger of summer and a paragon of virtue.'"

Aretha giggled.

"And you, mademoiselle, are the virgin spring and an enchantress of fetching beauty."

She smiled and blushed.

"*Fosssette,*" he said, touching her cheek. "That's the French word for dimple, *les fossettes* – two dimples, plural, feminine."

She leaned over and rested her head on his shoulder.

Above the trees and beyond was the needle of the Empire State Building.

After Union Square, Aretha took Jim to Harlem, where the name of the main Lennox Avenue has been changed to Malcom X Boulevard – a name not at first recognised by the post office – and apart from two blonde women walking together, everyone was black. They've had it rough there and now things are changing. Gentrification, it is called, developers buying up run-down properties and raising rents, forcing blacks to move again, further out. The Center for Research in Black Culture houses the nation's largest collection of documents, rare books, recordings and photographs relating to African American experience. Lectures and concerts are regularly held there, and nearby is the Apollo Theater. Three weeks after the election victory there were still freshly hand-painted posters proclaiming: *OH MAMA, WE GOT OBAMA* and *YES WE WILL, GODAMMIT*, and *PRAISE THE LORD*.

The weather turned bleak again – the grey sky threw inkblots on the paving. Fragile old people with the highest of human qualities were out shopping; some in dark clothing, aggrieved with sad eyes, held out a hand for money; one in a wheelchair refilled cigarette lighters; another wheeled a shopping trolley full of her life's belongings. A chestnut seller warmed his hands on his brazier; a fishmonger emptied a bucket of ice in the gutter; two little girls on a stoop played jacks, on the pavement their hopscotch chalk practically washed away. Lying dead on the kerb was an old TV, and posing as its widow, like a big, broken blackbird, a weather-beaten umbrella. Red and green traffic lights reflected on the road looked like pools of spilled blood and poison; a wild-eyed Jamaican exhaled a whiff of pot smoke. In shop windows they could see shrugged, mismatched suits and factory-discounted dresses, old black-and-white television sets for hire, and their reflections huddled together in the cold. A merry old man in a bowler hat and coattails, quietly singing a jazz lyric, broke into a tap dance. He danced around them, swaying his arms and clicking his fingers, and as he skipped away he took his song with him, homeless as the moon. Jim got a shot of him from behind looking like Charlie Chaplin. The jolt of what sounded like a gunshot let out; then a speeding police car with its siren wailing; then an ambulance wailing, then a graffiti-covered van – bumper sticker, *Going Nowhere Fast* – punching the air with gangsta rap; above, a helicopter fluttered. The air was spiced with fish gumbo, chicken stew and the blues. They realised they were hungry, so went into the Pokey Diner. The floor was bare boards and the wall a mural of a jungle of exaggerated Rousseau greens and a sky of enamel blue, added touches of a toucan, a hummingbird and some butterflies. Billie Holiday was singing God Bless the Child, two guys playing chess.

Over hot chicken stew with rice, Aretha, her hair now like wild scribble, wanted to know all about Paris. Jim told her the city centre is only about a hundred and fifty years-old, built in stone, that the townscape comprises five-storey apartment blocks huddled together with meandering streets and alleyways, the skyline of domes and jagged rooftops with thousands of terracotta chimney pots, and the River Seine, with two boat-like islands moored to each bank by beautiful bridges. There are grand boulevards, he said, lined with chestnut trees, manicured gardens with clipped hedgerows, squares with churches and fountains and fruit and flower markets, lamplit black-cobbled streets bathed in a soft yellow glow; and about the nightlife of Montmartre – the Moulin Rouge and the Folies-Bergère. Women are chic. He described side-street cafés and the tolling of distant bells. She knew of Shakespeare and Company, the bookshop. Another police car went by with its siren blaring.

"And can you speak French?" she asked, her face lovely and innocent with big brown eyes. He nodded. "I manage; *je me debrouille*. It is a big subject, full of silly, unnecessary complications. Every noun you see around us here is either masculine or feminine gender only, no neuters, and the adjectives that qualify them are correspondingly masculine or feminine. Crazy, eh? But it is nuanced and subtle and it sounds nice."

It was getting dark. The streetlights flickered. They seemed to have run out of ideas. All that remained now was their chicken bones.

"We should be getting back," she said.

"OK, let's go."

Jim bought his first ever pair of long johns, postcards for Ingrid and Svetlana Blum, and a packet of birdseed for Norma. Regrettably, he didn't make it to Nelson and Rita's for Thanksgiving.

Outside a neighbourhood café chubby old-timers passed the early-evening hours reminiscing about the good and bad old days in the Lower East Side – jazz singers, gangsters, baseball legends, boxing champions and movie stars: Sinatra, great in *The Man With the Golden Arm*, and Bogart: "Never met a dame yet who hasn't understood a good smack in the mouth." Laughter. It was an impromptu one-act play, their gestures were interesting. Jim got some shots of them when they weren't looking, something typically New York. Then the sudden alarm of an ambulance prevailed. He remembered it was Monday, time for his rendezvous. He got up and walked away.

Steam rose from grated drains; steel zigzag fire escapes bolted to the sides of blackened brick walls shook and rattled with the winds; downpipes made complicated geometry, and perched on top were ventilators and water tanks with conical roofs. Each morning Norma's church gave services in English, Sunday afternoons special services in Spanish, and Monday evenings they played bingo. Norma was waiting for him. She took him in as she said she would.

Inside the community hall a bulletin board announced the next Civic Improvement meeting, missionary work in Africa, Citizens for Yoga, fitness classes and Bingo. One wall was painted a depressing shade of green. A tail pinned to a paper donkey, smoke pouring from a gable house chimney, and a cut-out of van Gogh's *Sunflowers* indicated that it was also used as a day care centre. It was a gathering of about sixty old people, ladies mostly – fairly quiet for such a crowd.

After a bit of shuffling Jim bought his tickets, took his seat next to Norma and became a participant. There was an air of expectancy, bubbly excitement, and then quiet. During the calling out of the numbers his mind drifted to a prison joke someone once told him: in the refectory during mealtimes, to save telling the same jokes over and over for so many years, each joke was given a number, and so when somebody stood up and called out a number, if it was a good joke (Number 32 had a great punch-line), the whole gang would fall about laughing. But you had to tell it well otherwise it would fall flat. After about fifteen minutes, after a rally of numbers, the little lady on Jim's left spluttered, "Bingo."

Nobody else heard her, so with one hand on her shoulder and the other raised, he yelled, "Bingo!" Everyone looked at her with big eyes. Frightened and puzzled, she began to cry. Jim put his arm around her.

"I've never won anything in my life before," she sobbed.

She kept sobbing. Jim felt helpless. He and Norma didn't have the same luck.

Finally there was the clatter of standing up, chairs being folded, then everyone shuffled towards the rear where cups of tea and biscuits were being served – an opportunity to meet some of Norma's friends. She wanted to show him off as someone new, from Australia. They closed in around him, curious. One told him she had read the works of Patrick White, an Australian novelist who, in 1973, won the Nobel Prize for literature; another told him they have kangaroos in his country.

The famous boxer Joe Louis has been quoted as saying that everybody wants to go to heaven but nobody wants to die. Jim wants to live to be a hundred but to never get old. He vowed to himself he would never join a bingo club.

For the first few weeks he didn't have many photos to show. Now the freeze had abated he was able to walk the streets more freely. He saw images nobody else seemed to notice: the cloud-catching facades of skyscrapers that showed reflections of other skyscrapers, which appeared as impressionistic rippled distortions, fabulously rich in both design and colour – an astonishing effect that he thought could make a fascinating theme for an exhibition. As he stood on the middle islands of busy avenues taking shots, taxi drivers yelled, "Hey, you crazy or sumpin'?" He would throw back, "It's OK, I'm a recondite artist," and then they, "Yeah, well you'll be a f•••ing dead one you stay there."

He hadn't shaved for six weeks and his hair was longer than usual, so I suppose he did look a bit like an artist. But crazy? I don't think he is crazy, but who knows.

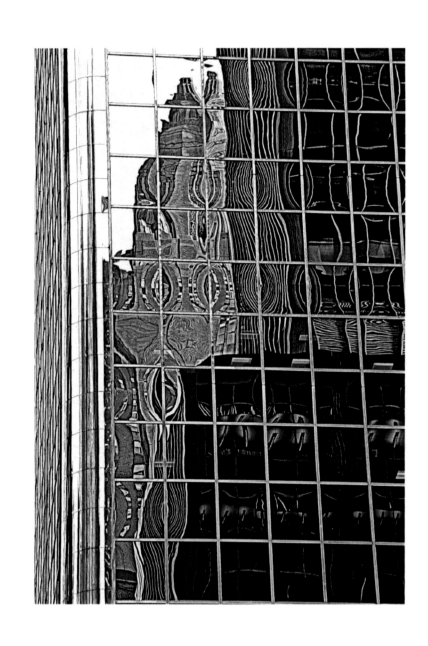

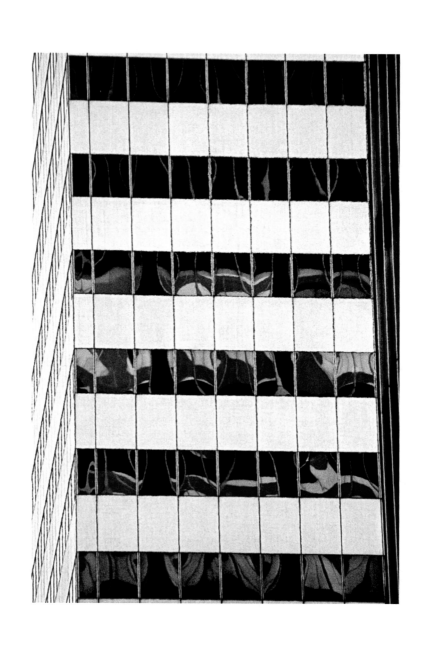

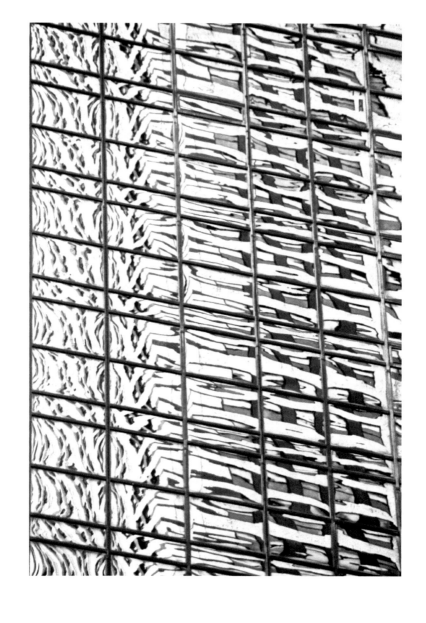

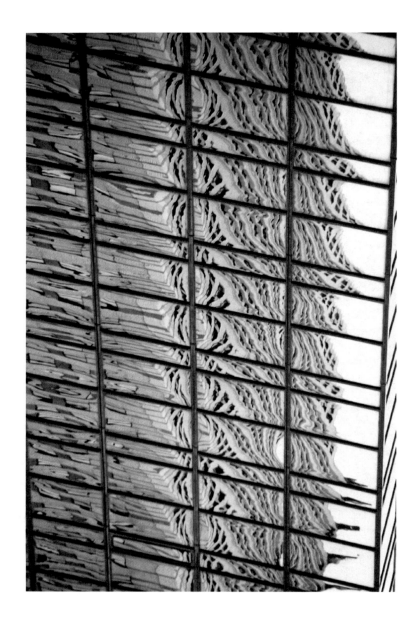

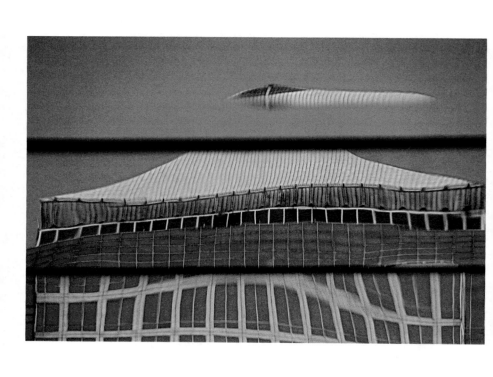

13

Chez Marcel

It was a cold, dark December morning.

Considering he'd never had any previous experience with white-water canoeing Jim was coping well, ducking and weaving, swerving around rocks with the sureness of a migrating salmon. He suddenly realised he was in grave danger – he was being drawn irrevocably towards a waterfall of perhaps a hundred metres' plunge. Frantically paddling, blinking his way out of the panic, he found he was not in a canoe at all but actually the turbulent disarray of his bed. He slowly calculated that he had been re-enacting the rapids scene from Deliverance, which he'd watched on DVD the night before. He lay there with that thought for a while, still feeling jittery, considering it, then he thought in advance about what this day could bring, even on one such as this.

There was a flutter of lightning followed by grumbling – resentment, or jealousy, it seemed, at having to do this sort of thing on a Sunday morning while everyone else, for the whole day if they liked, could luxuriate cocooned in the warmth of their beds. Soon after his arrival in Paris, Jim learned to never phone friends on Sundays before midday. *C'est interdit!* You would hear firstly a moan, then the phone drop on the floor.

He threw off the blankets, jumped up, stretched, and had a scratch. On his window he could hear spats of hail, and in his window box a happy little grub was wriggling like a baby's toe. Cauliflower clouds gathering in robust humanoid forms were shouldering one another into what looked like the formation of a huge rugby scrum. Having made probably the most difficult decision he would have to make all day, that of getting out of bed, he decided that since the worst was over he should keep the momentum going. He decided that on this day, Monsieur Turner shall have a nice, long, hot soak. His bed, which had so suddenly lost its warmth, was not happy; folds of unmade blankets were giving him pouts of disapproval and his slippers, like a pair of sleepy bunnies, were peeking from under his bed. The grumbling was turning spiteful. He turned on the radio.

Humming along with the *Four Seasons*, he skipped to the bathroom, tiptoed across the cold tiles, avoiding the mirror, and turned on the taps. He then emptied a sachet of blue-coloured bubble liquid into the steaming tub. He climbed in and submerged himself with just his nostrils exposed, à la hippopotamus style. Clasping his nose and rolling over, going completely under, fathoms below, he pretended he had gone down with the ship, drowned and lost on the sunless, sandy bottom, body inert, hair swaying with the swaying ocean weed. He could hear distinct breakfast clatter of a neighbour; sometimes water pipes muttering like fragments of human-speak (some psychotic huddled in a corner); caw-cawing of crow speak; chuckling; sometimes intestinal gurgling; cries like dolphins and whales. My God, the horrified shriek if Chitra should happen to walk in and see him like that – not the reclining painterly posed Marat with slashed wrist, but the drowned white body of the boy next door. He writhed and splashed about for a while until most of the heat was stolen by his iron bath. On his back again, with the little pink fingers of his right foot he pulled the plug chain. The bath deflated, the plughole chuckled and gurgled and slowly he changed from amphibian back into mammal, a species this time with a coat of thick white fleece.

In his bathrobe and red knitted house socks, his eyebrows slicked down, he set about preparing for himself probably the world's most famous and delectable breakfast: a porcelain-white, rubbery-soft medium-boiled egg with two slices of toast, strawberry jam, and a cup of Darjeeling tea. Maria Callas began to sing *Casta Diva*. What could be better than this, he thought? And, yes, if this day was the 19th, it was also his birthday. Carpe diem!

It was calm outside now, just a gentle applause of light rain on leaves gesticulating in their own quiet language, tears sliding down his fogged window in fits and starts. Through a wiped porthole, he could see across the courtyard to the pair of curtained windows opposite. As if with drug-distorted vision, he saw the rippled reflection of his twin brother and waved to wish him a happy birthday. He waved back. In the far corner of his room, between pregnant silences were the sounds of the tap's blunt drops – splat… splat… splat. To the sink I guess they sounded like the thud… thud… thud of spotted apples falling on a garden bench, or maybe the throbbing of its heart. Kicked out of its doze by its thermostat, the fridge began its quiet habitual muttering.

Then the sky was a nacreous glow; it had stopped raining. The bells of Église des Billettes nearby began their loud, delirious clanging for the ten o'clock service, and then over the next minutes other churches far away did the same.

Sitting at his window now, Jim decapitated his egg and took his first spoonful. Mm. He was about to take his first sip of tea… the telephone rang.

He recognised the voice immediately – pleasant, mellifluous, unmistakable, like Dean Martin's.

"Hello stranger," Jim said, "it's been a long time."

A one-time dealer in sporting goods, tennis coach in a girls' school, a part-time private detective, and now a sometimes moviemaker, it was Tony. For private reasons, he went by several different names: *Mario Crochetti, Private Detective* was one,

Tony Bonnano, Cinematographer was the one Jim knew him by. Of medium height, not bad-looking, dark complexion, and with black hair curled at the back, he did look a bit like Dean Martin; good on voices and accents, and always good for a laugh. They first met at a private informal dinner at Sonia's. Jim gave him his card and soon afterwards Tony rang and asked him if he would do some stills photos for him at a weekend conference he was to film on the northern coastal resort of Deauville. Michel Rocard and Valéry Giscard d'Estaing would be there.

It was a good job for both of them, especially Tony, because it was there he met Olga, a plump young Russian with a pretty face. She was new to France and on holiday. They met in the golf club bar. He was wearing an open-necked white silk shirt, white slacks and his lizard-skin boots. Over drinks he helped her with her English and made her laugh. He drank whisky, she vodka. He made films, he said, and gave her his card. He spoke knowledgeably about film noir and early Russian films she knew nothing about. He told her about his deprived Sicilian upbringing, his hard-working father and devout Catholic mother, that he was an only child, had never married (the six-month one with the checkout girl he didn't count) and was still alone. He told her, his hand on hers, "It isn't easy, being alone." The barstool worked her skirt a little, and it was cute, he thought, that she had only one dimple. He asked for a puff on her lipsticked cigarette. He had given up smoking. She worked as a clerk in a local courthouse where her father was the chief of police. She also took singing lessons and was hoping for a job in one of the nightclubs of Paris. The Les Welk Jazz Band struck up and they flew onto the dance floor and did the rock and roll. They were aware of eyes upon them but it didn't matter, nothing mattered.

To cool down they went wading and paddling together in the moonlight, Tony's trousers rolled up to his knees. On the pier after midnight they were heard singing to one another – Olga, *Bel Canto* and Tony, Dean Martin (*When the moon hits your eye like a big pizza pie, that's amoray...*). Back in The Paradise Lounge they ordered chicken sandwiches. She poured out the Champagne and he poured out his heart – they were intoxicated, they were in love.

The last one down for breakfast, Tony did not look his usual self. The crew, also looking rather worse for wear, laughed when he was made the butt of a rather crude joke. Later, in Paris, between them they chose the ornaments for their new apartment, the new doormat, found agreement on the yellow the kitchen chairs should be painted, and sort of agreed on the wallpaper for the spare room, decorated with the whole range of Old MacDonald's farmyard animals. The curtains were all hers.

But all that was years ago.

Jim could hardly make out a word he was saying.

"What's that you're listening to?"

"Dire Straits."

"Yes, well could you turn it down a bit?"

Tony apologised for ringing so early. He needed a favour.

He was to make a film clip for US TV – *Ripley's Believe It Or Not*. He asked Jim if he could come around midday to a restaurant in the Fifth Arrondisement just off Rue des Écoles where, believe it or not, doggies would be served their annual Christmas lunches. It was called Chez Marcel. The idea of the film was to make fun of the French and play on their infatuation with their adorable little four-legged friends. It sounded like a lot of fun so, yes, of course he would go. The only complication was that he was supposed to bring a four-legged partner.

Well, no problem. Thanks to the gracious generosity of Karl, his German neighbour (stage name La Baroness Karen von S), he was given approval to chaperone the beautiful Simone, a proud, snooty-nosed, *more*-than-beautiful, silken-haired Border collie. Simone knew Jim from across the courtyard – they had promenaded together on previous Sunday outings. When he rang their doorbell she (Simone) was coiffed to look like royalty, wearing, as she does for special occasions, her faceted glass necklace and matching tiara and the multifaceted brooch pinned in her Louis Vuitton scarf – a bit overdone for a Sunday lunch, Jim thought, but…. *ça va.*

"Remember, honey, be sensitive with her," Karl whispered. "The littlest things upset her."

Being such a cold Sunday morning there were only few people out on the streets; those who were looked and smiled politely, some giggled. An upstairs window was thrown open, a boy was pointing, and with three others laughed out loud and wolf-whistled. Simone couldn't give a damn; she was used to it. Plebs.

Chez Marcel had a welcoming feel. Its front window was filled with a miniature pine forest sprinkled with powdered snow, its tinsel-strewn branches strung with a hundred blinking coloured lights; and perched about like little red robins were many tiny rigid Santas. Reindeers chortled around on a train line to the tune of, over and over:

We wish you a merry Christmas,
We wish you a merry Christmas,
We wish you a merry Christmas,
And a happy New Year.

The window also displayed photos of famous French dog lovers. Brigitte Bardot was the only one Jim could recognise. A sprig of mistletoe had fallen down.

They arrived just when a girl on roller skates was being dragged through the doorway by an overexcited red setter – one of the regulars, obviously.

"Hey, Jim," Tony called, reaching for his hand, "thanks for coming."

"Thanks for inviting me. This is Simone."

"Wow, she looks gorgeous."

She turned her favoured profile.

Jim was surprised to see how overweight Tony had become, his hair longer at the back, thinner on top, and now he was walking with a slight limp. He was not in good shape.

"How's Olga and the kids?"

"Don't ask."

It was a hubbub of talk, clashing plates and spoons, and jolly-sounding Xmas cheer. Furry friends were all shapes and sizes – Jack Russells and cocker spaniels, Pekinese and poodles, boxers and bulldogs, their owners seeming to be mostly kids with their mothers, or ageing mothers who had never had any kids. A Great Dane seemed to be occupying a selfish amount of space. A tiny puppy in a doll's pram wrapped in a shawl and feeling a bit off, was being petted. A bosomy lady nursing her little terrier leaned with pursed her lips and he pecked her.

Marcel, the owner, a diminutive Mexican with little round eyes and elfin ears like a Chihuahua, was doing a great job serving plates of fish fillets, steak cuts, and meatballs with rice, and filling glasses from a jug of wine and bowls from a jug of water. His fat wife, Juanita, following him, was collecting the empty plates and mopping up the spillage. Pedro, their five year-old Chihuahua, was seated down near the kitchen with his younger sister, Fi Fi.

Their table had been reserved near the door with four others Jim already knew: Howard and Kate and their pretty little Christmas fairy, Olivia, and on Olivia's lap, wearing the colours of the French team that won last year's World Cup Final, was Rascal, big-eyed and excited, his mouth laughing. Jim stroked and ruffled him. Simone flicked her hair and looked down her long nose with mild disgust at Rascal's pedestrian taste and beastly behaviour. She wished he'd put his tongue away; she thought his Santa cap absurd.

Jim asked Olivia what it was like being seven because for him it was so long ago he couldn't remember.

"Well, I can't see over as many things as you can," she said.

"How's school?"

"OK, I suppose. I was the only one who knows what a baby kangaroo is called."

"What's your favourite subject?"

"Reading."

"What are you reading?"

"*Harry Potter* in English and *Le Petit Prince* in French. I have to write a poem about a dog. Do you know any?"

"Hmm, yes, I think I can remember one:
Hey diddle diddle
The cat and the fiddle,
The cow jumped over the moon.
The little dog laughed to see such fun,
And the dish ran away with the spoon."

She laughed and asked what a fiddle is.

"Anything exciting?" Jim asked.

"I can do cartwheels and handstands. And whistle through my teeth."

"Anything else?"

"Mm – we saw some kangaroos in the zoo, and a zebra. Daddy litrally climbed over the echidna fence and got some quills that were like litrally lying all over the ground. I was scared they were going to attack him. When we were eating our sandwiches a funny old man in a raincoat came up to us. He was like drinking this stuff from a bottle and he said I was pretty as a fairy. He said to Daddy, 'And you must be the fairy godfather.' I just giggled; Daddy gave him some money."

"Anything else?"

"Um… the old Chinese man at the back of us died in his kitchen. His cooking was burning. The firemen had to litrally break down his door. Mummy, I'm hungry."

They called for the waiter. Jim knew Her Ladyship liked fish, so he ordered it for both of them.

A fluffy little thing, not invited, attracted by the smell of meatballs, was outside touching his nose to the glass, begging to be let in. An elderly white-haired couple of American tourists sauntered in, friendly looking and tubby like a pair of Labradors. They took the only available table, sat down, and then noticed that something was unusual. They thought they'd made a mistake. They didn't know anything about 'doggy dinners'. But then they saw all the Christmas decorations and fancy dress and got the joke, and soon enough were being absorbed into the merriment as well.

Tony, in Private Detective Mario Conchetti's trench coat and his lizard-skin boots, with his motley camera crew, was beginning his interviews down at the other end of the room. Jim made conversation with Kate and Howard about their last sixteen years in Paris and the house they were about to begin building at Martha's Vineyard.

"Architect!" Howard bawled. "Who needs an architect?"

"You'll be sorry," Jim said.

He asked them if they had seen Deliverance, and did they remember the amazing canoeing scenes and the hillbilly banjo boy?

Tony asked each table the same set of questions:

"The world finds it strange that the French should have such a penchant for dogs; how pampered and domesticated they are. Can you explain?"

The owners were indignant. They said they are always surprised by this attitude. Even the little doggies seemed to take offence, being discriminated against like this, Tony intruding in the middle of their Christmas dinners, sticking the snout of his mike into their snouts, the blinding glare of the arc lights.

" *Mais, monsieur, c'est normal!* Eet ees like zat."

"What is strange, monsieur, considering what loyal, loving friends zay make, is why zee whole world hasn't take zem into zeir hearts," one said.

Tony had the impertinence to ask the mother of another, "What about the hygiene of dogs eating off plates in public restaurants?"

Dismissively, "*Bof*," was all she could say.

They must get tired of being badgered like this.

"What do you think of dogs being allowed three-course meals like this when there are millions of people in the world starving?"

"Those millions of people should be eating three-course meals too," she fired back. Touché.

The fish was fresh and delicious.

The cheese plate arrived.

Olivia came running to the table crying out, "Mummy, Mummy, come quick, Rascal is humping Fi Fi down near the toilet." I am not sure if Tony's mike quite picked that up. Kate jumped up and ran. Rascal was pulled back to their table and roused on. Looking up at Jim, panting, wagging his tail, innocent, he appealed for some support. Simone clearly had had enough. She wanted to leave.

At €8 a head, everyone had eaten and drunk very well. Jim made some new friends, and Tony got his TV clip. The American couple, turning at the door to say goodbye to everyone, said that now they can tell all their friends back home they know why the French have such fondness for their dogs. And, "Merry Christmas to you all."

Woof, woof.

Walking home, Rascal hoovered up all the street-corner smells. Simone, with her nose stuck up, caught the breeze. Howard and Kate told Jim they were expecting a couple of friends from Boston for dinner the following Friday – would he like to come and join them?

It snowed on Christmas Day, as it was supposed to.

14

Chez Howard and Kate

Howard L. Hattersley is bookish. He once worked behind the counter in Shakespeare and Company selling books, then in Norway for a season cutting cabbages, where he met Kate. He ended up as an archaeologist and marrying her. With his trimmed white beard and the mane that lies across his forehead like a seagull's wing, in his English tweed coat with patched elbows, and with his slightly elitist manner, he could easily have been mistaken for a pampered Eton grad, but it is his Boston accent that gives him away. And when he laughs he brays like a mule. Kate, also American, is moody and bookish, clever and pretty, and by day a business consultant. They suit one another.

They now occupy a first-floor apartment on rue Beaubourg, near Jim's, where they learned French together; had Olivia, their daughter; and got Rascal, their dog. The apartment is stuffed full of novels and books on archaeology, and beside each pair of French windows are large potted palms sheltering four jolly-looking garden gnomes. In the main room in glass cases are bone specimens, Neolithic bronze implements, arrowheads and primitive fishhooks, and on a shelf are a few small wood-carved African gods. And whereas the average person might display on his wall a set of four flying ducks, Howard has a compressed four-hundred-year-old, ten-foot-long crocodile. Rascal is a bit of a worry around the bones.

At eight o'clock precisely Jim rang the bell. At once the loud, excited barking of Rascal as he came careering down the hallway in leaps and bounds of madness. Kate opened the door and shouted, "Come in, come in. Rascal, you fuckwit, shut up! Come in, come in … shut up, dopey!"

He handed her a bottle. There was Mozart's *Clarinet Concerto* and the smell of curried lamb.

Howard greeted Jim in sandals, explained he had a couple of last-minute things to do, apologised, offered him a drink, then took him to his library to look through his collection. Minutes later the doorbell rang again, and again Rascal went crazy. It was Morgan and Stephanie from Boston. He was bearded too and handsome, a professor of fine arts whose special interest lay in sub-Saharan wood sculptures and tribal masks. He was wearing a black beret and a black cape. Stephanie, tall, sophisticated-looking, a lawyer for a humanitarian aid foundation, was wearing a black trouser suit, both of them full of smiles and immediately likeable. More drinks were offered. Kate went back to the kitchen to put on the rice and warm an apple pie, which left Jim with the two guests.

Stephanie told Jim they had met Howard and Kate whilst shopping one day at Martha's Vineyard and that now they were visiting Paris for the third time. They had loved their visits to Sydney and Melbourne. Jim said that he had enjoyed Boston so much during a thirty-minute stopover between Montreal and New York in the spring of 1991 he abandoned the bus and stayed for four days. Was Orpheo's still there on Charles Street? It was a popular late-night café run by a couple of retired Italian opera singers and he remembered the selection on their jukebox was only opera, and that the shop itself was like a stage set with theatrical lighting. Photos of famous contraltos, baritones and sopranos were fixed to the walls. Jim was welcomed at one table and he remembered being enthralled by Joan Sutherland's singing in the mad scene in *Lucia di Lammermoor.*

Stephanie knew Orpheo's well.

"We loved their chicken cacciatore with mushrooms. The old couple died," she said. "Their eldest son, who is also an aficionado, took it over and as far as I know he is still running it."

"Hello Olivia, hello Rascal, you old rascal," Jim said as they walked in together. Rascal remembered him and gave a woof and a wag.

"Mummy told me you were coming."

Olivia was shy with the couple she didn't know. Jim asked how her dog poem was coming along. She said it was about "a posh dog called Simone, who spent all her days on the phone, she tried to entice and be terribly nice but all she could do was to moan".

"Hmm, dependency-prone for a chaperone, was she?" Jim smiled.

Howard walked in and greeted his friends warmly.

Would they like to see the gold ring he had just found on the street, Jim asked? "Well, it was given to me actually." He showed them and let them fondle it.

"Awesome. Is it really gold?" Olivia asked.

"It was on the footpath, and just as I was about to pick it up a fat gypsy woman beat me to it. She examined it and cried out with wide-eyed amazement that it was gold. She asked if it was mine."

Howard interrupted, "Jim, you didn't – "

"Hold on a minute, I know what you are going to say."

"She said because I saw it first I should have it, and she put it in my hand. I insisted she should keep it. She explained that she was a Muslim and, therefore, she could not keep something that belonged to someone else. Yeah, sure."

Howard was smiling now.

"I played along and said, 'OK, if you are sure, I will keep it', then turned to leave. But she was hungry, she said, and could I spare some money? I gave her two euros. She asked if I could give her some more. I told her I knew she was being dishonest and so that was all I wanted to give, and then I walked away."

The ring was dull, chunky and heavy like gold, one of the latest scams to come from Eastern Europe.

"I looked back and she was gone, like a bad smell."

Kate came and announced, "*À table.*"

"Homework, Olivia."

Kate looked tired.

Wine was served. They drank to wish Morgan and Stephanie a happy stay in Paris.

Archaeology became the subject for table talk.

From the head of the table Howard began to recount the story of Roy Chapman Anderson. Jim had never heard of him; Morgan and Stephanie knew of the name but not the story. Kate had heard it all before.

"He was an archaeologist who began his learning in the early 1900s and developed his knowledge in New York's Museum of Natural History. He then became a traveller in search of treasures, and then a writer."

"He reminds me a bit of Bruce Chatwin," Jim said.

"Yes, it was in the '60s; Chatwin would certainly have known of Anderson." "Chatwin was English," Jim said to the others, "and became an expert on Impressionist art and antiques at Sotheby's in London, and then in the '70s he left and became a renowned travel writer and essayist. He died of AIDS in his forties in 1989."

Howard continued with his story.

"Anderson's fascination with archaeology grew, and so, apparently, did his charm and his ambitions. In 1920 he managed to raise $50,000 from philanthropists of the day, like J. P. Morgan and the Rothschilds, to lead an expedition into the Gobi Desert in search of the link between Neanderthal man and *Homo sapiens*. After nearly two years the search had come to nothing and with his funds practically gone he was on the point of giving up when, can you believe it, he discovered about two hundred sixty-five-million-year-old dinosaur eggs, and many, it was later discovered, contained near-perfect specimens of advanced embryos. The news exploded in New York, which, of course, won Anderson enormous popularity, especially coinciding with Howard Carter's discovery of Tutankhamen in the same time. Then he wanted to go back and, more as a publicity stunt that would add to his popularity (and, of course, his pocket), he organised for one of the eggs to be auctioned. The highest bid at $5,000 came from Mr Colgate of Colgate soap. Anderson returned to the desert and found another batch of eggs, sat upon by what was presumed to be a dinosaur but which, curiously, turned out to be another species. When the Mongolians heard about how much you could get for a dozen eggs they kicked him out and began scratching around for themselves. How about that?"

"Hmm, fascinating," said Morgan. "What a great story." He turned to Jim. "And how many dinosaurs have you discovered lately, Jim?"

Now the centre of attention, Jim returned his smile, sipped some wine, dabbed his mouth and thought. He could recall only one archaeological discovery. It was back in 1985, in the central Australian desert.

"A couple of friends and I drove from Sydney down to Melbourne, across to Adelaide, then up through the Simpson Desert to finally arrive at Alice Springs. After hours of driving in the desert Terrence was bored and complained about how hot it was, wondering if the trip was really worth it. I told him there were subtle colour changes he wasn't noticing, and to prove it I asked him to stop every fifty miles or so. We sampled specimens of soil with varying coloured minerals. Different species of plants, too, with tiny flowers had broken through, depending on the soil type.

"We arrived at Coober Pedy, a small mining town and the world's second largest producer of opals; the summer heat is so intense there that everybody lives underground. When we arrived we parked outside the town pub. Aborigines were lying about in various states of inebriation, some comatose, flies on their faces, forbidden to go inside. The beer tasted good and talk was easy. One of the miners told us that about forty-minutes drive due east was the Stony Desert. It was once a shallow lake and people have been known to find fossils out there – seahorses, bones, shells and the like. I pleaded with Terrence to drive us out there. I wanted to take something back with me."

The telephone rang and was ignored.

"Well, we did drive out and sure enough the desert was suddenly covered with stones as far as the eye could see – smooth, grey, granite-hard, like river stones, about the size of coconuts and spaced about a foot apart. Amazingly, a straight fence divided the plain, flat desert on one side and the stone-covered desert on the other. We wheeled in across the gateway and parked next to the fence. Terrence and Mat stayed in the car to have a smoke while I walked slowly away in a roughly diagonal direction to my left, my eyes scouring the sand floor. After about twenty minutes or so I was beginning to lose hope. I did find, though, that some of the stones had subtle sculptural qualities and if you wiped a bit of spittle on some, veins of colours jumped out. I gathered a few in the crook of my arm. Then I found one that was very different to the others – it was flattish in the shape of an elliptical disc, its two faces convex, one smooth and the other brittle. It looked like a tortoise shell, a neatly sculptured tortoise shell. I dropped the others and decided that was the one I would take."

The telephone rang again and was ignored.

"Then I heard the car horn beeping and Terrence was waving to say it was time to go. He'd driven some way up along the fence to shorten my walk and save time. Even while walking towards the car I was still looking for something. Now, this is the really interesting part. When I arrived next to the car an extraordinary synchronicity occurred. I looked down and saw a slightly larger than average stone with a scoop out of it. No, could it be? I reached down, and my stone fitted perfectly in place. I lifted the whole stone and took it with me back to my all-night coffee shop in Sydney ... as a conversation piece."

"Ah, yes, that was man-made, all right," Howard said, nodding, "I've seen that sort of thing myself. What probably happened, some Aborigine – it could have been hundreds of years ago – wanting to make an axe head, struck this stone with some kind of implement, the piece chipped off, he carried it for a while, thinking about it, and decided for some reason it wasn't quite right, then dropped it. Then many moons later, you, with your inquisitive eye, came along and discovered it. Voila."

He was right; there was a small indentation where it had been struck.

"But think about it," Jim said, "the chances of that stone ever being made whole again: firstly, the chip being 'found' in a desert in the middle of Australia where people never go, picked up, carried in exactly the direction of its parent stone some fifty metres away, then being recognised as 'belonging' together, and then fitted together. Then transported to a coffee shop in Sydney, and now being talked about over dinner in an archaeologist's apartment in Paris." They agreed the serendipity was rather remarkable.

There were a few more exchanges before they rose to leave: tribal groups and rituals in sub-Saharan Africa, the drought emergency in Ethiopia, cabbage cutting in Norway, Claude Monet's Japanese collection....

Howard had planned that early the next morning he would take his couple of Boston friends to Giverny, a couple of hours' drive away, to see Monet's home and studio, his collection of Japanese art and, of course, his beautiful, celebrated garden. After that they would go not far from there to a site which archaeologists know to have been civilised more than thirty thousand years ago. It had recently been ploughed, exposing, possibly, potsherds or flint-stone implements. Since Kate was unwell, Howard asked Jim if he would like to occupy the available car seat. Jim had been to Giverny before, but said, yes, he would like that very much.

Monet's house and garden were, of course, wonderful.

They fanned apart in the ploughed field and set out walking. The wind was icy cold, so Jim's heart wasn't really in it. Howard, though, with his trained eye, came up with a fine specimen of a spearhead, which will probably be of some interest to a museum. At the end of the day Jim invited Howard and Kate to come to the picnics he organises on the Pont des Arts during the summer months.

Le Pont des Arts is the footbridge that links the Louvre on the Right Bank of the river with Quai de Conti on the Left, and during the last four summers it has been a favourite place to gather for evening picnics, about fifty on average. In September there are a certain few days that are very special. This day was one of those. At its equinox the sun arrives at its westernmost position directly above the river and hovers there like a huge drop of glowing, golden honey, a truly amazing spectacle. Many Parisians and passers-by come and stand to watch it go down. It is rather, of course, that the Earth is rotating upwards, the river reaching for the sun. They draw closer, closer and closer – you can see the movement – and then when they touch there seems to be a moment of indecision – does the sun sink into the river and find its place among all the other buried treasures, or does it continue on its vast orbital path? The wavelets, like a myriad scales on a golden carp, shimmer with blinding brilliance. The river engorges the sun, as a python might a suckling pig, slowly, slowly, until in the last moment it is reduced to just a speck of bright molten gold. Then it is gone. The sky is Prussian blue with a blush of crimson; the clouds are in tatters, they drift almost imperceptibly, and, lit from below the horizon, they begin their spectacular, magical colour transformations – lapis to violet, amber to alizarin, plum red darkening to purple red, to black red; finally there is only the night's blackness adorned with sequins, the city skyline a dark profile.

The lamps along the bridge flicker and come alive. The breeze is cool, and over on the Left Bank, above the spire of the Palais de Justice, the moon shows her face and slowly floats up like an errant toy balloon.

Newcomers and invited guests are welcomed with hugs and laughter. Food offerings are plentiful, and the wine puts everyone in a good humour. About 60 are present this time.

At around midnight someone proposes a toast to Jim, the genius whose idea it was in the first place. He takes this with good grace. The attention makes him feel rich, and the wine, as usual, makes him frivolous, boastful and unashamedly silly.

Olivia, sitting next to him, asks, "Do you really have a chateau, Jim?"

"No, my dear little sweetie, I don't have a chateau, I have three – one in Spain, one in Versailles, and the one I live in not far from you. My Paris one has been in my family for many generations. It has seen plagues and famine, marauding armies, peasant revolts, and on the square knights jousting for the heart of a princess like you. From the top they dropped rocks and molten lead on the marauders below, and sometimes the town's scoundrels got their heads chopped off. It was set on fire once."

"Really?" she says, her eyes astonished.

"I am, what you might say, a link in the dynastic chain, a latter day knight-errant, if you know what I mean."

He raises his glass to his chin, causing a bit of spillage.

"Awesome."

They were the leftovers, about a dozen now, talking quietly in the lamps' glow, sipping the last of the wine. Peter had just told his joke about what the drunk said to the Pope; Pascal was quietly humming and strumming his guitar; Veronique, in the moonlight with a change of hairstyle, looked more beautiful than ever; Tony had taken up smoking again; Howard was seated against the rail beside Kate, who had Olivia tucked under her wing; Rascal was curled up on Olivia's lap, and Jim was sitting cross-legged, raising his glass and inventing more tall stories about his French ancestry. Max, the spoiler, a little drunk and a bit slower on this night, said in his acquired Scottish accent, "Don't take any notice of him, lassie, he tells that to all the wee gals. Chateau my toe, he lives in a filthy shoebox up in the Marais."

"*Mais, non,*" Jim insisted to the few who were still listening, "it is absolutely true. We can all go now, if you like, and carry on up at the old fort. We could feast on the balcony with pheasant sandwiches and caviar, imbibe some Cointreau in the tower, have a splash in the fountain, or whatever. *Comme il veut.* If my *femme de ménage* is not up I will bloody well get her up. Hic."

"Yeah, yeah."

Then suddenly, somebody pointed and cried out, "Hey, look at that!"

Everybody's attention turned to the Louvre end of the bridge. A lone man was coming in their direction. It was one of the most pathetically funny things you could ever see. He was so obviously and completely stone-drunk. Starkly silhouetted against the museum lighting, he was going through all the extravagant motions of inebriation, trying to find his way across. The deck of the bridge for him was the deck of a ship caught in a wild storm. He lurched forward three steps, backwards two, was thrown to one side, then to the other near the railing where he nearly went overboard. Righting himself, he swayed about some more. Finding focus, he stumbled forward again, and again had to catch himself to keep from falling down. They were all of them in fits of laughter seeing him so determined to make his way across. He carried on like this for some minutes until he came to within a few metres of them. At that point he fell quite heavily, as if he'd been shot in the back. Rascal barked loudly and wanted to attack him. He took a few moments to regain his breath then struggled to get up.

Jim felt sorry for him and so went to do his knight-errantly duty. He knelt beside him, put his hand on the man's shoulder and had a few quiet words in his ear. He was in his twenties and looked Polish, wearing a dark suit and a white shirt buttoned at the collar, his hair stuck down with perspiration, and stinking like a brewery. His eyes were rolling like a roulette wheel, and when they narrowed to find focus he wondered who Jim was. He gave a silly grin then burped. Jim told him to wait there a moment. He returned to his group to announce that he was going home. He told everybody how pleased he was that they had all had such a good time, thanked them for coming, and hoped to see them again next week.

"No, no, Jim, don't go yet, it's too early," said one.

"There's still plenty of wine," said another, beckoning.

"Jim, stay," the whole chorus said. "It's too early – come, come and sing with us."

"*Merci beaucoup*, no, I must go. Philippe here, my chauffeur, has just arrived to tell me my car is waiting."

And with that, Jim lifted his new-found friend, held him tightly with an arm around him, then, like two war-wounded comrades, they proceeded back to the end of the bridge whence the poor fellow had come, to where Jim's limousine was supposed to be waiting, and where he found for him a taxi.

"Don't forget next Tuesday!" Max called out.

15

Didier

At a certain night-time hour depending on the season and the moon, like chrysalid moths do when they twitch to unwrap themselves, or like the street lamps when they flicker to come alive, there are those too for whom, after a few drinks, at around midnight, observable transformations take place – they change and become who they really are. This night, the moon was waxing to near full.

It was late, not too late, and being a Tuesday there were only a dozen or so in the bar. Because Hernan, the barman, is Chilean, loud-ish, lively Latin American music was playing. It was his idea to stock the bar with books ... it is, in fact, a *bar/librairie*. Max had not yet arrived. Jim ordered another wine. Without a companion you may find yourself lost and forget why you are there.

Laurent, charming and good-looking, just returned from Barcelona with a Picasso tan, gulping down a carafe of white to get himself going, was laughing out loud, prodding Xavier, one of the pseudo-intellectual riff-raff, good at chess and a flamboyant painter. Jean–Camille, too, who the week before was seen at Le Connetable playing his own particular jazzy version of Chopin; and Ruby, gosh, Jim hadn't seen her for maybe ten, twelve years. He was sure it was her; she had such striking looks, even now – fifty-ish, buxom, peroxided if ever you saw one, her mouth drawn with fire-engine-red lipstick, a miniskirt with fishnet stockings that went all the way up, nibbling a cheese plate. Alesio, an Argentinian photographer who became quite well known for his Parisian scenes, dead now, had told Jim about her. He said he used to see Ruby fairly often at the hotel on the Carrefour de Buci. She was madly in love with an American pornographer, Jimmy somebody with some kind of speech impediment, a lisp, he thought… she stalked him endlessly. She had a baby by the fascinating method of standing in the street vetting passing men until she saw the one she wanted, then taking him home. She used to wheel her child in a wonderful English pram, a spiffy Daimler, and made a living by going to artists' studios and demanding a little sketch or two, which she then peddled in exclusive clubs. She sold a César drawing to the Aga Khan in the Club Olympique in St. Germain for five hundred francs, which in those days was a lot of *sous*. Alesio thought she was *le vrai Paris*, the original amour fou, until it transpired that she was a country girl and the black ewe of a respectable village family… it all came out when she was visited by her shocked younger sister. Ruby was at this moment dodging the predatory stares of Henri, a corpulent, balding philanderer with that menacing look of innocence, garnishing some lie to a timid, pretty Japanese tourist, his knee accidentally touching hers. Sitting at the end of the bar in a corner, never troubled by imagination or men, was Tsarina Katharina, a shy little Russian creature with grass-green eyes and fox-red hair wearing grass-green beads and a red fox fur, reading in French, *Alice in Wonderland,* nibbling a raw carrot. Absorbed into the background darkness, near the bookshelves with his glass of Bordeaux, frequenting the bar more regularly now, never saying a word to anyone, was that same sullen Dostoevskyan-looking character. Telu Khan, a shy, diabetic Bangladeshi, was shuffling among them peddling cellophane-wrapped red and white roses; a couple stayed for a drink, then left, as did a collared priest who came in searching for someone who wasn't there. Outside were four young Americans from NYU, laughing loudly and drunk, all smoking cigars – a birthday celebration, it appeared to be – and in a dark doorway, pretty Valerie, Jean-Marc's girlfriend, was being naughty, sticking kisses like postage stamps on somebody she'd never seen before. Hernan wiped the bar and took a sip of his own wine.

Max was late. He phoned to say he would be. Max is Jim's friend. Just beginning to go grey, he is tall and so handsome he is noticed everywhere he goes. Dark eyes, dark complexion, dark demeanour, his black hair tied at the back – Jim imagines Heathcliff, with a hint of more refined menace. He is sixty-one but can pass as fifty-one. Typically he dresses in a thick-knit pullover, baggy corduroys and brogues; sometimes in the dark blue jacket of a Scottish military uniform he bought in London. Sometimes he sports a black fedora, and occasionally is seen smoking a pipe. Coming from a rich, bohemian English background he sometimes seems pompous, but he doesn't mean to be. His home in the Sixth Arrondissement, bequeathed to him by a much older brother, is a large apartment with chandeliers and cracked ceilings, and shelves full of books, music and alcohol… some of the easy pleasures that surround lonely people. As he has known only acquaintances, he never married, never really wanted to. He likes to spend money on the cinema, theatre, books and generous servings of food. He works as a proof reader with the *International New York Times*. Once, when asked what he does Jim heard him say he is a Collector of Old Masters and young mistresses. He looks like he could be. There is something of the poet in him, too – lines pencilled on the backs of envelopes, that sort of thing. Jim enjoys his company, his dry sense of humour. Max comes to the picnics most weeks, and from time to time they ring one another to get together for a drink.

This evening they had arranged to see a play at a small amateur theatre and then afterwards go for a drink at Jim's neighbourhood bar, here on Rue Vieille du Temple. After the play, however, Max was called to his office for an emergency. "Some crazy Pakistani of British nationality," he sighed, shaking his head, referring to the Lufthansa hijacking that had come into the newsroom that afternoon. "It shouldn't take long," he said.

Jim was still on his second glass when Max finally arrived.

"So sorry old chap, had to make an appearance. They got him, nobody killed, all safe."

Max ordered, and as he drank he recounted office anecdotes, drolly describing the eccentricities of some fellow journalists and the amount of booze they drank. He was funny. There was an aura of good-humoured complacency about him.

The play they saw was called *East of Almeria*. It began in a pub after a day's catch – a room with a low ceiling and small windows; a fireplace; a table lit by an oil lamp; a small dark painting on one wall. Stolley, a grey-bearded fishing captain who lived on his boat, was having his usual drink at the bar. He was reminiscing with three others about when he was young, in Genoa. There was what sounded like the beginning of an interesting character story. He was telling his mates about that hot summer's day, about thirty years ago, when he saw this woman in a street café, the same one he'd seen singing the night before in El Paradiso. Admittedly he was drunk then, and it was dark, but not so dark that he couldn't see she was beautiful. She was alone reading *The Magus*, lovely long hair, her blouse half open to catch the breeze. Aware that he was standing there, she glanced up from her book.

"Excuse me, Signora, but your hair…"

He sat with her, ordered drinks and offered a Gitane. She was a painter, she said, and in between times a nightclub singer. Her studio above the café was little more than an iron bed, some shelves and an easel, in one corner a sink with brushes in jars, a small cooking stove, some potted plants in the window and, usually sleeping in the sun, her spoiled and lazy night-black cat. Three of her paintings were on a wall – Cubist Abstract or something. She also gave evening art classes in one of the schools. He charmed her, cared for her, shared a love for music with her – bluesy jazz. They talked about their pasts, made the most of the present, and touched on a possible future. He even gave up the drink, for a while. As soon as he mentioned marriage that day, he knew he shouldn't have.

Stolley, our sea captain, a man among men, unfortunately, turned out to be not at all the feisty stuff of hero. He was, rather, a weak character – not very sexy, not very self-assured, a dull sense of humour, his colours getting darker as he got older, an object of ridicule: "Why don't you drink beer like proper fishermen?" and "Ah, don't get him started on that again." He is a sentimentalist who speaks the 'language of the brook and the dove...soft as the rain on the meadows.' Hmm. He was drunk and maudlin. He had hardly begun his story when the others went to the table to talk about more important things like the day's catch, the price of bream, and extolling the virtues of brown ale. They had heard it all before. *But then, how can you tell a crowd like this?* Stolley thinks, rubbing where his head ached. Rosa, the barmaid, divorced, about Stolley's age, buxom and bountiful, pencilled eyebrows and a kind of hair that reminded him again of his Signora, seemed sympathetic, but she had her job to do. Others came to the bar and talked, but not to him. Soon forgotten, he turned away, found his way to the door and left. His life has never changed, as if he had no choice in it. In short, he was a bit of a bore.

Hernan put on *The Girl from Ipanema.*

"So what do you do with a character like this," Jim asked Max, catching Ruby's smile, "to avoid having the thing descend into a mawkish, dead-end love story?"

Max swallowed back the remains of his drink, drew a grey

nose-rag from his pocket, blew his nose, stuffed it back, and thoughtfully pursed his lips.

"Well, I think the trouble with Stolley is he doesn't know how to tell a good story. It was piss-weak on plot. He had to develop in some way for him to get our interest. He needed to earn his place on the centre stage. We needed some action, some drama – wild sex, some madness, a smoking gun… something. Maybe he needed to get off that aniseed muck and back into the old Genovese grappa – the real stuff, get some of that bloody flamethrower lighting up those salty old veins again."

Yes, Jim supposed, beneath that rather banal exterior there could have been something toxic or idiosyncratic or degenerate, like, for example, that little grotesquerie Jean-Baptiste in Suskind's *Perfume,* or a perverted mind, perhaps, like Humbert Humbert's in *Lolita,* or the passion of Roth's Mickey Sabbath. He could have been heroic or despicable or in some way truly admirable, ordinary even, but ordinary in an interesting way. He could even have been made great. They say behind every great man there is a good woman, and who better than a good, streetwise Italian momma like Rosa? But we didn't know if she felt the same way about him, though, did we? She had work to do. And, by the way, whatever happened to her pipe-smoking daughter who dropped in, the graduate from Dublin Drama School with the trace of moustache and hairy armpits, with the 'sea in her blood'? She could have given him a run for his money. The play's dialogue didn't exactly crackle with wit. The acting was good, though.

Max had caught up with him by now. Jim told him about the film festival he had recently attended in Bombay, the best film he thought, The Feast of the Goat by Mario Vargas Llosa, set in Santa Domingo in the fifties during the ruthless dictatorship of President Trujillo. And then afterwards his meetings with farmers and villagers in Maharashtra. He took out a few photos from his bag to show him. They changed the subject to Max's brother's success with a London firm of architects, and the Canadian girl Max had been bedding before she went back to Montreal.

"*Bon,*" he said, coming from the toilet zipping himself up, announcing his departure. It was around one and his face was a little wine-blushed.

"Must go, old chap; don't forget Saturday. Don't be late. Bring a good bottle. Au Revoir." He gave a friendly slap on Jim's shoulder.

Ruby Red Lips made that she was also about to leave. Max introduced himself, then after a few words, they went off together, laughing – incorrigible, our Max.

There were only a few left: Hernan, who had given up smoking, at the door outside for a break, lit up a cigarette; the tsarina was still reading and nibbling; the thin Dostoevskyan character (Raskolnikov, was it?), his stooped countenance unchanged, his head partly submerged between the shoulders of a thick, shapeless coat, still in the dark with his Bordeaux, just looking. Brooding? Shifty? Max said he thought he was a weirdo. What was he thinking? Find out …. invite him to the bar for a drink. And so Jim did. He seemed surprised that somebody would just walk up to him like that, a bit suspicious even.

"*Hernan, deux Cointreau s'il te plaît.*"

He said his name was Didier. He spoke no English. His awkwardness seemed to be due to shyness. Jim wanted him to feel relaxed, so he asked with a smile what his special talent was, the one he was born with, the thing he could do better than anyone else in the world. He shrugged and shook his head. "*Je ne sais pas.*" Jim told him he was a retired architect with an interest in photography, and that he had lived in the quarter for some years. He showed him some of his Indian photos. Didier's appearance now, in the light of the bar, *was* odd, rather like some

Nordic character in a kids' colouring book, his cheeks pencilled red and to each side a scribble of ginger moss, on his head a topiaried kind of grizzled shrubbery. Oddest of all was the way he looked at you when he was being attentive – his rimless glasses, thick as bottles, perched low on his nose, tilted his head back, which pulled his mouth agape, and breathing through his mouth like that made him seem slightly deranged. In those enlarged, pencilled-in eyes, the colour of sea monsters', were glints of something small and sharp, like tiny chips of glass. His teeth were like oatmeal, and his fingernails, Jim noticed, were chewed. Beneath his unseasonal coat he was wearing a green corduroy suit, at odds with his pair of white joggers.

Didier had been living modestly in Paris since the '80s. He said he was divorced, had a seven-year-old son, and was a biologist with a passion for opera. He took his spectacles off, wiped a small blemish, then put them on again. What he said next surprised Jim. He said he had just come into a fortune and had to decide what to do with it. When things are sorted out he thought he would like to buy a house with a garden in Paris, an apartment near his aunt's in Manhattan, and the chateau that had once belonged to his family, the one a French heroine's name is associated with. He would write a libretto about her. And he will see to it, he said, that his son gets the best education.

His new status, it turned out, was due to an inheritance, which involved his family and the house he grew up in. Yes, he said, he could talk about it. They sat down on the bar stools.

After another drink Jim was gaining Didier's confidence. His family, he said, was of Flemish-Belgian provenance. It was his grandfather, mainly. His name was Monsieur Forget. In the photos Jim was to see of Monsieur Forget in midlife he appeared as a tall, handsome man with a full head of hair, enthusiastic-looking. After graduating at the Sorbonne he began his career as a geologist. Instead of returning to Belgium he went to Canada to work on the construction of the Canadian Pacific Railway. From there he went on down to Mexico where he was employed as a supervisor in a small gold mine. This was in 1921. One day, an Indian with a ponytail of long black hair rode into town to claim back the son he had abandoned some two of three years earlier. He found him in the care of a Monsieur Forget. The youth had been injured in the mine and with nobody else to care for him Monsieur Forget considered it his duty to take him in. The father was very grateful. Anyway, they became quite good friends.

In a conversation, the boy's father recounted how, in crossing a creek the week before, in some large territory further south, he saw sprinkled glints of gold. He showed the sample he had collected. Monsieur Forget, the geologist, inspected them. He asked if he could remember where it was, and could he take him there. Yes, he said, though it would take maybe two or three days of tough riding through hills and forests. They set out early the next day.

At the same spot, there were more traces. Monsieur Forget was sure that the gold had not been washed down from somewhere upstream, more likely eroded from the adjacent hillside. He took out a mining lease, constructed a mine and subsequently found the area to be very rich not only in gold, but silver as well. He became extremely wealthy. The boy's father was well rewarded.

With all his wealth, then, Monsieur Forget went out on a spending spree. He bought up huge tracts of Mexican rainforest and built a logging plant; in France he bought a chateau; and down off the south coast in the Mediterranean, not far from Marseilles, he bought a virgin island. There he set about building for himself and his new wife, in the Spanish style, a rambling brick-and-tile villa. They raised a family there – three daughters: one emigrated to America, one went to Belgium, and Suskia, the youngest, went to live in Paris, where she met Monsieur Genet and had their son, Didier. When Didier was only six months old his father abandoned them and was never seen again. Paris was under Nazi occupation at that time. They managed to escape to the island home to be in the safe company of her parents once again.

During the years we are talking about – the late 1920s, '30s and '40s – Monsieur Forget, himself a personable dilettante and a good drinker, mixed in the milieu of many aspiring artists. He even had his own studio where he dabbled a bit. The island home became something of a bohemian meeting place. People on shore wove fantasies around the house. They leaned to one another to hear the rumours that passed between them and then passed them on, about banquets that sometimes lasted for days, the singing, the laughter and crashing noises. It earned Monsieur Forget quite a reputation. Guests could sometimes be seen through binoculars having their breakfasts at two o'clock in the afternoon, naked, according to the rumours. It was the debauchery that cost him his marriage.

Monsieur Forget's coterie included the abstract artist Lucille Barrymore, who had been a brilliant student at the London College of Art. She enjoyed a successful career as an artist and later became a respected art critic. Monsieur Forget admired her collection, which included little-known painters such as Chagall and Picabia, unsigned pencil sketches that turned out to be by Dufy, landscapes by Cézanne, early experiments in Cubism and Surrealism, and some rare but not very fine works of Russian socialist realism. Monsieur Forget offered to buy some from her for a good price and she accepted.

"Are you following me?" Didier asked.

"Yes, yes, go on," Jim said.

Now, on the same day when Matisse died in November of 1954 came the news of Monsieur Forget's death. It was a great farewell. Madame Genet continued living there. In her lonely last years the island home had become overgrown with shrubs and vines, the whitewash flaked away, the pointing crumbled; and the island, too, subdivided and was being sold off as building sites. She inhabited only one part of the house then, living the life of a hermit, scratching around in her garden and caring for her twelve-year-old dog, Capitaine, who was fat and slow and half blind – she was getting that way herself. An odd couple, people said. One morning – a Friday it was, a day of the social worker's visit – Capitaine was heard whining at the foot of the stairs next to Madame Genet's broken dead body. Capitaine died the next day.

The flip side of *The Girl from Ipanema* was playing now, and Hernan was counting his takings.

Didier continued.

He said he and an uncle have been searching the family records to sort out the estate, which meant having to go to the island home. An agent had rung to say there was a lot of interest in the property. In one of the outhouses with its wooden doors rotted away there was an early-model Citroen with flat tyres, a tractor, a lawnmower, and six antiquated tennis racquets – the tennis court lay buried beneath tall grass and brambles. Inside the house on the walls of the salon were gilt-framed paintings of Flemish ancestors, and on the fireplace mantel a collection of tarnished pewter mugs. Most of the nomadic rugs had come from the region of Baluchistan; platters on a pinewood kitchen dresser were decorated with bucolic scenes; bed sheets and lace lay folded in wooden chests; Madame Genet's collection of cameos in silver boxes; and in one corner, near a sunny window, her old sewing machine. Didier could feel his mother's recent presence, he said.

Rooms that had remained locked for years were prised open. Tucked away in drawers in the studio were four works by Picasso, four by Cézanne, one by Salvador Dali, a page of very fine pen-and ink sketches to be verified, and others that couldn't be attributed to anyone.

The artworks are now in Paris, kept in a small bank managed by a close friend of the family. A photographer goes there each day to catalogue the collection.

Hernan leaned over with his pleasant smile.

"Closed, Jim. Katharina, *Fermé,*"

Outside the bar, Didier told Jim that that week he had received copies of the first sets of photographs. Not wanting to cast doubts on his story, Jim asked if it would be possible for him to see them. They arranged to meet a few days later.

When the day of their meeting came, Didier seemed to have lost his shyness completely. He began by showing Jim some of the family photos he'd discovered in the house: a sepia print of his mother; his grandfather in middle age with a group of artists, one of whom could have been Picasso; one of his two aunts as little girls; himself as a boy; and early shots of the house – a complex of single-pitched tiled roofs set in the rugged island landscape. He remembered the beach of his childhood, their pet puppy, riding on the back of the tractor, and some of the wild goings-on at the parties.

Of the photos of the artworks, he first showed one in a style Jim immediately recognised.

"Toulouse-Lautrec, as well?" Jim stammered.

"No, no," Didier said, *"regardez"*, and showed him the photo of what was written on the back: *"D'après Toulouse-Lautrec"* and signed, *Picasso*.

Similarly, the signature on the back of the second painting, much in the style of Raphael, was Picasso. There were what could have been some ideas for his early Guernica sketches. Then Didier showed Jim a photo of a painting with a muddy-brown background and two small female figures – Salvador Dalí's mother and sister, done by him at the age of thirteen. The surprise that was to come from that painting was the discovery that beneath the surface was another he had painted over. The page of pen-and-ink sketches, four poses of the same male figure in a toga, where every fold was an exercise in light and shade, executed with superb aplomb, unsigned, was discovered to be by Poussin. Being rare examples of his early works, these aroused some interest from Le Louvre. That was all Didier could show at that stage – nothing yet by Cézanne.

16

Israel

A t an author's reading at the Village Voice Bookshop in Paris was a woman with a particularly lovely, interesting face. In the gathering afterwards Jim found the opportunity to meet and talk with her. Her name, she said, was Sarah and she was from Jerusalem. She was staying at the Cité des Arts, improving her skills in making sculptured jewellery. They saw one another only a few times over the following months and each time they had a lot to talk about. On the last occasion, just before her departure for Jerusalem, she invited Jim, should he ever be there, to come and meet her family. Her son, David, was studying architecture and her husband a practising architect. That opportunity arose the following year when he was assigned to a job in Egypt.

From Cairo Jim took a bus to Luxor where he marvelled at hieroglyphics inscribed on stonewall temples, and then through the rocky desert to the Valley of the Kings where he entered the tomb of Tutankhamun. Past fissured sandstone cliffs he visited Queen Hatshepsut's Temple. His final destination was the town built in the 1930's called New Gurna. Here, with a team of consultants he was to advise on the restoration of its open-air theatre.

On his return to Cairo he visited the Cairo Museum to see the more than 5,000 fabulous objects discovered by Howard Carter in Tutankhamun's tomb in 1921. The first ever known example of blown glass was the small round-bottom bottle, translucent olive green with fire marks; fold-up beds and fans and fabulous jewelry, and, most personal, was the bouqet of flowers his young wife had placed on his brow just before the sarcophagus was sealed four thousand years ago. The petals were a dark blood red. There was the young Pharaoh's favourite reed stick too that he took with him on his walks along the Nile, knocking off the heads of flowers.

16th March 1997

The security check Jim got from El Al (the Israeli airline) at Cairo Airport before boarding his 10.30pm flight to Tel Aviv was very impressive – his first encounter with Israeli efficiency. Everybody had to be checked, of course, but especially him, it seemed. Why him? I am still not sure. I suppose, on paper, he did look a bit suspect – non-Jewish, a man travelling on his own, a week spent in Egypt, intending a brief stay in Israel with no stated address, his passport photo looking like a mug shot photo on Interpol. Firstly, he was interrogated about his week spent in Egypt. He said that, yes, all the contents of his bags were his. He was then asked to lay them on the table. The seams of every item of clothing and the buckles and clips of his shoulder bag were fingered with the skill of a professional safe-breaker; even his toothpaste tube was inspected and his shoes taken away to be X-rayed. His body was searched behind closed curtains; his camera and shaver, confiscated for 'technical reasons' were to travel unaccompanied in some other compartment of the plane.

I guess one reason for the extra-tight security was that this week there would begin the construction of a new neighbourhood of 930 apartments in the Har Homa district of southern Jerusalem that was annexed to Israel after the 1967 war. It was considered an illegal settlement under international law; barriers would separate the West Bank from parts of

East Jerusalem where Palestinians go to pray. Hezbollah, the
military wing of the Palestine Liberation Organisation warned
of reprisals. This week, too, was the annual biblical celebration
of Purim when, for three days, all the Israelis in Tel Aviv would
come and crowd the streets in high spirits to shop and fill coffee
shops. It had been on the same occasion the year before when a
bomb ripped through a busy department store in the centre of
Tel Aviv, killing twenty-two.

Finally satisfied, to compensate for Jim's exasperation
and by way of apology for having put him through such a
procedure, he was handed an invitation to go up and wait for
his flight as a guest in the El Al VIP lounge where he could
avail himself of snacks and drinks, and the lounge-chair
comfort of English-language newspapers. He would have the
peace-of-mind comfort, too, of knowing that with security like
this, the flight was probably going to be safe. On his way to
the lounge he walked through Egyptian personnel-only areas
without even being noticed.

Shuffling in the queue towards the plane, he could see they
were probably a full load, Americans mostly – business-suited
men; black-bearded and black-attired Orthodox Jews; tired kids,
and a group of garrulous Christians – southern blacks (*The Good
News Is Jesus* printed on their T-shirts) going to celebrate Easter
at the biblical Church of the Holy Sepulchre in Jerusalem. In
front of him was an Arabic-looking man with a thin moustache.
No sooner was he in his allocated seat than a gorgeous hostess
came to escort him down to the front of the plane to fly, for
his first time ever, first class. She offered a glass of Israeli red
wine. *Why me?* he asked himself again. An Israeli businessman
next to him insisted that the honey, figs and oranges of Israel are
the best in the world. He urged him to see Yad Vashem and to
honour the martyrs of Masad, and learn a few words of Hebrew.
He warned against Arab street traders.

Needless to say, the flight was otherwise uneventful.

It was after midnight when he arrived in Tel Aviv. He retrieved his bags, camera and shaver, changed some money, then stepped outside into a temperature much colder than he was prepared for. A taxi driver took him to a hotel he knew in Disengorf Street in the city centre – anything would do at that late hour.

As if to spite him for his dislike of things in Cairo – the hot, heavily polluted air; the overcrowding of narrow footpaths and bus stops; the men's shoving and lack of consideration for women when a bus finally did come; the neglect of decaying historic buildings and appalling workmanship of the new; the incessant, neurotic blowing of horns in standstill traffic; and his frustration of not knowing the language – it had managed to give him a parting sweet kiss of dysentery, probably thanks to that last doubtful snack at Cairo Airport, or it could have been the day before in Luxor. For the first three days in Tel Aviv he felt drained; the weather was days of rain and bluster and nights of numbing cold.

19th March 1997

Lodging was found in a small family-run hostel off Dizengoff Street in the central shopping district of Tel Aviv. In the entry there was a large framed photograph of Theodor Herzl, founder of modern Zionism. Jim's room was small but airy and clean with a steel-framed bed, a basin and a plain, unsteady wardrobe bereft of coat hangers, whose doors had the teasing habit of swinging open each time he went near them, as if in need of a friendly embrace. Amos, the manager, was an affable, complicated man living a simple life. His whole body limped heavily away from the leg crushed ten years earlier in the car accident that killed his wife and two friends. In conversation he talked too loudly and would often cut Jim in mid-sentence to talk about some new personal frustration he was suffering.

Jim commiserated. "Oh well, life goes on," he would sigh. Jim was his only guest for the first few days. Jim felt his eyes watching his comings and goings through a chink in his door. It was OK. He thought he would probably keep the room for the duration of his stay.

Around the corner was the city centre's fruit and vegetable market. On this, his first day of regained health, and with an improvement in the weather, he ambled out to do his first shopping. Direct from the cultivated farms of western Israel, the produce was best quality and abundant. After Egypt it reminded him of how he felt on his arrival by bus at the first rest station in Finland in 1991 after a few impoverished weeks in Russia. The refreshment rooms were polished, immaculate white tiles and chrome taps, and the shop displayed the full range of everything Scandinavian – yoghurts, cheeses, unsweetened biscuits and fresh, rich-coloured fruits (shining apples like bursting ripe bosoms) – all the things he had been craving. The Israeli figs and oranges *did* look to be the best in the world. One peculiarity, apart from melon-sized grapefruit, was large, lidded water jars of long, skinned carrots all so uniformly cut to size they looked manufactured, like laboratory clones.

21st March 1997

There are beautiful women to be found everywhere, of course, all over the world. On the streets of Tel Aviv Jim thought he was just having an exceptionally good day, but by evening he came to believe it must be a national trait. The post-war Jewish migrants came from all over Eastern Europe – the blue-eyed blonde Ashkenazim from Russia, Poland, Hungary, Germany and Lithuania; and fewer dark-skinned Sephardic Jews from Spain and Morocco, with prodigious curly or tightly crimped hair gathered behind into bunches like wild brambles, sometimes wisps of it escaping around their faces. It seemed to be a marriage of both of these groups that produced the people he saw over the next few weeks in the streets of Tel Aviv.

When adolescent friends meet they do so with an embrace, a real embrace. They throw their arms around one another and hug with a long, strong, affectionate hug, as if it is a homecoming. It is, in a way – they are family with ties that go back through many generations, either here or abroad. But just being Jewish is enough; they are all in the same stream of history bearing the weight of a burdensome past, suffering the racial tensions of today's reality and the fears of tomorrow's uncertainties. At the heart of the Jewish embrace, it seemed there was something desperate and tragic.

This was the first of three days of annual celebration of the biblical occasion called Purim. The wind and rain of previous days had gone and it was now calm with sunshine and blue sky. It was a perfect day. Crowds were coming into the park and all along Sheinken Street and, again, it seemed everybody knew one another, all laughing at their fancy-dress costumes – the girls dressed as cats, vampires, Santa Clauses, schoolboys and nuns; the men, ironically, made great-looking Roman warriors or Egyptian pharaohs. A businessman in his car nudged his way through the crowd with a stuck-on nose and a long curlicue moustache. Jim made his way to Nahalat Binyamin Street, recently closed to all vehicles to allow a pedestrian flea market. All street terraces were crowded. To be able to watch the passing parade in comfort, Jim was welcomed at a table with four others who were all enjoying the spirit of the occasion. He ordered an omelette breakfast. It was so good to have regained his appetite and to be feeling normal again.

Strolling around the market he met Riki, yet another exotic-looking young lady with tresses down her back. She lived in the neighbourhood and was a regular stallholder – she sold her own hand-dyed silk scarves. It was amusing to see one of the market eccentrics walking by, a whiskered old man, sinister-looking, shrugged in a heavy overcoat, and dangling from his nose a long rubber penis. He walked up to people and sniggered in their faces. Riki said there were quite a few like him.

Riki accepted Jim's offer of a fresh-squeezed fruit juice from a nearby stall. A small crowd was gathered there. Everyone's attention was drawn to a TV screen mounted above. Something was wrong. On the screen was a street scene – tables and chairs were strewn all over the place, and there was panic, people being rushed away on stretchers. Jim appealed to the person next to him to tell him what was happening. He said it was live reportage outside a coffee shop on David Ben-Gurion Street, around the next corner, about two hundred metres away. A bomb had been planted there. Now you could actually hear the police and ambulance sirens. Of the faces of the people around Jim none showed the panic he was feeling; just a quiet sadness. While politicians continue to wrangle, this has become a way of life.

24th March 1997

Sarah sounded pleased when Jim rang her. She said if he could make it to their home in Jerusalem by 11am on Sunday, he would be welcome to attend a musical recital to be given for about thirty guests. It was only about one hour away by bus. Yes, he said, he would love to come.

On the early bus from Tel Aviv, his concentration was divided between the young conscript seated beside him and the barren hills of rocky desert that were passing by. The lad was eighteen years old and doing the three years' army service every Israeli youth is obliged to do (teenage women do one year and nine months). He was in uniform and armed with an Uzi rifle. Most of the soldiers patrolling Tel Aviv each day are armed with U.S. made M16s – much more lethal. He was taking two days' leave from duty to be with his family who were living just south of Jerusalem. In conversation he was friendly, intelligent and responded carefully to Jim's questions. He didn't like having to be in the army, he said, but even if he had the choice, in the circumstances it would be what he would want to do, have to do. If not, he would shame his parents, and his country, and himself, as well as the many Jews who had fought and died in their struggle for a homeland. He had a great love for Israel, he said.

Barren hills persisted with no villages, not even a single farmhouse. Sometimes a clump of cypresses or a single olive tree had managed to break through. Grapes and figs could manage, Jim thought, and certainly lizards and scorpions. Approaching Jerusalem, new apartment blocks appeared spasmodically on the hills, some still under construction, and then in the valleys many more were gathered.

A few miles before Jerusalem they arrived at Mea She'arim. This was the first settlement to be built outside the Old City a hundred years ago. In the narrow, un-guttered streets was a traditional way of life that has never changed: pedlars, beggars, quacks and bent-over old people with beards making their ways with sticks, others carrying heavy loads or wheeling barrows. It was the lifestyle that existed for centuries in the ghettos of Eastern Europe. There was not a flower, a leaf, or even a blade of grass, only the dirt colour of neglect and dilapidation, things falling apart. A classroom full of boys recited passages of religious learning; in an overcrowded, airless yeshiva, behind small black holes for windows, disciples of the ultra doctrines were engaged in full-time study. Prayers and texts are not spoken in common Hebrew but only in Yiddish, the archaic language of Eastern Europe. This town described the ultra-Orthodox Jewish way of life. Their savage bigotry and fanatical intolerance of others' ways places them in the far right of Israeli politics. What a strange sight to see so many of them dressed in their customary attire. Jim had seen some of this before in the Jewish Quarter of Paris – Mormon-length black coats or silk caftans belted and tied at the waist, some with trousers gathered into black or white knee-high socks. Some donned black wide-brimmed black hats like Roman cardinals; some, Borsalinos; others, cylindrical fur hats; others, less extreme, just the simple kippa – a knitted skullcap of pure wool. Faces were typically pale as lard with full, bushy black beards, wearing heavy black-framed spectacles and sometimes, strangest of all, single shoulder-length ringlets dangling down on each side. The young boys, as far as possible, are attired as junior versions. The moderate Jews refer to these ultra Orthodox men as 'penguins'. Jim was tempted to get down from the bus to take photographs, but feared he might get pelted with stones.

After Mea She'arim the bus was making its stops along the way. Some of the religious were boarding to go to the Old City to make their daily prayers at the Wall of Lamentation, known commonly as the Wailing Wall, the only remnant of the Jewish temple that was destroyed by Nebuchadnezzar II in 587 BC. Seated with their holy books open before them (the Talmud or Old Testament), not looking up or seeing anything else, their lips recited passages of the text over and over. He caught himself staring at them like an innocent child does when fascinated by an unfortunate person's obvious affliction. The teenage girl opposite had her eyes tightly closed while she memorised passages, nodding as if in a mesmerised trance. A woman with a strikingly beautiful face, wearing a black scarf around her head, indicating she was probably married into Orthodoxy, looked to be from the Middle Ages. She, too, was reciting in whispers, and, sensing Jim's curiosity and catching his gaze, gave him a lovely smile, then went back to her book and was reabsorbed. Jim resumed reading in the *Jerusalem Post* the aftermath of the bombing in Tel Aviv of three days ago while she still had not progressed beyond the beginnings of Jewish monotheism of three thousand years ago.

As the bus was descending there was an exciting moment when, from between two houses, he caught a glimpse of the Old City. Then, rounding a bend, it was there again, caught in the foliage of a tree this time. As the bus swung onto the open road, suddenly there it all was, laid out before him in a small valley, dazzling in its whiteness, an ancient archaeological treasure – Jerusalem!

Not much larger than a small suburb, you could see a massive wall snaked around it in a protective embrace. Churches, mosques, more than a thousand synagogues, the vaulted humps of the bazaars and the parapets of flat-roofed houses, all densely packed, made a fantastic sight. It was nearing midday so the city, without its shadows, only bright light reflecting off white stone, was literally dazzling. And there to his left and beyond, on a plateau, with a bright white point of the sun's reflection, was the city's most prominent feature, the golden dome of the Mosque of Omar, eight hundred years old. Jim's eyes devoured everything. Down one of the banks sloping towards the city was the litter of what looked like chips of stone. On the map he found this to be one of the vast burial grounds – the Necropolis.

The bus pulled up beside the huge gateway known as the Dung Gate, the entry into the Jewish Quarter. In the ancient wall that surrounds the Old City the only breaches are the eight huge double wooden gates. It was the ancient wall the Romans scaled in the year 70 to cast out the Jews; the same one the Crusaders scaled in 1099 to massacre Jews and Muslims; and near the same one from which the Palestinian youths of today, with slings like David used against Goliath, pelt the armoured Israeli police cars.

To enter through the gateway Jim had to have his bag searched by Israeli soldiers. From this elevated position one could look down to the massive stone wall, the Wailing Wall, about sixty feet high, its large square spacious enough for a congregation of maybe five thousand visitors and worshippers. Each Saturday thousands of local and overseas Jews visit the wall to pray, standing next to it, often alone, nodding and whispering to it, sometimes tucking into its hollow joints folded bits of paper scribbled with prayers or pleas for help – a kind of letter box to God. A family had gathered there to celebrate a young man's bar mitzvah. There were hundreds of tourists behind a barrier looking on and taking photographs. Nobody else seemed to notice that high up on parapets, keeping constant vigil, were armed Israeli soldiers.

Jim wanted to visit the Golden Mosque. Crossing from the Jewish Quarter into the Muslim Quarter, he was subjected to another bag search by Israeli soldiers. The lanes of the bazaar, narrow as footpaths, were crowded; the daylight under the cover of muslin sunshades was subdued. Objects for sale were mostly handmade – bags, sandals, carpets, clothing or incense – and farm-produced spices and herbs. Looking beyond the ends of these shaded corridors, sometimes framed by a stone archway, turbaned men in djellaba could be seen in bright sunlight, and then beyond them, in another subdued stretch of lane, people were dark forms again. This kind of modulation of light and shade Jim remembered from the souks of Marrakech and Istanbul.

Away from the bazaar, in the neighbourhood of the Muslim Quarter, the walls of the houses which form the lanes were typically eroded or in a state of ruin. Some were gone altogether. Over an arched doorway into somebody's home there was carved into its headstone an intricate design of Arabic geometry, and painted above that, some beautiful Arabic script. Further on, displayed as a curtain behind a window, was an Israeli flag. The window's glass was smashed. Kids were kicking a plastic ball about, while others were breaking up some thrown-out furniture to carry home for firewood. Along the approach to the entry gates of the Golden Mosque, in a deep open drainage culvert half full of stagnating acid-green water, there was an accumulation of neighbourhood garbage.

At the gate Jim was told brusquely by an Israeli soldier that to enter he had to wait half an hour till after the Muslim prayers. A stallholder nearby was selling postcards and Kodak film. As an excuse to meet him Jim asked if he had any black-and-white film. He didn't. Jim told him he was Australian and waiting for the mosque to open; would he mind talking with him? The stallholder smiled, pulled up a stool and asked Jim if he would like some tea. The name he gave was Joe. He was a big man who looked moderately well off. Jim asked him about his life. His family had lived in the city for seventy years, he said. The Israeli government had offered to buy his home, but each time he refused. He knew others who had sold out and said he wanted to cut their throats. Seven years ago he had been offered US$90,000, now he was being offered $3 million. He will never sell, he said, not at any price.

"We'll get it back, we'll fight them, without Arafat if we have to. He is not only a bad politician but a bad soldier; he doesn't know how to fight."

Joe showed his anguish, shifting restlessly from one position to another.

"Hussain, too, was a traitor for coming over to lick the arse of the Jew Prime Minister." (Jordan's Prime Minister came to give his condolences and regrets for the shooting the previous week of seven Israeli girls by a crazed Jordanian soldier.)

"Couldn't there be some sort of compromise?" Jim asked.

"No! We get it all, it's ours."

"All of what?"

"All that's ours, our homeland, everything from the Mediterranean to the Jordan River."

Joe knew, of course, that would not be possible.

Thousands of Palestinians have been forcibly expelled from their homes, their homes destroyed and their land of grape and olive seized and built upon by Israeli settlers. This, of course, is illegal. The US administration says it wants to broker a two-state solution, but the gap of disagreements is still too wide. More likely it is a play for more time to allow more occupation? A Paelstinian demand the Israelis say they will never agree to is a right for the exiled Palestinians to return.

"Wouldn't a guarantee of full and equal rights for all in some form of confederation or unitary state be possible?" Jim asked.

Joe was steaming. He was not even listening any more. He was really only thinking of revenge. After a tense pause, he leaned to Jim so nobody else could hear.

"There will be another explosion in Tel Aviv this weekend, for sure, you'll see."

The gate to the sacred site was opening now for visitors. Jim turned to him with his last question:

"Joe, since you feel so strongly about your land and your people, why do you choose to wear Western-style clothing instead of the keffiyeh, like Yasser Arafat?"

"I buy my clothes in Canada," he replied, "and I prefer this style."

At the entry gate, Jim underwent another search by Israeli soldiers.

It was quiet in there, in the garden – other tourists had not yet arrived. This sacred Muslim site is known to the Muslims as the Noble Sanctuary, and contains the Mosque of Omar and Al-Aqsa Mosque. To the Jews it is the Temple Mount (because it is located on the same site of what, more than two thousand years ago, was the original Jewish temple). The ground was level and about the size of a playing field, and its enclosure all round was a high stone wall. Olive trees were growing in groves, each one stooped, gnarled, scarred and twisted into the grotesque forms of old age, symbolic, it seemed. The ground was scattered with the same chips of white stone Jim had seen from the bus in the desert. He picked up a few to study their subtle tinges of grey and pink and, for a souvenir, put one in his pocket.

Central to the garden, were wide steps that formed the stone podium of the grand mosque. Over at the southern corner of the garden, a literal stone's throw away from the mosque, he could see that one wall retaining the garden was the parapet of the Wailing Wall below, the only remnant of that first Jewish temple. And from the elevated position on the podium, looking eastwards beyond the city wall, one could see the distant hills of the Mount of Olives, and beyond that the Judean Desert, and Jericho – the oldest known habitation in the world. There also was the northernmost tip of the Dead Sea in the rift valley – a valley 820 feet below sea level, the lowest known land spot on Earth – and beyond that, about twenty miles away, was Jordan. He took some photographs of the surrounding hills and urban expansion.

On the southern side of the garden is Al-Aqsa, another very significant mosque – much smaller in size than the Mosque of Omar. There was an incident at Al-Aqsa one morning in 1969, instigated by a mentally disturbed twenty-nine-year old Australian named Denis Rohan. He was a member of a Protestant Christian sect who was 'called' by the Radio Church of God in Australia to remove this 'abomination' so as not to delay any longer the second coming of Christ. He stuffed wads of kerosene-soaked cotton under the exquisitely carved wooden pulpit and set it on fire. There was serious damage. The Muslim world, of course, believed it was a Jewish plot of premeditated arson. Incensed crowds from Morocco to Pakistan clamoured for jihad. A preacher on Radio Baghdad announced that rivers of blood would not atone for this unspeakable outrage. Things almost got very dangerously out of control. Very.

Jim walked to a secluded part of the garden where only the sounds of a few small birds could be heard. There were very few people still. Two seated Muslim women were talking together. He wondered what they might be able to tell him about their lives. He smiled a hello and began to speak. Predictably, politely, they immediately retreated behind their protective veils and waved him away. He was infringing on their customs, but they probably couldn't speak English anyway. Just when he was ready to go and see inside the mosque, he was being shouted at by the Israeli soldiers at the gate – they were angrily waving him towards them because the visiting period was now over.

A few Israeli flags were draped on walls and flying from rooftops in the Muslm Quarter. To be mischievous, he stopped a young Orthodox Jew hurrying on a main street and asked why there were no Palestinian flags in the Muslim Quarter. The youth glared with contempt.

"Because it is forbidden," he said. "What some people refer to as the 'Muslim Quarter' does not exist. It is an area that Muslims may inhabit, but they must never forget that it is only because we give them permission to do so."

From one of the backstreets Jim could see through a vaulted passageway a small courtyard with potted trees, arched windows with fine filigree-carved screens, and above a doorway on its lintel some beautiful carved Arabic ornamentation, and above that some ornate Arabic script. He walked into the passageway to get a closer look. Two young Palestinian boys, aged about fifteen, followed him in and began jostling him. In the scuffle, the one behind tugged at his camera strap and shoulder bag, then his back pocket. Jim pushed back, choking out something about them being stupid. They forced him up against the wall. One, his eyes inches from Jim's and his dagger resting gently on his cheek, snarled, "I kill you" – the face of a career sadist, and his breath was fair indication that inside, deep down, there was something really rotten. Jim was able to quickly force his way to one side just as another older boy came shouting at them, abusing them, telling them to get away before the soldiers came. As they ran off, he clipped one of them and then turned to Jim to help brush the dust off his back. Jim pulled in a deep breath and actually thanked him. He was later reminded of that day on an industrial wasteland just outside Rome when a pack of feral urchins, girls and boys, came at him begging for money, then were all around him, forcing his pockets, pulling his bag and camera and ripping his shirt, the way animal predators taunt weak or wounded prey, debilitating it, forcing it into submission, then finishing it off. They were not malicious but did manage to run off with his bag, which had only changes of clothing and spools of unspent film – not so much a pack of wolfish predators as a band of ill-bred Lilliputians.

Leaving the Muslim Quarter, Jim began to make his way towards the Christian precinct to visit the Church of the Holy Sepulchre. He walked there indirectly through the Jewish Quarter. Within this narrow triangle formed by the Mosque of Omar, the Wailing Wall and the Church of the Holy Sepulchre, these three extremes of creed represented most of all religion of the entire Eastern and Western worlds. Going from one site to another like this, he was beginning to feel that he had come into some great living museum.

The whole of the Jewish Quarter was immaculately clean, gentrified in white stone – modern banks, fashionable clothing shops, designer jewellery, espresso coffee and fast food and wifi. The Postmodern-style apartments accommodated mostly middle-class professionals, many immigrants from the USA and born-again, like the young man he met from Los Angeles with the incipient ultra beard studying in one of the many religious seminaries. Jim asked him for directions to a cash distributor outlet. As they walked together, the man told him about his commitment, his new spiritual life and how good it could be for Jim as well. His persistence became a nuisance. Jim left him and walked across some grass to a quiet place to see engraved on a sunlit wall the following inscription from Zechariah:

> *Thus saith the Lord of Hosts: there shall yet old men*
> *And old women dwell in the streets of Jerusalem,*
> *And every man with his staff in his hand for every age.*
> *And the streets of the city shall be full of boys and girls playing.*

What of the Palestinian kids, he thought, playing in their dirty, rubble-strewn alleyways, kicking their plastic ball around; those in tiny stalls selling cellophane packets of local spices, locally crafted leather bags and sandals, T-shirts and fake antiques; even Mike, with his postcards nearby? Jim wondered what chance they might have for an improved future.

The Church of the Holy Sepulchre, actually a domed basilica, has nothing of the architectural scale of St. Peter's in Rome or St. Paul's in London, but in terms of its Christian significance it is bigger than both put together. It is believed to be located on the site where Christ's body was laid after the crucifixion. A commemorative stone slab in a small tomb in the main chapel (had it not been for the steel frame bolted around it, the tomb would surely have collapsed by now) is where Christians have worshipped since the church's construction by the Byzantines in the year 335. A continuous stream of tourists flowed through the main doorway into the main chapel, past the tomb, then in semi-darkness filed down a maze of corridors to Adam's tomb, and from there finally back into the bright sunlit forecourt, where kids eagerly sold folded postcard photos of what they had just seen. Buses were waiting to then transport them up to the Mount of Olives.

Jim arrived in the church's interior darkness at about four in the afternoon, just in time to see a procession of a dozen or so Catholic monks mount some narrow steps to a mezzanine floor, singing, in lovely harmony, in Latin, Gregorian chant. From there the singing lasted half an hour. A monk hissed down at the crowds of tourists below for more quiet. The monks descended and then they, too, were swallowed by the darkness. One, however, was left behind. He had a thin, handsome face, long hair gathered behind, and the kindest, most professionally engaging smile Jim had ever seen. Jim told him how much he loves Gregorian chant and asked when there might be another opportunity to hear such beautiful singing. He explained that because so many Christian religious orders come for services, each must be allocated its time and place within the church. There are the Benedictines from France, Franciscans from Italy, Copts from Egypt, Armenians, Greeks, Russians, Syrians, and the kind, gentle-looking Ethiopians, who have been allocated a confined space up in the roof by their adversaries, the Copts. Each order wears different habits and tolls different bells – the noisy clanking coming from the rooftops while they were talking, sounding more like saucepans, came from the Ethiopians'. Finally, in answer to his question, he told Jim one could come every day at five minutes to four to hear Gregorian chant.

At this stage Jim was beginning to feel the fatigue of trying to fathom so much history. He decided he'd had enough for one day and would look for somewhere he could stay for the night. Being the week of Easter, hotel after hotel was booked out. Finally, near the Damascus Gate, he found St. Thomas' Hospice and was kindly received by Raphael, a humble Palestinian Christian with a stubble beard. This particular religious group makes up only two per cent of Jerusalem's Christian population.

Later, after taking a shower, on his way out for dinner Jim found Raphael alone at the reception. They engaged in some friendly conversation.

Although he was born in Jerusalem, Raphael had never been granted citizenship. His two sons and daughter, like him, had only ID cards. Without any show of bitterness, he told of the Israeli practice of stripping non-Jews, particularly the east Jerusalem Arabs, of their legal papers. This began in the last months of the previous government and had increased since Benjamin Netanyahu came to power. Those affected became illegal immigrants in the city of their birth. Raphael said he was convinced now that the Israeli government intends to impose its will instead of negotiating, as promised, on the Holy City's future. His daughter, he said, would soon go to Ramallah, about twenty kilometres north of Jerusalem, to marry. Under the new restrictions she would not be able to return to Jerusalem with her husband, and she would never be permitted to return by herself if she were to be away longer than the two-year limit. If Raphael wanted to visit them in Ramallah he, too, would be subjected to the same restrictions.

At the hospice there were also territorial rules Jim had to abide by: the gate closed promptly at 10 pm each evening and any guest arriving back after that hour would remain locked out. Raphael, bless him, did Jim a special favour: after Jim had dined with others, he unlocked the gate for him at around midnight.

30th March 1997
Sunday. This was the morning Jim was expected at Sarah's home, to meet her family and friends and enjoy a musical recital. He arrived at the appointed hour of 11am and was immediately and warmly welcomed. Their rather spacious, open-planned home, designed by Moshe, her architect husband, was mostly concealed in an informal bush garden. About thirty guests

were in attendance. There was not much time for introductions before seats were taken. Around Jim were bearded academics, bohemian-looking artists, independent-looking women who appeared comfortably well off, all in fresh attire, all relaxed. The two young musicians, twin sisters, began with a duet for piano and cello. Bright sunlight pierced a mesh of vines covering full-height windows and warmed the colourful rugs. Peeping from behind leaves, curious about the new sounds, a variety of small birds came and went, the sun intensifying their yellows and flashing their purple gloss. The room offered space also for large, modern paintings; a suspended mobile sculpture; and figurative ceramic sculptures. The girls joined hands and joyfully skipped their way through fields of Beethoven, displaying deeper concentration on the less coherent architecture of Benjamin Britten.

After the recital, drinks were served. Everybody seemed to be one another's friend, so it was easy for Jim, with Sarah's help, to mingle and meet them all. Moshe, wearing thick-framed Le Corbusier spectacles and white braces stretched over a colourful floral shirt, seemed very much at ease in his role as host. The family's name was well respected in Jerusalem, and as a senior partner in a well-known firm of architects, Moshe was highly regarded. For his liberal views on religion and criticism of the government he was liked by some and criticised by others. His brother had a similar leaning, employed in the office of a national newspaper known for its left-wing, anti-government journalism.

Through a window, seated alone under a tree, Jim could see Sarah's mother, Yoheved, who was probably not used to this kind of social life. He went to her and introduced himself. She smiled and asked him to sit. She apologised for her English. She and her husband had helped administer the first kibbutz in Israel, she said, north of Haifa, where Sarah was born and raised till the age of seven. She described her younger years, the pioneering years of the new settlers. Since the death of her husband Yoheved has lived in Tel Aviv. She wanted to talk about her new life here in Tel Aviv, how she discovered she could paint pictures. In halting but passionate English she told how painting had become a force in her life – colours, bold prime colours, as if colour had become some new kind of extravagant luxury. She said it was as if, walking onto a stage before an audience, she had found the courage to reveal her inner self. She was working towards an exhibition. Jim said he would love to see her work. She pointed to a painting that was hanging inside. It was one of the large ones he had noticed before. In her hair was snared a small yellow flower. They were called inside to prepare for lunch.

Jim was privileged to be the only guest outside of the family to be invited to stay for lunch. As well as Sarah's mother, son and daughter being present, so too were her lovely sister and niece down from Geneva, and two or three other more distant relatives. Moshe asked Jim about his architectural work. He took him and seated him in his office to show examples of the work his firm had completed, large-scale commercial buildings mostly, nothing very exciting. But Jim wanted to know more about Jerusalem.

"Hmm, it's a long complicated story, there is so much to say. I don't know how much you already know but I can give you a rundown. Over four thousand years there have been at least eleven transitions from one warring faction to another – Egyptians, Assyrians, Babylonians, Persians, Greeks, Romans, Byzantines, the Crusaders, the Ottoman Turks, again the Egyptians, and again the Turks. They all came with swords and territorial ambitions. Why, for this barren, remote piece of desert, has so much blood been shed for so long, you might well ask? In 1917, the British seized control of Jerusalem from the Ottoman Turkish defenders. In 1947, the United Nations Resolution 181 approved a partition plan that provided for two states – one Jewish, one Arab, with Jerusalem as a separate entity to be administered by the United Nations.

"In 1948, the state of Israel declared its sovereignty and independence. For the Arabs this was totally unacceptable, and they declared war, lost, and under the armistice Israel took control of West Jerusalem, which became its capital. The Jordanians were furious; they annexed East Jerusalem and took the South-East Quarter. The occupying Jews were forced out, their quarter looted and burned by mobs, synagogues were razed, street names were obliterated and homes dynamited by the Jordanian Army. But no event has shaped the modern contest over Jerusalem as much as the Arab-Israeli War of 1967. Israel not only defeated invading Arab armies in six days, but also seized control of the Gaza Strip and the Sinai Peninsula from Egypt, the Golan Heights from Syria, and the land west of the Jordan River – Palestine – internationally known now, though not internationally recognised, as the West Bank. Most significantly, Israel captured East Jerusalem and declared the whole city reunited as its capital.

"It is this and the disputed West Bank land entitlement which are at the core of the on-going war with the Palestinians: the land is theirs, the Israelis claim, because it was given to them by God 3,700 years ago; the Palestinians claim the land is theirs for the same reasons. As the occupying power, Israel has violated international laws with impunity. It has committed grave breaches of the Geneva Convention against the Palestinian people, including crimes against humanity, again with impunity. The intention is obvious: that one day the West Bank will become locked into a greater Israel. Since 1967 the occupation has grown into huge housing estates on the West Bank, and in Jerusalem new synagogues, the House of Parliament, high office buildings, hotels, universities and museums, on land mostly expropriated from legal Palestinian owners."

He laid out a plan of Jerusalem.

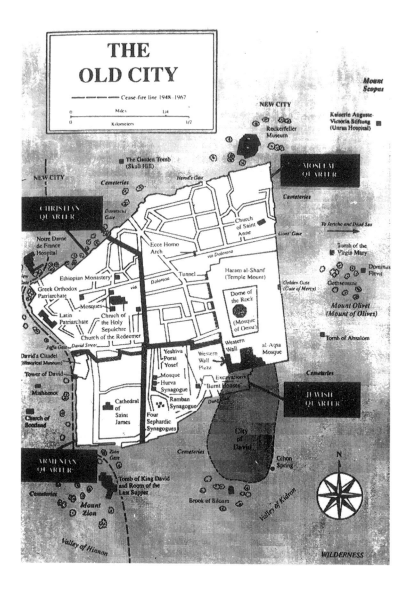

"You know the city is sharply divided by invisible boundaries into four quarters: this, the Muslim Quarter, having the largest area, and the other three, these, all about equal, Christian, Jewish and, of all things, Armenian. Each has its own religion, distinctive tongue or tongues, and its own particular alphabet. Within each quarter there are divisions and subdivisions. The principal languages are Hebrew, Arabic and Armenian, but also Greek, French, Yiddish, English, Latin, Russian, Ethiopian and Assyrian-Syriac (*the language spoken by Jesus*). Thirty religious denominations worshipping in at least fifteen national languages and with seven different alphabets congregate within these few hectares. The two main national and religious groups – Israelis and Palestinians – live apart within the city and are each other's bitterest enemy. Each can walk routes in the city where they know they need never see one another.

"There are three holy days each week, one for each main religion: on Sundays different bells toll and roll over all the rooftops all day while processions of Christians wind through the narrow lanes to reach the Church of the Holy Sepulchre. Saturday is the Jewish Sabbath, when all Jewish commercial life closes down and more than a thousand synagogues fill with worshippers. Friday is the Muslim holy day, when the call of the muezzin, amplified from the minarets of the mosques, floats over the city like a thin veil, drawing many of the faithful to pray under the golden dome of the Mosque of Omar. This mosque is built on the same site as the Jewish temple was, built upon by King Solomon three thousand years ago, making it the most sacred Jewish site in the world. After Mecca, it is also the second most sacred Muslim site in the world, a problem, it would seem, of insurmountable complexity."

"It was there, too, so it is claimed, that the Garden of Eden was located, where the world began, and where – it is sometimes conjectured, as a consequence of this on-going struggle over

Jerusalem, and particularly over this Jewish-Muslim site – it will end."

"And so there you have it, Jim. You see, life wasn't meant to be easy."

"Thank you so much, Moshe," Jim said. "That was very, very interesting."

And then, just on time, they were called to the table for lunch.

It began with succulent, warm artichokes. Jim learned more about typical life on a kibbutz and they asked about some of his travel experiences, his life in Paris, and what life was like in Australia. Lastly, after figs and cheese and halva had been served, Moshe said, "Come, Jim, follow me, I have a treat for you."

After a twenty-minute drive both were climbing into the cockpit of a purring two-seater Cessna aeroplane.

At about four thousand feet, clouds like big fish drifted around beneath them. Flying below that zone would have given excellent visibility, but Sunday peace needed to be respected. Enough of the city could be seen, though, for Jim to be able to shoot two rolls of film. In the sprawling conglomerate, the definition of the Old City was the first landmark he looked for and there it was, quite visible, the clearly scribed polygonal outline of the ancient city wall. It rides atop deep ravines along the eastern and southern sides, and then slides away to the west, down into the pastoral-looking Valley of Hinnom. The land all across the northern side of the city was a plateau, making the wall there, in the event of an invasion, its most vulnerable point. It was there that most conquerors during the last 2,500 years, from Nebuchadnezzar 11 to Dayan, had penetrated. The texture of most of the city was a peppering of houses with a conspicuous expanse of open space in the south-east corner – the garden setting of the two mosques, the Mosque of Omar and Al-Aqsa. Clearly discernable was the thick, heavy demarcation

of the Wailing Wall, separating the praying Jews from the praying Muslims. The Jewish Quarter was easily discernible, too, by its white newness – nearly all of it was rebuilt after its destruction during the Jordanian and Palestinian occupation between 1948 and 1967. A covenant required that every new building be finished externally with the local white stone. It was amazing to be able to see from this height the extent of the tombs and graves, like a spill of marble chips covering the whole western slope of the Mount of Olives. The city was ringed with cemeteries to the south, east and west, some of them stretching back in time as far as the eighth century, some of them new and still growing. Commanding city views from their eastern heights were the three buildings that represent Israel's main preoccupations – politics, education and history: the Knesset, Qiryat University and the Israel Museum. Here and there, there seemed to be attempts at creating parkland forestation, but not on the scale that would make it the oasis city once envisioned. Outside the Old City, reaching further into the desert and surrounding hills, one could see the enormous scope of new housing development that has taken place during the last thirty years. New roads snaked their ways all through and around the upper contours; low apartment blocks linked together came around bends like train carriages. From this height the hillsides formed with steppes looked like Balinese rice paddies.

4th April 1997

On the way back to Tel Aviv, a young woman soldier this time was seated next to Jim. When he told her he was from Australia, she lit up and wanted to know all about it. During the hour-long trip he talked to her about Australian history – from tribal Aboriginal habitation that went back further than the time of Moses, to the cruel English colonisation at the time of the French Revolution, and the multicultural present. He told her how easy-going and lucky Australians are, with enormous mineral wealth, good grazing land, northern rainforests, and pristine beaches that stretch all the way up the east coast, as well as a vast central desert. A north-south mountain range runs parallel to the east coast and forms a barrier to the ocean rain clouds that would otherwise reach into the dry hinterland. Now run-off water on the eastern slopes of the range is dammed and tunnelled through the range for widespread irrigation. There is only one season, a long, warm and hot summer. There are problems sometimes with droughts and flooding and bushfires, but never with warfare.

Finally, pulling into the bus station, she told Jim how much she was looking forward to finishing her duty in the army so she could return to her studies. She would search for a worthwhile vocation in what she hoped for most of all – a peaceful world.

"Like Australia," she said.

17

Bogart in Istanbul

Istanbul... the sound of its name had the same allure as Kathmandu did for Jim in 1963 – he had to go there then, and he had to come here now.

What did he expect? The clichés he pictured were mostly true: an ancient, densely packed city, labyrinthine laneways seething with life; domes and minarets of a thousand mosques silhouetted against glowing golden sunsets; the hubbub and bustle of great bazaars; extravagant palaces set in clipped gardens; marble steam baths. He had heard of the whirling dervishes – Sufi monks who dance themselves round and round into a frenzy of dizzy religious ecstasy, then what – collapse exhausted on the floor? He even imagined worming his way into one of the sultan's harems and could picture himself in exquisite polished surroundings floating on a sea of cushions, allowing himself to be petted, his feet caressed by a dream full of gorgeous, brown-bellied concubines. Perhaps he would solve the riddle of another murder mystery between Paris and Istanbul on the Orient Express, or add a tale or two to *One Thousand and One Nights* – how incredibly exotic.

This great city had its beginning three thousand years ago as a fishing village. Considering its location, between Europe and the Orient, where the West borders with the East and at the junction of four seas, it was inevitable that Istanbul should also become a centre of trade and commerce. Constantinople in the twelfth century was the largest and wealthiest city in all of Europe. It also became the capital city of the Roman Empire, then the capital of the Byzantine Empire, and then in the sixteenth century, when it changed its name to Istanbul, the capital of the vast Ottoman Empire. The Ottoman period of conquests spanned more than six hundred years throughout the south-eastern regions of Europe, Arabic northern Africa, and most of the Middle East including Jerusalem. In 1683, the Ottoman Army reached as far north in Europe as the gates of the walled city of Vienna. It was thought this would be its final conquest, but it was there that it suffered its final defeat. The Siege of Vienna in 1683 was aborted when the Polish Army, in league with the Viennese, overpowered the invading Ottomans. Strewn on the battlefield, as well as hundreds of slain soldiers, horses and camels; saddles; tents and rugs, were cooking utensils and foodstuffs, including many large sacks filled with a curious black bean. Everything useless was meant be destroyed.

Some enterprising Viennese, who realised what the beans were, managed to inveigle a supervising officer, took possession of them, ground them up and opened Vienna's first coffee shop. To frequent such a place, to sip this exotic, sour-tasting black beverage, as the English sahibs did with tea in India at about the same time, was, for some, a snobbish thing to do. Our clever Viennese entrepreneur was doing brisk business; he would invent a cake that would complement his coffee. Of all the shapes he could have chosen he decided, in celebration of the Ottoman defeat, and the four crescent moons represented on their flag, that the shape would be a crescent. It worked a treat. In 1770 Marie Antoinette from Vienna introduced this flaky pastry into Paris society.

"Let them eat cake," she said.

Et voila, le croissant!

"Ooh la la, mais oui, c'est déliceux."

This is one version of the story, but the best croissants in Paris today can still be found in the *Viennoiseries.*

At the bustling city centre, beside the floating bridge that spans the Bosporus, there are many fishmongers' boats moored to the railings, bobbing and swaying in the choppy waters. You can see some of the day's catch sizzling on an open grille on each deck. The fishermen, in a dexterous balancing act, while taking your money in one hand, with the other slap a delicious fish sandwich into yours. But all around the water's edge are suppliers of fresh fish, as well as vegetables, fruit and grain.

Caravans and boats used to bring goods from all parts of the empire and beyond – silks, spices, precious stones, rugs, metals, everything – to be unloaded here and traded from under tents or huts. Eventually, in the 1660s, to ensure safekeeping and permanence of place, and to give cover, vaulted concrete domes were constructed; goods could be locked behind closed doors and the market itself locked behind large gates. That place today is known as the Egyptian Bazaar or the Spice Market. On entering the dim light of its enormous interior your senses are immediately smacked by all the colours and aromas of powdered condiments displayed in open sacks or piled into cones; dyes, sandalwood and henna, as well as a large variety of nuts, teas, dates, figs, raisins, royal jelly, and a delightful range of Turkish Delight.

The Grand Bazaar, not far away, is truly grand. Admitting light through small cupolas, its single roof of multiple domes covers more than four thousand shops and several kilometres of streets and alleyways. It sells everything from the finest swords to beautiful striped Tunisian scarves; exquisitely embroidered shawls; rugs, of course; mirrors inlaid with mother-of-pearl; intricately carved wooden lecterns for reading the Koran; phials for perfume, not only glass but gold, silver, and enamelled brass; bells pitched to many different sounds; a treasure trove of jewellery, and for scratching one's back, little hands on long stems sculptured out of ivory or tortoiseshell. Meerschaum, a white magnesium silicate clay found only in Turkey, like cedar and marble, is ideal for carving. Because of its other qualities of porosity and heat resistance it is ideal for making bowls of smoking pipes. The pipe carving you see in the bazaar is very impressive for its fineness of detail: every hair and fold of bearded, turbaned pashas, mythological figures, and the most intricate of Islamic designs; or, if you prefer, not carved at all, just plain white. And just when you feel the need to rest, you can sit and take mint tea served in small, traditional tulip-shaped glasses.

Jim found a very reasonably priced hotel room in the city centre with a view just opposite of the magnificent Blue Mosque of Sultan Ahmet. The problem of being so close soon became obvious: five times each day the call to pray reaches out from multidirectional loudspeakers fixed to each minaret. On his first morning, at sunrise, with his window open, Jim awoke in fright thinking some intruder was at his side. But there are mosques everywhere in Istanbul, so this can hardly be avoided.

Santa Sophia, also nearby, originally a Christian basilica from the year 325 became a mosque in the 1300s. Around its interior courtyard walls, verses from the Koran are depicted in beautiful, elegant calligraphy, like a spill of writhing eels. There is flow and harmony and a sense of order in the script, suggesting a language of music. Islamic art forbids the depiction of figurative images in any form, for that would be to commit the sin of idolatry – no animals, fish or birds, or anything else with a 'mortal soul'. Flowers – the tulip and the carnation, typically – are common decorative motifs.

The evenings, one after another, were balmy with comforting breezes. The Blue Mosque itself was set majestically against a star-filled sky. From his hotel room each evening Jim could see across the park that a large, wide canopy strung from the mosque's high wall to some trees provided cover for taking tea or coffee, or smoking *narguileh*, the water pipe. It was the dancing firelight from a row of flaming oil lamps, the kilim wall hangings and camel-bag cushions strewn around low tables that made it most enticing.

When he had nothing else to do, or was too tired to do anything else, he would go there to take apple tea and relax in an atmosphere of patchouli and joss, and also in the hope of finding someone he could talk with. He would place himself as close as possible to the light of a lamp so that, at least, he would be able to read another chapter or two of an Anthony Burgess novel he was enjoying. A heavy man in a musician's costume was always there, seated at the wall, and beside him his young boy. The musician came to recognise Jim and threw him a smile each time he arrived. He played on his lap a *kanun*, the stringed instrument in the triangular form of a harp, and as he picked his way through some popular racy tunes, some tables joined in with song; others, causing an unpleasant distraction, made loud bubbling sounds on their water pipes. The smoke itself, though, had a not-unpleasant, mildly pungent, sweet smell. On one evening he found himself seated beside a young lady of dark Mediterranean beauty. She was alone with a pen and paper and he could see through the corner of his eye that she was studying some English text of Henry James. Well, how could he resist the opportunity? He could tell by her concentration and the way she was chewing her gum she was not aware of his presence. He slicked down his eyebrows, smiled her way, excused himself, and told her his English was good, and that if she liked, they could try to make conversation. She blushed with sudden embarrassment, sneaked the gum from her mouth, then smiled. Yes, she said, she would like that.

Her name was Naile, and she was from a small town on the Turkish Mediterranean coast, here to attend the University of Istanbul. Her ambition was to one day become a teacher of English. It was a difficult subject, she said, and yet apart from the usual problems with prepositions and conjugations, she spoke quite well. He was able to give some help with her essay. She spoke of her desire to travel. London and Paris were the cities that interested her most. Eventually, she asked about him. He told her of his interest in photography, the countries he had visited, and now his intention to capture the typical street life of Istanbul, mostly in the poorer quarters. She indicated places she knew on his city map, but for her the city was still mostly unexplored. She asked if the next day she could accompany him.

She brought her own tiny camera. Because of the attention he was giving her, he was missing photographs and took only a few. He took some photo portraits of her and some when she wasn't looking. They met one another to take tea a few more times and became friends. Freedom of personal choice, especially for women, is made easier in Turkey than in most other Islamic countries in the East. One evening, however, in the shadows of the park, she said if she were discovered in his embrace she would bring shame on herself.

Istanbul, like Rome, is said to be a city of seven hills, but it has many more than that. Turkey is part of the same eruptions that produced the myriad of Greek islands. Traipsing up and down on cobbled streets was tiring. Cushioned footwear is essential. He avoided most of the famous places and concentrated more on exploring typical living quarters.

It is a satisfying experience, having the fascination and the vagabond freedom to walk the streets of an exotic city with a ready camera, alert to the possibility that at any moment the forces playing all around you could synchronise in such a way as to compose the elements for a nice picture. If you are quick enough and have a good eye you might capture a photograph that can be appraised on some later day, not just for what was the main focus in that moment, but also the devils that were lurking in the details. What it cannot show is your look of concentration and the pleasure you, the photographer, were feeling at the time.

Walking the poor quarters, where tourists seldom go, he knew could be risky. Empty houses had fallen into desuetude – rotting timber and broken windows, flaking paint and torn slogans, deathly quiet at night. There was much in need of restoration. In the afternoons, mothers dressed according to the customs of their provenance gathered on their front steps or on street kerbs and talked while embroidering cushion covers, darning rugs or mending tears, while tiny children sat and watched and listened. Older children home from school played among the ruins, or skipped ropes or played marbles and, of course, kicked footballs. Where would the world's kids be without a football? One can buy them here, light, plastic, candy-coloured things for the price of a candy.

He was noticed everywhere and their smiles made him feel at ease. They sometimes beckoned to him and cried out "*Chek, chek!*" (Yes, take – take as many photos as you like!). There were some, though, who were superstitious, older women mostly, who believed if you take their photo you rob them of their soul. They took sudden fright at the sight of his camera, recoiled behind their scarves and then turned their backs, crying, "*Hah yuhr, hah yuhr!*" (No, no!). He regretted this intrusion, but if he were to ask permission to take a photo, the natural scene would be forsaken for a posed one, which was not what he wanted. With his long lens he did steal away some souls without them realising it. Children ran to him and giggled and jostled to have their photos taken. Once, as he was taking a group photo, a respectable-looking old man suddenly came at him from behind and angrily wrestled to take hold of his camera. He wanted to break it. I think he saw Jim as an intrusion into the privacy of the neighbourhood, though it may have been the same superstition. Jim couldn't understand his Turkish tirade, of course, but it was clear that he wanted him to leave, which he did.

Where he was permitted, he was able to shoot through open doorways to catch the family life at home; in more difficult light he was able to catch tradesmen in workshop caves shaping metal, mending shoes or tailoring; street vendors under canopies selling nuts and fruit.

He found the most challenging time for his camera was in the early evenings, when the brightness of the sun was mostly spent, at around 7 or 8pm The light then was softening, so the images, instead of being cast with contrasting hard edges of chiaroscuro black shadow and featureless white, would rather, in around seven tones of grey, be modelled with more surface detail.

One morning, early, in the town centre a bus was about to depart – to where he knew not, and didn't care. He quickly hopped on board. After about thirty minutes he signalled to the driver to let him down. There was a steep laneway leading up to his left. Was it serendipity again that beckoned him? A little way up he came upon the window of a tailor's shop, and sitting alone in the half-lit interior was a white-bearded old man. He was wearing a suit and the traditional fez, his hands clasped on a walking stick; there were piled bolts of fabric, but most of all it was the lighting – it was subdued with the dark tones of a Rembrandt painting. Jim gasped.

He entered. He smiled in greeting, and gestured in the best way he knew how for the old man's permission to take a photo. No, no – he waved him away. He seemed shy and a little embarrassed. Very politely, Jim appealed to him, and again he waved him away. *Why would any one want to take a photo of an old man?* his expression seemed to say. Just then a man entered bearing a tray with a cup of coffee. Jim asked him if he could speak English. A little, he said. He asked him if he could please explain to the old man that he was a photographer and that his interest was Turkish people. He turned and spoke to the old man, their conversation was brief. The man turned back to Jim and asked if he was American. When the tailor learned that Jim was Australian he nodded – yes, he could take his photo. He was old enough to remember the aftermath of the war in Gallipoli. The result was what Jim hoped for.

One hot afternoon, with the discomfort of an itchy ten-day stubble, Jim decided it was time for a shave and a haircut. He chose the same barber's shop he had noticed the day before, a small three-step walk down. On entering he saw an old man in plain clothes sitting in one corner dozing. It was the rattle of the bead curtain that aroused him. Suddenly awakened, he was a little flustered. He rushed to Jim, made a smile, then courteously ushered him into his copious chair. His own face unshaven, fully awake now as he wrapped the white apron and tucked Jim in, looked pleasant.

As expected, he could not speak a word of English. It was to be a one-act mime for two. Scene: a barbershop in Istanbul. Jim observed the stage set: laid out before him on a glass shelf, scissors, a comb, a cutthroat razor, and squatted on the shelf of the basin, a rather bedraggled-looking shaving brush. Taped to the wall next to the mirror's frame was a faded photograph, of the barber's wife, he supposed, when she was young, squinting at the sun and holding their squinting baby, or, the photo looked so old it might even have been the barber himself in the arms of his mother. Suspended from the frame by a cotton thread was a blue glass bauble – a talisman to protect against the evil eye. A book calendar had not been changed since probably the old man decided there was no point; and a tiny cassette radio was playing faint Turkish music. The walls were old-age yellow. On the end wall hung an aerial photo of Mecca on a day of hajj, and beside it a portrait photo of a man dressed as he nearly always appeared, looking like an executive banker – the much-revered father of the republic, Mustafa Kemal Atatürk. A coloured regional map of Turkey was there, and most conspicuously, most unlikely, a large Hollywood poster. In its original brash '50s colours it depicted a jungle scene: waist-deep in a jungle swamp, hauling behind him the wooden hull of the *African Queen*, was Humphrey Bogart. In the mirror's reflection, across the room over near the entry door, stood the skeleton of an old wooden coat stand, and in another corner, mumbling and trembling with what seemed like some kind of old-age disorder, a blue-painted refrigerator.

As he snipped away, Jim sensed the old man's awkwardness at not being able to offer his usual barbershop chat. They caught one another's eyes momentarily in the mirror and smiled.

The haircut ended up being exactly what he'd hoped for – shaped nicely with a light trim. For the shave he was soothed under a steaming face towel while a creamy lather was prepared.

After scrubbing it well into his stubble, the barber smoothed it with his brush. He took his strop and began to sweeten the edge of his razor, offering Jim in the mirror another modest smile. That slapping, stropping sound, steel on dull leather – he'd heard those sounds before, long ago, but where? Ha, it was his father, he remembered, in their bathroom mirror, and then scraping away the lather, the funny contortions with his mouth.

The barber abruptly swung him backwards to face the ceiling. He noticed an antiquated fan was going slowly round and round like a lazy old housefly, round and round, hardly stirring the air. Lulled and relaxed by this careful attention, Jim began to feel drowsy. That old poster, the one with Humphrey Bogart... Jim smiled and gestured towards it. Ah – the barber's eyes lit up. He turned, went to the radio, inserted a cassette, switched it on, then came back with his razor and a wider smile. Then, just as he began the shave, a song came on that again threw Jim back into his childhood past. He couldn't believe it; it was Bing Crosby singing:

The rich maharajah of Magador
Had ten thousand camels or maybe more,
He had diamonds and pearls and the most beautiful girls
But he didn't know how to do-oo the rumba.

And so forth, each time the same refrain embellished with a shrill, Turkish-sounding, belly-dancing flute, seeming to give some bizarre kind of relevance to the present.

How refreshing it was to be shaved like this.

Without asking for it, Jim was given, as a trial offer, a genuine, original (if somewhat pale), Turkish moustache. Well, he thought, why not – when in Istanbul do as the Romans do. He had never seen himself in that disguise before. He was dusted off with some talcum powder. For the price of a few old coins, he emerged shining like a new one. He was ready then, he thought, slicking down his eyebrows, to go and check out the sultan's harem. He went off humming the *The Maharajah of Magador* and soon found himself entering another poor quarter.

Just like he remembered in the poor quarters in Naples, laundry was strung across the streets from upper windows for drying – sparkling white sheets billowing like spinnakers, many-coloured shirts waving like flags – a hero's welcome, it seemed. Also like in Naples, housewives in windows pulled up baskets of shopping from children in the streets below. Coincidentally, Naples and Istanbul lie on the same northern latitude.

As much as slums can be kept clean, these neighbourhoods were not too bad. He was surprised when sometimes banana skins, plastic bottles and all manner of domestic garbage would fly out of windows and slap and tumble on the street, not at him but around him. At the same time some youths, appointed presumably by the neighbourhood community, were on their haunches, scraping around with hand-brooms, gathering it all up and throwing it into the street bins. How strange. A few times he saw three or four women carry rolled-up rugs onto the streets, unroll them flat on the cobblestones, then, with a running hose, plastic tubs, sturdy brushes and lots of soap, scrub them spotlessly clean.

Winding down in a bus from Taksim, tired after a day's shoot, the large, imposing facade of the Pera Palace Hotel came into view, the same one in which Agatha Christie wrote *Murder on the Orient Express*. At that stop the doors opened onto two old men, one short, one tall, both with white walking sticks. Jim thought they were going to get on, but they didn't. The doors closed, the bus pulled away and he looked back to see them, arm in arm, continuing on up the hill – the blind leading the blind leading a lopsided, four-legged shadow barely able to keep up.

Naile sent a carefully, beautifully written reply to Jim's letter from Paris with the photos he took of her that afternoon when she looked so happy and lovely. She spoke again of her dream of one day being able to come to visit Paris.

18

Chopin in Kraków

2006.

After a few days' stopover in Prague Jim boarded a Czech Airlines twin-propeller plane, so small it could carry a maximum of only forty-six passengers. Its wings were positioned atop the carriage, allowing an uninterrupted view for all, which was ideal for him. He was on his way to Kraków.

The terrain below was mainly flat with only sparse vegetation and mounds of hills blackened in parts by fire; practically no farmed land like he had seen over much of Western Europe. In the long descent to Kraków he wanted to find clues as to why, centuries ago, this particular site had been chosen to form a community. For one thing, the discovery that salt could be used as a preservative for meat meant nomadic tribes could sit and wait for the migrating herds to come around again, and in the meantime work the land. Arable land, therefore, would have been one reason. Forested land would have been another for timber construction. Security, too – even at that time, these tribal people subsisting between two expanding powers – Germany (the Holy Roman Empire in those days) and Russia – were continually caught between their conflicts. So, a site high up would give good surveillance against advancing armies and marauding invaders. And if, eventually, a protective wall were to be built around the town, the region should, ideally, be rich in alluvial stone. A river nearby would be a source of water and moreover serve as a route for the transport of goods

to and from farms and other villages. The riverside would thus
be a convenient site for a marketplace. For most medieval towns
the marketplace was the germ from which they grew, like an
organism.

And, yes, there it came into view: firstly the river, and
contained in its loop a land formation that rose steeply from its
bank to a high plateau, and on the plateau, a medieval kingdom
– a magnificent sight: the castle, a cathedral, a palace, chapels,
churches and various ministries, all clustered in a millennium
of architectural styles. Spreading down and around, like an
apron and then flattening outwards was the city proper. At its
heart, near the river, he could see the Main Square, the site of the
original marketplace. From the square, streets radiated outwards
through what would have been the gates of of the protective
wall, and then beyond into the boroughs and farmland of
countryside. Where the protective wall was (it was demolished
in 1800), there is now a thin band, like a necklace, of forested
parkland.

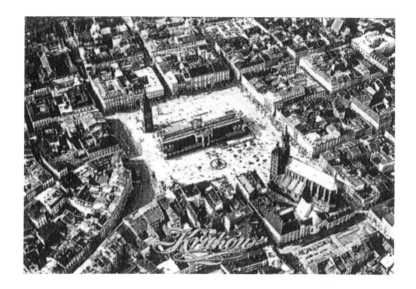

Taxiing to the airport terminal, on display was a series of vintage warplanes, a reminder of this country's terrible war-torn history. The terminal was new, though its design was old school – a functional box concept with little imagination, pragmatic, a hallmark of the Soviet mind-set – symbolic, not aesthetic. It was planned much smaller, too, than it should have been if it is to cope with the inevitable increase in tourism.

On exiting the terminal Jim had to wait a few minutes for a shuttle bus that would transport him a few hundred metres to where he would then catch a small train to the city centre. He was only a few kilometres from the centre, and yet in a semi-rural setting. Across the road, through a wire fence, was an old-style timber cottage with fruit trees and a vegetable patch, and picking through the dry grass, on their day's outing, were a most regal-looking Polish rooster, his clucky mate, and their brood of tiny chicks.

The train was only four carriages, and travelled at a tram's pace. Through a web of elms, chestnut trees, silver birches and the odd willow, he could see abandoned brick factories whose roofs were mostly gone and all their windows smashed; in a clearing further on, several magnificent vintage steam trains came into view. They had been laid to rest long ago, forgotten, it seemed, rusting and rotting in a field of tall weeds. After all those years of faithful service, he thought, if it was not too late, they deserved better – to be restored and placed in museums, perhaps. He thought he would try to make it back to photograph them.

At the train terminus, just outside the park fringe, construction of a large shopping and housing complex was under way, large in area but not more than five storeys high, not the high-rise office buildings you find in big cities that become dark mausoleums after working hours. Kraków is preserving the heart of its old city for the livelihood of its people and the interest of tourists. During periods of mild weather, thousands throng to the main square to admire the architecture, to shop, or take lunch or coffee under table parasols; in the evenings dining tables are candlelit and light music sweetens the air – it is like attending a big open-air banquet to which everyone is invited.

Poor Poland. Its tragedy, throughout its history, has been its location between the bludgeons, east and west, of Germany and Russia. In 1795, Poland's sovereignty was lost entirely when the three occupying powers – Russia, Prussia and Austria – divided its territory among themselves, Kraków coming under Austrian rule. Poland's identity would remain a ghost for the next 123 years until the end of the First World War, with the collapse of Austria and forced withdrawal of Germany. It regained its sovereignty, but for only twenty years, after which, on 1st September 1939, Poland, poor Poland, was the first domino to fall under Hitler's Blitzkrieg. On 27th September, Poland surrendered. The Soviets helped themselves to the eastern half. 1.2 million Poles were deported to the U.S.S.R. For the following five years, Kraków – its castle, no less – served as a Nazi headquarter, which is why, of all the large Polish cities, it was the only one that was not decimated. By the war's end in 1945, of the estimated 5.7 million Europeans killed in the Holocaust, some three and and a half million were Polish. After the war, Poland's 'liberation' came in the form of Soviet domination – communism under Stalin until his death in 1953. In 1980 there was a popular uprising against the autocratic communist leader General Jaruzelski, who responded with a decree of martial law. In 1990, through opposition from the Workers' Union (*Solidarność*), condemnation by 'Polish Pope' John Paul II, and encouragement from the newly elected president of the USSR, Mikhail Gorbachev, the hand of government was forced and totalitarianism was abolished, hopefully forever. The Poles were the first to have a free election in post-Soviet Eastern Europe.

Poland's priorities since then have been to develop a market economy, a parliamentary democracy and the rule of law. Now, in 2006, sixty per cent of Poland's workforce is now employed in the private sector; GDP growth is about five per cent, inflation about five per cent, unemployment about eight per cent, and, mainly because of foreign investment, prices for housing in the cities are spiralling upwards. In 2001 Poland joined NATO, and in 2004 the European Union. So the Polish people, with their backs to the east and facing west, look hopeful and optimistic.

What a lovely city, its streets lit by wall lamps that give a warm glow, like in Paris, and no neon advertising; no commercial advertising at all. There were no cars, only a tramline that circles the inner city and bus routes to the outer regions.

Accommodation for the first night was not difficult to find even though it was peak tourist season. Jim knocked on doors and found a room just off the Main Square. It was managed by two lovely old sisters. The room was clean, quiet and airy, and only fifty zloty (€13) a night. On one wall was a framed photo of a Paris café, one he couldn't recognise, and a painting by Gauguin. He slept well and decided on his way out for breakfast that he would keep the room for his three-week stay.

Like everybody else, Jim was inevitably drawn into the six-hundred-year-old main market Square. The five-storey facades that contain the square were mostly constructed during the late nineteenth century, most bearing motifs similar to those you can find on the Parthenon. What a profound influence the ancient Greeks have had on nineteenth-century architecture – seriously academic, totally unoriginal. Their stone-vaulted cellars, though, as he was to discover one evening while listening to jazz, date from medieval times. Like the Campanile, the bell tower in St. Mark's Square in Venice, the most conspicuous feature on the main square is the Town Hall Tower – the only remnant of the fourteenth-century town hall. In the centre of the square, dividing it into two spaces is the colonnaded Cloth Hall, once a marketplace for the cloth trade in the fourteenth century, and now a mecca for collectors of kitsch souvenirs (see aerial photo). Small carts sell traditional *obwarzanki* – fresh, crusty, donut-shaped bread rolls sprinkled with poppy seeds or sesame seeds or salt crystals – and other snack food. Dancers, jugglers and musicians enliven the square, flower stalls add colour, and plumed horses trot tourists around in elegant carriages. Jim sat at one of the tables with a coffee and snack to take it all in. He had never seen so many pigeons in one place. He referred to his guidebook to polish up his Polish. "*Dzień dobry*" (good morning), he said pleasantly to one pigeon, and to another with more difficulty, "*Przepraszam, czy Pan mowi po angielsku?*" No, he did not speak English, but it was clear that he wanted some of Jim's *obwarzanki*.

There were so many tourists taking photographs Jim found himself accidentally stepping into and out of people's frames. Who is this mystery man they will one day wonder, who keeps turning up in the family photo albums, upstaging kings and emperors? Sometimes, though, his photo was taken on purpose as if he were someone well known. How intriguing. From a street table, someone would notice him and point, and then everybody cheered. How very unusual. On the third occasion he decided he should get to the bottom of it. His popularity was due to mistaken identity, him being the spitting image, apparently, of the Dutch coach of the Polish football team that had just beaten Italy.

At the Main Square, some evenings he strolled among the respectable elderly crowd of diners and tried to guess their languages – German, Dutch, Swedish, Polish and English. He thought he might find some who would like some conversational company. He came to recognise the notorious Gang of Twelve, an early-divorce-age bunch of Mancunians who arrived each afternoon at about 3pm for breakfast. They formed a corral with the tables, ordered beers, then began to make each other laugh out loud by telling lewd jokes or lying about girls they'd spent with the night before. The biggest, with thick, equine muscles through his neck and shoulders, was the loudest, and also the ugliest.

"I says, 'Darlin', we live in the same neighbourhood so we should get to know one anuvver. Come and meet the boys, have a few, then we can go up to the old chateau and see the Rembrandts I was tellin' you about."

She had said something sarcastic about his appearance and manner, which Jim couldn't quite hear but made everyone else guffaw.

"Ay, ay", the same loudmouth shouted, poking the air at one, "tell you wo', my boy, I'm ten times better f***in' -lookin' than you."

Guffaw. The respectable people cringing around them knew they were from England. At about 9pm, after a good round of steak and chips, more gallons of beer, some loud belching and flatulence, they went off again on the hunt for sexy, saucy, out-on-the-town Polish women. Lovely.

More tourism: one morning Jim came into the square and saw a group seated on the benches at the base of the tower – retired citizens, ladies in pressed jeans, white-haired men in joggers. They were already scrubbed, combed and breakfasted, and there was something familiarly home-grown about their manner. Jim sat nearby to catch their conversation:

"Didja see the beggars on the streets?" one woman said.

The other; "I commented on that yesterday. I seen three; two of 'em was little kids."

Their group leader arrived: "OK, yez ready? Come on, off we go."

They lifted themselves up and Jim reached over to one of the women.

"Excuse me, which part of Australia are you from?"

One of the blokes looked askance and was on the defensive.

"Adelaide," she said.

He spotted Jim's lapel badge and lit up.

"'E's got a kangaroo, 'e's a bloody Aussie!" He then shot out his hand to shake and said, with a grin,

"'Ow yer goin', mate, orright?"

All smiles, then they toddled off.

Nice friendly lot, Aussies.

One afternoon, on one side of the Main Square, at the doorway of the Historical Museum of Kraków a poster advertised a temporary exhibition of Giovanni Piranesi's 1740 engravings of Rome. Hmm. Jim entered. The foyer led to a winding stair. In the first-floor gallery, in glass cases, silver coins that looked like scraps of tin foil bore images of the faces of eleventh-century saints and bishops; some archaeological finds of the thirteenth century included oil lamps, iron keys, spurs, arrowheads and flint strikers. Occupying nearly the whole of the next gallery was a large layout of what Kraków looked like in the fifteenth century.

He then mounted the stairs that led to the main exhibition: the large Piranesi engravings.

They were dystopian scenes of Roman antiquity depicted in ruins: the Pantheon in ruins, the Colosseum decimated; in the Piazza del Campidoglio, the statues of Marcus Aurelius and Ottaviano Augustus barely recognisable. Huge engulfing arches supporting gaping roofs that let in the sky; interior walls were being consumed by foliage. In rubble-strewn streets were a small population of survivors: men in capes and breeches trading wood or grain; stout women in headscarves washing clothes at a fountain; hermits in caves; beggars and madmen lurking in dark shadows; oxen, mules and goats shifting freely about; and scavenging dogs. Pestilence and starvation were in evidence. This was the capital of an empire reduced to rubble and dust. The cause? Jim never found out.

In the historical gallery on the floor above he found gilt-framed paintings of a long lineage of kings and queens. There was a large depiction of the Great Fire of Kraków in 1850 destroying all the buildings on this side of the square. During the next forty years they were rebuilt in the Neo-classical style.

On his way out of the museum he bought a postcard photo taken long ago of three firemen posed in uniform, each strapped to a portable breathing apparatus, and beside them a bizarre range of things to put out a fire – sticks and hessian bags, mostly. Ingrid will be amused.

It was mid-afternoon. Jim wanted to do some historical research. He was told a good source was the library in the EMPIK Cultural Centre. There he found at the end of a long, cavernous corridor of locked doors, behind a glass-fronted reception desk, a rigid, heavy, pale-faced woman pinched in a dark, buttoned-up suit; her eyes looked blank, she might have been embalmed. Was she in pain? He underwent the humiliation of having to bend down to speak through the small aperture. Her mouth moved.

"Closed," it said.

That was it, nothing more was on offer. He was expected to walk away. A bit peeved, and leaning down again he had to ask, "Closed—what, for lunch, for the afternoon, forever; what do you mean?"

In robotic monotone: "Closed for September."

"But it is not September," he persisted, "Today is the 25th of August."

Again the jaw dropped and the mouth said, "Closed."

She was a puppet. Imprinted on her bosom was a government badge of officialdom. Her condition was probably pathological, that which characterised functionaries who served perverse abstractions created for them by others. She was a relic – she had survived but had not escaped totalitarianism. He left her like that. It gave him a taste of what it must have been like.

Back on the square he noticed, on a first-floor window, a sign saying: *BRITISH COUNCIL*. Ha – that looked more encouraging. He went up and got a smiling welcome from a gorgeous young receptionist – peaches-and-cream British. There was a large TV screen showing live BBC news and commentary, and in the reading room were the day's English newspapers. And yes, in another room, there was Internet access, which she said he was welcome to use. In his inbox he found a long (for her) email letter from Ingrid, a happy letter – she was in love again. Seated beside him at the next laptop, tapping away, was a sad-faced fellow dropping sounds of frustration. Jim got two cups of cold water from the dispenser and offered him one.

He said his name was Paul, an English bachelor here on vacation. He worked in some auction house in London as a storeman and packer. He liked his job, he said, but when he's not there it all goes to pot. For the last five years he came to Kraków for his annual holidays, and each day here he trawled the dating websites in search of a nice Polish woman. So far he had not had much luck. Needless to say, he was a lonely soul. He sighed another sigh, stood, and took his cup to the window. Pointing, he said, "She's nice" and, "She's nice" and, "She's nice." It's true, the Polish women are especially lovely – typically slim, blonde, blue-eyed, warmly feminine and happy, most of them you would want to keep permanently tucked under your arm.

Paul was not bad-looking, forty-ish, still with a full crop of hair, his eyes magnified slightly behind thick spectacles, his business shirt the typical English blue-and-white pinstripes, a safe blue tie with a touch of design and food stains, grey trousers, and a trimmed grey beard which helped to give his face a bit of character. He was not overweight; never touched a drop and never smoked, he said. His teeth, though, were not the best – something about their arrangement, one or two too many – but his most unfortunate quality, probably the one that mattered most, and he admitted it, was his personality.

"But, hey, there are women out there who are shy too," Jim said encouragingly. He said he thought Paul was not going to get far if he spent all his time indoors like this, that he should go out and join in the hunt and gather. Ruefully, Paul agreed. Jim changed the subject to Kraków and Paul was able to suggest some useful websites.

A statistical aside: in Kraków there are dozens of museums, 160 Roman Catholic churches and chapels (seventy-two historic), thirteen universities, thirteen theatres, twenty cinemas, seventeen hospitals and nine sports stadiums.

One evening Jim saw a film. It was called *House by the Lake* – American, and such a wacky story it is not worth talking about. On another evening he saw John Malkovich demeaning himself in the role of a boring, stupid, camp impersonation of a fictitious Stanley Kubrick in *Colour Me Kubrick*. It was unbearable. Peeved, he walked out to look for a coffee shop.

There is a good coffee shop near the cinema on Tomasza Street called Camelot, facing a Baroque church, and far enough away from the square to be tourist-free. It attracts bearded Polish film enthusiasts who like to discuss subjects and read books in candlelit darkness. Apart from the waiter, practically no one spoke English or French – Russian and German, yes, but surprisingly, not English. Anyway, Jim had the book he had just bought, called *History of the Present: Essays, Sketches and Dispatches from Europe in the 1990s* by prize-winning journalist Timothy Garton Ash. On this Kubrick evening, however, when he was walking out of the cinema, the ticket-seller told him his favourite coffee shop was Nowa Prowincja. "The best coffee in Kraków," he said, "down on Bracka Street, not far away."

OK, Jim would try this one for a change.

It was another dark, candlelit shop for discerning people, mostly university students this time. He took his coffee at an outside table. The flavour was a strong blend of Italian, very nice. As he was reading about the war over Kosovo, a lady from the next table asked in good English if he would take a photo of her sitting with her friend. It was a good enough excuse to start a conversation. Her name was Grażyna and she was Polish, spirited and very glamorous. Her friend, Ulrich, looked sick with sadness. He was going through a divorce. He had come here from Wroclaw for the weekend to pour his heart out to Grażyna, poor fellow. Poor Grażyna. Her conversation with Jim was interrupted by her mobile phone – her brother was calling to tell her that she was at that moment on television, a film she had performed in some years earlier. So, she was an actress. But she had to attend to Ulrich, who couldn't speak a word of English, or didn't want to. Jim went back to his book. On parting, however,

Grażyna said she'd never met an Australian before and asked if they could meet again sometime for dinner. A bit too quickly Jim jumped to it and said yes, he'd love to. She gave him her card. The following Friday evening, his penultimate day in Kraków, they did meet again, at the same coffee shop. She was dressed beautifully. He wanted to know all about her – her life story, her acting career and her love life. She had once played a role in an Andrzej Wajda film, and had done a number of stage performances, including Ibsen, and some television. Now she was finished with acting, she said, and was employed in an architectural publishing office. She had never heard of Jean Nouvelle or Santiago Calatrava but would look them up. She had once been married to an actor, who was quite well known, and they had a twenty-five-year-old daughter named Gabriela.

After coffee she walked him to her favourite Italian restaurant, called Soprano. Grażyna was recognised by the staff and diners, which made Jim feel even more special. The dinner was superb and she was wonderful company. A bit reluctant to think about it again, she nonetheless told him what it was like to grow up in Poland during the years of repression – the cold bleakness of it, personal relationships among trusted friends, the forbidden books they smuggled to one another. Popular entertainment was the cinema. Under Communist rule, Eastern European film-makers were obliged to produce works of socialist realism, anthems to the workers' state. Many of its directors emigrated to Hollywood where they helped to create American film noir. People were influenced by propaganda, of course they were, but many who knew better held on to their revolutionary beliefs; there was no dissident who didn't feel passionately about her country. And she smiled her lovely smile when she described the overwhelming joy they all felt during 1989 and 1990, glued to their radios, hearing the day-to-day news of the events that were making history and delivering them ever closer to freedom.

"And what about the church?" Jim asked. "What about religion in a country where eighty per cent of its people are supposed to be Catholic?"

"In the fifties the Party tried to neutralise the influence of the church. Church schools were nationalised; monasteries and seminaries were shut down; Catholic hospitals, nursing homes, and charities were closed. Church leaders were blackmailed, persecuted, harassed, and jailed.

"Now the churches are full of old women. When the Polish Pope visited Poland there was some revived fervour, but now, with the death of communism, religion is slowly dying too. With improved education and freedom people are finally thinking more for themselves and realising that the dogmas of religion, like the dogmas of communism, are a colossal hoax. It's difficult for those of faith to live in an age of reason."

She wanted to know his impressions of Kraków, what life in Australia was like, and asked him to describe his life in Paris. She wanted to practise her schoolgirl French, which made the evening more amusing. In the end she insisted on paying the bill. Jim suggested they go back to Nowa Prowincja for a coffee, but she had to find her car for an early rise. They walked through a dozen tree-filled streets, past the Jagiellonian University, the monument to Nicolaus Copernicus, and the theatre in which Grażyna had so often performed. As she spoke she held her arm affectionately in his and her manner was light and gay.

The next morning he rang to thank her once again for her kindness. She promised they would meet again, but this time it would be on his terms, in Paris. After their conversation Jim went to the British Council to check his email. Paul was there again, stooped over his laptop and his half-eaten apple, earnestly tapping away. It was a bit cruel, I suppose, of Jim to tell him of his good luck of the night before. Paul was amazed and crumpled into a whimper.

Kazimierz is one of Kraków's inner suburbs and is known as the Jewish Quarter. The biggest second-hand English-language bookshop in Poland is there. What a goldmine. It is called Massolit Books on Felicjanek Street, and was run by a personable young man from West Virginia. One could sit comfortably, tasting fresh muffins or croissants, and good coffee. Jim spent the three days it rained browsing and reading journals. Every book is properly catalogued, and a movable stepladder reaches up to near the ceiling. In another room there is a whole wall of Jewish history.

Jews began settling in Poland in the fourteenth century and continued for those fleeing persecution from all corners of Europe. Before the Second World War 3.5 million Jews were living in Poland; today there are only three to four thousand. Of the approximately seventy thousand who were living in Kraków in 1939, only some six thousand survived the war. In the quarter today there are only about 150, though there are always many visitors, especially these days since Steven Spielberg shot his film *Schindler's List*, here. Oskar Schindler saved twelve thousand lives from the concentration camps by employing and protecting them in his factory. Today, around the world, there are about seven thousand descendants of those on Schindler's list. Seven synagogues survived the war, but only one of them continues to function as a place of worship; two others have been turned into museums. The Jewish cemetery in the quarter was closed for burials in the early nineteenth century. Auschwitz was nearby, but Jim didn't want to go there.

Among the other books he bought from Massolit was the hefty volume, recently published, of the autobiography of Gabriel García Márquez. He won the Nobel Prize in 1982 for his epic, *One Hundred Years of Solitude*. The autobiography Jim found to be disappointingly dull.

Nowa Huta means 'New Steelworks'. In the early 1950s the communist regime built a gigantic steelworks and a new town for its employees about ten kilometres east of Kraków. It was supposed to give a 'healthy' working-class injection to the strong aristocratic, cultural and religious traditions of the city. It didn't matter that this region had neither ores nor coal deposits and that virtually all the raw materials had to be transported from distant locations, that the site had the most fertile soil in the region for farming, and that there were important villages that went back to the Middle Ages wiped away. Because the environmental pollution became catastrophic the management was forced to cut production, but the steelworks still functions, even though it is unprofitable.

Jim went to the steelworks by tram and found that living standards declined the further out he went. Unfortunately for him, entry into the mill was only for those granted official permission. From behind the high steel fence he could see the afternoon shift arriving, a plodding, disparate army of stooped grey men being drawn towards tall, smoking brick chimneys under a pall of grey sky. He thought of Fritz Lang. He walked to the original residential sector where some steelworkers still lived. The neighbourhood layout reminded him of Victorian England – blocks of smoke-blackened three-storey brick terraced houses enclosing grassed, treeless squares where children were meant to play. In the main public square where a giant statue of Lenin once stood, many residents were gathered in an air of jollity to celebrate a neighbourhood wedding. The groom, formally attired, arrived on a bicycle, and side-saddled was his ravishing bride.

Chopin is, perhaps, Poland's most celebrated artist. When Jim found that on his last evening in Kraków there was to be a full evening performance of the *Nocturnes* at the city's Filharmonia Krakówska, home to one of the best symphonic orchestras in the land, his memory took him back to his student years, to his attic room, burning the midnight oil, drawing and listening for hours those wistful, lilting piano pieces by Chopin. He rang to invite Grażyna but she was not at home.

In a fathomless hush, more than a thousand were there, mostly plain-dressed, middle-aged citizens with enthusiastic faces. All listened with reverence and obvious satisfaction. Why had he left it so long to listen again to those beautiful, mystifying sounds? At the end there was mild, respectful applause, then everybody quietly shuffled away.

As Jim was walking back through the park in a special mood, there was, watching him through the trees and drifting clouds, following him, a lovely, bright, enchanting moon.